Gale Borger

Totally Evil

A Miller Sisters Mystery
Book Three

Totally Evil
A Miller Sisters Mystery
Book Three
An Echelon Press Book

All rights Reserved.
Copyright © 2013 by Gale Borger

Cover Art © Nathalie Moore
With Karen L. Syed

Echelon Press
2721 Village Pine Terrace
Orlando, FL 32833
www.echelonpress.com

ISBN: 978-1-59080-889-4
10-digit: 1-59080-889-4
eBook: 978-1-59080-889-4

Published by Echelon Press Enterprises LLC.

To my sisters, Robin, Dawn, and Sam. From painting the tree house to the cow in the kitchen, growing up with you guys was the best, and your laughter still rings in my dreams. No worries though, your secrets are safe with me. The people who read my books think I really make up all those stories.

And to Bob and Shannon, with whom, all things are possible. I love you both.

Chicken around the parking lot made for a short outtake of levity on an otherwise dismal day.

The gawkers applauded, very entertained. *Sure glad I could provide the half-time entertainment for all the laughing hyenas standing behind the police tape.* I hoped they were as cold and miserable as me. Wouldn't you think one of them would offer to share an umbrella? Their collective teeth clacking together in counter rhythm sounded like a marching band cadence at half time.

The aroma of soggy hot dogs, donuts, and hot coffee provided by Sal's Diner made it seem like a town festival–only smelly and gruesome.

I saw a flash of silver off someone's flask, and realized the dollop of brandy they just dumped in their coffee might have something to do with the crowd's high spirits. They laughed and cheered on the body extraction, and it all added to the half-time atmosphere of a rainout, dead-guy show. Thank God the football cheerleaders had enough sense to stay home–but with most of the geriatric SWAT team present; the crowd didn't need any more encouragement.

"Don't you people know it's raining out? Go home and read about it tomorrow in the paper!"

They laughed and waved from behind the tape. Someone gave me the thumbs up sign and someone else gave me the finger. I squinted through the rain. *Hey! That almost looks like Mom back there...naw, must be my imagination*–but I snuck one more peek to make sure.

I'd been so busy trying to make out the finger flipper under all the rain gear I didn't notice I closed in fast on the dumpster. The crowd frantically waved and pointed again. I raised a hand to wave back...and slammed right into the side of the dumpster, jarring the lid and dislodging the garbage which had been piled up there after the discovery of the body.

With leftover pizza and congealed, unmentionable glop

I hate dead bodies. Have I mentioned that before? Dead bodies in the pouring rain are exceptionally objectionable. I sighed as I eyeballed the leg sticking up out of the dumpster. *Crap.* I knew this would happen. It's me. My fault. I'm a jinx!

Murphy's Law runs rampant in police work, as it does in my Irish family. If anything can make a crime scene more miserable, it'll happen when I'm around–guar-an-teed! If someone gets himself knocked off outside, it's either fifty degrees below zero, raining, snowing, or 110 degrees in the shade.

Today, I stood in an ice-cold late spring deluge behind Sal's Diner. I was soggy, crabby, talking to myself, and in desperate need of a cup of coffee and a roaring fire. Warm June showers my foot. I snorted. *Hah! July is just a few weeks away. We'll be lucky if we get above fifty by the fourth the way we're going*!

I moved my frozen toes around in my very cool paisley rain boots. *Should have worn your Sorrels, Buzz. Spring in Wisconsin is always iffy.*

I peeked over the side of the dumpster and almost tossed my cookies. *Yuck, this stuff is way gross. You should be happy you're retired, Buzz, at least you aren't on dumpster duty. If you're lucky, the rain will wash some of the maggots off the corpse before you have to handle it.*

I always like to keep a positive attitude.

Trying to look professional in front of the gathering crowd, I stepped away from the rancid odor and pulled up the collar of my raincoat. About a half-gallon of icy rainwater ran down my back. Cussing a blue streak and dancing the *Funky* journalism professor to get a "B." At the time I asked her if the grade was for journalism or did he think she's just a lousy lay.

Since that fateful day, she has reciprocated our mutual loathing, and about thirty years later, we still banter back and forth in a totally immature way.

Rosie tried her journalistic *luck* in Milwaukee and Madison, but no matter how many news executives and politicians she got *lucky* with, she kept ending up hung over and alone in the morning, and no job with big network television.

Five years later, she came crawling home with her tail between her legs and a reputation for doing just about anything (or anyone) to get a story, and Rosie has since been dubbed "Rosie the News Whore," and will forever go down in history as the Monica Lewinski of White Bass Lake.

Sitting in her warm van with her pug nose against the glass, she reminded me of my Bulldog, Hillary making those wet-nose trails across the window when she saw a stray hound dog lifting his leg on a hydrant.

I didn't see anyone lifting his leg anywhere, so Rosie must have been entertaining herself by watching J.J. fork garbage from the dumpster into Sal's parking lot. Though J.J. never treated Rosie with anything worse than polite disdain, it still made my blood pressure skyrocket when she twitched her rear in his direction. I'd already chased her off with the pitchfork once today, and had a wonderful, warm moment of imagining Rosie accidentally tumbling head first into the rancid dumpster, her stilettos flipping helplessly in the air.

Tugging my green-eyed fantasies back to the cold, wet parking lot, I watched as J.J.'s deputies, Moe (Darryl) and Larry (Phil) sifted through the trash J.J. and Luke tossed out of the dumpster, onto the plastic sheeting spread across three parking spaces.

Sal poked his head out the back door of his diner for what must have been the fiftieth time. He bounced on the balls of his feet and stood on his toes, waving a spatula in my direction. I waved and called "No updates yet, Sal!"

He waved his spatula again and bits of egg flew into the air. "Okey dokey, Buzz, you gonna tell me first 'cuz it's my dumpster and my dead guy, right?"

I smiled and nodded and lifted an arm to wave back. Water trickled down my arm and all humor vanished.

Geez. I shook my sleeve. *His dead guy? Since when does ending up in a rented dumpster define ownership of a corpse? What the heck is this sick town coming to?*

I summoned up what I thought looked like a smile "Sure, Sal," I half-heartedly yelled back, "I'll give you a holler when we get something."

Sal looked confused and a little scared.

Shaking my soggy sleeve I thought, *why the heck do I do this? Buzz Miller,* You *are an idiot!*

Sal rewarded me with a beautiful smile. "Good, good. Uh, thanks, Buzz, I'll send out more coffee!" Satisfied, he hustled back inside.

That's why you do it, Buzz. You get free coffee. "Thanks, Sal," I yelled to the closed door. My mood lightened considerably as I speculated on the probability of Sal throwing in a donut along with the coffee.

My newly found positive attitude took a dump right there in the pouring rain when I heard the roar of eight glorious cylinders of a Crown Victoria engine eating up the road, jolting me out of my donut dream world.

2

Oh no. Now we're in real trouble. A very red and very unwelcomed Crown Vic threw gravel as it careened around the corner, blasting Rosie and her crew right in the rear quarter panel with pea gravel. I took a breath to scream a warning to the crowd. The crowd screamed and jumped back just as the Crown Vic swerved at the last moment and slid to a stop, creating a tidal wave in the parking lot and nosing the police tape. The deluge struck the front row. Dripping and angry, the crowd surged forward. I thought for a moment that I might have a riot on my hands.

My mom's friend Mary Cromwell kicked the driver's door open. Levering her boney elbows against the doorframe, she struggled out into the rain. I barked out a laugh at her get-up. She looked sort of like the Gorton Fisherman meets Underdog.

Eighty-one-year-old Mary Cromwell sported a funky hat with earflaps and a red poncho raincoat which flapped in the breeze with all the flamboyance of a cartoon cape. She had bird watching binoculars around her neck and her huge pink purse overflowed with a magnifying glass, wet sidewalk chalk, a 100-foot reel tape measure, and a thermos. She looked so outrageous, even the crowd froze in mid-mutiny as they stopped to stare at the little old woman clomping across the parking lot.

Her arms pumped like pistons and her orthopedic shoes slapped at the puddles like cement flippers as she slowly made her way toward me. She looked like she might be going the speed of sound, but I had to line her up with a light pole to make sure she continued to make forward progress at all.

She inched her way past me and I snagged the thermos out of her bag. Mary might be a little wacky (okay, a lot wacky), but she made a heck of a cup of coffee. I opened the thermos and smelled the rich, aromatic brew, noting the hint of Jameson's and I sighed with anticipation.

At J.J.'s shout, I stashed the thermos in the pocket of my rain jacket and wandered toward the dumpster. I passed Mary on the way. Her seventy-eight pound frame began to sag under the weight of her stupid pink bag, so I plucked it off her shoulder and dropped it near the dumpster.

"Yo, J.J., you bellowed?"

"Come on, Buzz, what's up with Mary? I thought you secured the perimeter." I tossed the thermos up to him and he caught it. "Mmm, is Mary's special coffee in there?"

"Yeah," I said. "I thought it was a good enough bribe to let her in."

"You can't take a bribe, it's against the law."

I stuck out my tongue. "You forget, I'm not the law anymore."

He rolled his eyes. "Really. Well, did she at least bring donuts?"

"Don't know, but here she comes, you can ask her yourself."

I snatched the thermos out of his hand while he focused his attention on Mary and slipped around the side of the dumpster. I heard him say, "Mornin', Miz Cromwell, what brings you out on such a nasty day?" I had to giggle as I listened to him schmooze our most notorious senior citizen and I cracked open the thermos. I slugged the delicious brew straight from the bottle and immediately felt its warmth penetrate the bone-deep cold.

I had just taken my second swig when J.J. scared the crap out of me. He appeared out of nowhere and poked me in the side. I choked on the coffee and it shot out my nose.

Just as I recovered from the hot brew and the Irish whiskey singeing my nose hairs, J.J. whipped off his plastic gloves and made a grab for the thermos. "Hey, quit wasting good coffee and save some for me."

I caught a whiff of his coveralls. "Ick, you smell like a dumpster, pal."

He smiled. "Trivial matters such as smell do not get in the way of Mary's coffee. Here, she gave me the donuts."

He hit me in the arm with a bakery bag. While I put the grab on the potential donut lead, he grabbed the thermos.

I looked in the bag and almost sank down into the puddle at my feet. Inside, I found one of those exquisite bear claws from Brody's spectacular bakeshop. I snagged it and had it half gone before J.J. realized I scarfed most of it down.

He took a big slug of coffee and belched. "Man that is *good* coffee." He looked up and shivered. "Is this damn rain ever going to stop? At least it's good for the crops. Speaking of gardens, Buzz, how *does* your garden grow? Or should I say, *not* grow. Heh heh!"

I took his sarcasm as a rhetorical question and ignored him. My arthritis must've been acting up as well, because my middle finger rose slowly on its own. "Go ahead, make fun of me. I know you all call me The Black Thumb Gardener, but I'll have you know I learned a lot about vegetables and flowers over the winter. I'll show you all who can grow container tomatoes!"

He laughed. "Figured out how you're going to cheat already, eh?" I popped him one in the arm.

"Can I have the other half of that?" He reached for the bear claw.

I surrendered the uneaten half unwillingly and took my turn with the coffee. "By the way, no."

"No what?"

"What?"

"No."

"Know what?"

"Knock it off, Miller. You said no."

"You asked if the rain would stop. I said no. It's supposed to keep drizzling until early tomorrow." I leaned over and took another bite.

"Oh."

"No?"

"No, what?"

I smiled. "What?"

"I said, no, *what*?"

"Just between you and me, no my garden does not grow at all, I can admit as much. I suck at gardening even when I follow directions. I put my tomato outside just like they told me and it croaked. But hey, I am going to win the Miller Sister's First Annual Tomato Growing Contest if it kills me and whoever gets in my way."

J.J. laughed. "Tomato growing? You? Hah! You can't even keep grass alive, and you think you're going to grow tomatoes?"

I swallowed my injured pride and lifted my nose in the air. "I'll have you know I am in possession of one new tomato plant, and detailed instructions from Ollie Boothe over at The Olive Branch Garden Center on how not to kill it."

J.J. slapped the side of the dumpster. "Oh my God, I can't wait to tell your sisters!"

"They already know, Mr. Insensitive. We each have the same kind of tomato–Early…uh, whatever–and we each are going to raise them up by our own secret methods. I–"

"Your method will be how to cheat and not get caught, right, oh Black Thumb Gardener Extraordinaire?"

Feeling a little guilty because it was exactly what I planned, I sent an evil look his way. "You know everything about everything, don't you, Green? You just wait and see. I'll show you all! Ollie Booth gave me her never fail tomato secrets." I kicked the side of the dumpster.

Luke poked his head over the edge of the dumpster. "Hey, knock it off, you two, I'm getting a headache. In case you wanted to know, I got our guy uncovered in here and ready to go. Buzz, you take this camera. You can record the removal from the outside. We're through with it in here."

He saw J.J. stuff the last of the bear claw in his mouth. "Hey, are you selfish hogs eating donuts while I'm in here slogging through maggots and meatballs?"

J.J. quickly shoved the thermos my way and dusted his chin. Trying to swallow and talk at the same time he said, "Wow, Luke, you already took pictures and everything?"

He winked and flashed me a grin. "Okay everyone, let's get this show on the road!"

Taking a deep breath, J.J. heaved himself over the side and back into the dumpster.

I turned away and heard Luke say, "Yeah, yeah, I finished with the camera and he's ready to go. We can move him."

Let them handle it; I'm freezing to death. I ducked low so they couldn't see me back away from their conversation and around the corner of the dumpster.

I swigged down the last of the coffee as I continued to back away from the dumpster and I backed right into Mary. She had her measuring tape out and busied herself measuring lord knew what. I dropped the thermos, and she turned quickly. Startled silly, I jumped out of my skin and snorted coffee through my nose again. Mary jumped too and the measuring tape went flying out of her hands. J.J. poked his head out of the dumpster and got whacked in the forehead with the tape.

He held up a finger if to say, "Point of Order" and I watched his eyeballs roll back into his head and he slithered

15

back into the dumpster.

Mary stood dripping and staring, magnifying glass in one hand and binoculars zeroed in on the dumpster. "Oh my, did I just clock Sheriff Green?"

Recovering from drowning for the second time that day, I stood gasping and laughing. Holding a bakery napkin to my nose, tears dripping off my face, I nodded furiously. I picked up the empty thermos, shoved it into her hands, and splashed my way back to the dumpster. The coroner's truck had arrived and Ivan backed across the parking lot, heading in our direction.

I stood on my toes and looked over the side of the dumpster. Luke laughed and slapped J.J.'s cheek. "Come on, buddy, it was a cloth tape measure, don't be a girl."

I opened my mouth to point out the tape measure had a steel case, but Mary startled me by yelling at the top of her lungs. She stood at the edge of the crowd jumping up and down waving her arms yelling, "Meat wagon's here! Everyone move back. *Move back*, I said!"

Directing traffic with her magnifying glass, the crowd parted like the Red Sea. The ambulance backed in with no problem.

J.J. smirked. "Great coffee, great donuts, *supremo* traffic control, hey, Luke, maybe we should hire Mary on a permanent basis."

I gave him the evil eye. "Wait 'til I get you home, Green."

He smiled and those long dimples creased his face. "I look forward to it with great anticipation, my dear Alice Christine."

I snorted and felt my ears grow hot. I pulled the camera strap up on my shoulder, stuffed my hands in my pockets, and made my way over to brief our medical examiner.

Fire and Rescue had already arrived on scene to assist in

the unloading of the body. They piled out of the fire truck like clowns out of a Volkswagen. Big Mike Bradley crawled into the dumpster with J.J. and Luke. How they all fit remains a mystery; Mike's built like a linebacker, J.J.'s got to be six-two or three, and Luke might be skinny, but add the garbage and one very dead guy, and I couldn't help but think, *wow*. Good thing there's a lot of grease in there. They'll need it to get out.

Larry the Deputy ran the video and I took the still pictures. Curly and Shemp pulled up in the other squad car, and donning rain gear, joined us to help with the removal. The men gently lifted the body onto a stretcher and hauled it straight up and over the side of the dumpster into other gloved hands. The crowd strained to see if anyone recognized the dead guy as the outside rescue team gently laid the corpse on the open body bag. I clicked away as our ME, Malcolm Evans, and the assistant ME, Ivan Sligorsky, zipped him up and loaded the bag onto a stretcher. My job on stretcher duty was to run interference for Malcolm and Ivan.

I immediately saw trouble brewing. I jumped over a huge puddle to place myself between the stretcher and Rosie and her camera crew, as they splashed their way toward the coroner's van. Because the news crew's camera rolled on, I held up my hands, and in my most authoritative voice said, "Ladies and gentlemen, Coroner Evans has no comment as to the victim's identity or any facts regarding cause of death at this time. There will be a news conference later this afternoon where Sheriff Green and Coroner Evans will issue their official statements; so please step back and let them do their job. Thank you."

I let that sink in as I watched Malcolm and Ivan sprint toward the truck, stretcher bouncing between them with each stride. Actually, Malcolm sprinted and Ivan strolled–his stride equaling about three of Malcolm's.

The television crew advanced on me, and I backed up,

still holding my hands out. "We appreciate your concern and support, but you must understand, after identification of the body, notifications of family members is in order, so please, turn off the cameras. Sheriff Green will issue an official press release later today. Again, thank you all for your concern."

I noticed the camera man turned off his equipment, but realized too late he acted as a diversion so Rosie could sneak past me. She totally ignored my little speech, and went splashing after Ivan, balancing precariously on those ridiculous stilettos she always wore.

Ivan and Malcolm transferred the body onto a gurney and rolled the body to the back of the ambulance. They picked up speed as Rosie bore down on them. I took off after her, determined to waylay her before she interfered with, or touched the body. I splashed within shouting distance just in time to hear Rosie croon to Ivan through the back door of the ambulance, "Just a little bitty peekie to see if I can help you identify the victim, Ivan honey?"

I skid around the side of the van. Ivan plucked Rosie's hand off his coat and stood very tall—about six-feet-seven inches tall. He held up one hand and intoned in his best Dracula voice, "You cannot come in here, Miss Rose. There is bad blood at play, *moo-hoo-hoo-hooo-hah-ha*!" He looked over his shoulder. "Some pretty odiferous odors too, come to think about it. So take your little peep show on the road, Miss Rose, before you contaminate the evidence. Shoo now." His hands flapped in her face.

Rosie looked taken aback, but recovered quickly. "So, you're saying this is a murder, Ivan?"

Ivan looked slowly left and right, "No, I'm saying it smells pretty ripe in here. I'm clearing out, but by all means, come on in if you want to hang out in the stench for a while."

Rosie huffed, Malcolm wheezed, Ivan quirked a smile and glanced in my direction. Rosie didn't know I stood behind

18

the door.

Ivan worked at positioning the gurney. "Please, speak to Buzz Miller, Miz Rose, as she is our communications liaison on this case."

Rosie put her nose in the air and crossed her arms. "I wouldn't ask Buzz Miller for a crumb if I lost my way and starving to death."

I bristled and stared in wonder as her expression instantly changed from evil to coy. She pulled on his pant leg. I thought maybe she intended stay attached like a terrier in love. "But, Ivan Honey—"

Ivan dramatically placed a hand over his heart and looked down at her. "I am naught but the resident body snatcher, Miz Rose, on his way to the big cooler downtown."

He beetled his eyebrows and leveled a look at her. "Now, excuse me please, *some* of us have work to do." He disengaged his leg, turned his back on Rosie, and secured the body in the van.

Rosie stood stunned and watched Ivan lean across the body bag, tightening the straps. She spotted me and it startled her out of her reverie. She curled her lip in my direction. I just smiled and twiddled my fingers at her. "Hey, Rose, trying you luck with Ivan?"

She ignored me, I insulted her, and everything became right with the world.

Ivan hopped out of the van and looked down at Rosie one last time before he slammed the back door. She had a hand on his sleeve and stroked his forearm in blatant invitation.

"C'mon, Ivan, just one statement. Hey, I could come down to the morgue. I'm sure we could find something to talk about there. What do you say?"

Ivan looked down at her hand, and then at me. He winked at me before he turned back to Rosie. Waggling his eyebrows, Ivan tapped an imaginary cigar. He leaned forward like Groucho Marx and said, "Nice try, but hey Rose, if you're still offering a piece of tush when I get off work, come on over to the morgue and I'll show you my stiffy."

You had to love Ivan; he really had a great–if warped– sense of humor.

I laughed and Rosie sputtered as Ivan jumped into the driver's side of the van.

"Hey, Rosie," I yelled and saw her jump. Her shoulders stiffened as I approached. *Getting into witch mode, eh, Rose, old gal? You'd better not offer me what you just offered Ivan; I might have to kill you.* "Yo, Rose, I think the guy in the ambulance is more your type."

"What do you mean my *type*?"

"Dead, Ha, ha–kind of like your last boyfriend, eh?"

"You are such a bitch, Buzz Miller, but say, you'll look smashing on television tonight with jelly donut dripping off your chin."

I looked at the rolling camera and ran a hand over my chin. I pulled away with raspberry bear claw on my fingers. *Crap. Oh no, Rosie, is not going to get the last word in. Think, Miller, try for mature, but think fast.*

"At least I don't have to feel up the Assistant ME while trying to get information." *Real mature, Buzz, you idiot.*

Rosie held up a middle finger and spun on her heel. The thought crossed my mind there was an awfully lot of finger flipping going on this morning when I heard the coroner's van start up behind me. I turned to see Ivan grinning from ear to ear. He looked like a demented Doberman as he nodded to me and revved the engine. I jumped back onto the curb. Ivan gunned the engine, nodded once, and took off toward the giant lake flooding the street.

Seeing the writing on the wall, I immediately dove toward the bushes on my right.

Now I hadn't been bush jumping since college, and we had all been extremely intoxicated at the time. This day, thirty-some years later though, full of Mary Cromwell's spiked coffee and a half a bear claw, I flew through the air with the greatest of ease and cleared the junipers which divided Sal's Diner from the folks next door. I hit the turf on the other side and rolled to my feet just in time to see the show.

From my perch, I had a bird's eye view of the wall of water Ivan created as the van tore through the flooded street. Rosie stood there struck dumb, a stunned look on her face as filthy water plumed over her head like a giant tsunami.

Mary Cromwell stood behind her, sporting her Gorton Fisherman's hat and a huge umbrella. "*Surf's up*," she hollered, and cackled gleefully when the wave crashed over Rosie's head.

Drenched from head to toe, mascara running down her face, Rosie raised her middle finger (there's that flying finger again) at the retreating coroner's van and yelled, "Ivan, you son of a biiiii–"

She never finished cursing Ivan, because another vehicle flashed by and another tidal wave of muddy water hit her open mouth. She sputtered and gasped while a suspiciously familiar GMC dually zoomed past and drenched her again.

Mary jumped up and down, punching the air. "Good shot, Gerry," she yelled at my mother.

The dually stopped and Mary clambered into the passenger's seat. I looked in the side mirror of the truck and saw my mother grin and give me a two-fingered salute as she revved the engine and disappeared around the corner.

I waded back through the junipers and warily checked the street in case someone else had lined up to pelt Rosie with muddy water. Must have been a slow day, because the streets were clear and my vehicle sat on the other side of Sal's.

Hmmm, too far away to get her again. Drat, another missed opportunity.

I smiled widely as Rosie staggered to the curb, shaking her leg like a cat with tape stuck to its foot. "A little humid out today, wouldn't you say, Rose?"

"Oh shut up, Buzz Miller. That was your mother's pick-up truck and you know it!" She wiped a hand over her mouth and smeared a mud mustache across her upper lip. I didn't tell her about it. Let her see it on the 6:00 news.

I spotted an inconspicuous little man holding a small camera about fifty feet up the street. He pointed it in our direction. Curious, I turned to Rosie. "Hey, Rosie, is that guy over there one of yours?"

She squinted hard and I could almost see her hackles rise. "No! That's the little rat from the Chicago affiliate! What's he doing here, do you think?"

"Aside from filming you for the 6:00 news?"

It took a split second for it to sink in. Rosie let out a blood curdling scream and took off down the street at a dead run after the little camera man. He wisely hoofed it to a nearby minivan and gunned the engine. He sent up a rooster tail of street water under his spinning tires, and shot forward about the time Rosie made it to the back bumper. Catching another face full of water, she sputtered and screeched. She stood in the street, a vision in her red and mud slimed outfit, and dripping yuck from her hundred-dollar hairdo.

I shook my head. *Show over except for the rolling credits.* I sighed and looked around. I dusted my hands and looked smugly at the crowd, who stood silently in the frigid rain, mouths open. "Well folks, I think the fat lady has sung."

I mentally patted myself on the back for a job well done. It made the raspberry glob on my chin worth the 6:00 humiliation knowing Rosie would star on the late Chicago news tonight. I sighed and strolled toward the dumpster, wondering for the hundredth time if the rain would ever stop. I turned up my collar and headed back across the parking lot, doing a little shivery dance as the cold water trickled down my neck again.

Luke and J.J. had climbed out of the dumpster and Moe and Larry began to shovel the trash back into it. Luke and J.J. peeled off their long rubber gloves. I grabbed the shoulders of J.J.'s coveralls and helped him tug them off. I did the same for Luke. They dropped everything into black plastic bags and J.J. stuffed them into the trunk of his squad.

Mrs. Murphy, or Mother Nature, or the Goddess of icy spring rains seemed to be having a grand time at our expense, because the drizzle stopped drizzling and the clouds began to break up.

I looked at the crowd and everyone looked up, as if waiting for a divine sign. J.J. sighed and slipped into a jacket. "Well, the rain is over, the excitement is over, sounds like a good time to have coffee. Buzz? How 'bout it? Your house or Sal's?"

"Since you both smell like the inside of a dumpster, we're not going into Sal's. Why don't you two go back to your house, shower, change, and come over? I have to get the dogs out anyway. By the time you get beautiful, you'll be off duty. I'll have pizza waiting."

J.J. grinned. "Sounds great."

"Don't buy any beer, I've got the coffee and antifreeze covered too."

Luke sighed blissfully. "Buzz Miller, will you marry me?"

J.J. looked over his shoulder. "Not so fast, Casanova, you've got to stand in line, small fry."

"You're both nuts." I laughed and took off toward my SUV.

3

I walked back to my vehicle, preoccupied with thoughts of Luke and J.J. Watching Luke in "official mode" was sure a lot different than watching Luke the first time I met him. About ten years ago during a late February blizzard when I still was a member of the Sheriff's Department, my partner Chet Arsenal and I pulled the late shift in booking. Just when we thought we were going to breeze through an uneventful evening, a call came in from the emergency room across town–a jurisdiction from the opposite end of the county was bringing in a drunken juvenile on a B&E, Burglary to a Dwelling, DC, Resisting Arrest, as well as Prohibited Alcohol Content, and Under Aged Drinking.

Chet snorted. "Sounds like loads of fun."

"Yeah, you know how I love drunk punks. They e-deed him too, but the hospital gave him medical clearance, so now he's ours. So much for emergency detentions, eh, Chet?"

Chet grinned large. "Yup, they clear them so they don't have to deal with them. He'll be a fighter, so I'll be waiting in the reception line. That means you get to book him. Besides, you're the only one who knows the new booking program." He smiled a little smile. "Oh, and you're the girl, so you can do the 'mom' thing and counsel the poor misunderstood boy."

I gave him the stink eye. "Poor misunderstood boy my sweet patootie, Arsenal. I don't have kids. I don't want kids, and I especially don't want to deal with fighting, puking, drunken, felonious, punk-assed kids!"

Chet laughed at me and we strolled over to the coffee pot.

I grumbled and filled my coffee cup. "Maybe we'll get lucky and he'll sleep through it."

Chet laughed and held out his cup. "Fat chance, Pollyanna. He'll probably kick and scream so loud I won't be able to take my three-a.m. nap. Come on-bet me. Loser makes coffee for a month."

"Forget it."

"A week?"

"You're on, pal. Remember, I like my coffee ground from whole bean."

Chet choked on his coffee and some squirted out of his mouth. "Hah! I'll bet Murphy's Law is against you tonight, *DE-tective*."

Suddenly irritated–probably in part because Chet dribbled coffee on my pant leg–I blasted him. "Shut up, Arsenal, you know I hate that 'Detective' crap. If it weren't for this, uh, Irish *thing* I have, I'd be as lousy at police work as you are."

Chet snorted. "Yeah, as lousy as I am. I only meant–wait a minute. What do you mean, 'as lousy' as I am at it? My track record is almost as good as yours... Well, not almost, but it's pretty good! Why, the investigation we worked together on last May would have gone south if I hadn't discovered the body."

"You weren't on that investigation Chet; you were diving on the old car wreck in the middle of the lake with your friends when you found him."

Working up a full head of steam, Chet barely heard me. "Yeah, uh, well, I was all over it after I found the stiff, right?"

"More like stiff when your intoxicated girlie friend almost threw up on it after they dragged him out. What the heck was her name again? Bambi? Bunny? Bombo the trained ape?"

"I'll have you know–"

From the rear of the building we heard. "Arsenal, you couldn't find a stiff with two hands and a map."

I hooted and Chet snorted more coffee–this time in the direction of Scott Brown, social worker and child advocate for our county's Human Services Department.

Chet wiped his chin with his sleeve. "Scott, what brings you out on such a fine evening?"

Scott stroked his jaw. *He's trying to find a way to break something to us gently.*

"Well, it's about the kid who is due here in just a few minutes. I've been over to the hospital, and wanted to bring you guys up to speed on him."

My apprehension grew. "Up to speed?"

"Yeah. While the kid is actually a resident of Jefferson County, he committed the crimes here. The house-dad of the halfway house where he lived called to say he ran off again."

I groaned and Chet chuckled. Scott continued.: "He is still on juvenile paper in Jefferson County until he's of age, and now because these new charges carry a felony as an adult, we have a sticky situation."

I swallowed. "A juvie, or not a juvie? That is the question."

"You have the right of it, Buzz. So I'm asking that he be held here until the two counties and court systems straighten out the legal mess."

"But Ed, the state burglary charge is a felony. It would naturally take precedence over any juvenile misdemeanor he has on record."

"Were that the case, I would agree. But its felony *juvenile* paper he's on, and that opens up a whole new can of worms."

I swore. "Yup. Big ugly worms. Okay, Scott. We'll book him and keep him here for now. We can hold him as an adult because of the new felonies. Anyone contact his P.O.?"

"Yes, I did. The apprehension request should be coming over the fax any time now. His probation agent is really pissed. Don't know if it's from being woke up at two in the morning, or the fact she's mad enough to revoke him this time. I got to tell you though; this kid has some deep-seated emotional trauma from his past."

Chet snorted. "Great, a psycho drunk punk."

Scott looked up from his paperwork. I mean it, Chet. I've been his case worker for three years and I haven't been able to scratch the surface with him, but he's as damaged as they come. He has a strong will and a sharp mind. Be careful with him—I don't know how dangerous he can be. The cops had a hell of a time with him, but he's too drunk to sedate—God knows what's in his system, beside the alcohol, you know?"

Jeff and I sat and stared. I got up and walked toward the other room. Jeff looked startled. "Hey Miller, where do you think you're going?"

I sighed. "Thought I'd get started on that first pot of coffee—looks like I lost the bet already. How 'bout it, Scott? Can I pour you a cup?"

The dubious expression on Scott's face almost made me laugh. "Uh, no thanks, Buzz. The rot-gut you guys call coffee will keep me up for days. Think I'll go home and try to get an hour or two in before I have to start it all over again." He turned and headed for the back door.

"Okay Scott, thanks. If we have any problems, we'll call you."

Scott called over his shoulder, "Good, I'll be sure to unplug the phone."

Chet and I had a good chuckle.

Chet sighed and heaved his donut-laded butt out of his chair. "Guess I'd better get started."

He stretched and walked over to the rubber room. Turning on the lights, he checked it over for any signs of abuse, or anything another inmate might have left behind which could be used as either a weapon or a tool for suicide.

He walked out and held up a dime. "Hey look, Buzz, someone left a tip."

I shook my head and Chet pocketed the dime. Several beeps from the county repeater followed by a blast of static signaled a forthcoming transmission from the police radio. The golden tones of Rita Ballard, our night dispatcher announced the arrival of two squads and an ambulance entering our Sallyport.

Chet looked at me. "*Two* squads? You are making coffee for a month, Miller!"

I pulled on my trusty nitrile gloves. "Shut up, Chet."

He smiled as he took off his glasses. "Yeah I know. I'm a pain in your butt. It's part of my charm."

We rounded the booking counter together. Chet looked at me and held up a fist. "Loser gets the kid's head."

I hate rock, scissors, paper. I always lose."

"Even better. And it's called rock, paper, scissors."

"No, rock, scissors, paper."

"Nah-ah. It's paper-scissors."

"It is not. It's scissors-paper!"

"Look it up. It's paper-scissors"

I hated the game to begin with, and Chet had just got on my last nerve. "If you insist on being infantile about a stupid game, let's get it over with before I shoot you."

"Fine with me, Buzz. Now get your fist up and we'll do rock, uh, you know."

I nodded and we rock-scissored-papered. I lost–of course. "Crap, loser again. You must cheat. My sister Fred cheats. She probably taught you." I stomped away grumbling. "Damn cheaters."

He grinned and followed. "I don't cheat–admit it; you got a big 'L' engraved on your forehead. That stands for la-la-la-l-oozer!"

4

I elbowed Chet out of the way and grabbed a spit shield on the way out the door. A wall of freezing air hit us as we stepped into the garage/pole barn we affectionately called the Sallyport, as if we worked for a big, well equipped department.

The ambulance backed toward the door, and four doors on two squads flew open. Four huge men climbed out of each squad.

Chet nudged me and said through chattering teeth. "Eight guys? Take a look at all that beef, Buzz. Where do they *grow* those guys? I'd bet not-a-one is under six-three! How did they all fit in those two squads?"

I stepped on his toe. "Close your mouth, Arsenal, you look like a fish on a hook. *Try* to pretend you're a professional."

Chet poked me in the side. "Like you're not staring like a high school prom date at King James Green over there. Pick your jaw up off the floor and wipe the drool off your chin."

I could feel the heat infuse my cheeks. "I am not drooling, you idiot. I've known J.J. since we were kids. Now leave me alone before I knock you down." I left his side and stepped between two deputies. I am rather tall, but my head didn't even reach their shoulders.

I heard Chet in the background. "Riiii-ght. Anything you say, *Dee-fective Miller*."

J.J. ruffled my hair. "How's it going, Miz Defective?"

I pushed his hand off my head. "Not you too!"

He chuckled. "Naw, I'm just a follower. Looks like you're a little irritated with 'Ass-enal' though. I don't poke sharp sticks into irate bears, so let's start over. You must be freezing to death, you're cheeks are pink."

I eyeballed Chet. "Yeah, I'm cold. So where's this big bad felon you guys brought in?"

The back doors of the ambulance opened to reveal a skinny young man in his late teens strapped to a gurney. His head popped up and his lips drew back in a sneer. "Motherfuckers. You can't do this to me. I have rights!"

I eyeballed the kid. "Yup. I guess that answers the one hundred-thousand-dollar question."

J.J. patted the kid's shackled foot. "Rights? Yeah, kid, we know all about your rights. Now calm down like we talked about across the street, and we'll talk about your rights, your charges, and perhaps your future, okay?"

"You're just another clown in brown, pig. You don't give two shits about my future."

The kid's head flopped down on the gurney and he kicked his feet, rattling the shackles and straps holding him down. The hospital staff unlocked the gurney and began to unload him. His left leg quivered and his foot tapped at the empty air. The gurney tilted slightly forward as the Paramedics waited for the legs underneath the gurney to snap into place.

I sensed rather than heard the kid's sudden indrawn breath. His head popped up again and I shoved the spit shield over it at the exact moment he spit a mouthful of phlegm in the general direction of the deputies. He screeched like a girl as the phlegm coated the inside of the spit shield and dripped back onto his own face.

A Jefferson County deputy was the first to respond. "Wow-ee! High five, man. What a catch!"

Chet recovered next. "Geez, Buzz, good job—and don't worry about the coffee, I got it."

"Yeah man, that was a close one—he'd a had me for sure."

30

"She might be little, but she sure is quick."

Little? I shook my head. A deputy stopped and leaned on the gurney.

"Did I ever tell you about the time this punk hocked the loogie of the century into a crowd at the..."

General chaos ensued as the four giants resorted to back slapping and loogie stories. The Paramedics joined in with the hospital version of the same stories.

Feeling a little queasy, I turned away and looked at the kid. Tears of rage and frustration filled his eyes, and through his gritted teeth, he ground out, "Please lady, get me outta here before I go postal, Would ya?"

I patted his shoulder and said in my most soothing voice, "We have to make sure you're not going to hurt yourself or any of us before we let you out of the restraints."

"Lady, I'm going to die on you if you don't let me out. I can't breathe. Please, I'm okay."

I smiled benignly, "I know you must be uncomfortable, young man, but–"

I made the mistake of resting my hand on his wrist, and my world tilted and spun. Frozen, I could only stare into the kid's eyes. It felt like there was no barrier between us, but I did feel the life seeping away. His wide eyes drilled into mine. His pulse began to flutter and I yelled, "Chet!"

I felt my knees give way and strong arms kept me from falling. When I let go of the kid, everything came back into focus, and I stood. Staring at the kid on the gurney, I said, "We need to get him inside and off this gurney–quick!"

I spotted the paramedics by the open ambulance door. "You two–grab the oxygen!"

Chet opened his mouth and I held up a hand. Wobbly as I was, my focus stayed on the teen on the gurney. "Questions later. We got ya now, kid. Are you going to cooperate, or are we going to leave you trussed up like a pig on a spit? I mean it, kid. Work with me here."

I looked over my shoulder. My knees wobbled again. "Where's the Oh-Two, Chet?"

I heard J.J.'s voice as he propped me up. "Buzz, are you okay?"

Another deputy sneered, "That's reason one-hundred-and-one why girls shouldn't be cops. They're pansies."

J.J. and Chet whirled on the deputy, and I swayed and grabbed the straps on the gurney. J.J. got in the deputy's face. "You don't know a thing, about her, cowboy, so shut your pie hole. She's more cop than you will ever be, now back off." No wonder I adored that man.

Chet didn't look like he had anything to add, so he just hitched his pants and said, "Yeah, shut up, dick head."

I had to smile. Chet didn't possess a stellar vocabulary, but his heart was always in the right place.

I ignored them all and stumbled into the Intake area with the Paramedics–leaving the he-men arguing in the garage.

Paramedic Number One ran out the door with the bottle of oxygen. He slapped the bottle on the floor and attached the tube. He ripped a plastic bag open with his teeth, and pulled a mask out, attaching it to the tube. I moved back to get out of the way, and found the paramedic following me.

I held up a hand. "Not me, you moron, the kid!"

He had the grace to turn pink, and faced the kid on the gurney.

I looked at the kid through the slimy spit shield. "Okay kid, what's your name?" I looked at Paramedic #1. "Well? Get the oxygen on him." He jumped to comply.

The kid stared at me, and I again asked his name.

"L-Luke," he whispered.

"Okay Luke, We're going to undo you now. Understand you hold your immediate future in your own hands. You can cooperate and get through this, or you can fight, and those eight goons over there will jump on you. They will strip you naked and this," I gestured toward the rubber room, "will be your accommodations for at least twenty-four hours."

The kid opened his mouth to speak and I stopped him. "*Ehh*! Before you say something stupid, may I remind you, you are now charged as an adult, and we do not coddle you like they do in Juvenile Detention. You screwed up big time, and now you're playing with the big boys."

He started to turn away. The paramedic fit the mask over his mouth and nose and I held his head so it faced me.

I stared at him hard. "Do. I. Make. Myself. Clear?"

He swallowed and nodded.

"So we have an understanding?"

I held out my hand and he stared at it without making an effort to shake it. "Uh, yeah, I understand, but I don't think I'm ready to touch you again just now, okay? I might be drunk, lady, but not drunk enough to not get the woo-woo vibes you give off."

I smiled at the puzzled looks of the Paramedics and patted Luke's arm. "That's okay, Luke, as long as we have an accord, I won't touch any exposed skin until you're ready."

"A cord? Naw, I ain't got no rope, but I won't fight no more or hang myself or something equally stupid, if that's what you mean."

I let out a breath. "Okay." I looked at the paramedics. "Gentlemen? If you would loosen the straps please? Have the oxygen ready."

The Paramedics gaped at me like I was from outer space. Paramedic #1 said, "Are you kidding, lady? You got to be nuts if you think I'm turning that deranged cave man loose in here!"

I stepped to within a couple of inches of Paramedic #1 and spoke softly but vehemently. I poked him in the chest as I spoke, and he slowly stepped backward. "I am *not* kidding, *nor* am I nuts. And I am *Detective* Miller, not 'lady', understood?"

Paramedic #1 turned a lovely shade of red. "Uh, yes, ma'am."

I gave him another nasty look and stepped toward him. He flinched. "Detective, I mean. Sorry."

I kept my eyes on his. "Thank you. Now will you please ease the restraints on Luke?"

He gulped. "Yes, Detective Miller." The two paramedics went to work on Luke, and the rest of the deputies piled in from the garage.

I looked at Chet. "Grab a towel for his face, would you, please?"

Chet tossed a towel onto the gurney.

J.J. slapped a hand on my shoulder. "Got him under control now?"

I grinned. "Which one? If you mean Luke, here, he has himself under control. I just explained the consequences of his actions from here on out. I don't know what he's on, but he needs some oh-two. He knows he's headed for the master suite if he messes with us."

"Ah, the old rubber room treatment. That's the way to calm them down in a hurry." I rolled my eyes at him and he smiled back.

I removed the spit shield and Luke jerked his head around to eyeball the deputies. A hunk of phlegm flew off his head and headed straight for them. They all jumped aside—except Chet, who had his back turned and caught it on the back of his neck. He froze in place, and very carefully reached for his handkerchief as the nasty goo slithered inside his collar.

The guys from Jefferson giggled and J.J. put his hand on Chet's clean shoulder. "Cop rule one-oh-two: Never turn your back on a subject; you might get a loogie down your shirt."

We all laughed, and I gestured for Luke to sit up. I gave the kid the rag to wipe off his face, and I hooked up the oxygen back up. He made to move off the gurney. He still looked a little wobbly so I put a hand out to stop him. He avoided my touch but allowed J.J. and one of the Jefferson guys help him down. Luke stumbled over to the chair in front of my station and held on. He swallowed several times and had a distinct green cast to his skin.

I took one look at him and called to the other cops. "Uh, would you guys mind escorting him to the bathroom where he can uh, clean up a little? There are towels in the cabinet. Thank you."

They quickly took him back, O2 bottle and all. I prepared the paperwork we needed for booking. I heard the water running, and the gut wrenching sounds of Luke retching whatever he had left in his stomach. *Hope he hit the toilet.*

One of the Jefferson guys looked at the bathroom door and snickered. "Wow, would ya listen to that? I sure hope he hit the toilet."

Chet appeared from the staff bathroom on the other side of the room. Drying his neck with a paper towel he stopped to listen. "Geez, I hope the kid at least hit the toilet, I'd hate to clean that up."

J.J. appeared from the break room, sporting a stale donut and a cup of killer coffee. Taking a bite, he said with his mouth full, "Man, hope the kid at least hit the toilet!"

I sighed and returned to my booking form.

Another Jefferson guy walked in from the garage, paperwork in hand. He stopped and cocked an ear toward the bathroom. He looked back at us. "Boy-oh-boy, I hope–"

We all held up our hands. I said, "We know! You sure hope he hits the toilet!"

"Uh, no. I was going to say I hope I have all the hospital

paperwork, because it looks like the medical clearance is missing." He looked at me with a puzzled expression. "What's this about something hitting what toil–"

J.J. threw his hands up "Nothing! Never mind! Let's get this show on the road, people." He bent to pick paperwork up off the floor. He shuffled through it and pulled out a sheet. "Here's your clearance, Barney Fife, now don't lose it on your way to the counter."

The deputy slapped the hospital form on the counter in front of me. Grumbling to themselves, the cops in the room prepared to leave. They emptied our coffee pot and swiped the last of our stale donuts before piling out the door. I sorted through the mess of paperwork the Jefferson County deputy dumped in front of me and tried to read the chicken scratch which appeared to be his version of what happened.

The bathroom doorknob rattled and I looked up to see Luke stumble into the squad room, pasty and shaken. He looked around as if he just realized he wasn't in Kansas anymore. The oxygen mask hung around his neck by a piece of green elastic. Chet took the bottle from him, turned it off, and set it on the floor. Luke took off the mask and dropped it next to the bottle.

The kid still looked around the room like he'd landed on Mars. He watched Chet lumber around the corner. I indicated the plastic chair in front of me and said, "Pay no attention to the man behind the curtain, kid, have a seat."

He scowled at me and lumbered flat-footed toward the booking desk. I had a chance to observe him for a few seconds. He was a kid like a thousand other kids who had passed through the system before him. Thin bordering on skeletal; Luke Hall's clothes seemed to hang on his scarecrow-like frame. *Needs a haircut and a shower too. Looks like someone ought to hang him in the corn field to chase crows. Hoo-whee! The smell alone would chase them away*!

According to the paperwork, Luke blew over a .25 blood-alcohol content on the road, and the high BAC led to the need for medical clearance, the subsequent nasty scene at the hospital, followed by the DC ticket. They drew blood to determine if anything else was floating around in his system. Bruises covered him head to toe and I cringed inside while I gently questioned him on the subject of what might have happened. I asked him about being involved in an accident, I asked about fighting, drugs, bullying, falling out of trees in a blizzard, skateboarding, hate crime–all the ways kids can get the crap knocked out of them when they get drunk and stupid. Luke wouldn't give me a straight answer, but it didn't surprise me much. What did surprise me was the open hostility I felt pouring off his body and aimed in my direction.

I ignored him and turned to my trusty computer. My fingers were loaded and the safety was off as I began hunting and pecking my way through the new booking program the County sprang for. Though I acted like I ignored the kid, I kept an eye on him for the most part. I sat grumbling and cussing to myself because the program was designed for a large metropolitan police force and not compatible with our equipment. Leave it to administration to make decisions without consulting the people who had to actually use the product.

I could hear Chet abusing the old Royal typewriter in the next room as he hammered out his report. *At least he's doing something more productive than eating donuts and watching infomercials*, I grumbled to myself.

I looked up from the computer and I was struck again by the outward calm shown by this obviously tensed up teen. Battered and drunk as he was, Luke took a deep breath, pulled his head up and looked at me. No other movement marred his vacant expression as he gave me the once-over with very old eyes. Then it struck me; where's the attitude I so despise in teens? Where's the loud-mouthed-know-it-all the cops wrestled with at the hospital? Where did the belligerent-and-immature kid under the spit shield go? Was this the calm before the storm? I felt the rage bottled up inside him, the hatred bubbling to the surface, but nothing showed on the outside...weird. Very weird.

He almost seemed to be waiting for something. *What are you waiting for, kid? 'Cuz we ain't sitting around here playing Parcheesi.* He knew who I was–all the kids did in a small burg like ours, but he didn't acknowledge Buzz Miller the person either, he just sat there in eerie silence.

He answered some of my preliminary questions, but he did not invite conversation; he just stared, and I stared back. *Come on kid, give me a hand here. I don't read minds. I only get creepy feelings about people and places sometimes. You gotta help me out if I am going to help you, and you aren't going to make the first move so...*

I reached out and touched the back of his hand. "Look, Luke." He snatched it back like he had touched fire, but not before the familiar vertigo-like feeling washed over me and I had to blink to clear my head. Pain like I had never known flashed through me. Desperation so grievous it would have bowled me over had I not been sitting, surged on a current from him into me. Flashing through my mind like an 8mm movie, the rage, hatred, and despair flickered in my mind's eye. I took a shuddering breath and looked up to see Luke ready to bolt.

I had always tended to feel funky when I "read" something from another person or when I knew something was about to happen. Don't ask me how; my mom says it's the Irish and my friends called it freaky. Don't ask me why– because I sure as heck didn't know then and I don't know now. And I *don't* call it a gift because it about ruined my life.

Back then I had a bleeding ulcer from stress which about killed me and insomnia which I self-medicated with copious amounts of alcohol. I also thought (faulty logic I know now) it was my personal mission to save the world. Heck, I was a one-woman superhero show–the only thing missing was the dumb red cape...what a dope I was back then.

I looked up sharply but the kid still stared at his hand. "So, you felt it too, eh bonsai?"

He stared at me.

I got up and walked slowly around the counter. He once again looked down at the floor. Speaking softly and careful not to touch him, I asked, "Are you going to tell me what happened here, Luke? Or are you going to let me keep playing twenty questions?"

He shrugged his shoulders. "Whatever. Do you worst, lady," and laid his head on the counter as if resigned to his fate.

"I know you don't trust me, but I won't hurt you, Luke." I laid a hand on his shoulder. He flinched and dizzying waves of black and red swept over me as the Irish "sheeney" allowed me a glimpse into the horror of the life of the man-child before me.

* * *

I am an eight-year old boy screaming for Mommy from inside a really small room–a closet I'd bet– but she never comes. I know the monster will come soon and beat me so I try to not make noise, but he will also shoot me with drugs. I am forced by fear and pain to cry out. My mind rejects the drugs while my body craves them like a gnawing hunger. I'm sweating and shaking. I itch all over. My stomach hurts. Oh man, I'm gonna puke! I need to crawl out of my skin. The itch is worse. The monster is coming back, and I gotta pee bad, but I don't want him to hurt me again. Fat chance, moron.

I try to move. I'm very weak and I stumble and fall

against the door. I make a thump. Oh no, no, no! I think he heard me. I see a flash of light as the door is snatched open, and I cram myself into a corner. I cannot see him, but I smell his rancid odor. I flinch because he wants me to, and I couldn't help it even if I wanted to.

He wants me to cower, to cry. I want to refuse, but I'm so scared I think I'm going to pee myself. I feel the sharp stab of pain. "Shut Up, Freak." Fists, belts, hangars, feet, whatever else is handy rain down on my body. Something cuts me and the umbrella pokes. I try not to cry out, but it's too much this time. I hear someone scream–I think it's me. I cower like the beaten dog I am. Freak. Baby pissy boy.

I uncover my head and a take a peek, his fists find my face. I cry like a blubbering baby and pee myself just like one. I puke all over myself, but the beatings continue. I gasp and choke on my own puke, and I figure he's going to kill me this time. Thank God because I don't want to live...I don't want to live. The world shrinks down into the black cocoon. Velvet blackness envelops me in her welcoming arms...

I must've passed out again, I'm trying to remember. I pinch my arm and I feel it. Oh crap, I'm not dead. Dead could not feel this bad. I hoped he would kill me this time.

Opening an eye just a slit, I see I am in my closet. I lie on the floor, my face stuffed in a corner, my twisted body battered and bloody. I hear the door creak. I force my swollen eyes open and I see a sliver of light. The light invades my cocoon but I cannot overpower the pain left by the beating and the wracking pain of jonesing for drugs.

I lay there like a pile of rags. I feel the prick of the needle and warmth rushes up my arm. Relief. I can feel the warmth separate and flow into other veins. Warmth spreads through my chest, the pain recedes, and I relax. I can trace the warmth as it rushes to my hands and toward my feet. This is the best part. Blessed warmth, blessed oblivion. The door slams closed and the velvet dark envelops me once again. Pain recedes, I can relax. The dark is my friend. The dark is my only friend.

For just a second I think of my mother and I feel loneliness so acute it's almost a physical pain, but the hatred seeps in and festers like an open sore in my heart. I hate her for leaving me with him. I hate her for not coming back. I despise the monster with every painful breath I take, and I hate myself for being what I am. The drug dulls my pain as the hatred feeds my soul. I begin to fade away again. Blessed oblivion...

I let go of the kid. I stumbled backward, sucking in great gulps of air. Luke sat in his chair, face down on the counter not moving. I felt terrified to intrude again on this kid's horror, but I was compelled to reach out. He had no one else in the world but an abusive old man who beat, drugged, and continuously abused him.

He turned his head toward me and opened an eye. "I don't know what you're doing, lady, but it's giving me a buzz." He turned his head away from me and I sighed. Tamping down the sudden need for my usual stiff belt of Jack Daniels, I leaned forward. I fought the need to know with all my being, as his past had nothing to do with what happened this night. Luke didn't move, and I felt myself move. I watched in a kind of trance as my hand moved toward this broken and battered man-child. I knew it would fry my senses. I knew I would re-live Luke's nightmare, but it was like I sat watching an Alfred Hitchcock movie. I silently screamed at my hand to stop, but watched helplessly as it hovered over Luke's tee shirt, and dropped lightly to his shoulder. Luke shuddered once, and I launched back into an eight-year-old's horror.

Another scene. Lights hurt my eyes; I must still be drugged. Claw-like hands grab at my arms and drag me

41

unceremoniously over the splintery floor. I fight free and fall. Pain explodes in my head and blackness engulfs me. Safety in darkness. Safe for a while.

Odd odors surround me. The smell of old sneakers and of powder and lavender. Grandma's room? Comforting. I remember feeling safe with my grandma. Where is my grandma now? Why doesn't she come and save me?

Then another smell permeates my senses like a black fog and I freeze in terror. The smell of dirty underwear and B.O. and the rancid smell of the monster. I begin to sweat. Hands hold me down. Oh no, I know what's coming. Make them stop, oh please, someone make them stop! I feel the needle prick. I feel a little muzzzzyyy.

I am jarred away by blasts of lightning pain, oh my God, burning, tortuous pain. Fight back, dirty boy! I'm too weak to make him stop. Make it stop! Mommy! Oh God, oh god-oh-god–blackness.

I am older now, and something is different. I jerk up my head. I'm in a windowless room. Not in my closet. Where's my closet? I want my closet. I hurt. Pain reminds me I am still alive. Panic... panic! Breathe. Slow down and breathe in, and out, slow in, slow out. Can they hear me? I hurt. My whole body hurts. Will the voices know where I am? I smell mildew and cat pee. I reach down and feel a cold floor. Bone deep cold. Scratching. Sounds as if something is eating cracker crumbs. Rats. I hate rats.

I hear footsteps. He's coming for me again. I can't breathe. Has it been hours, weeks, months, or years since I last saw daylight? Nothing has changed after all. I'm starving. I need water. I try to be strong but I start to sweat. I start to shake. I hurt so bad.

Be strong dirty boy. I start to cry. I hate my weakness, but I fear the monster even more. The voices whisper, "Dirty boy, bad boy, bad boy, dirty..."

42

Escape. I have to escape now or die.....

I tore myself away from Luke and out of his nightmare. The force of it knocked me back and onto the floor. I didn't want to see anymore. Oh my God, how this child had suffered at the hands of a monster. Tears streaming down my face and gasping for air, Chet ran from the office, pepper spray at the ready, and blood in his eye. "What the heck, Buzz?" He spun toward Luke and thumbed the tab up on the can. "Don't move, kid, or you won't be able to see the commissioner tomorrow!"

"Chet," I wheezed.

He looked at me, pepper spray still trained on Luke. "You okay? Did he hit you?"

"I'm okay, back off, Chet. Not the kid! The kid's okay Chet. Not his fault."

My heart rate slowed and I crawled to my knees, shaking. "Put the spray away and call J.J. back. Tell him I need him. The kid needs him. He'll come, I know he will."

Chet slid a look toward Luke one more time before shoving his spray in the holder and turning to the phone. Luke didn't move. I slowly got up and went into the bathroom, looking neither left nor right. I flipped up the toilet seat and proceeded to toss up whatever I had in me. I began to shake. Falling to my knees, I wrapped both arms around my middle and silently cried for the child who suffered such heinous abuse.

How did this crime escape school, police, and neighbors? While I contemplated the possibilities, I stood and flushed. I cupped cold water in my hands and bathed my ravaged face.

Stepping out of the bathroom, Chet stared at me; concern darkening his features. The outer door slammed open.

J.J. stomped snow off his boots and clomped into the room. I guess I didn't do such a good job of disguising the greenish tone to my face, because he came straight for me and took me by arm. He half–dragged me toward the break room. "Chet, book the kid, would you? Buzz, come with me."

Like I had a choice. I followed like a sheep and he sat me down on the short couch in the break room. He closed the door, pulled up a chair and sat nose-to-nose with me. I must have looked like a chewed up limp noodle–I know I felt like one.

He took my hands and lifted my chin. He stared into my eyes. The corners of his crinkled with compassionate humor. "Now tell me." And I did.

5

Memories of that horrible first night faded as I watched Luke from across the parking lot. I saw J.J. and Luke head for J.J.'s squad. I opened the back end of my vehicle and began stripping. Shucking my rain gear, I tossed it into the back and slammed the tail gate. Watching the comfortable banter between Luke and J.J. brought back more memories, and the rest of Luke's story.

Horace Hall was a surly old fart on a good day and a sloppy, mean drunk pretty much every other day. No one in town had any idea of the evil lurking in the heart of that mean old bastard, or of the abuse one young boy suffered at his hands.

Beginning on that long ago frigid February night, seventeen-year-old Luke Hall finally ceased to remain a high, drunken, and beaten throw-away child. In the end, the courts awarded our local sheriff, J.J. Green, full custodial rights. J.J. suffered alongside Luke through the hell of alcoholism and drug recovery over the next year. Trying to fix the emotional damage however, took much longer.

Slowly Luke came around, and after Horace Hall got out of prison, he rotted alone in that broken down and decaying old house at the edge of the dead end road. One thing always stuck in my craw. Horace Hall was never really brought to justice for his crimes against Luke. A couple years in prison, some parole time, then free as a bird, the monster slithered back into the old house. Unless, of course you believe in what-goes-around-comes-around, because he ended up getting his arm sucked into his wood chipper and he bled to death alone, out behind his shed. Most folks thought even that gruesome end was too good for him.

Only Luke, J.J., and I knew how much he had made a small boy suffer those many years ago. Luke somehow survived his hell at the hands of a worthless waste of skin, but through it all he remained the great kid he still is.

When the old buzzard got himself wood chopped, Luke seemed to stand little straighter and talk a little easier, as though a tremendous weight had been lifted from his shoulders. Some idiots ugly enough to whisper behind their hands might have insinuated Luke knew a little more about Horace's grisly demise than he let on, and maybe our good sheriff didn't investigate deep enough into "poor Horace's" death, but no one was stupid enough to say it within earshot of J.J. or me.

Two years down the road, a clean and sober Luke finished high school. I was there to kiss his cheek when he loaded his worldly possessions into the back of J.J.'s truck, ready to face college head-on. He had a full ride academic scholarship to U. W. Madison, and J.J. couldn't have been more proud if Luke had been his own son. Tears and cheers surrounded the stuffed-full truck as well wishers arrived to see Luke off to college, then onto the FBI Academy and the Forensic Sciences Division.

Enough with the reminiscing Miller. Shaking my head and bringing myself back to the business at hand, I climbed into my SUV.

I barely had the door closed when movement by the dumpster caught my eye. Luke and J.J. ran across Sal's parking lot. Luke jumped into the Sheriff's squad. J.J. had the cell phone to his ear, and slapped it closed in time to duck into the car a second behind Luke. They took off after the coroner's van and left the other deputies to finish cleaning up the crime scene.

Not one to be left out, I revved the engine and tore after

them—a pretty dumb move now that I think about it because Sal's is about two blocks away from everywhere in White Bass Lake, so where else would they be going but the morgue? But who thinks of logistics when they are in the midst of chasing a meat wagon, a sheriff, and an FBI agent through town? Obviously not me, uh, until I tried to turn into the morgue parking lot and my SUV began to hydroplane on the flooded street. It was like driving in a crazed mini-sprint on a wet clay track in the clubhouse turn.

Fighting the urge to yank the wheel and slam on the brakes, I gently turned the wheel into the spin and hoped I would miss the coroner's van and J.J., who, at this point had not noticed me heading straight for him. I laid on the horn. Thank heaven Mrs. Murphy lost out on this one, because my wheels grabbed hold of the crown in the parking lot at the last second and jerked my SUV to the side. Ivan grabbed J.J. and yanked him out of the way as I flew past, but the gurney he held on to did not fare as well.

I whipped my head around in time to watch the gurney creep away from the back of the van in slo-mo, and slowly roll its way toward the center of the parking lot...the same parking lot I currently careened through at a high rate of speed.

In a total panic I slammed on the brakes—breathing a prayer of thanks for anti-lock brakes. I barely heard the yelling from the guys in the parking lot. Clenching the wheel in both hands, I gritted my teeth and stood on the brakes.

"Buzz!"

"Watch Out!"

"Ohmygod Stooop!"

"DON'T KILL THE DEAD GUY!"

Don't kill the what?

The SUV came screeching to a halt, spinning in a half-circle. The gurney met my bumper head-on as my SUV came to a jolting stop. I had no time to check my vitals as my body pitched violently backward against the headrest. Adding insult to injury, the airbag exploded in my face and the force of the contact with the gurney flipped it and the dead guy into the air and over the hood ornament of my SUV.

I had no idea how long I sat before I could hear the commotion outside my SUV, but I must have come-to, because the first thing I remember was beating frantically against the deflating bag only to stare stunned and grossed out at a naked, maggoty butt half through my windshield.

I take no responsibility for my actions which followed, as I am a consummate professional, and will forever claim I was totally disoriented. I freaked. I screamed like a girl. I momentarily thought I had run over J.J., and he somehow got naked and plastered against my windshield. Dumb, I know, but what the heck, I had just been blasted into la-la land by an airbag.

"AAAAHHH! J.J.!"

Screaming bloody murder and staring at the dead butt in my face, I must have sounded like the Demented Banshee from Madagascar. I clawed at the seatbelt, hysterical and screeching. The driver's door flew open and thought I heard people yelling, but nothing penetrated through the dense fog of my concussed brain. I thought I had just croaked my childhood friend and man of my dreams by being a stupid ambulance chaser.

Yanking the driver's door open, J.J. yelled in my face he was alive and well, and his butt was not maggoty thank-you-very-much. His voice kicked me out of my mania, because one look into those beautiful green eyes had me blubbering nonsensically. I threw my arms around his neck and sobbed.

J.J. fought me for the seatbelt, all the time trying to calm me down. Ivan had come through the passenger door, and tore the airbag away from the steering wheel one-handed, and peeled me off J.J. He leaned in and laid his left arm across my chest, pinning me against the seat while J.J. scrambled to get the seatbelt undone.

Once free, I catapulted out of the driver's seat onto J.J., crying and bleeding all over him. He kept up his reassurances he was indeed, alive and well, and I kept apologizing and uh, probably babbled some things I shouldn't have.

As J.J. carried me to the curb I thought, *this guy is a lot stronger than he looks,* and knew I slowly made my way back to coherent thought. He set me down and tilted my face toward his. J.J. pulled my soaked, bloody hair off my face and Luke held a flashlight up so J.J. could assess the damage. The beam sent shards of pain shooting through my head, I flinched, and the lights went out–in more ways than one.

I next woke in unfamiliar surroundings. Pain knifed through my head as I looked around the brightly lit room. Moving only my eyeballs, I realized I was inside the morgue, and Mike Dudley stared at me from about three inches away.

"Uh, Mike? Am I alive?"

His eyes crinkled at the corners. "Yeah, Buzz, you're alive. A little worse for wear, but you're alive."

"Did someone call in a dead horse or something?"

He chuckled and looked up. "Hey J.J., she's okay because she's joking."

"Who's joking? You're a veterinarian."

Mike looked back at me. "I know I'm a vet, but Frank is at the hospital delivering a baby, so J.J. called me. He figured you'd be pissed if you woke up in a hospital."

"Uh, yeah, but waking up in the county morgue with a neuterer of goats staring me in the eyeball is better?"

"Apparently J.J. thought so."

"No offense, Mike, but he called the pig doctor."

"No offense taken, my friend, but after all, he is my best friend, and I am pretty good to have around in a crisis."

"Sorry, Mike, thanks for coming down. I guess I'm still a little foggy." I touched my nose. "And my nose hurts."

He patted my shoulder. "Atta girl. You're lucky if you didn't break your cute little Irish schnoz. Now let me get J.J. in here–he's still fit to be tied."

At my puzzled expression, he leaned in closer and whispered, "Personally, I think he's pretty worked up over you and not thinking straight."

"I know. I almost ran over him. I thought–"

He pressed a hand to my shoulder. "Whoa, Buzz, save it. Tell it to 'da-man'. You need to concentrate on staying calm and awake. You have a pretty good nick above your right eye, and your nose bled pretty heavily from contact with the airbag, but like I said, I don't think it's broken. It does look to me like you have a concussion, though. Let me call your guy in and you can discuss it with him."

"My guy?"

Mike shook his head and walked out of the room. I smiled as what he said clicked. "Ohhh, right. My guy. Right." I'd have rolled my eyes, but they hurt too much.

J.J. skid through the door. To my humiliation, tears began to stream out of my eyes and run into my ears. I tilted my head to shake them out and pain throbbed in my temples.

J.J. sat in the chair Mike had vacated and we both spoke at once. He leaned forward and my arms slid around his waist.

"J.J., I'm s-sorry. I–"

"Buzz, are you okay?"

"J.J., I almost killed you!"

"You scared the crap out of me!"

Silence fell like a stone. J.J. tried to catch his breath. Suddenly his brow furrowed and those green eyes flashed like flint. He kissed me on the forehead. I felt warm and loved–for about two seconds.

"Buzz, what in Sam Hill were you thinking?"

"I–I wasn't thinking, I guess. I tried to catch up to–"

"Damn right you weren't thinking!"

"I just said that."

He continued to holler at me. He jumped up from the chair and started to pace, gesturing wildly. "I know what you said. I said it too, and I'll say it again. You could have been killed driving like an idiot! If you died, how would I tell your mother? How would I tell your sisters?" He stopped suddenly. "How would I tell the dogs?"

I smiled a little and closed my eyes (I still couldn't roll them) at his melodrama. I guess he caught me. He got in my face. "You think this is funny? You took ten years off my life out there."

I tried to look contrite, but my head really hurt. He flopped back in the chair and ran a hand through his hair. He grabbed the hand nearest him and wrapped both of his around it.

"Look, Buzz, I know we avoid talking about personal stuff like the plague but I uh, you should know uh, I mean if anything ever happened to you I'd uh–"

I panicked. "Wait. You don't have to do this."

"Huh?"

"Yeah. I know what you're going to say, and I know."

"You know?"

"Stop repeating me, Green. I know you'd take my dogs if anything happened to me, and for that I'd be grateful."

He scowled at me. "Really, J.J., I appreciate it. I do–"

"What the heck are you talking about the dogs for? Every time I try to talk seriously to you, you change the subject. Would you just shut the heck up for once and listen? I'm not talking about the damn dogs, Buzz, I'm talking about us. *Us*!"

He stood over me, looking really pissed. I didn't want

51

him saying anything he would regret when the shock wore off, but I really hoped he was about to say what I'd wanted to hear for as long as I could remember. It was like a tragic accident you're compelled to look at even though you knew it would be devastating. I stared at him like a dope.

J.J. now had a death grip on my hand. "Buzz."

"James?"

I felt my heart thump as he leaned in closer. He took a breath and I held mine. The moment stretched and I felt ready to explode. I felt my eyelids droop and my mouth tilt toward him.

His lips parted. I waited. "Buzz, listen to me. I, I–"

The tinkling of the bell above the entrance to the morgue halted him in mid-sentence. J.J. jerked to attention and the air whooshed out of my lungs.

"Hold on second."

He vanished out the door. The breath I held whooshed out and my head fell back on the pillow. "Ow."

I heard a shrill voice and knew any hope of regaining the moment flew out the window. I hefted myself into a sitting position and tested my balance. I was a little dizzy, so I took it slow. I rose in inches, teetered on my feet, and grabbed a table. Blinking hard I tried to clear my vision. Geez, it even hurt to blink. I took a deep breath and took a couple steps. That seemed to go pretty well so I tried a couple more. By the time I made it to the door I heard J.J. talking to my mother in the vestibule.

I shook my head to clear it and was immediately sorry I did so. Nausea rolled through my belly and my hand missed the table. I fell across the surface and hit my chin. Tears sprang to my eyes and the opening bars of Beethoven's Fifth pounded through my head.

Mom prattled on about the time and some meeting....

Meeting! I had forgotten about the fair meeting. I looked

at my watch and sighed. I had about an hour to finish up here, get home to take care of the dogs and pick up my fair board packet, and get back to town. Taking a deep breath I cautiously put one foot in front of the other. By the time I hit the door, I was moving pretty well. I slipped out of the office and headed for the door.

I didn't even wait to see if J.J. followed me. I could hear him in the cold room yakking it up with Mom and Ivan. I moved at what seemed like a fast clip down the hall. I didn't want to face Mom or J.J. right now. My only thought was escape.

I had already scoped out Malcolm's inner office and didn't see my keys anywhere. My head felt like someone blindsided me with a baseball bat, and I fought the nausea, and blinked my teary-eyes. I checked the reception area for any keys lying around. No luck. I slid around the reception counter, using it to prop me up.

The longer I stayed upright, the better I felt so I stayed focused on the task at hand...whatever that was.

I looked up and saw the exit sign over the door. Ah-ha! Escape. Forgetting about mundane things like car keys, I concentrated on getting out of the morgue.

I put my hand on the door handle and drew up short. There J.J.'s jacket laid, draped across a chair in the waiting area. Keys! I stumbled across the room and fell on J.J.'s jacket like a starving man on a steak dinner. I dug around in his pockets until I felt my key ring. Eureka! I snatched the sucker and started for the door.

My head pounded and my vision blurred. I blinked and reached for the door. I missed the handle the first time. I had a vision of me driving my SUV out of the parking lot into a ditch. In my cracked-brained state, I justified it because there I knew there was no ditch across the street. I hesitated, however, knowing there was going to be big trouble coming from Mom and J.J. if I left and drove myself. Oh, and Malcolm and Luke would probably yell at me too. What the heck, I might as well include Ivan and the Tooth Fairy while I was at it. Any way I looked at it, the only intelligent option was to crawl back to Malcolm's office and lie down until someone fetched me... Not!

I peered down the long hall and heard muffled voices coming from the cold room. I panned in on the squad in the parking lot. I shook and panned in on the closed cold room door, like a heroine in a Hitchcock film. I drew a close-up on the keys in my hand. My fingers curled around them until I could feel the teeth biting into my palm. *Don't do it, Buzz!*

And so it came to pass, I crept out of the morgue like a thief in the night and drove myself to my house, where I cleaned up and ate a few ibuprofens, and then took myself off to the county fair meeting.

The thunderstorm outside my vehicle matched the thundering of my headache as I rolled into the town hall parking lot about an hour later.

6

"... So the carnival will be rolling into White Bass Lake early next week for the County Fair."

I stood in front of the County Fair Board of Directors and the various sub-committees and read my notes. I leaned on the podium for support. The stuffy room closed in on me and sweat ran down my back. *Smells like feet in here. Maybe I got clunked on the head harder than I thought. My head hurts and my nose feels like a balloon. I wonder if anyone in the audience has any aspirin.*

Local hair salon owner Lee Ann Swanson beamed at me in the front row. *How does she do it? Doesn't that woman ever sweat? It's got to be a hundred and ten in here.* The room became awfully quiet and I realized I had stopped speaking. Everyone stared, waiting for me to muddle through the rest of the progress report. *My brains must still be a little scrambled. Focus, Miller, Where the heck were you? Ohh, yeah, "Little Miss Never Sweat."* I cleared my throat and tried to focus.

"Lee Ann Never Sweat—I—I mean Swanson here is in charge of the makeup and hair for the beauty contestants. Her sister Sherry is in charge of the pageant itself. Do you have anything needing attention tonight, ladies?" The two women shook their heads in unison, smiled, and waved to the crowd. Sherry smiled. "We're all set, Buzz. The last contract was turned in yesterday."

Lee Ann nodded. "Yup. We at Ready, Set, Blow are ready and set to go!"

I forced myself not to roll my eyes, remembering how much they hurt, and continued. "Okay. I'm sure the girls are in great hands. Thank you, ladies. They waved at the audience and I noticed Lee Ann had a small wet spot under her arm. "Hah!"

Lee Ann yanked down her arm. "What? What is it, Buzz?"

A wave of dizziness and contrition swept through me. "Nothing, Lee. Just proud to call you friend and neighbor."

She smiled and wrinkled her nose. "Thanks, pal."

I cleared my throat and continued. "Gerry Miller, Jane Knight and Joy Broussard are taking care of the organization, judging and security of the Agriculture Building where everything from flowers to fruits and vegetables will be judged." I saw Mom and J.J. enter the room. J.J. stood glaring at me from the back and Mom slid into a seat next to Jane.

I looked at my notes. "The ladies want you to remember we have yet to catch the notorious phantom garlic thief who strikes the Ag Building every year, but with the newly installed security cameras along with our crack security team they have confidence the garlic thief will finally be brought to task."

I heard a sharp intake of breath before Mom, Jane, and Joy waved. The crowd hooted and whistled.

I figured whoever sucked in the air must have been the garlic thief, but looking over the crowd, the only person not clapping was Bucket the Clown. He sat, silently staring and scowling at the SWAT team. *Strange, why would the clown be glaring at a group of little old ladies?* I took a moment to pretend to look over my chicken scratched notes, trying to get J.J.'s attention. No go. Bucket finally looked forward and our eyes met. He looked away first. I knew that had to be significant, but I just couldn't figure out why.

I continued pawing through my notes, wishing not for the first time I had the talent to organize as well as my baby sister Al. Though my youngest sister prided herself on being a royal pain in the buttski, she really was a tremendous organizer. Must be because the anal retentive gene zinged right past me.

I sighed. Old Al was also a shyster. How I got hooked into standing up here reading the committee notes I had no idea. She worked like a dog and almost single-handedly organized the entire fair. Why she preferred to stay in the background was beyond me, because Al always seemed to be first in line to be the center of attention. But there she sat, in the back of the room furiously typing away on her laptop; pencil between her teeth and her half–glasses sliding down her nose. She was probably organizing world peace while the rest of the room patted each other on the back for their very small jobs well done. I sighed and continued.

"Alexandra Miller has a hospitality tent set up in the oak grove near the big stage. The stage will feature local talent. The refreshments donated by White Bass Lake Business Owners Association will be sold by the county 4-H kids to provide money for next year's tent, and the 4-H scholarship program. "The fair board donated the cost of the space, but we still have to pay for the tent and the electric. Bucket the Clown will be our emcee." Bucket started like someone jabbed him with a pin. He realized he was in the spotlight and cranked a corner of his mouth up while waving his hand. *Hmmm, what a weirdo.*

"Mary Cromwell volunteered to take care of the lineup of talent, and Gary Conway is sitting in as her co-chair."

Gary lifted a hand to the crowd and Mary jumped up like something bit her. She gave him the stink eye and he waggled his eyebrows at her. She bared her teeth and hissed, "Keep it zipped, you old goat!" She smacked his arm, and Gary just smiled a secret little smile and settled back in his chair. I almost fell down trying not to laugh.

I tried to find my place in my notes. While I fumbled

with the papers in my hand, I spotted old Gary's hand as it snaked under the table and grabbed a hold of Mary's kneecap. She wound up like a pro-ball pitcher and jabbed a boney elbow into his side. I knew she landed a direct hit because Gary wheezed and gasped, and dropped her knee like a hot potato. I had to look away and bite my lip to keep from totally losing it.

With great effort I continued. "Sheriff Green has enlisted the help of village and city police officers throughout the county for security. I saw J.J. duck through the door and his eyes immediately met mine. His green eyes seared into mine and my headache grew worse. I gulped. "Uh, the police officers will all be wearing red polo shirts with the county emblem on the front." My eyes flicked over the crowd and stopped on J.J. again. He glared daggers and made a cutting motion with his index finger across his throat. I'll admit it, I flinched.

"I, uh, there will be eyes..." I stopped. "I-I mean green eyes–"

I took a deep breath. J.J. glared at me, but one side of his mouth jerked up. *He knows how intimidating he is.* I fumbled with my notes and stared over his head. "I meant to say there will be out-posts marked on the fair map for citizen access. Each team will have a radio and will be assigned a walking beat; this way we won't have ten guys hanging out at the queen contest and no one on the carnival grounds." I leveled a look at the cop table and Moe and Curly, two of J.J.'s deputies, had the grace to blush.

"The Sheriff's Department tent will be manned by Sheriff Green, Dr. Ian Connor, FBI Agent Bob Haskins and me, along with volunteers from the Citizen's Police Academy. Edie will be running the dispatch center from the motor home loaned to us by Dr. Tony Castillo." Tony smiled, lifted a hand and the crowd applauded politely.

"Kurt & Larry's Flying School will provide helicopter rides in the infield of the track. They'll also donate a hot air balloon anchored to the ground. It'll lift approximately thirty feet in the air for demonstration purposes; so parents and kids can experience what it feels like to lift off in a balloon.

"Kurt will also demonstrate flying an ultra-light, and has arranged to have local collectors exhibit their planes on Saturday and Sunday on the infield of the grandstand." Larry sat quietly snoring in the back row, while Kurt sat next to him waving enthusiastically. He sat back and jostled Larry, who snorted and made "yum-yum" sounds before drifting off once again. Kurt shrugged and popped a Pez candy in his mouth. You had to love those guys.

I quickly ran down the rest of the list. "Al also has planned for the kids, a greased pig contest, a pedal power contest, and a pet parade. For the adults, a chili cook-off, a chicken dinner picnic basket competition, a home-brew beer competition, a best dessert contest, jams, jellies and cake decorating, and the pie auction on Saturday."

The crowd *oood*, and Sal Garcia jumped out of his chair and rubbed his hands together at the mention of cake decorating. "Competitors beware! I am not just another pretty face. Hah! I will create a masterpiece which will stand above the rest!"

His wife Amy grabbed his shirt tail and yanked him back into his chair. "Yeah, well don't get too cocky, Mr. Ace of Cake. Fanny McCabe from Kenosha kicked your butt two years ago."

"Yes, but I have it on good authority Miss McCabe is visiting her daughter in Door County this summer and will not be attending the fair this year." Sal smiled smugly, and fisted his hands above his head like a champion prizefighter. The crowd hooted and applauded. Amy just sighed and shook her head.

7

The meeting broke up shortly after, and everyone headed for air conditioning and home.

I headed for the door when Al said from the back row, "Uh, Buzz, what about the tomato contest?"

I ducked my head. Ouch. "Tomato contest? Uh, I don't know anything about-oh no, you're not talking about *our* tomato contest, are you?"

She grinned. "I sure am. I contacted an old friend who now works for Channel 13, and she is going to do a special interest piece on the fair and cover the judging of the First Annual Miller Sister's Tomato Growing Contest."

My headache reached epic proportions and I started to sweat. "But...but...I uh, Channel 13...you don't mean like television Channel 13, do you? We can't...you can't...Alexandra, no one is going to be interested in a dumb tomato contest! That was just a family joke last winter. No one actually is interested if we can grow a tomato or not, especially at the fair."

"Sure they are. You're a legend in the tri-county area! Everyone wants to see if their advice helped you to actually grow something."

I thought a minute. "I guess I have been getting a lot of mail with tips on growing stuff. Heck, I've gotten so much gardening advice lately; I could hand out little cards with gardening tips on them!"

Al smiled. "Yeah, you could be the 'Dear Abby' of gardening. Newspaper syndicates all over the country would pick you up."

Al didn't see me turning as red as one of my so-called

tomatoes.

She babbled on. "My friend Laura at Channel 13 is thrilled with the small town family competition angle. We all started with the same variety of tomato, and we're all growing them to maturity. Ollie Boothe said she'd be our judge. The SWAT girls have agreed to provide the picnic supplies, and Dad is going to grill uh, whatever he wants to grill. Come on, Buzz, it'll be fun."

My mind worked 90 miles a minute. I thought about the dead sticks in the tomato pot at home and knew I was doomed.

Think, Buzz! How are you going to get out of this pickle? Wait! Cukes are pickles and tomatoes are, uh....dead. My tomatoes. Croaked. Ka-put. Lifeless, deceased, expired, dearly departed, gone, lamented, perished, fallen, slain, slaughtered, killed, murdered (by me!), dead as a doornail, six feet under, pushing up daisies...

Shut up, Buzz, you're an idiot. Oh no, my tomatoes are dead and I've been lying to my sisters for months; bragging about my beautiful plants just to shut them up. What the heck am I going to do now?

"Buzz! I said snap out of it! Are you okay? You look a little sick. I thought this would please you. You've been telling us all spring how well your 'maters are doing, so I thought this could be a little celebratory event for your first gardening success. This is history!"

I pasted a sick smile on my face and turned to Al. "Th-thanks so much for going through the trouble of setting this up. I hope I can live down to expectations."

Al missed my sarcasm and waved a hand in the air. She went back to typing. "No prob."

"But not at the fair, okay Al?"

"Mmm hmm."

I sure didn't like the sound of her "mmm hmm" but

watching her, I had to admit she looked a little ragged. No wonder. She almost single handedly accomplished what it usually takes a committee of six an entire year to do. Were I she, I'd have looked like last week's moldy pizza by now. I picked up my notes and wandered over to see what she was working on. "Are you about finished yet? What are you doing, transcribing the Dead Sea Scrolls or what?"

"Naw, jussa mint, Buth." She spit the pencil onto the table. "Sorry, Buzz, just a minute—I'm almost done."

Her fingers flew over the keys. I watched in envy of her talent. "Al, how do you *do* that?"

She saved her data and shut down the laptop. In a flip manner she said, "I guess we all have our talents, Buzz. Take you for instance." She stood and plunked her laptop tote on the table. "You jump on bad guys and get yourself shot. You always were good with puzzles, and you have the annoying habit of knowing either what's going to happen or what someone is thinking. You've always been the hero. You lead the charmed life. You are the one the town looks up to. Me, I'm just the ditzy blonde who can type fast and run in stilettos."

Al picked up her tote and slapped it on the table. Shuffling papers and stuffing her briefcase full, she was oblivious as to how her words cut me like a knife. Green smoke came out of my ears. I glared daggers at her, but she was too dumb to dive for cover. With my scrambled brains, I never realized her fatigue and stress levels reached far beyond human endurance at this point.

I spun her around and poked her in the chest. "Al, you are such a moron sometimes! The real story is, I spent a career with a bleeding ulcer and night terrors. You think this sheeny-Irish thing is a blessing? Every time I had a vision, I suffered as the victim suffered. I bled when the children bled. I felt their pain. I sometimes still hear them cry out.

"I drank way too much and waded through gallons of blood and guts and gore. It got so bad, I was deathly afraid to sleep at night because I thought I'd witness another child being torn apart or smell the putrid flesh of another decaying corpse."

She shook her head, "I didn't mean...I'm sor–, I mean I didn't know–"

I ran a shaky hand over my face. "And one day I found myself a victim. Old Superwoman here lived a private hell in a physically and mentally abusive marriage."

I turned toward her. "Yeah, me. Wonder Woman. Sure, people looked up to me. They actually waited for me to fall apart. They watched for signs showing the crap sifting through my brain finally drove me over the brink. I was interviewed, tested, threatened, counseled, and tested again. When I did finally flip out, I didn't tell anyone because I didn't want to pull anyone else down the sewer with me, and God help me if I besmirched the Miller name by seeking professional help."

I swiped a hand over my hair. "And somewhere in my screwed-up brain I thought if I just worked a little harder, if I worked just one more case, saved one more kid, if I proved just a little more perfect, everything would fix itself. What a delusional hell-hole I had to climb out of.

"I should have joined Psychos-R-Us, but they would have probably kicked me out. Thank God I retired early or I would have ended up a psychotic alcoholic with a bashed in face and no stomach lining. As it was, I almost succeeded."

Al stared at me silently, eyes wide and teary. I took a shuddering breath. "Charmed, Al? For a librarian, you sure have a screwed up definition of the word."

I grabbed my notes and stomped toward the door. I slipped around the corner and stood, sucking in air and trying not to lose it. I peeked back to make sure no one was coming, and saw J.J. as he walked past where Al still stood with her mouth hanging open. "Screwed that one up good, eh Al?"

Red faced and stammering, Al looked up at J.J. "Sorry. I must be more tired than I thought. What could have possessed me to—"

"Buzz is tired too. That and the fact she probably has a concussion and should be at home in bed might make her a little cranky. Why don't you sleep on it and talk to her tomorrow?"

Al ignored him. "No, I have to catch her now."

Suddenly she stood, shoved the laptop in the bag, hitched her tote over her shoulder, and headed after me. I could hear those obnoxious stilettos clicking a staccato beat down the tiled hall. Swiping at the tear running down my face, I picked up speed. Al did the same.

Damn. That's all I need. I knew I was being a wienie, but I picked up the pace to a sprint, hoping to avoid her altogether. Rounding a corner, I ducked into the bathroom and barricaded myself in the end stall. Trying not to breathe, I waited about five minutes before I exited.

I peeked out the bathroom door like the coward I was and found the the coast was clear. I didn't have much time to pout over Al's misconception of my life, but it what a slap in the face to think my own sister knew so little about me—let alone thought so little of me. Stepping into the hall, I dumped my stuff in a chair. By the time I finished putting my notes in order I felt much more myself again. I thought maybe I'd take some aspirin, call J.J. and maybe we could do something with the dogs tonight, or take in a movie, but I felt so rotten, I figured I'd just go home. Alone—which made me feel even more rotten.

I lamented the fact outdoor movie theaters were almost extinct around here anymore. Watching movies alone sucks. Microwave popcorn sucks. *I can't even take in a good movie with the dogs anymore unless I stay home. And I don't care what Orville Redenbacher says; the popcorn at the movies tastes different than it does coming out of a microwave.*

Deep in conversation with myself, I stepped out of the building into a drizzle. It reminded me of the guy we pulled out of the dumpster earlier. I practically fell over J.J., who stood under the eaves out of the rain, waiting for me.

My luck is changing already. Maybe dinner, maybe a quiet night at home with Clark Gable and Claudette Colbert, the dogs AND the Sheriff!

I pushed Al's words into the far reaches of my brain. When I looked up, I smiled at J.J. "What ho, Mr. Sheriff? Why are you standing in the rain looking so perplexed? Wondering what movie we're watching tonight?"

He blinked and pinched the bridge of his nose. He held up an index finger. "Just wait a minute Buzz, let me think here a minute. I just had an idea."

"Uh, yeah. I can smell the rubber burning."

"What? Wait, was that sarcasm?"

"Oh, no, must be your imagination."

He took my arm and pulled me away from the milling crowd. I sighed, shoving the disappointment to the back of my mind alongside Al's junk and in front of the pounding headache. I would pull them out for analysis later, when I got home. Alone. Not watching a movie. Sigh. *How annoying.*

When we arrived at my SUV, J.J. consulted the little notebook I gave him last Christmas where he kept his life organized between the pages. He absently scratched his forehead with the pen as he ran down his lists. Still stinging from the rebuff, I didn't bother to tell him he was holding the pen ink-side up. It gave me an evil tingle of pleasure to know Mr. all-business-and-no-movie was currently writing in hieroglyphics all over his forehead. He glanced my way and ran the pen by his temple. I bit my lip and tried to focus, but those little black scratch marks on his forehead had me giggling inside. *Darn, where is someone to share a Kodak Moment when you need them?* At least my mood was changing for the better. *You are one sick individual, Buzz, tell him he's writing all over his face.*

"Not a chance."

J.J. looked at me, irritation written all over his face–along with several Chinese symbols. "What? Did you say something, Buzz?"

I gave him one of my most engaging smiles... I think it scared him. "No, no, go on; you were saying?"

He gave me a weird look and thumbed through a couple of pages. He absently scratched his ear with the pen. I felt my eyes water and choked back a chuckle. I had to look away after the pen colored in a dimple on his cheek, and suddenly wished I had actually *used* the facilities rather than just hide in them earlier.

J.J. looked perplexed. "I thought I had it right here." He looked up and scowled at me, and I wanted to laugh so bad I had a sudden urge to wet my pants.

I leaned on the car and crossed my legs and he went back to concentrating on what he searched for. I couldn't stand it any longer. I had to tell him. "Uh, J.J. –?"

"Not now, Buzz." He tapped the pen against his cheek and black freckles dotted the side of his face.

I couldn't hold it back any more. Barking out a laugh I had his full, irritated attention. "BWaaa-ha-ha! J.J., ha-ha, your pen, it-it–"

He let out an exasperated sigh. "Buzz, could you be serious for just one minute? I'm trying my best to–"

Just then I heard The Maggot say behind me, "Buzz, what the heck is wrong with you? You look like you're about to wet your nappies."

I burst out laughing, turned to her, and crooked an index

finger. Totally perplexed, she circled around so she could see J.J. He stood there, scowl on his face, reading his notebook, tapping rhythmically on his chin, pen still in hand, still ink-side up. He had about a dozen inky freckles on his chin, and I couldn't stand it anymore. As soon as Mag said, "J.J., what the–!" I lost it.

I collapsed on the hood of the SUV, crossing my legs and laughing my head off while tears streamed down my face. Mag sucked in great gulps of air as she guffawed loud enough to be heard across the parking lot. People were beginning to motivate in our direction, and poor J.J. stood there, innocent as a babe with black pen marks all over his face.

Now I don't mind letting J.J. humiliate himself in front of family, but I wasn't about to clue in half the town. I grabbed one arm and beeped open the door to my SUV. "Let's get him out of here before anyone sees this!" J.J. protested as we tried to shove him into the passenger seat.

"Hey, you guys, knock it off. What are you doing with me–" The crowd in the parking lot picked up speed when they saw the scuffle. They could smell gossip a block away, and the sheriff and I were gossip fodder on a good day. This was not a good day.

Still howling like a banshee, Mag grabbed for the other arm and together we stuffed one very confused and pissed off sheriff inside my vehicle.

"Buzz, what the heck? I drove myself–"

"I'll bring you–I made the mistake of looking at him. "B*waaa-hahaha!"* I sucked in a juicy breath. "Back later, J.J. Later!"

Mag slammed the passenger door and I ran around and jumped into the driver's seat. She dove into the back seat just as I gunned the engine and laid rubber on the pavement. I sped out of the parking lot and down the street.

I looked across at J.J. and tears blurred my vision. I laughed all over again at his irate expression. I could tell he was getting really pissed, and I had to get off the street. I turned left into the church parking lot before I ran over some little old lady because I couldn't see. J.J. grew angrier by the second, and every time he opened his mouth, Mag and I laughed louder.

My sides hurt, my eyes still blurry, and I was barely able to catch a breath. My headache hammered at my poor skull. I pulled down the visor on the passenger's side and pointed to the lighted mirror on the back. Between gasps I said, "Loo...look mirror!" He gave me an odd look, and I tried again. Taking a huge breath I said, "Look...face...mirror!"

I struggled for breath and looked to Mag for help. I looked into the rear-view mirror, but all I saw were Mag's legs kicking in the air, and I heard snorting and hiccupping coming from somewhere back there as well.

J.J. finally caught on and looked in the mirror. We watched his expression change as he comprehended the ink marks, looking at the end of his pen like it was the pen's fault. That single movement sent Mag and I into gales of laughter all over again.

He turned toward me and spoke in a calm, soft voice. "You let me do this for what—a half-hour and never said a word?"

Laughing helplessly, I could only nod.

"You didn't say anything on purpose, didn't you?"

I couldn't speak, so I nodded again.

"So what's her excuse?" He jerked his head toward Mag which sent her into gales of laughter.

Mag gulped in air. "Got none. Guess I'm just a weasel." That set us off again.

Grumbling loudly, J.J. opened the glove box and fished around for the baby wipes he knew I kept in there.

Mumbling mostly to himself he scrubbed at his forehead. He gave me a sidelong glance. "How old are you two anyway?"

We laughed harder.

"Couldn't you have *told* me or something?"

Wiping my face on my sleeve I tried for contrite. It came out unashamedly unrepentant. "Yeah, but it was just too good to pass up. You are such an easy target, J.J."

"Turkey Butt."

Mag kicked the back of my seat. "Yeah, Buzz, you turkey butt. Why didn't you stop Picasso here from drawing all over his face? What kind of a friend are you, anyway?" We laughed some more.

J.J. heaved a long suffering sigh. "Why do I keep hanging out with you guys? I must be a closet masochist or something."

From the back seat, Mag grabbed him around the throat and noogied his head. "You know you love us, Green. Just think about how dull your life would be without us around to torment you?"

He rubbed his throat and croaked, "Yeah, I think about how peaceful, *sane*, quiet and uh, almost *normal* life would be."

I wiped my eyes. "Green, you wouldn't know normal if it bit you in the butt."

Mag ruffled his hair. "Yeah, you'd die of boredom in less than a month."

"Mag's got the right of it," I said. "In no time you'd be jonesin' for 'Miller Time'."

He scratched his head and smiled, the faint pen marks disappearing inside those long dimples. "You got me there. Wait! I almost forgot. Speaking of dying, I have more information on the body we pulled out of the dumpster."

I put the SUV in gear and prepared to pull out of the

church parking lot.

"Yeah, I know. That's what started this whole thing. I was thinking *It Happened One Night* and you're thinking what happened *last* night."

He leaned my way and smooched my cheek. "Sorry, Buzz, I had this idea but I couldn't quite put it together. We'll just have to rain check movie night." He ran a thumb across my cheek. "I'll make it up to you, okay?"

I stole a look at Mag. My cheeks turned pink and Mag grinned from ear-to-ear. I felt her kick the back of my seat. J.J. glanced in my direction when I suddenly flew forward, but made no comment.

No one said a thing while I drove back to the Village Hall parking lot. Mag jumped out and J.J. gathered his notes.

She poked her head in the window. "Tomorrow, coffee, right, Buzz?"

"You betcha, kiddo-bye."

8

J.J. showed no intention of getting out of my vehicle, so I wondered if he might have been there to stay. We sat in the nearly deserted parking lot and talked over the case.

Finally, the subject of murder waned, and J.J. climbed out of my SUV. He seemed to be scanning the parking lot and finally asked, "And do you know who our victim ended up being?"

"Now how the heck would I know who it was, James Green? Between the blunt head trauma and the dumpster gook all over the body, we could have found Jimmy Hoffa, and I wouldn't have known."

"Ivan got the body cleaned up and when Malcolm went in to begin his autopsy, he realized it was no transient we pulled out of the muck."

"Who is it then, and don't tell me it's someone from town!"

He scanned the few people left. "Have you seen Mary Cromwell, Buzz? I have to talk to her."

"Not since the meeting. Why do you need Mary? She left before we did..."

At that moment, J.J. saw Mary Cromwell backing stealthily around the corner of the building and smoothly placed himself in her path. She ran butt first right into him and shrieked. She stood ram rod straight and dropped her purse on the sidewalk. It clanked like she had an anvil inside. She raised her hands over her head. "Alright, you got me–Oh, J.J., it's you. Sorry. I thought you might be ole bean head Cab Walker. Or maybe the creepy rodeo clown fella. What's his name again? Butter? Buttons? Butt Head? Confounded clowns, why can't they have normal names like Willy or Jim? All I know is someone followed me, and I wasn't going to be no sitting duck, waiting for him to get me."

At J.J.'s doubtful gaze, Mary raised her right hand. "I swear, J.J.! I tell ya true, I felt someone lurkin' back there, a-grinning like he knew he had me cornered!" She shivered delicately. "I can't tell you how many times someone has snuck up on me lately. *Brrrr*! creeps me out, it does. One of these days I'm going to give whoever it is what for!"

Digging around inside the pink monstrosity, she pulled out her mean looking sap. She snapped her head around and raised her hands like the world's oldest Karate Kid. It looked as if she expected old Cab to jump out from behind a rock.

J.J. grabbed the sap in mid-swing and wrestled it away from her. "Whoa there, Mary! You'd better not be beating up our senior citizen population just because they find you irresistible."

She preened as he guided her over toward me. "Now you told me earlier you have not seen Cab for a couple days; ever since he went missing from the assisted living place."

"Missing, schmissing! He probably went to see his sister up in Whitewater and forgot to tell anyone he when he left. He's probably snortin' flank on them little co-eds, that skirt chasin' old fart."

She thought a moment. "Or maybe he found someone else to stalk. I don't care either way, as long as he leaves me alone."

She put her arm through J.J.'s and strolled across the parking lot. I hefted her pink purse and wished I had a fork lift. I wondered, not for the first time, how little bitty Mary lifted the monstrosity, let alone lug it all over town.

"You know what, J.J.? I was about to sap Cab upside the head the other night. He kept grabbing at my knee under the table while we played in the Euchre tournament down at

Pauly's tavern. He kept saying he needed to talk to me in private, said it was urgent." She snorted. "Yeah, I gave him urgent! Like I never heard *that* one before!"

J.J. looked extremely uncomfortable. "Uh, Mary? Maybe you shouldn't be telling me you sapped some poor guy–"

"Poor guy my old patootie, the man is a masher! Can't you like, TASER him or something? Maybe he's got an electrical short in that pea brain of his and you can jolt him back to normal or something."

Her faded blue eyes darted left and right. She turned and grabbed her purse and rummaged around inside. "I'll tell you what I did do though! Wait 'til you see this." J.J. stepped back and she looked up at him with fire in her eyes. She pulled out a tiny pen knife sharp enough to puncture what she aimed at. Light flashed off the blade as she waved it in front of her. "But I sure gave *him* what for! Thought he wanted a *poke*. Heh heh; so I gave him one! Right through the hand the next time he slid it past my knee!"

"You stabbed Cab in the hand?" I gasped in shock. J.J. froze again and grabbed my arm.

Mary continued. "You betcha, I did. That old geezer's a-thinkin' I'd play patty-fingers with him in the back row at the Senior Center on Bingo night too. He kept trying to drag me out into the hall. Once he tried to corner me in the kitchen– kept sayin' he had to talk to me, private-like." She winked at me. "He had the gall to mess with me with there being a $100.00 pot at stake! So I let the old goat know in no uncertain terms where the bear dookies in the buckwheat. Say, I won't get a ticket for stabbing the old coot, will I? It was self-defense, I swear!" She stubbed her toe into the ground. "It *was* really only a little poke."

J.J. made a non-committal noise and opened the passenger side of my SUV. He helped Mary into the front seat. "Mary, I need your help with something. Did you happen to get a look at the victim while we were at the morgue earlier today?"

Mary shook her head. "Nope. There wasn't time, what, with the county fair meeting and all. Why, J.J.? Is the stiff someone I should know?"

J.J. sighed. "I'm not sure. Would you mind coming with us over to the morgue for a minute?"

Marty bit her lip and nodded. "Okay, J.J. if you think I can help, I'll come."

J.J. fired up the SUV and I crawled into the back seat. I couldn't stand the suspense any longer. "By the way, Mary, what did you tell Cab when he asked where the bear goes dookie in the buckwheat?"

"Wherever the bear wants!" She slapped J.J. on the arm and the SUV swerved. "Oops, watch the road young fella."

She closed up her purse with a snap and winked. "That's when I stabbed the old buzzard."

I bit my lip. J.J. sent me a warning glance, but there was no stopping Mary when she was on a roll. "But if Cab touches me again, he'll know he has stepped in it deep. I know what I'm doing, I saw Lorena Bobbit on the news!"

"Mary, you cannot take the law into your own hands. If someone harasses you, you need to call me. If you don't want to call me, call Constable Puetz; he *is* your son for heaven's sake!"

Mary looked at her knees and shook her head. "Poor Teddy is so useless even *I* call him Dead Butz. But ya know what? Lately he's been acting a little weirder than usual. He's been following me around a lot. Takin' notes and talking into a recorder. I think he's trying to get me locked up in one of them old people hoosegows. You know, like 'One flew Over the Cuckoo's Nest'."

Mary struggled with the seatbelt and finally got it to click closed. She smiled and sighed. Looking up, all traces of

74

melancholy gone, she smiled and patted J.J. on the head like nothing happened. "So how can I help in the investigation, Jimmy-Joe?" I saw J.J. wince.

J.J. sat in the parking lot. He patted his pockets, looking for something. He pulled out Mary's keys and dropped them in my hand. "Buzz, follow us over to the morgue in Mary's car, would you please? I'd like to talk with her a bit."

I sat there with my mouth open and my hand dangling in midair. Mary winked at me. "Seems like your fella needs a little one-on-one with me, Buzz. Don't worry, I'll give him back to you in one piece."

I got out and stood in the parking lot, staring at my vehicle, wondering what happened, when I heard her start up. I stood there, doing the fish out of water thing with my mouth, and no sound came out. Mary leaned out the window.

"About my car? Sometimes you have to talk to her real gentle-like to get her going, then she purrs like a kitten. Don't worry, Buzz." She patted J.J.'s thigh. "I'll take real good care of your man here!"

J.J. pinched the bridge of his nose. "Just follow me, Buzz, would you please?"

"Really. Thanks. I guess I'll follow—where are we going?"

"Back to the ME's office. I'll explain later."

"Wha—" but J.J. had already taken off.

I fumbled with the door to the Crown Victoria and slid into the driver's seat. Compared to most vehicles these days, it felt like sinking into the sofa at home, except, my knees came up to my ears. I slid the seat back and looked over the dashboard. *No wonder you can only see the top of her head,* I thought.

The car started right up, but the sound she gave off was anything but a purr. I craned my neck so I could see over the dash and put her into gear. Backing out of the parking space,

I took off through the alley which runs alongside Sal's place, and drove the side streets to the morgue.

J.J. and Mary were just exiting my SUV when I trundled into the parking lot in the Crown Vic. Mary hopped down and turned to grab her pink purse. She was about to slam the door when I called, "Remember, Mary, no weapons of any kind through the door of a county building."

9

Mary stopped dead in her tracks. "Huh?" She stared wide-eyed and clutched her pink purse with both hands. "What are you babbling about, Buzz Miller?"

J.J. stopped and scratched his head. "Uh, she's right, Mary, the law says no weapons of any kind through the door of a county building. If you don't want to go through it now, you can just leave your purse in the car."

That shook Mary out of her trance. "Are you kidding me, James Green? You and me, we know there's something totally evil going around here and I ain't leaving my purse behind! You're a nice boy and real good at your job, but I got my rights. I gotta protect myself! Clint Eastwood said so, right on TV."

"Uh, Mary, don't you mean Charlton Heston in the NRA commercial?"

"No, I mean Clint Eastwood, 'cuz I'm going to make someone's day if'n anyone messes with me."

Her piercing voice shot shards of electricity through my poor sore head, and the pain took away my breath. I swayed and J.J. put a hand on my shoulder. "Mary, the concealed/carry law says no guns, and that includes *all* government buildings, not just the ones you pick and choose." J.J. turned and went toward the morgue.

Through my bleary eyes I could see Mary's forehead furrow, and her eyes narrow. She spun to follow J.J.

I peeked around the car and almost chuckled when I saw little Mary Cromwell in a standoff with a six-foot-three man of the law. Rather than look intimidated, Mary looked ready to kick some booty.

Shuffling a couple steps on wobbly knees, I placed a gentle hand on her shoulder. "He's right, Mary. Since we're with the Sheriff, we have to look to him for protection against the bad guys while we're here. Why don't we pull out anything considered a weapon and you can bring your purse with you? Malcolm is a real stickler for rules, and we don't want to set him off, do we? We can leave everything in your trunk, and I'll help you load it back up when we're finished inside."

Mary bit her lip and scuffed her toe on the pavement. The hollow sound of her orthopedic shoe reverberated off the parking lot. It kept time with the pounding in my head. She drew a deep breath. "Well, I don't know...." She stared at me and jerked her head toward J.J. I had no clue what she spazzed about. I must have had a dumb look on my face because she narrowed her eyes and jerked her head several times in J.J.'s direction.

The light bulb went on and I turned to face J.J. I took his arm and all but shoved him through the glass doors leading inside. "Why don't you go in and see what Malcolm found out about our dead guy, J.J.? I'll help Mary take care of her purse and we'll meet you inside."

"Uh, okay, I guess, if you're sure." He eyed Mary's innocent expression and started pushing back. "Uh, Buzz? Is there something I should know ab–?"

I must have panicked a bit, because I shoved him a little harder than I thought, and he went tumbling toward the morgue door. He regained his balance and put his hands on his hips. He marched up to within a foot of me and leaned in until we were nose-to-nose. I tried for an innocent look and he narrowed his eyes.

Without turning his head, his gaze slid to Mary. She began to whistle and roll her eyes skyward. Rocking back and forth, she clasped her hands behind her back and looked guilty as heck.

"Buuuzz?" He looked at Mary, and then he looked at me. He looked at Mary again and drew in a breath. "If you ask me, there's something fishy going on here."

I gripped his arm and urged him toward the morgue. "Come on, J.J. We'll be along in a minute." I gritted my teeth and gave J.J. what I thought was another gentle push. How he stumbled and ended up plastered to the door still escapes me, but he finally straightened, and holding his crunched nose, disappeared inside the building. I figured I'd apologize later.

I stomped back to Mary and her super-sized lethal weapon and opened the clasp. I shook my head at the array of junk I saw inside. I popped the Crown Vic's trunk, and braced myself. "All right, Mary Cromwell, toss whatever you didn't want Sheriff Green to see into the trunk."

Wide-eyed, Mary blinked slowly at me while she reached inside the pink monstrosity. She proceeded to pull out a sap, two pair of handcuffs, four cans of pepper spray, a Bodyguard .380, and Model 29 Smith with an eight-and-three-eighths barrel *in chrome*. It would have made Harry Callahan weep. I finally understood the Clint Eastwood line. She pulled out pliers, a Slim Jim, a pair of nun-chucks, a sock monkey (a sock monkey? Involuntarily I shivered), and the largest box of condoms I'd ever seen (No, I did *not* ask). I found myself drooling over the .380 and Mary snapped her fingers in front of my nose. "Buzz! Snap out of it!"

"Huh? I-I uh just, uh, never mind. Is that it, Mary? I mean, can Sheriff Green find fault with anything else in there?"

"Wellllll," she said as she looked furtively around the parking lot.

"Mary! Please stop messing around and tell me what you need to tell me!"

She stepped close enough for me to count the hairs in

her facial mole. Her claw-like fingers clamped onto my arm in a death grip. She yanked me down to her level and in a quavering voice said, "I uh, I think I found the murder weapon."

"You *what?*" I winced as pain exploded in my head.

"*Shh!* The murder weapon! I said I think I got the murder weapon!" I opened my mouth and she slapped a boney hand across my lips hard enough to rattle my teeth. I gasped when I thought my eye exploded.

"*Shh!* Don't spray it all over the neighborhood, Buzz Miller," I made a grab for her purse and she slapped at my grappling hands. I stumbled backward, a little dizzy. My hands itched to choke the story out of her. I eyed her sap and shook my head. Too messy. Instead I reached out and grabbed her by the raincoat. I lifted her off her feet. Taking in a long, calming breath, I said through my teeth, "Explain... and *FAST!*"

She eyed me like a wounded puppy and clutched her purse against her breast. "Well, uh, let's see. I watched them guys on CSI once, and I remembered they found the murder weapon inside a bag of garbage away from the crime scene. So I took my show on the road after everyone left and lookee here what I found behind "*Ready, Set, Blow!*"

She opened her purse and pulled out a brown paper bag. Inside lay a Wonder Bread wrapper. She unrolled it and opened the top. She reached past me for a latex glove and slid it over her hand. Holding the closed end of the bag, she peeled back the bread wrapper, and unveiled an antique filet knife.

Holy crap, I thought. *That sucker is so razor sharp it could probably have gutted a Coho with one swipe!*

Mary waved it around pretending she was Errol Flynn. "Ain't she a beauty?"

I grabbed her wrist and steadied it. The Wonder Bread

bag crackled as I inspected the knife. "I need to take this in and check the blood to see if it is Coho or *oh-oh*. Did you touch–?"

"No way! What kind of private eye would I be if I touched the ev-ee-dense?" I picked this baby up wearing my rubber gloves and dropped her into the bag just like you see." She grinned proudly. "I took me some pictures, too! Jest like they do on T.V. You think J.J.'s gonna be mad on account of I found it first?"

"No, but he will be mad if you moved evidence or wrecked the crime scene. You should have called on the phone and had J.J. go out and check the area."

She stubbed her toe into the pavement. "I thought about it, but there wasn't nothin' else laying around, so I figgered the morning monsoon washed any other evidence away."

I shook my head while I examined the knife. "I wonder whose knife it is..."

"I bet it's Captain Bob Otto's."

"Captain Bob's? How would you know this?"

"Aside from the "CB" carved into the handle, let's just say I've had cause to see him whip it out a time or two." She grinned mysteriously.

I held up my hands. "Yuck, Mary, too much information! Tell it to J.J."

"I was going to, as soon as I escaped octopus man, Cab Walker with the groping hands." She paused a moment and scratched her head. "At least I hope it was Cab, because who else could it-a been? I figgered he must've followed me from Sal's. He's been pressuring me to go out with him lately. Anyway, whoever it was, I clocked him with my purse back over yonder and beat feet back here."

Mary began stuffing stuff into her purse, mumbling the entire time. "Between Cab and the dumb clown asking me questions all the time, I hardly had time to shake 'em so's I could investigate on my own!"

About to ask what dumb clown asked all the questions, a sick feeling in the pit of my stomach had me groping for words. *What if the guy she clocked was actually the murderer, and Mary, almost his next victim?*

I did *not* want to bring up the fact we might have a murderer running around town to Mary. She'd probably think of it as a personal challenge to wrap up the case by rounding up the geriatric SWAT girls and arming them with assault rifles.

I glanced at Mary to see if she had put two-and two together. "Mary, stay here for a minute, would you? I'm going to walk over to *Ready, Set, Blow* to make sure Cab is okay. We don't want him getting sick if he's knocked out cold on the wet pavement, do we?"

I began walking away, but good old Mary can spot a phony a mile away. "Buzz Miller, you slow right down. I'm coming too!"

Rather than argue, I waited until she fell in behind me. Few lights lit our way, but I heard a click and Mary smiled when I turned to see she had a huge flashlight in her hand.

The beauty shop was only a few doors down from the morgue, so we were there in two shakes of a lamb's tail. Mary sure called one thing right; the parking lot was totally empty. "See? I told you. Lee Ann Swanson don't even have a dumpster back here."

I marveled at the cleanliness of the area. There wasn't so much as a gum wrapper on the ground. We spread out and snooped around the perimeter. Mary waved me over to the south end and pointed to the ground. "Over here's where I found the knife."

I looked down and noticed a red "X" on the pavement.

"Mary, what is this?"

"Why, "X" marks the spot, Buzz. I used my Maybelline

Miracle All Day Color Stay Lipstick to mark where I found the knife. It's waterproof and has lasting color all day long." She pointed down. "See? It's still there, even though it's been raining!"

I closed my eyes and inhaled deeply. I planned to give Mary another speech about preserving evidence, but one look at her bright button eyes and her eager smile had me patting her shoulder and telling her she did a good job.

We were about to leave and I noticed something on the pavement about three feet away. "Odd."

Mary looked up. "Who, me?"

"What?"

"Me. Am I odd?"

"Well, yes, Mary, but in a very nice way. Why do you ask?"

"You said 'odd', I thought you were talking about me."

I pointed over a white substance on the ground. Mary shoved the flashlight at me and pulled out a giant magnifying glass from God knows where. I pointed. "I was talking about the stuff over there and thought it odd that it messed up this otherwise pristine parking lot."

She stepped closer to the stuff on the ground and see-sawed the magnifying glass in front of her face. She bent, broke off a piece and popped it into her mouth. I covered my mouth, horrified.

"Mary, spit that out! You don't know what that is or where it's been!"

She straightened and let out a long breath. "Popcorn."

"Popcorn?"

She dusted her hands on her bony hips and looked up at me with a satisfied grin. "Yup, popcorn. Little bitty pieces of popcorn. Take a look."

She shoved the magnifying glass into my hand and I bent to inspect the white flecks. "By golly, you're right. It looks like popcorn. And lint." *Lightbulb*. "Mary, is this about the place you hit whoever trailed you?"

Mary looked around. "Yup, you betcha it is. Right over here." She bent at the waist. "See? I bent over to pick up the knife like this here, and the air like shifted around me." She swirled her hands dramatically. "Now you're gonna think I'm a batty old broad, but it's like I felt the air move, and when I stood, someone-I thought it was Cab-grabbed my leg. Well, I kicked him in the head, and swung my trusty purse as hard as I could. It sounded like a hammer hitting a ripe melon, and I knew I hit a grand slam."

"What happened next?"

"Well, I didn't turn around to look if that's what you mean, cuz I figured whoever it was might steal my evidence and take credit for the find, so I high-tailed it outta here and ran into you." She furrowed her brow, scratched her head, and looked at the ground. "At least, I think that's how it happened. At my age you never know."

I couldn't help it. I grinned.

She brightened. "Anyway, I looked back and saw him lying on the ground, the toes of his cowboy boots cocked up, pointing to the stars, and knew I'd be okay." She cackled and slapped her boney knee.

My face must have registered shock.

She sobered when she saw my expression. "What?"

"Did you say cowboy boots?"

She scratched her chin. "Yeah, I did. 'Cept come to think of it, Cab always wore sneakers, on account of his bad balance and plantar fasciitis. That's what you thought too, right?"

I nodded. "But if it wasn't Cab who grabbed you–"

She twirled the hair growing out of her mole. "Then we don't know who was out here." She brightened. "Well, at least I knocked him out before he could do any real damage, eh?"

I sighed. "I hope your good mood lasts when you tell J.J. about all this."

"Don't know if I will, but I feel better getting it off my chest."

I said nothing, but headed back toward the morgue. Mary trotted behind me, trying to keep up. "Hey, Buzz, (*puff, puff*), you don't think he'll (*puff*) arrest me or nothin', do you? Say, you can put in a good word for me on account of he's your fella, right?"

I looked over my shoulder. "No, Mary, withholding evidence or lying to him is what would anger J.J... I think he knows you well enough not to jump to any conclusions, and I am not putting in a good word for you." I looked at her and she really did look scared. I patted her shoulder. "Just kidding, Mary. It'll be okay, just talk to him like you do me."

I slowed my pace and Mary caught up. "*Whew*, Buzz, ya really had me going there for a minute. Whew, I feel better. Thanks for the help. Can we slow down now?"

We walked slowly back to the morgue. Mary gathered up her purse and slammed the trunk. She hustled off to the door of the morgue. She paused, waiting for me to move. I tried to figure out how I was going to drop this new little bomb on Green. *Hey, J.J., guess what Mary found?* No, too direct. *Uh, J.J., remember how worried you were over the police scanner Mary bought? Heh, heh, wait 'til you hear this one! .... No, he'll probably throw her in jail. Hey Green, wanna see what your deputies missed this time?* No, that approach was sure to get me killed. I began to sweat. I couldn't very well run away, he'd find me. I heard a hollow thumping and looked up to see Mary impatiently waiting in the open door, her orthopedic shoe thumping on the morgue floor. *No wonder she was out of breath, running with those cement shoes on her feet.*

By now I had a death grip on the Wonder Bread bag, and

I'd had about enough of feeling guilty over something I didn't even do.

Concentrating as I was, I bumped into Mary when she stopped in the hallway. "You know, that Green boy can be such a stick sometimes. How the heck is a lady supposed to protect herself in her own home or feel safe on the streets if she is forced to leave her .44 at home? Why, it's an open invitation for some bad guy to break into my house and steal my Dirty Harry Special! So I gotta carry it with me so I have it when I need it. If I don't *then* what am I gonna shoot a bad guy with, this pop-gun?"

She lifted her pant leg, and I cringed when I saw a. 22 tucked into the top of her rolled down support stocking. She snatched it out and waved it in my direction. I ducked.

"Take this little pea shooter, she said. It's fine if I'm up close and personal; I can pop me a cap into his eyeball and listen while it rattles around in his cranial cavity. But it sure ain't gonna stop some hopped-up gooney bird bent on robbing a poor defenseless little old lady now is it?"

I couldn't help it. I bit back a smile and told her the hopped up gooney bird would be in major trouble if he tangled with Mary Cromwell. Easing the gun out of her hand, I unloaded it and dropped it into the waste basket by Malcolm's office. "We'll pick it up on the way out."

I studied the contents of her purse for a moment before I turned back to her. "Mary, I'm sorry, and I know I'm going to regret this but I have to ask one more question." I held up the king-sized condom box and shook it.

Mary smiled a secret smile and crooked her finger at me. I leaned in and she checked for eavesdroppers before she whispered, "I have a dream, kid. And I'm going to be prepared for the time when dreams comes true, ha-ha get it?"

My stomach churned and bile fought its way up my throat. I nodded vaguely and prepared to get the heck out of there. *No wonder Ted's so screwed up.* I heard her chuckling softly as I dropped the offending box in with the other stuff I found, in her purse.

I went to pass her in the doorway and she stopped me. "I'm teasing you, Buzz. I emptied a box of "Crunch-O-Munch into the condom box. I'm going to slap it on the table at Bunko Night down at the seniors' center and watch 'em all scramble for cover!"

"Mary, That's terrible! What if you give one of them a heart attack?"

"Heh, heh! They all got pacemakers anyway; I'll let 'em have a laugh over it. They'll just get zapped back to normal."

We both laughed over the thought, but a voice calling our names from the autopsy room had us sobering. I wiped my eyes and took a couple of fortifying breaths. I picked up the alleged murder weapon from where I dropped it. Turning to face Mary, I hitched my head in the direction of the autopsy room. "Let's go."

Mary hesitated and I had to give her a little prodding to move her along. "A-are you sure he wants me in there, Buzz? Maybe I should just go home. You know, I got re-runs of Lawrence Welk I don't want to miss tonight, and I want to–"

I spoke out of the side of my mouth. "Too late, here he comes."

I tried to keep her in front, but she grabbed me and shoved me forward.

J.J. came out of the cold room and stood staring at us. "What took you so long? Malcolm wants to go home sometime tonight."

Mary started backing up. "I, uh, forgot to uh..."

I grabbed her by the arm. "J.J., you'll never guess what Mary found."

Later on the thought crossed my mind I should have just gone home.

10

J.J. stood staring at the Wonder bread wrapper. "You did what?"

Mary hung her head. "I'm sorry, I was just trying to help, J.J."

I chimed in, "She marked everything in the parking lot, and took pictures too."

J.J. sent me a stern look. "I appreciate your defense of Mary, Buzz, but you need to stay out of this."

I stood and worked myself up into a self-righteous huff. "Fine. I'm outta here."

J.J. passed his hand over his face again.

I turned to leave and Mary grabbed my leg. "Oh no you don't. I ain't doing this by myself. You've got to stay and...and...oh I don't know, but you ain't leaving yet, Buzz Miller."

I settled her in a chair. "It's okay, Mary, I'll stay." I shot J.J. an evil look. "Maybe I can be of some use to *someone*."

J.J. sighed and stepped forward. He gently took Mary by the arm. "Mary, the reason I asked you down here is I think you might be able to help us find out who we pulled out of the dumpster." He stopped in front of the doors to the cold room. "It's not going to be easy, nor is it pleasant. Do you think you can help me with this?"

She gulped. She looked at me and grabbed my arm. "Can Buzz come too?"

J.J. looked at me. "Buzz?"

I nodded, and Mary gripped my hand as we slowly made our way to the swinging doors. White as a sheet, I realized J.J. thought Mary might not want to help, but I knew she would. Mary was too afraid of the interview regarding the knife to care about a few maggots and a naked dead guy. She's nothing, if not a trooper. Malcolm and Ivan waited by the stainless steel table, and stepped forward when we approached.

Malcolm cleared his throat, ready to go into a long orientation. "Now, Mary, we–"

Mary snapped, "Just shut up Malcolm, and pull back the sheet."

She had a death grip on my hand which belied her brave front. Ivan pulled the sheet back and Mary sucked in a breath. She pulled me with her, and we shuffled around to the other side of the table. J.J. followed. She carefully lifted the sheet to reveal the body's left hand. There between the first two knuckles we found a small cut. Mary took a step back, but never faltered. "Dang, I was afraid of this." She pointed. "There Sheriff, see? Right there on his knuckle. That's where I nailed him. It's Cab all right."

It was my turn to turn green. "Cab Walker? Are you saying this is poor Cab Walker under the sheet?"

J.J. nodded. "I put it together when Mary mentioned him earlier. Now all we have to figure out is why."

"And who did him."

He nodded. "And who." He shook Malcolm and Ivan's hands. "Thank you, gentlemen, for coming back down here, I appreciate it." They both nodded and prepared to move the body.

I cringed at the sound of the squeaking wheels of the gurney, and hustled Mary out into the hall. "Whew," she said. Pulling a hanky out of her sleeve, she dabbed her eyes. "He may have been a grope-happy S.O.B., but nobody deserves to go like yesterday's garbage."

What could I say? "You're right, Mary, no one does; which is why we need your help on this." I led her to a chair.

"So, Buzz, do you think I can just leave the knife here with a note, and let the coppers take care of it from here?"

I heard J.J's footsteps coming down the hall. "Too late, here he comes now."

She sat and primly folded her hands in her lap. I stood alongside and put my hand on her shoulder as J.J. came in and dragged another chair over to face her.

He sat and took her hands in his. "Mary, I know this is difficult for you, but try to remember if you can, the last time you saw Cab?"

"I told you, J.J., last Tuesday at Bingo night. He seemed hale and hearty."

"Do you remember him saying anything else to you?"

Mary bit her lip. "Nothing important, he just compl–"

"Just what?"

J.J. leaned forward. Mary bit her lip in concentration. "He complained, just like me about clowny boy asking questions again. Cab was kind-of spooked by him too."

"What clown, Mary? Some bone-head at the assisted living place?"

She looked up. "No, no, a real clown! That creepy clown who's always butting in where he's not wanted. You know, Anthony Parks I think is his name. You could ask Al she did all the contracts for the fair. She'd have his real name on file, I'm guessin'. Kind-of new to town. Been here a couple months. Says he's looking up people his mother knew, but like I said, he's kind-of creepy and asks a lot of odd questions."

J.J. and I looked at each other. J.J. leaned forward. "What kind of odd questions?"

"Well, he asked me how old I was back in '29. I told him I was just a young lady and didn't hang around people like he was looking for, but some of the real old timers like Cab still lived around here and maybe he'd remember life back then.

90

He wanted to talk to Cab and me in 'private', you know? That's when we had a, uh...difference of opinion—Oh my God, you don't think what I told him could have gotten Cab killed, do you?"

J.J. patted her hand and told her no, he didn't think so, but Mary watched him while he avoided meeting her eyes.

Mary shook off J.J.'s hands and stood. She brushed off some non-existent lint from her dress and picked up her jacket. "Well!" She huffed, "I guess this interview is over."

J.J. stood. "But, Mary, I—"

"I, nothing, James Green! When you are ready to be honest with me, you'll find me at Gerry Miller's house. Buzz, if you would be so kind as to call her and tell her I'm coming, I'll be on my way." She fussed with her jacket and I pulled out my cell.

"Uh, Mary, didn't you forget something?"

She stopped and stared at me. "What?"

I nodded to the Wonder Bread bag.

"Oh. Uh, J.J? You'll never guess what happened on my way over here."

J.J.'s lips said nothing, but his raised eyebrow said it all.

Mary scooted forward and held out the bag. "Well, it was like this..."

J.J. waited until she finished before starting the tirade we knew was coming. He yelled at Mary, Mary yelled back, I yelled at him for yelling at Mary, and he yelled at me for yelling at all.

By the time Mary stormed out of the ME.'s office, J.J. had the full story and I had Mom on speaker phone, briefing her on Mary.

"That's okay, Buzz, don't worry about Mary, I'll put her in your old room tonight. She probably shouldn't be alone. Does J.J. want me to interrogate her? I've been reading up on interrogation tactics, and watching a lot of Perry Mason re-runs lately."

I looked at J.J. He made a frantic slicing gesture by his throat. "Uh, thanks, Mom, but J.J.'s got that part covered. But you're probably right about not leaving Mary to her own devices tonight. Even though she didn't like Cab much, she might take this pretty hard. I think she might believe his death might be her fault. She'll be needing a friend tonight, Mom, not the Spanish Inquisition."

"I'll ply her with my special stash of Hennessy and knock her out. We'll be toastin' a few to old Killian Hennessy, and Mary will be back to her old self by tomorrow morning. Trust me, honey."

I smiled. "I do, Mom, and thanks. But you do know old Mr. Hennessy passed into the great vineyard in the sky in 2010, don't you?"

A moment of silence. "Uh, no, I hadn't heard."

"He was a hundred and three years old."

"Well bless his memory. We'll drink an extra toast to him, we will."

I chuckled. "You do that, Mom, but don't go driving anywhere tonight, okay?"

She laughed. "Not on your life, but won't Bill be havin' a fit when he finds the good brandy gone from the liquor cabinet?"

"Just pour him a glass, and enjoy your evening. Thanks for everything, Mom."

"Any time, dear."

J.J. yelled into the speaker phone, "Yeah, Thanks, Mom Miller!"

I could hear Mom chuckling. "Hug J.J. for me, Buzz, I'll see you in the morning. Love you, bye!"

I rolled my eyes. "Love you too, Mom, bye now."

I slipped my phone in my pocket. "Well, at least we know Mary will be all right this evening. Good old Mom."

J.J. dragged the chair he used across the room. "Yeah, between your mom and Mr. Hennessy, Mary will be in good spirits."

"Bad joke, Green." He shrugged and smiled.

I grabbed my jacket. "Come on, I'll give you a ride back to your squad."

"Naw, I'll call Curly and have him and Shemp pick it up. What say we go to your house and watch a movie?"

"But I thought–"

He cornered me by the door and leaned in close. "Well, you thought wrong, didn't you?" He tapped the end of my nose and reached for the light switch. I ducked out from under his arm and headed out the door. I rummaged in my pocket for my keys, and realized J.J. still had them. Turning back I saw J.J. dangling my keys between two fingers. "Lose something?"

"No, I forgot you had them."

He smiled. "Hop in babe, I'll drive."

Who was I to argue?

11

With pain medication in my system, my head felt much better. Snuggled on my fluffy couch with a big bowl of popcorn between J.J., Wesley, Hillary, and me, is about my number one favorite happy place in the world. Watching "Young Frankenstein" for about the hundredth time and laughing at the same dumb lines made the evening perfect.

By the time the final credits rolled, I was mostly asleep. I looked at J.J. and saw his mouth hung open, his breathing suspiciously deep and even. Picking up the remote, I turned off the television and snuggled under the comforter. *Just a couple minutes and I'll get up and go to bed.*

* * *

I woke to sunlight streaming through the crack where the drapes met. My neck hurt, my head pounded, and I had a feeling of being hemmed in. Thinking the big dog slept most of the night on me, I made to push him off. I heard a distinctly human snort. I turned my sore neck and saw a scruffy chin dotted with a couple ink marks a couple inches north of my nose. *Hmm. Definitely not Wes, but suspiciously familiar.*

I realized I sprawled across the couch, mostly under J.J.'s chest. His arm behind me, I leaned over the arm, which put the rest of me at an odd angle. I snuggled up against him, with my head under his chin. I checked his shirt to make sure I didn't do anything as indelicate as drool on him, and tried to ease my way back into an upright position. I slowly backed away and he came with me, ending up with his head conveniently pillowed in my cleavage.

"Now what?" I whispered. Not wanting to rock the boat,

and frankly feeling a little too cozy, I lay there waiting for him to wake. Feeling his breath on my skin sent little shivers up my spine, and telling myself I shouldn't disrupt his sleep justified staying right where I was. My eyes drooped and I felt myself drifting off again.

Later on I was loathe to open my eyes, my dream so vivid I knew it had to be fake. As I gained semi-consciousness, even I could tell my dream was just a little too 3-D and definitely in Technicolor. I cracked open an eye and looked down. J.J.'s smiling face, inches from mine, was buried deep in my shirt. I smiled and sighed.

"You're as bad an opportunist as Wes."

I heard a muffled "Yesssss, I am."

I plinked him on the back of the head, and he came up for air. Wearing a sheepish grin he said, "Well hey there, Buzz, don't mind me, I'm uh, just nosin' around."

"I can see that, James Green. Why don't you nose around the kitchen and see if we have anything for breakfast?"

He rolled to his feet grumbling. "Spoiled sport."

While J.J. stumbled to the bathroom, I limped to the back door and let the dogs out into the back yard. While they responded to the call of nature, I grabbed the coffee beans out of the freezer. By the time I had the coffee going, the dogs were ready to come in. They each grabbed a doggie cookie and ran to roust J.J. from wherever he hibernated.

The dogs loudly announced they had successfully recovered J.J. and Hillary proudly led the procession into the kitchen. I pretended to be engrossed with my first cup of coffee, and J.J. reached over me to grab a traveler cup out of the cupboard.

He snatched up the pot and filled his cup. "Gotta get down to the office early if I am ever going to get back here this afternoon."

I pushed the hair out of my eyes. "This afternoon?"

He gave me a funny look. "Yeah. Luke is meeting me at the office and we're coming over here around 4:30 or so to compare notes. Don't tell me you forgot?"

I just stared at him. He took my face in his hands and spoke gently. "Are you sure your head is okay? I told you I thought you should go to the hospital, but *nooo*."

Dumbly, I nodded. "It still aches a little, but I must've forgotten the meeting in all the chaos. I'll set up a whiteboard and get my notes ready. We'll order in pizza or something."

He plastered a big ole smooch on my lips and grinned large. "That's another thing I love about you, Buzz. You can adapt without freaking out. See you a little later, babe."

J.J. turned to go and froze half way out the back door. He turned back to me. I held out my hand and he gingerly picked up the SUV's keys. "Uh, are you going to be okay without a car today?"

I grinned. "If not, I'll give you a call."

He winked and turned to go. I pushed away from the counter, sloshing coffee as I slid my mug across the surface. I strode to the door and grabbed a hold of his shirt. Giving it a good yank, J.J. stumbled forward.

"One more thing, Green."

I caught his lips with mine, and when I let him go, neither one of us stood steady on our feet.

"Wow," I breathed, still clinging to his shirt.

I blinked and found J.J. staring intently at my mouth. "Somehow 'wow' doesn't quite cover it."

His chest heaved and he wore a determined look on his face. He slammed the back door. "To hell with the office. Come here, woman."

He took a step forward and I shoved his coffee cup into his hand. "Hey, pal. No time for fooling around. You have to go to work, remember?"

He continued to advance. One hand clamped on my

shoulder, and the other aimed for the counter. I heard my coffee cup fall into the sink and crash against his, but I could not for the life of me look away from those eyes. He leaned in close. I stared into those emerald depths and I was a goner. J.J. backed me up against the kitchen door jamb and I tingled where his fingers trailed down my arm to my hand.

He lifted my hand and gently kissed the palm. I about melted into the floor. He smiled. "Why Ms. Miller, weren't you just telling me I was going somewhere this morning?"

I turned toward my bedroom, his hand still in mine. I raised his hand and placed it on my shoulder, and led him down the hallway. I smiled. "Uh huh. You're going somewhere, alright, Mr. Green."

J.J. grabbed the phone as we passed it and threw it on the couch. Wes promptly jumped up and laid his massive body on top of it. J.J. rubbed his ears. "Good boy, Wes."

He wiggled with glee. Grin, wag, grin.

Hillary jumped up and snuggled next to him. Wes slurped her face. She calmly passed gas and sighed. We picked up speed. Outside my bedroom J.J. drew me to a halt. He pressed me against the bedroom door and devoured my mouth. He came up for air and I felt him smile. "I uh, think I'm going to be late for work."

I felt behind me for the doorknob and turned it slowly. I backed in to the room. He entered and walked past me. I clicked the door shut and turned toward him. "I *know* you're going to be late for work. The question is, however, how late do you want to be?"

* * *

Later in the afternoon, I recovered enough to get everything set for the evening, and by the time Luke and J.J. piled in the back door, I was ready to go.

I stood tearing lettuce at the sink, and J.J. patted my butt on the way to the fridge. I felt as red as the tomato salad, and for once, had nothing to say. J.J. grabbed my arm and spun me around. He dipped me backward and kissed me silly. The lettuce flew out of my hand, but I didn't much care where it landed. We'd go without a salad tonight.

He finally came up for air and set me back on my feet. My head cleared and I stared into his eyes. "Buzz, I think perhaps, our relationship has headed down a new path."

I could only stare. "Uh, new path?"

Luke snorted. "Path my foot. You two finally woke up and started your engines. You just figured out what the rest of us have known for years."

J.J. smiled and ducked his head toward me again.

Luke put his hands over his eyes. "Please guys, not in front of the kid! I might be permanently damaged."

J.J. laughed and let me go. The vertigo had me grabbing the counter top and he chuckled. He and opened the fridge, grabbed two beers, and tossed one to Luke.

Luke snagged it out of the air and popped the top. "Ah, reinforcements." He sucked the suds off the top, belched, and smiled. The atmosphere in the kitchen cooled and we were back to our normal (for us) selves.

Supper went well, I decided to grill steaks rather than order pizza, so it was late when we got started on the case.

We sat around my den, discussing dumpster possibilities, noting the evidence on my trusty whiteboard. The hours passed and I found my head drooping. I shook myself awake. J.J. stared at the autopsy photos, and Luke thunked his pen rhythmically against his head.

The dogs snored softly nearby–the only ones with brains enough to go to bed.

The fourth or fifth time my head almost collided with the desk, I decided to hit the hay, leaving Luke and J.J. to fend for themselves. I must have slept hard, because I never heard them leave.

12

In the wee hours of the morning a rumbling outside woke the dogs, who in turn woke me. I listened. Holy cow, I knew that sound! Instantaneous child-like excitement propelled me out of bed and across the room. I yanked the street side curtains aside just in time to see a trio of huge, lumbering semi tractors toting a super spectacular carnival ride down my street.

Someday someone will have to explain to me why an over 50, average (notice I did *not* say "normal?") woman who hasn't ridden a carnival ride in over twenty years would jump around at three in the morning and scramble for the phone to call her sister; whom she knows is wide awake, on the other side of town, doing the same thing.

Breathless and humming with adrenalin, I waited impatiently while my speed dial took forever to connect. A click sounded at the other end and Fred's voice blasted my sleep-heavy ears.

"Buzz! Did you hear them? The carnival is pulling in! Woo-hoo! I want to run down to the fairgrounds, but Mom says no, I'd just be in the way and probably get squished by a semi putting a ride on location. I feel like a little kid, I am so excited! Tony thinks I am absolutely insane to be so spastic about it. I tried explaining to him how it's perfectly alright to call you because I knew you'd be up, so I'm glad you called me first."

"Uh Fred, did you say Tony? As in Dr. Tony Castillo? Hey, I don't want to sound like Mom, but what the heck is Tony doing at your house at three in the morning? Aren't you dating Mark Malone, or should I mind my own business?" I bounced down the hall, dragging a shirt over my head, with the dogs hot on my trail.

"You should mind your own business, and yes I am dating Mark *very* seriously. He's here too. Want to talk to him?"

"Uh, not necessary."

"But just to get your mind out of the gutter, Buzz–oh wait! Isn't that like the pot calling the kettle black big sister? Word has it James Green left your house at an extremely late hour in your vehicle today. Just what do you suppose went on at your house this morning?

I panicked. "What? How did you find out? What do you mean?"

She laughed. "Nothing, Buzz, I'm razzing you. But just to ease your mind, Tony and Mark are not the only ones here. I'm having a 'Carnival is Coming' party and there are several people here, and no, no one is engaging in deviate sexual acts; but the night is still young, so I remain hopeful."

"Smart ass. I should tell Mom on you."

"Hold on; you can tell her yourself."

"I...what? Mom?"

"Yes, Buzz, this is your mother. Too bad you couldn't make it, but I realize spending all morning in a dumpster can take a lot out of a person."

"That was yesterday, Mom."

"Oh, thanks for reminding me. Today was spent in bed over at your house, wasn't it, Alice Christine? Was James Green rubbing your temples to ease your headache, dear?"

"Uh...yes?"

She sighed. "Well, it sure beats slogging through a dumpster, I suppose. Hope you're feeling better, dear, here's Freddie."

I finished up making a date with Fred to go to the carnival later in the morning to watch the carnies set up, and hung up the phone.

As I walked through my kitchen on the way to the back door, I thought briefly about asking my mother how she knew what it felt like to spend all day in a dumpster, but I figured this was one of those things I just did *not* want to know.

The phone rang and I grabbed it. Mom again. She asked if I was really feeling okay, because I had a standing invite to Fred's tonight, but she was concerned about my brain sloshing around.

"I'm okay. Just stayed in, took in a movie...you know, the usual. I'm just tired and forgot Fred's get-together last night."

I half-listened to my mom prattling away as I put my hand on the back door to let the dogs out. I had barely touched it when the door flew out of my hand. I squeaked and jumped back as the dogs jumped forward. J.J. caught Hillary in midair and rubbed her ears. "Hello beautiful, feel like a party for two?"

I heard Mom's excited voice on the other end of the phone. J.J. teetered on one foot as Wes decided whether he should be up with Hillary.

"Beautiful? Buzz, is J.J. in the background coming over to your house again? I thought he just left." She covered the phone and spoke excitedly to the crowd at Fred's. I sighed and saw J.J. falling sideways under Wesley's exuberant hello, the back door slamming against the wall, and Hillary slithering out of his grasp.

Oh crap, I thought. I hit "speaker phone" and slapped the phone on the counter so I could haul Wesley off J.J. I could hear my mother on the phone giving someone a blow-by blow report of everything she thought happened at my house since yesterday. I heard one smart ass humming *The Wedding March* and my eyes flew to J.J.'s. He grinned and set Hillary on the floor, rubbed Wes's ears and ruffled my hair. I huffed

101

and he turned and headed back out the door.

I was still on the phone with Mom and Fred when J.J. struggled through the back door carrying a grocery bag in one hand and soda in the other. His eyes crinkled at the corner and he hollered "Hi, Mom Miller! I'm here to ravish your daughter and steal her dogs!"

I glared daggers at him while gales of laughter and wolf whistles could be heard over the phone. J.J. smiled and set Hillary on the floor...again. He began to unload the grocery bag, leaving me to handle damage control. Wes danced and woofed, and Hillary sat on my foot and batted adoring eyes at J.J..

Here we go. "Wait, Mom? J.J.'s just kidding. Mom, listen! I'm not beautiful, Hillary is. No–I mean yes J.J. is here, but he was talking to the dog." More laughter and whistling followed and I slumped in a chair. *Does the whole town know my business? Is the whole damn town over at Fred's?*

My mother continued in the annoying *Mom knows best* voice. "Dogs do not party Alice Christine Miller–well, maybe yours do–but I can tell you one thing, James Green is not at your house at three in the morning to party with your dogs. I'll hang up now so you can get to work on him." J.J.'s brows flew up to his hairline.

I slapped my forehead. *Geez, more damage control.* "Mom!"

"Well, you know what I mean, dear. You two have fun. Toodles!" And the phone clicked off.

J.J. and I stared at the phone. Our eyes met. "Toodles?" We both said and cracked up.

"Your mom is a hoot."

"My mother is insane." The awkward moment disappeared and I breathed a sigh of relief. I hoped last night, and yesterday morning didn't make things awkward for us, but I should have known better. J.J. is one in a million. And

102

he's mine. I savored the little tingle creeping deliciously up my spine.

Booting the dogs out the back door, we watched as they completed their separate missions. They tumbled back through the door, smiling their doggy smiles and looking for snacks.

I turned and a Miller High Life appeared in my hand. I looked at the kitchen clock "J.J., it's almost four in the morning, and I have a concussion! What the heck is with the beer?"

He grinned as he dropped a cracker in each of the dog's mouths. "So we're starting the carnival party a little late. We're both off work today, we have nowhere to be, you're not on drugs, so why the heck not?"

He shoved a cracker into his mouth and washed it down with the ice cold High Life. "I love the way you think, mister." I took a swig. "*Ahhh*, the beer that made the Miller Sisters famous!" J.J. threw an arm around me and smooched me a good one. I had to grin. "*Mmm*, I feel better already."

I stood and marveled at this man as he pulled a movie out of the grocery bag and carried it, as well as two kinds of crackers, dip, his beer, and a hand full of dog treats into the living room.

With nothing better to do, I took a long pull on my beer and followed J.J. and his two new best friends (or traitors, as I call them) into the living room.

If I were someone else, I might be expecting a nice romantic movie and a little kanoodling now and maybe something very civilized and boring a little bit later, but I knew better. I really love my life...have I mentioned that before?

My heart melted when I stepped into the room and saw J.J. and the dogs on the couch amid the pillows and snacks, and a scant six inches left for me to squeeze into. I heard the opening credits for *Homeward Bound* playing, and all three of them turned to me with smiling faces. J.J. ruffled the top of Wesley's head. "It's his favorite movie, and I figured it was his turn to pick."

To hell with romantic movies. This man loves my dogs. Hillary stepped onto J.J.'s lap, which opened up another few inches of couch space. I hopped over the arm of the couch and sank into the cushions. Wes stretched across my lap as I heard the voice of Michael J. Fox say, *"My name, is Chance..."* Wes woofed and we all settled in to enjoy the movie.

Déjà vu. I looked over at J.J. He looked over the top of Hillary's head. "I had so much fun last night I thought we'd have a repeat performance."

I smiled back and ruffled his hair. "Perfect."

I switched to Diet Pepsi, and J.J. had another beer. Wes looked up when J.J. came back into the room and his hopeful expression, along with the crumbs clinging to his lips made us both laugh. As Chance came bounding over the hill at the end of the movie, J.J.'s cell phone rang. He heaved a sigh and pulled it out, squinting at the number which flashed up on the screen. Our eyes met over the dogs and he flipped it open. "Green here, and this better be good. Nope. No. No. Not today. It's Sunday morning, are you kidding me? Forget it. No, it's your problem today. Yup. Don't call me again unless it's a *real* emergency, you got it? Good. I'll see you tomorrow morning."

He flipped the phone closed and pinched the bridge of his nose. I knew that gesture well. I clicked the movie off, took our leftovers to the kitchen, and turned the dogs out into the back yard. It was almost 6:00 in the morning, and the coffee maker had already done its automatic magic. I figured what the heck, and poured a cup.

I heard the front door open and grabbed another mug

from the cabinet. J.J. came strolling through the door with the Sunday paper as I set the second mug on the kitchen table. I picked up my coffee and sat across from him. He thoughtfully thumbed through the paper and pulled out the sports section. He silently handed it to me and settled back to read the headlines. We sat absorbed in our reading when Wesley knocked on the back door. Hillary woofed and I got up to let them in. "So much for quiet."

I opened the back door and the dogs piled in. I was wondering if the Badgers could make a third seed in the tournament, and why the Packers hadn't settled yet with Greg Jennings. The door was almost closed when I heard an "*Oof*!" and turned to see I had squashed J.J.'s mom between the screen door and the wooden door. I quickly grabbed the inside door, swung it open and Sylvia Green stumbled into the kitchen. She dropped the crushed white paper bag she had been carrying and Hillary picked it up and brought it to J.J.

I heard a gurgling noise and watched as J.J. sat choking on his coffee and grabbed a napkin as it ran out of his nose. When he caught his breath he wiped his watering eyes and gasped. He must have noticed his shirt tail hung out of his jeans. He tried to smooth his hair, but there was nothing for it. He blushed a dark pink. "Uh, Mom, what the hell...er...heck are you doing on this side of town at six in the morning?"

Sylvia smiled a Mona Lisa smile and cocked her head. "Oh, I got a call bright and early this morning informing me my son had spent the night over here, so since I was going out for donuts anyway, I thought I'd bring you some–she looked at me and winked–thought you might need the energy."

"Uh, gee thanks, Mom, but it really wasn't necessary. And I uh, really didn't spend all of last night...uh, it was actually yesterday I–oh forget it." He looked at me with pleading eyes.

I took pity on him and set another mug of coffee on the table. I turned to his mom and said, "Come on, Mom Green, have a seat and help us out with these donuts. You still take your coffee black, don't you?"

With a twinkle in her eye, she replied, "Sure do, and thanks, Buzz." She pulled out a chair and sat while her red-faced son mopped up the coffee he had spit across the table. Silvia silently picked up her mug and sipped as J.J. wiped her side of the table. I could see her smiling behind the lip of the mug and sat back to enjoy the moment at J.J.'s expense.

The silence stretched as we all stared at each other. I tried for nonchalance and failed miserably and blurted instead, "So, J.J.," I said a bit too loudly, "Did one of your boys call you right before your mom came in?"

"Yeah, Moe the Moron. I left him in charge today, and he's already yapping in my ear about carnies and parking and noise. Seems the porta-potties aren't on site yet, and Mrs. Simmons is yelling about a carney watering her petunias."

Silvia chuckled. "It wouldn't be a Sunday morning if Sarah Simmons didn't have someone pis–tinkling in her petunias."

I imagined Mrs. Simmons cracking the curtains open to spy on her neighbors and coming face-to-face with a urinating carnival worker. "What did you tell Moe?"

"The same thing Max Dillard over at *Party Potties* told me. They're scheduled for a 7:00 this morning and they will be there by 7:00 this morning; arrest the guy pissing in the flowers, and I told Moe to stop pissing in my ear–oops, sorry, Mom."

J.J.'s cell phone rang with the third movement from the *William Tell Overture* and at Sylvia's startled expression J.J. gave her an indignant look. "What? So I like the Lone Ranger. He held up a finger. "Hold on a sec." He flipped open his phone again. "Green here. They did? He did? What happened? He did? Put him on the phone."

J.J. rolled his eyes and heaved a sigh. "Yo, Max? Got everything squared away? Naw, don't pay any attention to him, he's an idiot... Yeah. Go ahead and drop one by the office too. Have Mrs. Simmons make a report with Darryl or Phil; petunias are out of your realm of jurisdiction, and according to my watch, you are an hour and three minutes early with your delivery... Yeah, I agree; Carneys are full of it, but so is half the town, so it's a good thing you rolled in early." He shared a chuckle with Max. "Yeah, you too Max. Take care and thanks a lot–yep, I'll see you bright and early tomorrow morning."

He flipped the phone closed and glared at us. Obviously angry and hands in fists, he groped for words. "How... how did I ever get stuck with such idiots on my police force? Mo the Moron seemed so normal at his oral interview. Geez, any idiot ought to be able to put the donikers on location. He even had a map!"

Sylvia gave me a blank look and I whispered, "Doniker is carney-speak for toilet."

Sylvia nodded sagely and turned back to her coffee.

J.J. continued his tirade about his incompetent staff as his mother and I sipped our coffee. He was on such a roll I snatched another donut and finished the sports section before he took a breath.

Sylvia got up and re-filled all our cups. She sat and folded her hands in front of her. Leveling a look at her son, she got down to brass tacks. "Now, it seems you have thoroughly expounded on the genealogy of your law enforcement line staff, so let's talk about something fun. Since I seem to be the only sane person in town to stay dry and at home rather than crawl around inside a maggot infested dumpster yesterday in the torrential rain, why don't you give me the lowdown on what you found?"

J.J. looked at me and tried not to smile. I could see the condescending gesture made his mother furious; I'd be angry too if my son treated me as if he were humoring a senile but sweet little old lady. I had to give Sylvia credit, she neither decked him, nor did she storm out of the kitchen. She certainly contained herself better than I would have, were I in her shoes. J.J. ducked his head and covered the smile with a very unconvincing cough. He fidgeted in his chair to give himself a little more time to come up with a line of blarney to appease Sylvia. "Well you know Mom, there is an ongoing investigation here and I can't divulge most of the–"

"Cut the crap James Joseph Green. You know darn well I never poke my nose into police business. I only put two-and two together this morning." Her hands began to shake as her voice went up in pitch. "There is something going on here that goes beyond a typical murder and I want to know what it is."

I could see her tense up, and thought I'd rescue J.J. from his own stupidity. "J.J., the entire town knows by now. Just tell her what's going on."

J.J. shot me an annoyed look. "My mother does not need to worry about boring police business, Buzz. I don't want her upset–"

Sylvia may have been slow to burn, but she worked herself up a full head of steam. She slapped both hands on the table and I could almost see the green smoke pouring out of her ears. "Let me tell *you* something before you start handing me another line of crap, young man. I think I have information which will help in the investigation, or at least be of interest to you, and if you can get you arrogant ass off your high horse for one minute, I think I can help."

After J.J. picked his jaw up off the floor, he threw a confused look in my direction.

I shrugged and grinned. "I tried to tell you, ace."

Sylvia huffed out a sigh. "I was going to give it to you in a nut shell, but I think I'll go for the unabridged version."

J.J. sobered. "I'm sorry, Mom. Sometimes I get full of myself. Thank God I have you and Buzz to keep me grounded. Whadaya got?"

Sylvia eased back into her chair. "I'll have you know your Aunt Pearl in Baraboo called last week. While we caught up on family gossip, she mentioned Olin Norris Sr. had died." She turned to me and patted my leg. "I don't know if you remember Oly and Alyssa Norris from over on Vine Street? Alyssa was a 4-H leader at the same time as your mom, Buzz, and I think their third boy, Pat, is about your age."

At my dazed nod, she turned back to J.J. "Well, Pearl said her best friend Bertie has a daughter Ann who plays Euchre on Saturdays with Oly Jr.'s wife Betty."

My eyes crossed, but I continued to nod slowly. I noticed J.J. wore the look of a dumb sheep as his mom continued without taking a breath. "Well, Betty told Ann who told Bertie who told Pearl Oly Sr. disappeared from the assisted living facility about three weeks before she talked to me, which would have put his disappearance about five weeks ago."

At this, J.J. jerked to attention. His mother gave him a smug little smile as she delivered the one-two punch. She leaned in for effect as she delivered the final blow. "Two weeks ago last Tuesday Oly Sr. was found murdered and dumped in a dumpster out back of the souvenir shop at Circus World Museum right there in Baraboo."

J.J. let out a whoosh of air. "Holy crap, Mom."

His mother leaned back and sipped her coffee. "Son?"

J.J. turned a stunned expression toward me. "Buzz."

I, of course, came off as a class act and eloquent. "Crap-o Grandpa."

Sylvia stood and leaned across the table. She looked J.J. in the eye and said, "I see two and two gets four in your condescending little pea-brain, James Joseph. Now apologize for being rude and I'll leave you two alone to figure out the connection."

She looked at me. "Let me know how it turns out. If not I'll hear about it at the SWAT meeting. They re-scheduled it for today because your mother and Mary were schnockered up for the last one." She shook her head.

We sat stunned and staring as Sylvia took her cup to the sink and rinsed it out. On her way toward the back door, she turned, lifted a brow, and slipped a chunk of donut to each of the dogs. She brushed her hands on her slacks and finger waved over hear head as she slipped out the door. It banged and all four of us jumped.

J.J. eyed the closed door. "Uh, bye, Mom."

13

We sat back and thought about Sylvia's information, contemplating the possibilities. Since she didn't know the details of our dumpster guy, her information had no prejudice, and therefore was gold. I mulled over obvious questions in my head. *Were the two dumpster bodies related in any way? Were they random killings or the start of a pattern? Were there more bodies before this one? If there's a pattern here, were they two more in a series of murders, or two bodies as a part of a killing spree? How similar will the murders? How much in common did the two men have? Did they get viable prints?*

I could physically feel the adrenalin rush coming on. My heart rate accelerated and blood pulsed through my veins. My breaths started coming in shorter gasps and I had to remind myself to slow down. I chanced a look at J.J., and saw him still in deep thought. *Of course they're related, Buzz. Now get cracking and look for the connection.* I had to move, so I got up and went into my office—a. k. a. the den.

I had just finished adding to the whiteboard when J.J. appeared in the doorway. "Sorry I spaced out back there, I should have known you'd bring us up to speed. You are a woman after my own heart, Buzz Miller. I love it when you get into murder mode."

"Awe shucks, J.J. You say the sweetest things. You love my murder mode, you love my taste in movies, you love my dogs...heck you love almost everything about me, don't you?"

I turned back to the whiteboard and scribbled notes on the side. Not looking back I said, "Come on, Green. We don't have much time to devote to diddling around, so let's get our thoughts down in writing."

I felt his arms slide around my middle. His breath skittered across my neck as he nuzzled my earlobe. "Huh, that's what you say. I say there's always time for a little diddling. We can come back to the whiteboard tonight or tomorrow."

"Time for diddling? I'll show you time for diddling, mister." Before he could answer I slipped out of his grasp, ruffled his hair, and tossed him a dry marker on my way out the door.

I made more coffee and brought both mugs back to the office. I had a feeling my very short night was going to be followed by a very long day, and wished in a fit of whimsy I could just hook up the coffee intravenously. Sighing, I picked up my notes and made notations on the white board.

J.J. helped himself to my desk and computer and currently spoke on the phone with his office. His reading glasses slid down his nose, and his hair stood on end. He furiously scribbled on a piece of paper. Not wanting to bother him, I picked up my cell phone. After eight rings, a groggy Fred picked up on her end.

"Hey, little sister, rise and shine, the fair is probably half over by now!" I heard a grunt and interpreted it to say, "Okay, Buzz, I'm awake."

"Hop in a cold shower, Fred. We promised Mom we'd help get the Geriatric SWAT Team settled in the Ag building, and we need to get Tony's RV on location while there's still room enough to squeeze a vehicle of that acreage on location. My trailer is all set up at the campgrounds. I just need to fill the fridge and bring the dog bowls. Everything else is already there."

"What the heck time is it, Buzz? We were uh, up pretty late and I um, what the heck time is it, Buzz?"

"Seven-forty by my watch, Fred, and I haven't been to

bed yet, so quit your griping."

"Bugger it, Buzz, call me back at a decent hour."

"Wait! Don't hang up Fred. Just leave the keys to the motor home on your kitchen table and I'll come by and get them. Edie is going to meet me at ten at the Sheriff's tent with the electronics we need to set up inside the motor home, and the cops start with perimeter patrol this afternoon at three. We are due to have a meeting with the Chiefs and their officers assigned to the fair at 11:00, so I need to get rolling on this now."

"Okay, okay. I got it. The keys will be in the kitchen. Just give me a couple of hours and I'll make the meeting at 11:00. Al made up a patrol schedule for each shift, complete with walking maps and overlapping routes. It's amazing! I'll grab those on my way in. Hey, can you call her? Maybe she'll help you get the Ag building set up."

"Al? Heck no, she might break a nail, and we'd have to call an ambulance. Seriously, Al has enough on her plate, and I am not going to pile more on it. I'll call Mag instead, and Mom too. I know she'll come out. You get ready now. I'll pick you up with the keys."

I heard Fred moan and laugh. "But, Buzz—"

I could hear her blowing her bangs out of her face. "Whatever, okay, I'll get up. You're right about Al too. She worked her butt off on this fair, and I have to give her credit, I do love Al's organizational skills." I heard her blow out a huge breath. "Oh, Al reminds me, Buzz. When and where do we drop our tomatoes? Al said something about a special area, but is it located in the Ag building? Mag called and I told her I'd let her know."

"Uh, I don't remember. Tell me again why we have to bring our tomatoes to the fair?"

"Why, did you kill yours again?"

"What? Whatever gave you that idea? My tomatoes are

113

beautiful! Their huge! They'll knock your socks off."

I looked out my window for stray lightning bolts. "Did you kill yours, oh Grand Pooh-Bah of the Plant Growing Queen of the Tomato? No blossom end rot? No fusarium wilt? No early or late blight?"

"Don't start, Buzz. I'm not picking on your black thumb gardening skills."

Yes she was, but I wasn't going to start a fight over it...after all, my tomatoes *were* dead. "Okay, I'll pick on Mag instead. Get your butt out of bed and let's get going."

"*Riiight*. Hey I forgot, Buzz, remind me again. What was your one redeeming quality?"

"My sparkling personality. Now get your tomato-growing butt going-I'll be there in twenty minutes. Be ready."

I slapped my cell phone shut and looked up to see J.J. staring at me. "What?"

He smiled. "Oh, nothing. Was that one of your sisters you were oh-so-polite to?"

"Yes, as a matter of fact, yes, Fred. I'm picking up her and Tony's motor home on my way to the fairgrounds. I want to get 'Mom and company' settled in before our coordination meeting at 11:00. I'll be staying out there from tonight on, and I want to get the dogs settled as well."

I turned to leave, but J.J. grabbed a loop on the back of my jeans and I stopped when I pulled him half way across the kitchen. He grinned. "Uh, Buzz?"

I whirled on him. "What? I have to run out for a minute. I'm going to the garden center in Burlington. I'll be right back."

"Buzz?" I stopped. "You killed your tomato plant, didn't you?"

I bit my lip and looked anywhere but at J.J. "What?"

"You heard me, Buzz Miller. I looked out the back door. I see a pot with brown sticks in it, but no tomato plant."

I made a dash to the back door.

"Buzz?" With keys between my teeth and one hand on the doorknob, I stopped again and turned.

"You're going to cheat, aren't you?"

I stared into his eyes and slowly nodded.

"Buzz?"

I folded my arms across my chest and stuck out my chin. I was not going to start a long monologue about how I had been bragging about my non-existent tomatoes, and how I refused to suffer one more humiliation at the hands of my siblings because I have the blackest thumb in the Midwest. Was I going to cheat? Hell yes!

"*Buuuuzz*?"

His voice jolted me back to the kitchen. I took a deep breath. "I knew I'd probably kill one plant, so I started with four spares. I managed to discover damping off, verticililium wilt, aphids, thrips, and some black-spotty-yellow-yucky-buggy thing which ate my last tomato."

I hyperventilated by this time. "James, I don't know how, and I don't know where, but I am going out that door and I am going to find some tomatoes to bring to the fair if it kills me!"

He grinned.

"Don't try to stop me J.J."

He didn't move. I pointed a finger at him. "I mean it, Green."

He put his hands in the air. "Far be it from me to stand in the way of you when you get a head full of steam. I was just going to say before you go steal Mrs. Simmon's heirlooms, I happen to have a pretty good looking pot tomato on my patio in the back yard. It happens to be the same variety as the ones you started this spring, and I figure since we *are* a couple..."

I folded my arms across my chest. "A couple what?"

"Ha-ha. Don't interrupt while I'm abetting a cheater." I had to grin.

"Anyway, since we are uh, you know, a couple, and we share everything, I figure the tomato on my porch is half yours anyway. So if you were to borrow it for the week…"

I flew across the kitchen and grabbed him around the neck. I planted a big smack-a-roo right on his lips. "James Green, you are the absolute best! You'll even commit veggie felony with me. No wonder I love you!"

I ruffled his hair and dashed out the door. It only took me about two blocks to realize I'd blurt all over the place I loved him. *Hmmm, you realize there'll be no living with him after this...*

"Great, Buzz. You go and blab what you've kept to yourself for what...thirty years? What an idiot." I grinned. "I should have done it years ago."

I pulled into his driveway. I got out and slammed the door, stalked around the side of his house and slipped around the corner into the back yard.

There on the patio sat a huge, beautiful, bushy tomato plant. "Wow, this baby must be two feet across. How did he do this?"

I grabbed the pot and had to drag it down the sidewalk. I opened the back gate and struggled to get the monster tomato into my SUV.

Jumping into the driver's seat, I yanked out my cell phone. He picked it up on the first ring.

"Buzz?"

"J.J., this is about the most beautiful tomato plant I've ever seen. Where did you get it? I didn't think you liked tomatoes."

"I uh, well, I've been meaning to tell you–"

"Tell me what?" I thought a minute. "Wait a minute. Why did you grow a tomato plant?"

"I, uh, that is..."

"James Joseph Green?"

"Promise you won't get mad?"

I grumbled. "Okay."

"Promise for real?"

I crossed my fingers. "I said okay, so spit it out, ace."

I heard him draw in a breath. "Well, it went this way. I watched you try so hard when you were starting those plants a few months ago, and I heard all the usual razzing your sisters gave you. I wanted to make sure you had a tomato worthy of wiping the smirks off their faces."

I felt a loo-loo coming on, but I knew his heart was in the right place, so I mumbled in the appropriate places until he got to the point.

"... So I thought I'd better keep a spare tomato plant on hand because you would, in all likelihood, kill the ones you started."

I could hear the smile in his voice and I could tell he was very proud of himself. My eyes teared up and I sniffed my runny nose.

He must have heard me because he sounded anxious. "Hey, I didn't mean to hurt your feelings–"

I wiped my nose on my sleeve. "No, No! This is happy sniffing. I can't believe you actually went through all this trouble just to save my butt just to save face, in case."

"Uh, I think I understood your meaning, which is very scary."

"It is very sweet of you, James, thank you."

"Awe shucks, honey, 'dare ain't hardly nothin' ah wouldn't do fer yew."

I grasped my cell phone harder. "I think I am finally beginning to believe it, too. Thank you, James, you really are one in a million."

"Ah! You finally see my worth. Hold on a minute." In the moment of silence which followed, I heard him sigh.

"J.J.? Are you still there?"

He sighed. "Yes, just savoring the moment. It might be a long time before I can savor another."

"Knock it off, Green. Seriously, this tomato plant is worth Christmas, several birthdays, Valentine's Day all in one. Thank you. Gotta go soon though, I'm driving." I backed out of his driveway and headed back to my house.

"Buzz, you have got to be the only woman in the world who would rather have a tomato plant rather than a diamond ring. It took me a long time to get used to the idea."

I turned onto my street. "Aw shucks, mister, ain't hardly nothin' in the world ah wouldn't–"

"Hah, I cannot tell you how much I look forward to reaping the benefits of your gratitude, my dear."

I turned back into my driveway. "Do we have to wait until tonight?"

"Huh? Why, change of plans?"

I turned off the SUV and hopped out. "Open the back door, Green."

The door swung open as I rounded the corner of the house. He stepped out and I grabbed the front of his shirt and walked him back inside, my lips plastered to his. My foot slammed against the inside, and the door closed.

J.J. came up for air when we started down the hall toward the bedroom. "Uh, Buzz, we both have full days ahead of us. Wasn't it you who said save the diddling for later?"

"It's later, sweetheart."

He backed down the hall. I reached for the top buttons of my blouse. I saw sweat bead on his upper lip. "Uh, Buzz, honey, don't you think we should–"

My shirt hit the floor. "Why yes, I think we definitely should–"

J.J. grinned large. He stopped and wrapped me up in his arms. I sighed when he ran those beautiful hands down my

118

back. I made short work of his shirt as we cleared the bedroom door. My hands touched his chest as his foot kicked the door closed. J.J. ducked his head toward mine. Stopping just inches from my lips, he smiled. "Yes, ma'am, you're right as usual. I think we *definitely* should."

14

Running a brush through my hair, I heard J.J. call my name. I knew I was running late, but I took a second and pondered my reflection in the mirror. *You don't look different, Alice Miller, you're not even drooling.* I stuck out my tongue and turned from the mirror.

I rounded the corner into the kitchen just as J.J. began to yell out the door. I put my hand over his mouth and he grinned. "You bellowed your majesty?"

He flicked the end of my nose. "What's up with 'Your Majesty'? Wasn't I 'Oh God' about twenty minutes ago? Have I been demoted?"

I rolled my eyes and poured coffee in a to-go cup. "I won't dignify such arrogance with a response."

J.J. smiled and tucked in his shirt. "I wanted to tell you I might be in for a long night tonight, because I'm the only one on. After today, the Four Stooges will be taking turns on regular patrol, so I'll be freed up for the fair. We'll be up and running from the motor home by ten tonight, so I'll just stay out there full time starting tomorrow. He strolled to the sink and rinsed his cup.

"You can crash at the fairgrounds with us if you end up there tonight, or the kids and I will expect you tomorrow, okay?"

He turned from the sink where he had been rinsing his glass and smiled his crooked smile I knew and loved so well. "Now who in their right mind could turn down an offer like that?"

"Do you want the list alphabetically, or in chronological order?"

He threw an arm around my neck and squeezed, making a loud smacking noise when he kissed my temple. "Oh, Buzz, how could anyone resist the company of you three?"

I looked down to see both dogs grinning large. Both their heads were cocked to the left, tongues lolling and their tails wagging–well, Wes wagged and Hill just wiggled her butt. I hugged both of them. "I don't know, J.J. We're a pretty irresistible group all right."

Hillary passed some superb gas and we jumped. Totally offended, Wes moved to the other side of the kitchen.

J.J. grabbed his ball cap off the table and fanned the air. He bent to rub Hillary's ears. "Yup, you're definitely a pretty special, girl." He straightened and headed out the door. "I'll most likely have a very late night, so I'll probably end up at home tonight. I'll toss some stuff in a duffel bag, and I'll see you guys in the morning. In the meantime, I'll call Chief Kimichik in Baraboo and see what's-what up there."

I grabbed a to-go cup of coffee for each of us. "Got it. Call me if you think I can do any leg work between now and then."

J.J. slapped the ball cap on his head, grabbed his coffee, and walked to the door. He hesitated and turned back. He gave me a slow squeeze and a long kiss. "Our timing isn't the best, but eventually we'll get this right."

I smiled. "I think we got it pretty right already, Green. Now get out of here so you can go out and serve and protect."

He tapped the end of my nose. "Okay. Until tomorrow, kid."

"Okay. When I get organized, I'll work Oly Norris from the local angle and see what he had in common with Cab Walker."

"Great. I sure hope we can connect up those bodies with a reasonable explanation. I'd like to wrap up this investigation before the fair starts tomorrow. I'll find out more and call you

121

later."

"Okay, if I think of anything, I'll make notes."

He winked and headed out the door. I heard him say under his breath, "I sure hope this is the end of it."

I hadn't the heart to tell him I had a feeling it was only the beginning.

15

Early morning on opening day at the fair is a flurry of activity. I opened the trailer door and took a deep breath. The sweet smell of cotton candy wafted gently on the breeze. The 4-H kids had already fed their animals, cleaned the barns, and wereat the wash racks bathing their animals for the livestock show. I took a deep breath. Wet pavement, clean straw, old corn dogs, diesel exhaust, and the animal barns combined to create a kaleidoscope of scents threatening to overwhelm my delicate, early morning sensibilities–and woo-hoo, today is opening day!

I took another breath and hesitated before I stepped out of the trailer. A feeling of light-headedness swept over me. I steadied myself on the trailer steps and took another tentative whiff and felt as if a fits punched me in the gut. "Oh crap. I smell death."

A nudge from behind reminded me the dogs had not yet been out this morning, so we took care of priority one. "Come on, guys."

I stumbled down the trailer steps; aided in my free fall by my loyal canine companions. They about bowled me over in their race to the parking lot. By the time I caught up with them, they had finished and waited for me; both with self-congratulatory grins on their doggy faces. Wes had a gum wrapper stuck to his chin. I yanked the foil off. "No chewing gum, Wes."

I ruffled the hair on their heads and we all took off toward Garcia's Grab and Go; run by none other than our favorite local diner owners, Sal and Amy Garcia. Actually, Amy did all the running and stocking since Sal had to see to the diner in town until the afternoon shift. The dogs and I passed by the full dressed Carousel at the entrance to the midway and Hillary slowed to a stop. The hair on the back of her shoulders lifted slowly and a low growl rumbled quietly into the morning air.

I stood next to her and listened. "What's the matter, Hill, do you feel it too?"

She stared down the midway and continued to growl. I took a tentative step toward the Carousel and Hill stepped in front of me, her growl becoming louder. I dug for my phone and speed-dialed J.J. I took in his low gravelly voice and felt almost sorry I woke him. "Sorry, J.J.," I said in a rush, "I didn't know you'd still be sleeping."

"Rough night; pulled in two drunks and a domestic off the fairgrounds last night. I got in a few hours ago. I didn't want to wake the dogs, so I just went home."

"The dogs?"

"Yeah. You I'll wake, but Wes would have been barking and spinning for an hour and I knew we'd get no sleep. What's up?"

"I got one of my feelings this morning. I thought I smelled death this morning, and Hillary is currently growling down the midway at God knows what. I got a bad feeling, J.J., so I called you before I check it–"

"Don't do a thing, Buzz, and for heaven's sake don't check out anything until I get there, promise?" I heard clunking. "I'm getting dressed as we speak."

"Are you sure, James? I could get Moe...."

"No Moe. No Miller Sisters, and for God's sake, don't tell your mother!"

I could hear clothes rustling in the background. "Buzz...."

I sighed. "Still here."

"Listen, Buzz, don't move. I'll be there in a couple

minutes."

"No, wait! It may be noth–"

Hill stared at me with watery eyes, and I knew I was only blowing smoke. "I don't want to bother you, stay in bed for now. You can check it out later. I can go see what she's–"

He chuckled. He tittered! He had the temerity to *laugh!* "Like I could sleep now. Man, sometimes you kill me!"

"I've come close a time or two," I said through my teeth, "But it is a subject which is sounding more tempting by the minute."

"Awe c'mon. Don't you see the humor here?"

"I wonder if poison is out of the question?"

"I'm sorry I got you going. Let me get dressed and I'll run over there."

"Not if I run you over first, pal..."

"Buzz, would you please calm down? What is your problem? Has the creepy feeling got you super freaked?"

"Now I'm freaked. Well, I'm a hungry freak, so the freaky kids and I are going to get breakfast at the cook shack. I'll meet up with you there, okay?"

"Good. You'll feel better with some food in you."

"On this we can agree, Amigo. Meet us at Sal's, but don't waste your time on clean clothes, because I'll have a knife in my hand by the time you get here, and I don't want to get blood all over your good uniform."

I heard him snicker as he hung up the phone.

I stuffed the phone into my jeans and looked down at the dogs. "Come on kids, eat now, work later." We took off past the donikers and all three of us held our breaths. We wove between a cat rack and a water race and hopped over the kiddie-canoe ride–I didn't think anyone had those anymore. I wondered not for the first time if they still used Tidy Bowl to turn the water blue.

I was reminded of a story about a carnival we played in

Chicago many years ago. It was an ethnic event, and many tents were set up serving traditional dishes and drinks. I was kind of grossed out at the time, because I didn't see any water hoses or sinks leading to the little tents so the venders could wash their hands after using the port-a-potties and before they plunged their hands back into the making of food. We all decided to steer clear of the vendor tents that week.

I was out one early morning walking Hillary and our foray took us past the kiddie canoe. I stopped dead in my tracks as I watched the local women dipping their drink jars in the canoe ride water. Since they had no water source, I guess they made their juice drinks with the only water they could find. One of the carneys tried to chase them away, but no one knew how to say toilet bowl cleaner in foreign languages. We finally found a bilingual cop, and he explained the facts of life to the locals. Must have been a run on Imodium that week in Chicago.

I could see the faded orange canvas top of the cook shack on the other side of the funhouse. The dogs must have smelled the bacon burning, because I had to trot to catch up.

The cook shack has been a mainstay at the county fair since we were all kids. Originally owned by old Mr. Riley, he retired six years ago and sold out to Sal. Mr. Riley still came out to the fair, and currently ran the cash register for Amy. I kissed his leathery cheek and hugged him close. He grinned widely and held my hand. "Why, Miss Buzz, did you come out this morning just to brighten up an old man's day?"

"Mr. Riley, hardly a week goes by I am not counting the days until I see you again."

"I miss you too, girl. How's your momma? I should've run off with her sixty years ago, but I never did have any sense." He shook his head in mock sadness.

We laughed over the same line he'd been telling me for forty years. "Mom will be over in a little while. I'll keep Dad busy while you sweet talk her, okay?"

He slapped his knee and cackled. "Ha-ha. No sass now." He hugged me again. "I sure do love you, little girl."

I bent to kiss his check again. "And I you, Mr. Riley."

He smiled and rubbed the ears of both dogs. "Ah, and how are my favorite Miller children? Miss Buzz a-treatin' you right?"

Mr. Riley remained a favorite of Wes and Hillary's, and they moved closer in doggy bliss as he continued to run his arthritic hands over their coats.

Wes grinned in ecstasy and in his typical over exuberance, leaned against Mr. Riley's spare frame. His back foot pumped up and down as Mr. Riley hit all the right itchy spots. I noticed Wes leaned closer, bending Mr. Riley into an unnatural position.

"Wes," I squeaked, and Wes spun around, his butt knocking into Mr. Riley, toppling him like a house of cards. I grabbed Mr. Riley's arms and jerked him to his feet, steadying him and picking up his chair before he sat back down.

"Whew," he said, "That was a close one. Good reaction time, Miss Buzz. You go on now and get these guys some breakfast. I'll still be here when you leave."

I thanked him and proceeded to the line of waiting people. I chatted with the town folk and nodded to those I did not know. Some of them eyed my dogs, wondering if they should eat in the same place where dogs were customers. It reminded me of the time Wes stole some lady's toast when her back was turned. I had been talking with Mom when we heard the commotion. I looked up to see a woman arguing with Sal, complaining she had not been given toast with her meal. Sal jumped up and down, pointing to the crumbs on her plate asking how stupid she thought he was. The argument escalated in volume, and Amy slipped around the counter and dropped two more slices of toast on the woman's plate.

She grabbed her toast and stalked off and I turned to talk to Mom. I happened to look down and there sat Wesley; a piece of crust between his toes and crumbs on his lips. I poked Mom, who gathered her purse while trying not to laugh. We slid out the back way like thieves in the night and laughed about Wes and the missing toast for days.

Christopher Pyle (of course the local idiots called him Gomer) stood at the grill, cooking bacon, sausage, pancakes and eggs. Seventeen and sullen, Chris had a tough childhood, and from the looks of him, his teens weren't going any better for him. With his dark, lank hair stuffed into a food service hat, his acne stood out in angry contrast against his pasty white complexion. "Hey Chris, what's news?"

He barely looked up. "Nothin'."

"What have you been up to lately? I haven't seen you around."

His head snapped up and he glared at me. He held up the spatula like he wanted to hit me with it. "What? Why? Who said something?"

Wes growled and I put my hands on his collar. "Whoa kid, calm down! I only asked because I care what is going on in your life."

He gave me the stink eye, looked down again, and mumbled, "Really? Well I know better, witchy woman. Nobody ever gave jack about me my whole life."

I leaned in and said softly, "That's where you're wrong, young man."

He slid his eyes to mine and stared hard at me for a couple of seconds and looked back at the grill. "Riiight." In a deft move, Chris flipped Bud Webb's pancakes onto a plate.

I gave it one more try. "Chris, you know you are always welcome at my house, and call me Buzz. Why don't you stop by once in a while and visit with the dogs? You can take them over to the dog walk, or just hang out in my back yard. You know the door is always open."

He took a deep breath and let it out slowly. He looked up and leaned on the counter. "Yeah, I guess I do know. Sorry, Miz Buzz, I know you don't mean nothin' by it. I kinda got a lot goin' on lately."

"If you want to talk, let me know." I reached out to touch his hand and he drew back.

"Uh. yeah. Just don't touch me right now, okay? No offense, Miz Buzz, but I don't want no psychic reading or woo-woo forecast, dig? He took a breath. "You want eggs?"

"No offense taken, and yes, eggs over easy, toast and bacon, please. Oh, and a couple extra orders of toast for my canine connoisseurs as well, please."

"Yeah, okay." He looked at the hopeful expressions on the dog's faces and almost cracked a smile. "You guys gonna bogart me outta some of this stuff?" He wiped two pieces of toast on the grill and tossed them over the counter. Hillary caught hers in midair and Wesley let his bounce off his head and hit the dirt. Hillary watched with the patience of Saint Francis while Wes snorked and snuffled the ground, gobbling up the treat in one gulp.

Chris did smile this time, and forgot to be rude. "Hey, Buzz, I think he snarfed up a piece of old bubblegum."

"He'll be fine, but gum gives him gas. I think I'll be in trouble later."

"Yeah, he might be blowin' double bubbles out his butt!" He handed me my plate.

"Thanks, Chris, I'll take pictures on my cell phone, and remember the invitation is good any time."

He sobered again and looked back at the grill. "Yeah, thanks."

I took my plate and worked my way down the line until I picked up my coffee and paid Mr. Riley. I went to the rear of the tent and sat at a corner table. I ate my eggs while the dogs munched on their toast.

I jumped when I heard, "Hey beautiful, are you buying breakfast?"

I looked over my shoulder and J.J. snagged a piece of bacon off my plate. He plopped down in the chair next to me and grinned as he bit down. "Don't look so crabby, toots. It could be worse, I could have been someone really, really obnoxious like Ted."

I put down my fork. "I don't think I could handle Dead Butz right now, but I can tell you one thing; had it been Ted who scraped the bacon off my plate, this fork would have slipped out of my hand and through his."

"Ouch, I'll remember those words of wisdom. Speaking of Ted, he's been pretty low key since the debacle at the garden center."

"You can't wet your pants in public and live it down in a small town–especially if you're the town constable."

"Yeah, you're right, but Ted has no shame. I honestly don't think he's bright enough to be embarrassed."

"Probably not, but you didn't come here to snitch my bacon and talk about Ted."

"No, I didn't." He suddenly smiled widely, leaned back and patted his flat belly. "Well lookee here, a woman after my own heart. Amy, I am in love. Thank you very much." Amy set a plate piled with eggs, bacon, pancakes, and potatoes in front of him. While J.J. whipped out a ten, I snatched a piece of bacon.

Amy started to wave her hand and J.J. said, "Remember? We agreed no special treatment."

"But, J.J...."

"But nothing." He pressed the ten-dollar bill into her palm. "No argument, Amy. Besides," he winked at her and waggled his eyebrows, "my girl here might find out about us and squeal to Sal." He nodded in my direction, and my jaw dropped to the table.

"J.J.!" I looked at Amy. "I will not, don't pay any attention to him, Amy. I have to return him to the asylum in an hour, and if I'm late they won't take him back."

Amy winked at me as she turned. "Can't have him missing his medication now, can we? After all, he does carry a gun." She patted J.J. on the shoulder. "I'll be back with your change." She turned and sashayed through the tent and J.J. turned back to me, still smiling at the encounter.

My expression must have betrayed my thoughts because he immediately looked contrite. "What? Was it something I said?"

At his innocent look, I dropped my voice to a stage whisper. "You had better watch what you say in Gossip Central, Green. They'll have us married off before you know it."

Saying nothing, J.J. tossed Wes a piece of toast. He stared at it while it bounced off his nose and hit the ground. We watched as Wes gobbled up the morsel.

J.J. rubbed his ears. "Know what? I don't think my man here is a dumb dog. I think he lets food hit the dirt on purpose. I think he likes the taste of turf dogs and dirt toast." He ruffed up the hair on the Newfie's head and Wes grinned back; crumbs on his nose and grass stuck to his lips. "You're just a four legged dirt delicatessen, aren't you Wes?"

Grin, wag, grin.

I concentrated on my eggs. "Yeah, it's all fun and games until your dog starts blowing bubble gum farts."

Grin, wag, grin. Wes didn't know what he did right, but he knew it deserved another treat. He stretched his nose toward J.J.'s plate and Hill stepped in front of him.

Amy returned with J.J.'s change and a couple of pieces of dry toast. Flipping one to each dog she smiled. "You guys

131

are on a diet. You've had enough butter for one day."

The dogs settled down to savor their latest score, and we settled back to enjoy our coffee. I sat thinking of the feeling death is hanging over the fairgrounds, and a shiver crawled up my neck. I tried to sort it out in my mind so I could explain it to J.J., when I looked up and saw him grinning at me. "What?"

"So tell me," he began, slowly folding his hands behind his head. "What had you so shook at the Carousel this morning?"

"Hillary. She never gets upset unless she is seriously spooked."

"What do you think we have out there?"

I eyed him over my coffee. "Something dead. I just hope it's not human."

J.J. polished off his coffee and stood. "Well, let's get moving, favorite detective of mine."

"Easy for you to say, I'm a sure thing," I mumbled.

He stood, picked up both plates, and winked. "So am I, pal, so am I."

We exited the tent and headed toward the front of the midway; oblivious to the knowing smiles of some of the patrons, and the betting money exchanging hands.

16

After leaving the cook shack, we sipped our coffee while following the dogs to the entrance of the midway.

We stopped and Hillary lifted her nose in the air. The hair slowly rose on her back, just as it did an hour ago. J.J. puffed out a breath. He bent and touched her head. "What do you smell, girl?"

Hill snuffled and took off at a slow trot. She focused on her business and never looked left or right. The slight limp from her long ago injury made her look a little lop-sided as she moved determinedly through the trailers and tents, meticulously inspecting each object in her path.

She slowed and stopped at the end of the game line-up. Wes ran in to the back of her and she snapped at him. I jumped and grabbed Wes. "Not now, big boy, she's on the job. Watch and learn."

A huge green garbage truck lumbered down the midway toward us and I grabbed J.J.'s sleeve. "Hey, let's cut behind the joints and see if Hill can pick up on anything back there. The garbage trucks are going to be emptying the dumpsters, and you know how Wesley gets around garbage."

J.J. nodded, and I made a sharp right between two carnival trailers. I looked behind me and J.J. shook his head. "Joints? The only joints I know Moe confiscated off Jimmy Mallory and his pot head brother last week."

I elbowed him and stepped over an electrical wire. "Joint, as in carnival trailer or tent, J.J." I rolled me eyes. "Food trailers are grab joints, because you grab the food and go. In general, game joints are hanky-panks, alibis, or flat stores, depending on how hard they are to win, and how bad you're getting cheated. The kind built out of lumber and canvas are called stick joints. Some games have specific names, but they are all joints."

"Sticks? As in 'stick it' to 'em?"

"No, as in made of a wooden frame, smart ass."

"Your carnival vernacular never ceases to amaze me, Buzz."

"I spent enough time around here to pick up stuff. These are some great people, Green. We've known a lot of these guys since we were kids."

"Not me."

"That's true, but only because you're a snob. Come on snob boy; let's check out the beef barn. Hillary looks as if she lost the trail, and the Junior Beef are being judged this morning."

He checked his watch. "Good idea, my cousin Katie is showing Herefords this morning. She's got a great little steer this year; calls him Bud."

"Well let's go root for Bud."

We rounded the corner just as a garbage truck picked up a dumpster outside the show ring. Annoyed because the guy blocked the entire row, I grabbed Wesley's collar and said, "Oh man, another truck. Grab the dogs."

J.J. caught Hillary's collar and we stood watching as the dumpster tipped his dumpster into the back of the big truck. Hillary lunged and began barking non-stop, and J.J. bent to settle her down. I felt a tingling at the back of my neck and looked up. As I watched the garbage roll slowly out of the dumpster, I touched J.J.'s shoulder. He looked up in time to see the head and shoulders of a man catch and hang for a moment on the lip of the dumpster before tumbling into the back of the garbage truck.

Caught in stunned silence, we stared as the truck gently set the dumpster on the ground. The hollow clunk of metal meeting blacktop galvanized J.J. into action. Leaping forward, J.J. jumped in front of the garbage truck, frantically waving his hands. The truck jerked to a halt, metal clanking and air brakes shushing. J.J. jumped onto the running board of the still rocking truck, yelling in the ear of Newt Johnson, the driver. Newt grabbed his cell phone and began yelling into it. J.J. grabbed his own phone, and began yelling into it, and I already had mine out, yelling into it.

We cordoned off the area with stock chains borrowed from a carney named Rubber Meat (I didn't ask), and by the time Larry and Shemp arrived, we looked a little more like a crime scene. Yellow tape replaced the stock chains and kept the gathering crowd at bay, and Malcolm arrived with an evidence collection kit, as did Moe. A blast of a dually horn had J.J. whipping his head around in my direction. He glared at me. "You called your *mother?*"

"I, uh, of course I did. I knew she had a ladder in the back of her truck, and I knew she'd be somewhere on the fairgrounds. Besides, she'd find out and hunt us down anyway. You know what they say, Keep your enemies close and your little old ladies with police scanners closer."

A rumbling in the distance had us turning. A familiar and slightly dented ugly red Crown Victoria came trundling around the pig barn, barely missing the garbage truck. It slid to a stop and sent a spray of pea gravel in our direction. Pebbles bounced off the garbage truck like a blast from a Remington 870 Express. Before the dust had a chance to settle, the door of the Crown Vic flew open and an orthopedic shoe appeared in the opening.

J.J. stood beside me and moaned. "I swear I'm going to take her scanner away from her and break it over Ted's head for buying it."

"Ted thought it would keep her company while he ignored her, good son that he is."

"Like he's so busy being an incompetent boob he couldn't find time to see after his mother?"

"Nope, her waking hours and the closing times of the donut shop openly conflicted, so the donuts won out. Ted got the jelly roll, and Mary got the scanner."

"Geez. Well, I guess I had better do damage control." J.J. sauntered off in the direction of the Crown Vic, and I scooted over to Mom's dually. She struggled with the tailgate, but by the time I got over there, Shemp and Larry grabbed the ladder and lifted, allowing her to drop the gate and slide the ladder out. The two deputies took the ladder to the garbage truck and stood at attention, awaiting J.J.'s orders.

The rest of the morning was spent extracting the body from the garbage truck. Malcolm and Ivan, looking sweaty and harassed, worked with police to gather what evidence could be collected before taking the body to the morgue.

I scanned the crowd, looking for my mother and Mary Cromwell, hoping to divert their attention from the crime scene, and hoping they didn't trample through the scene or make off with evidence, for which we already learned Mary could very well do. I found a couple kids snooping around behind the lineup, thinking it might be a good time to steal a couple teddy bears, and I chased them out to the front. Moe picked up on the little thieves, and ushered them aside for questioning. *Good, both the kids and Moe would be occupied for a while.*

Mary's son Ted lumbered around the corner, wearing a constable badge and wiping at copious amounts of powdered sugar from the funnel cake he had just polished off.

Mary rounded on him. "Ted, you lazy old coot, where the heck were you when the call came over the radio?" She eyeballed his sugar-coated uniform and flicked his tie. "*Humpf,* I should have remembered you have priorities. Isn't it a little early in the morning for elephant ears?"

Ted sniffed. "Funnel cake, Mother. Elephant ears are crispy and donut like, with butter, sugar and cinnamon. Funnel cakes are like pancakes with powdered sugar, at least the best ones are with strawberries and whipped cream."

Mom said nothing, but she and Mary headed around the front of the garbage truck. Ted followed and brushed at his dark blue shirt, managing to smear the powdered sugar in mini arches across his chest. He wasn't watching where he walked, and tripped over Bucket the Clown's oversized cowboy boots.

Bucket ignored Ted (most people did), and watched with avid interest as the police worked the scene. Ted perked up. "Well Tony, how ya been? Interested in police procedure, are you? I can walk you through the process if you want."

Bucket looked down his nose at Ted. "Constable Putz, if I wanted lessons from you, I'd leave a note on Dunkin' Donuts' cork board. Excuse me." He brushed by Ted and continued down the midway.

I elbowed Mom. "Wow, what a rude dog. We can poke fun at Ted, but he's not even from here."

"Maybe Bucket's mad because Ted called him Tony instead of Bucket. When clowns are in full makeup, you call them their character names. You don't want touchy clowns on your hands, believe me."

I watched the retreating figure of the old clown; hands fisted, head down, legs kicking out his feet so his boots didn't get snagged on the ground. "Hey, Mary, did you notice Bucket wears cowboy boots?"

Mary dropped her spy glass into her purse and busied herself with taking notes. "Nope, didn't notice, Buzz." She looked up. "So?"

"So, he's wearing cowboy boots, Mary. That could be significant."

Mom sighed. "So nothing, Buzz. Lighten up and quit

137

trying to make something out of nothing. Mary and I are leaving. Meet us at the talent show around three. We want to get a good seat, and Mary has to make sure the acts are lined up and ready to go before four. I've got the roller-cooler with drinks."

Mary piped up. "I'm bringing a cooler with sandwiches, unless you want to get us one of those eye-talian sausages with the onions and peppers glopped on top. Windfall Concessions always serve up a good dog. Gotta go now, stay out of trouble, and tell us all about the victim later, okay? That garbage smell is making me kind-of queasy."

Mary and Mom disappeared, so I moseyed over to where J.J., Malcolm, and Ivan transferred the body into the coroner's van. "Any ideas?"

J.J. looked at me over his shoulder. He talked quietly. "Initially, it looks like the same M. O. as the others. We'll know more later after Ivan and Malcolm finish with him."

"Does this mean you're going to be gone all afternoon?"

"No, Malcolm and Ivan can handle it from here. They already know what to look for, but they have to proceed like it's a new homicide so they don't miss any details. I'd only be in the way, and I have enough on my plate this afternoon."

He checked his watch and ran a hand through his hair. "The fair officially opens in about twenty-five minutes. Can you get these people with vehicles off the grounds? I'll have the Four Stooges disperse the crowd and pack up. We can pick up the interviews with the carnival personnel later. Let's get things back to normal as quick as we can. It's pay-one-price day and the kiddies will be lined up three deep at the ticket booth over there in about a half hour."

I nodded and waved the vehicles on their way.

J.J. strode toward his deputies. Last we heard was, "Hey Moe—er—Phil, come over here for a minute, would you?"

You have to love J.J.

138

17

With the crowd gone and the midway back to normal, I was hard pressed to find something to do. The kiddies lined up to get their wristbands. The Carneys looked haggard; standing around sucking coffee with one hand, and holding lit cigarettes in the other. They looked like they wanted to be anywhere else but here, and I didn't blame them. For the next five hours they would be running non-stop, controlling crowds, dealing with spoiled, screaming, and puking kids and cranky parents. How they kept their rides going and their patience from exploding is one of the mysteries of the world I have contemplated many times.

The independent ride owners who booked their spectacular rides with the show I really felt sorry for. They make their money off individual ticket sales. On Pay One Price Day they only received a cut of the gross. The kids ride the cheap ticket rides all week, but on Pay-One-Price Day, they converge on the expensive super-spectacular rides and work them to the max.

I shook my head and walked down the midway, avoiding eye contact with the agents in the games and trying not to look like a "mark."

Back at the trailer, I put the dogs away and grabbed some money. I checked in with Edie at "Motor Home Control." She assured me everything went off smoothly, and everyone showed up for foot patrol duty. I completed my initial report on the body, and by the time I finished, it was time to find something to eat again.

I bought three Italian sausages with everything on them, and smiled when the guy at the window yelled over his shoulder, "Three Dagos, and kill 'em!"

Not too politically correct, but it would not be me arguing semantics with a sweating, ornery Sereno brother.

At least he gave me a small box to carry my stash. I happily wove my way between a spoofer dime toss and a bottle-up stick. I twiddled my fingers at Big Dave in the duck pond and he yelled, "Hey, Buzz, where's the maggot and Freddie hiding?"

Harvey Spinner sat on his stool at the Skee Ball, his grind tape playing loudly in the background. "Whoa there, pardner, it's the family fun game, it's Skee Ball! Rolllll six balls up the lane and win a big State Fair Prize! Everyone is playing, and everyone is winning, it's Skee-Ball."

On and on it droned. Harvey must have heard it a thousand times a summer for the last thirty years.

I shook my head in wonder and waved to Harvey. "Hey girl, how's your momma?"

"Fine, Harvey, just fine. She'll be over to see you later today."

Harvey nodded and spit tobacco into the old coffee can at his feet.

I made it over to the oak glade on the west side of the fairgrounds and found a row of six empty seats about a third of the way back from the stage. I sat in the middle one and I didn't even have my sausage unwrapped when I saw Mary barreling down one end lugging a pull-behind cooler. It glanced off one guy's knees, but the other two people in the row had the good sense to jump out of her way. I hopped up and took it from her, carrying it to her seat. She flopped down and fanned herself with her program. "Hoo-wee, it's hot out here! They're all set to go backstage. Bucket is our emcee, so I left everything in his hands so I could enjoy the show. Did you bring me a sausage, Buzzi girl?" She craned her neck and smiled when she saw the box in my hand.

Mom chose the moment to come at me from the other end of the row, cooler in one hand and umbrella in the other. I helped her along by taking her cooler. I tried to crawl past Mary, but they sandwiched me between them and dug in to the sausages. Joy Broussard sat about five seats over, fanning herself with her program. I asked Mom for her program so I could see the star-studded line-up.

"Here, Buzz, I got you one of your own. Go ahead and keep it."

I fluttered my eyelashes and clutched the program to my heart.

"Oh thank you, one for my very own. Did you happen to get me a Lemonade Shake-Up?"

"Don't be smart young lady." She grabbed the other sausage.

Bucket stepped up to the microphone and began his opening patter. He announced the first act, Molly Olsen took center stage and sang a couple of lovely Irish ballads. She received great applause, and it proved to be a great opening act. The crowd buzzed with anticipation for what came next.

Bucket entertained the crowd between the acts with some of the magic tricks he did from his kid shows. He stayed away from the more risqué rodeo clown jokes, and brought up volunteers from the audience and the crowd loved him. I leaned over and said, "Nice choice in emcees, Mary. Bucket is great, a real crowd pleaser."

Mary and Mom agreed and we settled back for more.

Later in the show, we suffered through an excruciating singing performance by Sherry Riley. My ears still rang after the final notes died a terrible death.

I wondered what number performed next so I consulted my program. The setting sun was lovely to watch, but here in the oak grove, there was little light to be had, so I could barely see the writing on the program.

I felt a bump on my right. In a loud stage whisper, Mom leaned on my arm and said, "Whew, I'm glad she's done and over, what's next? That last act really stunk!"

"Shh," I said. "Sherry Riley's relatives are nearby. Her mother is sitting over there, so don't be rude." I indicated Bev sitting white faced at the end of the row.

Mary piped up from my left. She leaned across me from the other side and said in a louder voice, "Old Sherry howled and screeched so bad it sounded like she had her booby caught in a meat grinder! I told Bev Riley her daughter couldn't sing, but would she listen? *Noooooooo*! She made me book her anyway. Blackmailed me, she did. I sure hope the next act has more talent than Scary Sherry."

I could feel my face heat with embarrassment for Sherry's mom. "*Shh*, Mary, be nice!"

My mom nodded, ignored me, and leaned across my lap. "Whew, I'm with you, Mary. I don't care if Wesley gets up there and howls, as long as Scary Sherry doesn't try to sing Whitney Houston again." She shivered, and I almost smiled.

"*Shh*, Mom! Sherry's family might hear you." She tried to move closer and jostled my arm again. "Mom, sit still a minute; I'm trying to read–"

A jostle from my other side, and a boney elbow in the ribs had me gasping and crumpling the program. "*Pssst*! Gerry!" Mary leaned over my lap once more and balanced her boney elbow on my thigh, trying to read the program in the fading light. "When are Cameron McKenzie and his cousins going to play? I think they're doing '*Vehicle*,' I love that song!"

Mom nodded. "Doncha just love the brass section?"

Mary cooed. "Doncha just love Cam McKenzie's patootie?" Several grey heads nodded.

I eased Mary back into her chair. "Mary, you're drooling on my program. I like their harmony, myself."

Mary crossed her arms over her meager chest and pouted. "Sometimes I wonder who the old lady is in this town, Buzz Miller. You are such a stick sometimes."

I gasped and Mary chuckled. "Okay, okay, I've only heard the McKenzies a couple times. Last year they did a great job, didn't they?"

I smiled. "They did, eh?"

"You bet they did! Uh, I can't remember off the top of my head what they played last year. I remember it had a nice beat but I couldn't dance to it."

I bit my tongue and Mom sighed. "They played *The National Anthem*, Mary."

"Oh, uh...yeah...I forgot. That's why I couldn't dance to it. But they did have a nice beat, didn't they?"

I rolled my eyes as I struggled to keep a grip on the program as well as my sanity. While they chatted back and forth, I tried to lean back to avoid Mary's boney elbows. She belched loud and long, and the smell of the Italian sausage with onions she had an hour ago smothered me in a green fog. At the same time, Mom leaned in on my right, squishing me between her and Mary. While they critiqued the local talent, I could barely breathe. Sandwiched as I was between the two of them. I struggled to extricate my arms from under their bodies. I began to list to the right. Then the left side of my chair started to sink into the grass. I shifted my weight and my chair began to tilt backward. If I didn't do something fast, I was going to sink like the *Titanic* in fast forward. "If you two..." (gasp) "Would just move a little..." (huff) "I could see..." (puff) "The program..." (wheeze) is under your elbow, Mom!".

"*Shh*!" Came from behind us, and some kind soul shoved my chair forward. I crashed into the two of them, but aside from knocking Mary's pink sombrero askew, they never broke stride. They kept up a steady chatter about the

143

McKenzie cousins until the time the next act staged up and was ready to perform.

Bucket O'Donnell, aka Bucket the Clown, took the stage again. His banter began to pall, and I felt about ready to get out of Dodge. He thought to spruce up his act by adding the rodeo clown jokes, but they went over like a lead balloon, Still dressed in his clown get up from the kid's magic show, he ran through his old rodeo clown joke repertoire like he still shouting from the middle of a rodeo ring. I had about all the "suns along the beaches" and "booger bit it" punch lines I could handle. "What is taking so long? I thought the McKenzie's were going to perform. Hand me the program, someone, would you please?"

I shoved against Mom and Mary and my right arm popped free. I snatched up the program and tried to read it in the fading light. I held it over my head so I would be able to hold it steady enough to read. With my head tipped back as far as it would go and my arms outstretched trying to catch the last rays before dusk, I could finally make out the writing. *Oh no!* I groaned inwardly.

I whispered to Mom, "It says here the next one up is Tammy Grogan and her dancing Poodle, Snoodle. Who the heck booked them?"

Mom and I both looked to my left. "*Mary!*"

Mom sighed in exasperation. "How could you? I'd rather listen to Scary Sherrie sing the entire *Hallelujah Chorus* than suffer through Tammy's stupid poodle act again. McKenzie boys or not–let's get out of here!"

Mary slapped Mom on the thigh. "Hoo-hoo, come on, Gerry, where's your sense of humor?"

Mom quickly looked up and down the aisle for an escape route. "My humor went south as soon as I heard Snoodle the Poodle performed next, Mary. I sat through stupid Snoodle last year with Joy at the Pet Parade. I tell you it was torture the entire time! I felt embarrassed for poor Tammy."

Mary snorted. "Sure, humiliating, for Tammy and Joy, that is! Snoodle the Poodle did a doodle right on the judge's shoe! I tell you, Tammy fainted, but the crowd loved it-it seemed like part of the act, so I booked 'em here for their entertainment value. Just look how many people showed up. It might even settle their indigestion from Scary Sherry. You can bet your bucket Bucket doesn't realize his clown shoes are history."

Mary wheezed out a guffaw that had the crowd shushing us again. "I remember Joy about to have conniptions over Snoodle. I told her to stop wailing over her daughter-in-law's stupid dog act, and concentrate on potty training the stupid mutt."

Mom gave a stiff nod. "Yep, I really gave her the business about Tammy's poopin' poodle too—oh no look, there it is!"

Her voice faded out as Bucket boomed out the introduction. I looked down the row at Joy as she sat frozen in her seat, staring at the stage. A recording of *The Syncopated Clock* began and I looked up in time to see a ball of white fluff in a pink tutu hop across the stage on his hind legs in time to the music. He hopped back toward Tammy and stopped to twirl at center stage. He hopped over to Tammy, who bent to pick up the dog, but he squirmed out of her arms. The crowd clapped politely.

Flustered, Tammy picked up a small hoop, which I guessed Snoodle supposedly jumped through. She gave the command and Snoodle sat there panting, staring into space. Sherry bit her lip and looked over at Bucket, and so did I. He stood with hands on hips, glaring at Tammy with a cross between exasperation and disgust on his face. It looked especially evil on a face covered in clown-white.

I said out of the corner of my mouth, "I got a *bad* feeling about this." Mom chuckled and Mary put a bracing arm across my front, in case I tried to bolt.

Tammy snapped her fingers again, and Snoodle walked up to the hoop. "Come on Snoodie. Jump for Mommy!" Tammy gestured to him to jump and Snoodle ignored her. "Come on, baby. One little jumpy. Let's go!" She jumped up and down and Snoodle walked back to center stage.

Tammy dropped the hoop and fetched a ball and a small red bucket–personally I thought Tammy fetched better than her dog. Placing the bucket up stage and to the left, Tammy commanded Snoodle to fetch the ball and drop it in the bucket. Snoodle stood on his hind legs and proceeded to hop toward Stage Right. Tammy shouted, "Snoodle no, get the ball! Snoodle, come to Mommy... Snoodle stop!"

The little dog continued toward stage-right, and I could hear the panic creep into Tammy's voice.

Mary's bony elbow cracked a rib on my left. A decidedly sinister sound to her laugh flowed past me as she leaned my way. She whispered, "Just like watching a train wreck in slo-mo, ain't it?"

Tammy took quick, shuffling baby steps and retrieved the ball. "Lookie, Snoodie, I fetched the ball!"

She ran across the stage and dropped the ball in the bucket. A grinning Tammy jumped up and clapped her hands. The crowd clapped and shouted. Some idiot–it sounded suspiciously like my dear sister Mag–yelled, "Atta girl, Tammy!" Tammy turned red-faced and watched as Snoodle hopped away.

As Snoodle neared the edge of the stage, Tammy was galvanized into action. Tammy made a grab for his tail. "Snoooo–daaall!" I looked down our row of chairs, only to see Joy slumped back, her friends furiously fanning her face.

Bucket must not have realized his microphone was still live, because when Snoodle dropped to four legs and shifted into second gear, he quipped, "And good riddance to the dumb little bitch...*and* her damn dog, heh, heh."

He snorted and turned back to the crowd. He gazed out across a grove full of silent and staring faces. He made a valiant effort to recover. "Hey, folks, ever wonder how to become a steer wrestler? Well, you get a bunch of marbles and put 'em in your mouth–"

"Knock it off, Clowny!"

I guess the crowd was in no mood to mess with Bucket, but he plowed onward, his size 24 cowboy boot fitting more snuggly in his mouth. "Then you get up on the running board of a truck..."

"We want the dumb dog back!" Tammy may have had the worst dog act in the world, but when an outsider like Bucket disses the local dumb dog and his owner, an angry mob can pop out of nowhere.

Bucket stumbled over his words and tried to gain control. He didn't see the commotion off to the side, and found himself caught by surprise at what came next.

I panned in on Bucket, and noticed Tammy scuffling with her dog in the grass off to Bucket's right. I panned in on Snoodle as he squirted out of Tammy's hands and headed back up the stairs. A sick sense of dread settled in my stomach and I had visions of an Alfred Hitchcock heroine about to buy it in the shower stall.

Mary elbowed me hard and said out of the corner of her mouth, "Hah! Here comes the good part!" Snoodle ran back onto the stage. Tammy bent over and shuffled after her dog, trying to grab any body part she could. The dog headed for Bucket, and Tammy trailed after him. She made a running dive for Snoodle, catching a hind leg. Old Snoodle the poodle let out a vicious yap and chomped down on poor Tammy's thumb. Tammy in turn let out the wail heard around the world, and Snoodle scadoodled off the stage like a rocket.

147

The crowd went wild. Joy passed out. Tammy lay on the stage screeching like she just lost an arm. Bucket yelled into the microphone, "That's okay folks, everything's under control!" He whipped his huge rodeo clown bandanna out of his back pocket and proceeded to wipe his brow with one end and wrap Tammy's bleeding thumb with the other. Mike Dudley, veterinarian extraordinaire and rescuer of damsels in distress, jumped on stage just to have Tammy swoon in his arms.

Mom and Mary both looked at me and rolled their eyes. Mary snorted. "And you don't think the swoon wasn't planned? She just conveniently faints in the arms of the handsome veterinarian she's been chasing for two years?"

Both Mary and Mom turned back to the stage, nodding sagely. I looked at Joy, still lying on the ground. I noticed she had one eye open and glared at Mom and Mary.

I had to bite back a laugh. I looked over the crowd and saw a familiar Stetson bobbing its way toward the stage. My heart gave a little thump and I told it to shut up. J.J. had Wesley in tow. He left Wes at the base of the stairs and hopped up onto the stage. He trotted over to where Mike tried to revive Tammy.

They attempted to move her off stage. J.J. and Mike each grabbed an arm and they staggered under the weight of Tammy's not-so-petite body. They managed to get her about ten feet to the right and stopped. J.J. lost his hat in the process and Mike hauled in air like he just ran a marathon.

The crowd quieted as J.J. felt for a pulse and picked up Tammy's good hand. He held it directly over Tammy's face and I heard someone whisper, "What the heck is he doing?"

One hundred and fifteen people watched in silence as J.J. dropped Tammy's hand, and instead of hitting herself squarely on the nose, her hand suddenly jerked sideways and fell gracefully to the side of her head. J.J. stood and ran his hand through his hair.

Hands on hips he looked rather disgusted. "C'mon Tammy, show's over. Get up now." Mike still knelt by Tammy's side and looked knowingly up at J.J., and back down at Tammy.

The crowd *ooo*'d as Tammy's eyes fluttered open and her gaze landed on J.J. She shook her head and turned to gaze into Mike's face. "Oh, Mike, thank you!" She grabbed him around the neck and plastered her lips to his. The crowd gasped. Mike's arms flailed about. He grabbed Tammy's arms and tried to pull them from around his neck. He got his hands between them and pushed. J.J. grabbed Tammy around the waist and tried to pull her off Mike. Bucket crossed the stage to help, grabbing J.J. around the waist, he gave a mighty tug.

The crowd roared. Bucket lost his grip and let go. Mike struggled in vain to get free. Tammy swallowed Mike's tongue and Snoodle doodled on Bucket's oversized cowboy boots.

Bucket went ballistic. He tried to shake his boot and caught Snoodle under the tail. Snoodle flew through the air with the greatest of ease and disappeared off stage.

The crowd followed the dog's path until Mike finally broke the strangle hold Tammy had on his neck. They came apart with a sick sucking noise. The force sent J.J. flying backward into an unsuspecting Bucket, who still stood off to the side, trying to shake the doodle off his boot. J.J. lost his grip on Tammy and staggered backward. Tammy grabbed J.J. just as he tripped over Bucket's feet and they all went down, skidding backward across the stage on their butts. When they slid to a stop, Tammy turned and looked at J.J. and screeched, "Oh, J.J., Thank you!"

She put her hands on J.J. and I came up out of my chair. Mom grabbed me by the shirttail and yanked me back down. "Not now, Buzz. No need to create even more gossip, J.J. can handle himself."

Though I am not one to sit back and take it, I became distracted by Mom, and realized I was about to deny something but I couldn't remember what it was. I heard Mary behind me. "Gee, Gerry, I sure hope Buzz don't have a gun on her. She might just bust a cap on old Tammy's butt. I know if the little hussy put a lip lock on my old man, I'd have to kick her booty but good."

I lowered my head so Mary wouldn't see my smile, and I heard rustling coming from behind me. My mother gasped and I turned. Mary shoved her pink purse into my hands. "On second thought, here, Buzz. You can use my .44 on her. Let her have it right through the left cheek!"

I shoved the purse back at Mary, but murmurings fluttered through the crowd and we all turned to look at the stage.

Wesley took the moment to lumber up the stairs and stroll across the stage. He calmly stepped in between J.J. and Tammy and slurped her from chin to hairline. Gotta love my dog. Tammy squeaked and fell back in another false faint. She made quite the spectacle with dog slime dangling from her bangs and chin, and if I wasn't mistaken about the positioning of Tammy's body, she had just laid her head in the pile on stage, and had doggie doo under her head. I reminded myself to buy Wesley a steak.

Before I could stop her, Mary stood up and cupped her hands around her mouth. She bellowed into the silence, "Faking it is a pretty lame way to catch a man, Tammy! But I gotta say, you gave the Best Actress award for the night!"

Joy came out of her stunned state and yelled down the aisle, "What a terrible thing to say, Mary Cromwell! What would make you think my poor Tammy faked it?"

Mary yelled back, "I didn't get to be eighty-two years old and not know when some broad is 'faking it', Joy Broussard!"

She cackled at her own joke.

Mom tapped her on the arm when she sat. "Well said, Mary, but you know what? You don't look a day over seventy-eight."

Mary tapped her back. "Thanks, Gerry, because I'm really eighty-five."

I heard Joy yell, "But she acts about twelve years old!"

Mom smiled serenely. I could tell she was about to deliver a good punch line to Joy, but I wasn't about to let her cause more trouble. I put a hand on Mom's arm, but it came too late to stem the flow.

Mom said condescendingly, "If Tammy really passed out, her arm would have dropped right on her face and hit her right on the kisser! That's how Mary, and J.J., and me, and anybody else who ever watched *ER* knew she faked it."

Mom sighed. "Seems to me like a good excuse to display bad manners and kiss all the eligible males in the area."

"Well I never!" Joy huffed off in the direction of the stage.

Mary leaned across me and said to Mom, "I'll bet she never! That's probably why she always goes around with a stick up her butt! 'Cuz she *never*...you know...ha-ha," and waggled her eyebrows. Only Mary could get away with something like that.

Another commotion on the stage brought us back to the moment. Mike helped Tammy to her feet, and evidently, someone called the paramedics. They clambered onto the stage with their backboard and oxygen tanks, only to realize their patient only had a puncture wound on her thumb, and dog slime on her face. Two men helped her off stage and a woman paramedic followed; sniffing the air around Tammy's doggie (hair) doo, grimaced, and held the gauze she carried to her nose. A composed Bucket boomed, "Ladies and Gentlemen, let's hear it for Tammy Grogen and Snoodle the

151

Poodle!"

An anguished look came over Tammy's face and she looked around the stage. "Snoodle! Where's my baby? What happened to Snoodle?"

From the other end of the stage, my good boy Wesley lumbered up the stairs for a second time. Hanging out of his mouth was a suspiciously pink tutu. The crowd sucked in a collective breath. Tammy screamed and fainted for real. The paramedics were so busy watching Wes, they forgot to catch her, and Tammy's head sounded like a ripe melon squish when it hit the stage.

Bucket took one look at The huge Newfie and hunched his shoulders and let out with "*Blurp...ooo-blurp!*" He put a hand to his mouth and ran for the nearest bathroom.

J.J. calmly walked over to Wes, patted his head, and said, "Good boy; drop him now, Wes."

I sat smiling smugly as a tail wagging Wesley strolled up to where J.J. stood. He held his hand under Wesley's jaw, which he opened immediately. "That's a good boy, now give him back, please."

Wes opened his mouth, made a noise which sounded something like "*blec-c-ch*," and out rolled Snoodle–, but a little slimier for the experience. Snoodle leaned forward and gave Wes a big doggy kiss on the nose. Wes grinned and wagged his tail.

After a moment of stunned silence, the crowd went wild. J.J. returned Snoodle to Tammy, who covered his slimy little head with kisses. Bucket returned to the stage, looking a little green around the gills. "Well folks, this proved to be an interesting turn of events! I thought...I thought the big dog ate the little dog and...oops! *Blurp, Oof,*" and held another clown-sized bandanna to his mouth as he ran off stage.

Mom said, "*Eww!* Bucket doesn't look so good, Mary."

"Damn fool is going to toss his cookies all over stage left

in a minute. Wait here!" Mary took off in the direction of the stage.

I started forward and Mom grabbed me. "Buzz, do you really think you can stop Mary when she's under full steam? Sit back and enjoy the show. It should prove entertaining, to say the least."

Mom settled back and opened her cooler. She pulled out two bottles of cold water and gave me one. "Here, Buzz, have a belt on me."

I smiled and took one. We sat back and relaxed while chaos reigned around us. The microphone on stage howled with feedback and we looked at each other and grinned. Stage hands struggled and gagged as they cleaned up after Snoodle and Tammy, and to top it off, Mary's scratchy voice boomed over the crowd. "*TESTING! TESTING!* Okay, Hey, folks! Let's hear it for the great Wesley Miller and his rescue act!"

The crowd clapped and cheered. Wes basked in their admiration, and lumbered off the stage, trailing behind J.J. Mary took a deep breath. "Y'all don't go nowhere now, 'cuz we've got a talent show to finish up here. I don't care how entertaining you found it, I'm not going to go down in history as the one being in charge of the screamin' Mimi, barfin' clown, and poopin' poodle show! Stage hands, did you take care of our little, uh, mess over there?"

A voice off stage yelled, "I think Ms. Tammy mopped it all up with her head, ma'am!"

The crowd laughed uproariously. Mom smiled serenely and sipped her water. Mary took another breath. "Soooo-okay, last up we have those adorable McKenzie boys poundin' out some classic rock for us. So take a 'lude' and hold on to your tie-dyes you baby boomers, 'cuz these kids are *r-r-rockin'*!" She kicked a scrawny leg in the air and her orthopedic shoe thudded on the stage like a sand bag hitting turf.

153

The McKenzies took the cue and exploded with two trumpets and a trombone blasting out the first few bars of *Spinnin' Wheel* by Blood, Sweat, and Tears. Danny McKenzie played bass and trumpet, Evan played keyboards, and trumpet, Cousin Robbie played drums and trombone, and his brothers J. R. and Cameron both played guitars and switched off with the lead vocals, sax, baritone, and other percussion. They are a phenomenal talent, and they had people dancing in the aisles.

Mary squeezed her way back to her seat. She looked over the crowd and beamed. "Look at them, putty in their hands. Good thing I booked them toward the end, mayhap no one will remember Sherrie or Tammy tomorrow."

The crowd roared, and Mary slapped Mom's knee. "I knew those boys would steal the show! Old loose-lipped Tammy can take her poopin' poodle back home where it belongs. Wonder what her husband's going to make of the lip-lock she put on poor Doc Dudley?" She shook her head and cackled; settling back and grabbing a bottle of water out of Mom's cooler.

The crowd screamed for more, and Mary yelled, "Play some more, boys, we got all night!"

J. R. held up a thumb. "You rock, Miz Cromwell," and dove into some *Earth, Wind, and Fire*.

I leaned over and asked, "Mary, aren't you going to emcee the rest of the show?"

"Naw, I just gave old Bucket a breather. The last act packed up and went home, so these guys are it for the night. I told 'em to play as long as they wanted.

"Lately I heard talk Bucket's been pretty down about retirement and being useless and all, so I thought this might just be the ticket to perk up an old clown. He might be a skirt chasing dog, but he's been leaving me alone this week. He's been kind-of distracted of late, so I'm just trying to help him out a little. Bucket was a bit shook when he thought your dog ate the dancing ankle-biter, but he's coming around just fine. He'll probably talk about this until next year!"

I expelled a sigh of relief, Mom flopped back in her chair and put the cold bottle of water to her head, and Mary relaxed and sipped her bottled water, a grin forming at the corners of her mouth. She dug a crumpled bag of popcorn out of a pocket and began to munch, bobbing her head to the music on stage.

I sat back and Mom leaned over, a smile in her voice. "Isn't Mary just a pip sometimes?"

I sighed. "Yeah, Mom, she sure is. A real pip."

18

I left shortly thereafter and drove over to the morgue. I hoped we had some word about the body we found at the fair. I pushed through the swinging doors of the cold room and saw Luke playing around by a giant transparent box in the middle of the room.

"So whatcha up to, buddy-o-pal?"

Luke looked up from our John Doe and flashed me a quick grin before returning to focus on the job at hand. The body had been placed in what looked like a very large sealed aquarium attached to a long steel table. The aquarium had two round openings in the side where long gloves had been attached and allowed hands-on inside the aquarium. Luke's left hand currently was inside a glove and he tried to hold onto the victim's head while reaching for a camera outside the tank with the other. The tank was opaque with fog and I watched while Luke gently turned the head so it faced away from us.

"Hey, Buzz, grab my camera for me, would you?"

I picked the camera off the top of the tank and tried to place it in Luke's free hand. As the fumes dissipated, I saw dark patches appear on the body around the neck area as well as on the arms. I realized Luke and the body were immersed in a process of some strange forensic thingy I could not begin to comprehend. Luke had both hands inside the aquarium now and sighed in frustration.

"Damn, I can't get this head to lie still."

"Uh, do you want help?"

"Yeah, can you handle the camera while I position the head?"

I looked at the strange contraption in my hand. "No, but on a good day I can hold a head pretty steady, and I take direction well."

Luke let go of the head, looked up from the body, and smiled. I gloved up and switched places with him. I gently touched the head with only my fingertips, and only where I had seen Luke touch it. Slowly tilting it up and away from me, I exposed the neck and stretched the skin until the wrinkles smoothed out. To my surprise, a perfect thumb print stood out boldly in dark contrast to the ghostly white skin of the victim.

"Whoa," I whispered in hushed awe.

Luke grinned. "Yeah, pretty cool, eh? We've come a long way in the past two decades. Even as late as the 1990s the practice of trying to retrieve latent prints off human skin met with only rare success. Tilt the chin just a pinch more to the left, would you?"

I did as I was told. Luke messed with the camera and decided on an angle from left to right. He snapped off a rapid succession of frames and move inches to the right, repeating the process.

"You know," he said, "So many assailants grab the victim without thinking while trying to subdue and immobilize or when disposing of the body, they never think in many situations the prints can be preserved and recovered."

"So I've heard. I understand so many outside influences affect the prints, they are easily distorted or destroyed, so cops seldom bother with them. I've never actually seen it done. But this body lay in the sun and garbage Luke, prints can't be taken if they are washed away by tomato paste and funnel cake grease."

"That used to be true. Skin is constantly growing and shedding cells and the pliability factor alone lends itself to the distortion of what could have been a good set of prints. Plus the fact so few guys are expert in latent print recovery, beauties like these are often overlooked."

Luke leaned against the table and continued. "Sweat is also a huge factor-meaning the victim's and the perpetrator's sweat. It's the way the body rids itself of wastes, so prints can be washed away or smudged very easily. That does not even take into consideration the environmental factors of weather and decomposition, or if the body is mutilated and bodily fluids make it impossible to retrieve any prints. Now turn the head slightly your way."

"Okay, I get that part, but what's with the fish tank?"

"The fish t–oh."

He straightened and gestured to the very large glass rectangle in front of us. "This," he said like a proud papa, "Is the equivalent of a 900-gallon aquarium. It is what we call a cyanoacrylate fuming chamber. In order to do this, you need three basic elements–humidity, warmth, and Super Glue."

"Uh, Super Glue? Really, you've got to be kidding."

"Not kidding. This tank has its own heater and exhaust system, and uses a warmed super glue-type substance which is heated in a separate chamber. The humidity is controlled by the dial on your right, and the body should be warm–which is the biggest advantage in this case, but who knows how long John Doe here has been dead? The best thing we have going for us is though it's been pretty chilly at night for this time of year, the garbage probably kept the body relatively warm." He grinned at me. "That means odds are in our favor we will get positive results."

I touched my churning belly. It pretty much grossed me out, but I could tell Luke warmed to his subject. He patted the aquarium. "Anyway, the fumes from the glue flow into the chamber and are circulated by a small fan. When the fumes come into contact with a print, they show up dark against the skin. Notice those long gloves inside the tank are rather like

158

those used on a neo-natal care unit and allow hands-on manipulation of the body without allowing the fumes to escape the chamber. This enables us to photograph the prints much easier. Better pictures equal better chances of identifying and catching the bad guy, and more convincing courtroom evidence."

Luke took a couple more photos and again handed me the camera. "Here's where I come in. This is not an easy process, and takes countless hours of practice. I have about the most success with taking latent prints off skin and non-porous substances. He waggled his eyebrows. "That's why I make the big bucks." He quirked a smile. "Plus we have the added bonus of me being down here visiting family when the first guy was dug out of the dumpster a couple weeks ago."

At my raised brow he chuckled. "I bet you thought J.J. called me in because of our connection, but the truth is I messed around a lot with this stuff when it was still in its infancy, using everything from baby food jars and coffee cans to old refrigerators for fuming chambers. It seems practice is the only way to get good at this. These days they call me an expert and send me out in the field on special cases."

"Why is this case so special?"

Luke lowered his voice. "Because by all appearances these murders look serial."

"They're not serial, Luke. I know they are connected to the same crime. I don't know how I know, but there is a connection. What we need is for you to help us find it. What we have now are helter-skelter pieces, three dead bodies, and my gut feeling. It's very difficult harvesting forensic evidence off aged skin."

"I hate to admit it, but you're right. You basically have no solid leads. Also, when working with geriatric skin, it is especially tricky because the skin is so loose and hard to work with. Because I've had the best luck in this area, they thought

I was their best bet in gathering any useful prints. Most prints are distorted or negligible and you only get one shot at getting it right, so the big boys gave me the good equipment and the cool camera, but between you guys on recovery and Malcolm and Ivan's stellar handling of the body, it made my job much easier."

"Wow." I stared at John Doe in the glass case and felt new pride at being a special part of Luke's life.

He sighed his "get back to work" sigh, pulled a case out of his pocket and inside I saw a small brush and a tub of black magnetic print powder. Now this part of the process I understood.

Luke held the brush by the handle and twirled it between two fingers. "Now watch and learn my lady. This is the real reason why they tagged me with the 'Expert' moniker."

Luke removed a dish so shallow unless the light winked off the edge, one would think it was a flat piece of glass. "Henry Polanski–not the son, but the old man–hand-made me this dish for my graduation from the Academy."

"Nice," I replied, though I had no idea what the heck he babble about. A powder dish was a powder dish. He turned the dish slowly and I could see the tiny bubbles inside the glass which told me it was indeed, hand-blown.

"Yeah, it sure is a beauty. I've taken a lot of razzing-especially by those guys who just fold up the sides of a print card and tape the back–but I guess any port in a storm, eh?" I blushed because I was one of the ones folding and taping cards. Luke knew it too.

He stroked the glass. "I guess as long as the dish is real shallow, it doesn't much matter what you use unless you're looking to control the load on your brush, those guys wish they had my dish *and* my brush."

He set the dish on the steel table and picked up the brush.

"Here comes the tricky part. *The Brush*. There are a bazillion different brushes on the market, from feathers to carbon fiber, but for this type of work, I love a well broken in fiberglass brush and plain old black magnetic powder."

He brandished his brush with a flourish. "Wha-lah! My trusty little Zephyr."

"Show off."

He grinned. "Yeah, I know."

I watched as Luke shook about a half teaspoon of black powder into the glass dish, and proceeded to gently grind the powder–breaking up the tiny clods of by twirling the brush between thumb and forefinger–working the powder gently across the glass.

He grinned an evil grin and exaggerated an up-and-down wrist movement. "Notice the wrist action. It breaks up these little powder balls so the powder doesn't streak, and loads the brush evenly."

Tapping the brush ever-so-gently against his forefinger, he cackled like an old witch.

"Don't try this at home, boys and girls, *I* am a professional."

I ignored his antics, and he snickered.

With one hand he opened the end of the aquarium. The rolling table inside quietly swooshed and John Doe now stuck out of the end. I gloved up and held the head while Luke continued to swirl the black print powder.

Luke again tapped the brush against the finger he held over the dish, shedding any excess powder. "There we go boys and girls, now for the really *really* tricky part."

At this point I couldn't look away if I wanted to. "A lot of guys will stroke the powder on like they are painting a picture, but if I know a print is there, especially on aged or damaged skin, I like to add a twirling motion to the mix so the bristles on the brush flair and I get better coverage

161

without excessive powder. See how only the center of the brush touches the skin? I roll with the flow of the ridges of a print, rather than against them. You have to be careful not to overdevelop or erase the print, and I need to lift it as soon as I can."

He handed me the brush, snapped off a couple more pictures, pressed the tape over the print, and lifted. Securing it to a print card, he signed his John Hancock and straightened.

"Best case scenario would have been to take the prints at the scene, which was obviously impossible to do today with the fair crowds and the garbage all over. There's no one better at handling a body with care than Ivan, but many times what prints are left are unknowingly destroyed in transport."

Luke stowed his print kit and clipped the print card to the morgue file. "When Malcolm saw the damage to the neck, he immediately sent word I needed to get here fast–thus the mad dash to the morgue. As it was, Ivan had a fan ready to dry the body when I arrived and they wisely did not refrigerate or wash him down. Those two guys might have given us our first solid lead."

Luke patted the file and headed out the door. I looked down at John Doe as if he would give me answers. My eyes gazed upon his ravaged face. The putrid smell of garbage and decomposing flesh singed my nose hairs.

The fringes of my mind blurred, giving reality a dream-like ambience. Like a Hitchcock movie, the camera of my mind panned in on John Doe. Though I knew I shouldn't go there, the large autopsy room seemed to zoom in as if only John Doe and I were the last two people on earth.

The sterile, metallic silence deafened me and the smell dissipated as my senses other than sight ceased to function. My hand seemed compelled to reach out toward John Doe. My mind screamed to pull it back, but my heart told me I needed any answers this guy could give me. So I ignored my mind and went with my heart. The hand slowly reached out, hesitated, and touched.

A horrible moment of dead silence flashed through my mind and then a sudden cacophony of sounds, smells and visions, nearly knocked me off my feet. I grabbed for the glass aquarium and then–nothing. I never felt my head crack as it bounced off the cold tile floor.

Smells bombarded me–dirt yes, but something else-fresh cut grass and wait–straw. A barn. A cattle–no, a horse barn.

Sounds–music and a tractor–whose farm am I on? Wait! Not a farm. A flash of purple, a crowd. An auction? A horse show?

Another smell. Faint. Familiar. Burnt. Popcorn. Popcorn? Purple popcorn at a horse show? No, a fair! County Fair. The 4-H show at the County Fair.... .

Paper held tightly in knarled fingers. I have to remember my medication, this arthritis is killing me. The crowd erupts and I look up. Horray Deserae! A blue ribbon! Nine years old tomorrow and I've never met you, my granddaughter, but I love you. Grandpa Iggy loves you little girl!

The dirty piece of paper, worn soft from all the handling burns a hole in my hand. Not today. Let Deserae have her day. Maybe tomorrow. Definitely tomorrow. I'll have more courage then. It was worth every penny I paid to find them. I can't believe I ever came back here after what happened all those years ago.... I'll look up Miz Sweetwater one more time, that's what I'll do.

Yup, that's what I'll do... tomorrow.

Another scene. The carnival midway. I shuffle down the lineup. Paper still clutched in a painful hand, I have to hurry to meet him–oh no, I dropped the paper. I promised to delivered the information the guy wanted, and I have to get to the bank before it closes. Grandpa Iggy is going to give his little girl a surprise. College money. Lots of college money.

Darn! The paper blew away. The wind puffs and the paper floats just out of reach. Must have it... It's my only proof! Bend down to get it.

Bright flash. Pain! Can't breathe. Choking. The paper... must keep... he promised... colors blur, fading. Not now, please not yet! Deserae! I need... I need... fading...

"No, wait! What's on the paper? What happened Old Man? Come back dammit! Get back here!"

"Buzz! Wake up! What the heck–Buzz! You're scaring me babe, wake up!"

I didn't want to come back before I knew what happened to the old man, but the violent shaking would have awakened the dead. Tears ran down my face. My head hurt so bad I felt queasy–again–but my only thought was I would die before I threw up on J.J.

Slowly I opened my eyes and looked into the worried grass green eyes of my favorite Sheriff. "J.J."

"Buzz, are you okay? What the heck happened? Was it about our John Doe?"

My head pounded with my heartbeat, and my thoughts jumbled and merged together. I worked frantically to separate fact from fiction and tried to remember every detail of my vision. I knew I missed something. Some clue sat in the fog, just out of my reach and I forced myself to concentrate. Old man, little girl...I shook my head and squeezed my eyes shut, searching my mind for a spark of recognition. Elusive clouds wafted across my mind's eye and I concentrated harder. I smelled popcorn. I felt I needed to get somewhere...feeling lost–no, lost something...I had color. Flashes of colors. Rainbows reeling–a kaleidoscope swirling–red. I saw red.

J.J. must have taken my scrunched-up look as copious amounts of pain, because he took my chin in hand and turned my face toward his. He ran a knuckle down my cheek and I couldn't help but drag my focus kicking and screaming back to the present.

"Buzz, slow down, you're going to short circuit."

By now I was in a near panic. Why couldn't he understand? "The clue, J.J., the clue! Stop and let me think–I lost the clue!"

"Right now I don't give a damn about a clue. Alice Christine Miller, all I care about at this moment is you are okay. It's been a heck of an afternoon, and you need to slow down before you melt down."

I knew I was being irrational but I couldn't stop myself. The adrenalin pumped at full speed and my heart raced. I could barely breathe as I desperately groped to keep the picture in my mind. *Paper.*

"Paper... a kid... a girl. In his change pocket. Look in the jeans pocket."

J.J. cupped my chin. "Take it easy, Buzz. Let it go. We'll get it later. Relax, Honey. Sleep now, that's my girl."

I felt myself sliding. "Paper, J.J. Look. Promise you'll look."

I saw his lips move and he nodded. I made a feeble attempt to hold on to consciousness, but the picture I had faded into negative, the words blurred into nothingness.

I felt empty. Drained of life. As I slid into the darkness, I had no clue J.J. and Luke dragged me out of the autopsy room–again–, back to Malcolm's office.

Much later I emerged from the abyss with a monster headache and felt a moment of panic when I couldn't see. It took me a second to orient myself to my surroundings in the pitch dark, but by then things clicked slowly into place.

Staring at the ceiling, I took a calming breath. I went over what I could remember about the old man. I heard the crinkle of paper and felt the deep ache of arthritis. I flexed my hands as if I could dispel the pain with my own. Colors floated to my consciousness. I remembered–the county fair.

The 4-H horse show, and a little girl he called Deserae. Who was she? What connection did she share with the old man? And what about the paper?

My head hurt again-I really had to stop bashing in my brains every time we had a new corpse. What an imbie. I sat up. Whoa, I was a very dizzy imbie. Wait...*Imbie*. Something about an imbie...indy...no, iggy. Iggy. The guy's name was Iggy! Grandpa Iggy. Deserae was the granddaughter. "J.J.! Luke! I have something!"

No sound. I tried again. No sound.

Crap. That meant I had to go to them. I pinched the bridge of my nose, and scrunched my eyes tight, willing my head to stop throbbing. I opened my eyes. No good.

Malcolm's desk sat only a few feet away. It looked like fifty. "If Lassie made home it through a war, I can make it to the door."

No one said I had to be rational while in pain.

I grabbed the arm of the couch and heaved myself to my feet. I teetered there while I waited for my head to stop spinning. I put a hand to the back of my head and felt a bandage. *I'll think about that later.*

I carefully placed one foot in front of the other and lurched toward the desk. I hit the lamp with my hand, and it shot across the smooth wood surface and crashed against the wall.

By the clambering in the hallway, I realized they heard the crash. The door popped open and slammed against the wall. J.J. grabbed me around the waist and I leaned against Malcolm's desk. He smoothed the hair out of my eyes. "What is it? Are you okay?"

I nodded and immediately wished I hadn't. Pain exploded behind my eyes. I heaved and huffed like I just ran a mile. "Yeah, I have something. The old man called himself Grandpa Iggy. His granddaughter won a blue ribbon at the

166

fair."

J.J. leaned close. "What else?" Luke looked at both of us and hummed the Twilight Zone theme.

"The 4-H horse show and her name is Deserae." I rubbed my forehead. "And a paper. He had a piece of paper which he was going to sell to someone."

J.J. eased me back on the couch. "That's enough, Buzz, sit."

"But J.J., I—"

"But nothing. Rest."

I didn't have the strength to fight. I sat and closed my eyes.

Luke leaned against the wall with a thump. I winced. "Holy Cow. You used to creep me out with the woo-woo thing you do, and I still can't believe it, but I'm here watching it firsthand. Buzz, you are something else."

I rubbed my head. "Yeah, I know, something else. They just haven't figured out what, yet."

J.J. hugged me close. "Right now you're done." He kissed the top of my head. It was the only spot on my body not in pain. He looked back at Luke. "I'm taking this one home. Call me when you get something."

Luke flashed a grin. "Will do, and, Buzz, I'll check out the pocket. We have the clothes locked in evidence."

J.J. politely but firmly gripped my elbow and headed for the door. I twisted around. "Luke. Call the fair office. They'll be able to tell you who Deserae with the blue ribbon is. If not, call Al. She can get anything you want. We'll find Iggy. And find the paper. I keep thinking it is very important."

He smiled wider. "Okay, Buzz, you just get back to the trailer and rest. Can you drive?"

I rubbed my temple. I had a mongo headache, my hands hurt, and my knees hurt. *Sheesh, I am in rough shape.* "Well, sure. I—"

J.J. ran a hand over his hair. "If the dogs weren't already at the fair, I'd take you straight to your house." I'll get over there as soon as I can. Don't worry about a thing."

We were almost to the door when I had another thought. "Oh, and Luke, one more thing—"

J.J. covered my mouth. "Luke will do it, Buzz. It's his job. Let's get some aspirin in you and ice on your head."

I relented. "Sorry. I know you know your job, Luke. It's just—"

Luke kissed my cheek. "I know. It's the 'Mom Thing.' But don't worry, you taught me well. I'll call you right away if I find something, okay?"

I nodded, and wished I hadn't.

J.J. steadied me. I saw stars. Everything swam in and out of focus. *How the heck am I going to drive?*

J.J. turned and called over his shoulder, "I'll call you, Luke. Don't worry about this one, I'll look after her."

Luke stopped to wink. "Love you guys."

I smiled. "I know, and thanks. We love you too."

I let my head loll onto J.J.'s shoulder as he bundled me into the vehicle. I think I patted him on the head and thanked him for driving me, but he never mentioned it. I was getting fuzzier by the minute and uh, I think a little goofy. J.J. clicked the seatbelt in place and closed my door. When he slid into the driver's seat, he turned to look at me.

I knew I was close to passing out, but the need to say something kept me out of the black hole. J.J. stared at me. "Are you okay, Buzz?"

My mouth tried to form words, but it felt like I was trying to move through Jell-O.

"What is it? Should I take you to the ER instead of the trailer?"

My eyelids felt like manhole covers, and they refused to focus. "Jayyyy? Naw, just fly me to the moon." I began to hum *Fly Me to the Moon.*

"That's it. We're going to the hospital."

I kept singing like an old drunk at a New Year's party. *Fly me to the moon. Let me play among the stars. Let me see what spring is like on Jupiter and Mars"*

"Waiiii-t." He paused, hand on the ignition. I blinked to clear my muddled brain. "I–I, if I die, I want you to know."

He leaned close. "Know what, Buzz? What are you trying to say?"

I touched his cheek and whispered, "I love you, James."

He smiled and I heard the engine roar to life. "Now I know you're loopy. Hang on, Frank Sinatra, we're going to the hospital."

"Whaah? Wha'd I say?" I stared out the window and sang, *"Fill my heart with song and Let me sing for ever more. You are all I long for All I worship and adore"*

J.J. fumbled with his cell phone. He barked into the phone. "Luke! Yeah, it's me. I'm taking Buzz to the ER. Yeah, she's worse off than she led us to believe."

"Hi, Luke, I love you too!"

I wondered what the heck he was talking about, so I strained to listen. I guess I got bored, because I looked out the car window and song overcame me again. *"In other words, please be true, in other words, I love you."*

J.J. shook his head. "Just take my word for it, Luke. And hey, call her mom, would you? Gerry can call everyone else. Later."

* * *

I felt the transmission slam into drive and heard the tires chirp on the pavement. I must have passed out again, because in the next second, bright lights blazed and electric shards slashed through my brain, I was jostled around, my head felt like it was on fire, and I had a death grip on J.J.'s hand.

19

The next twenty-four hours were a series of, meds, me almost asleep, nurses from hell visit, me almost asleep, more meds, poke-prod, stick with a needle, me almost asleep, nurse from hell again... you get the picture.

I woke sometime later to stare into the puppy dog eyes of Dr. Frank Beth. "Hey, Buzz, back among the living?"

The inside of my mouth tasted like an old sneaker, and I'd have bet the bank my breath smelled like one too. I sealed my lips shut and nodded. I breathed shallowly while he backed away. *Smart man.* He smiled.

"I bet you want to know how long you've been here, right?

I eyed my water cup and nodded. Frank picked it up and went to the bathroom sink to dump it. I saw my hospital bin sitting on the table and snatched it up, grabbing the toothpaste and squirting a blob onto my tongue.

Frank strolled back into the room and poured me a fresh cup of water. I gratefully took it and sucked in a mouthful. I swished the toothpaste around and looked for a place to spit... Nothing. I squeezed my eyes shut and swallowed-yuck-but it tasted better than breathing sweaty sneaker in Frank's face.

"How long have I been here, Frank, a couple hours??"

He consulted his watch. "Well, in about forty minutes it'll be seventy-two hours."

"Get out! I'd have said four hours max. Did J.J. leave?" I snorted. "Of course J.J. left you dough head. He works for a living, plus he's got the county fair...." I looked up at Frank. "The county fair? Oh no, are you sure, Frank? J.J.'s going to kill me. After giving me the tomato...oh no! the tomato is in my car. Frank, tell me the truth, did I really miss the fair?"

"Yep, you missed it, I'm not kidding you, nor am getting out."

I rubbed my forehead. "I don't get it. How—"

Frank crossed his arms and tapped his chin with his pen—the capped end. "How indeed, Buzz. What the heck were you thinking? Usually when someone gets their brain sloshed around not once, but *twice*, they get checked out at the local ER, but you? Noooo. Bullet Proof Buzz thinks she can gallivant back to the county fair sporting a doozy of a concussion!"

My eyes began to squint. "Frank, you're yelling."

"Damn right I'm yelling! You watch enough sports. Have you ever heard of second impact syndrome?"

His yelling hurt my head. The backs of my eyes began to throb and I slid under the covers. Frank didn't seem to notice and continued to rant. "When you have one concussion on top of another, you raise the risk for brain swelling." He started pacing and gesturing wildly. "Do you know what's next?"

My eyes began to water and I shook my head... *very* slowly.

He spun around and yelled in my face. "Death, you imbecile! Death!"

By this time I cried all over myself and hid under the covers. Frank was immediately contrite. He grabbed a chair and dragged it to the bed. I cringed at the scraping noise, which sounded to me like ten thousand fingernails on a slate chalkboard.

Frank picked up my hand. He stuffed some Kleenex into my other hand. Softly, he spoke to me as he stroked my hair. "Gee, Buzz, I'm sorry about yelling, but you could have killed yourself."

He brushed the hair out of my eyes. "Do you know how worried we all were? You scared the crap out of everyone.

J.J. was fit to be tied by the time he got you here. I thought he was going to shoot me at one point."

I again shook my head and whispered, "Sorry, didn't know."

Frank smiled. "Thank God you're better now." He furrowed his brow. "Not that you're in any shape to do anything. But you're strong and healthy, and if you follow directions, you'll be fine." He absently patted my hand and I felt better. Frank checked the machines and looked at my clipboard.

I felt tears leaking out of my eyes again. "Am I gonna make it, Doc?"

His eyes crinkled.

"You're too mean to let a couple head injuries get you down, girl. Your MRI is clear, but you're not 100% yet."

I frowned. "But I can go home, right?"

"Not that I don't delight in your company, my dear, but I ought to be able to spring you tomorrow afternoon if you tolerate eating, or within the next couple days if you don't. We'll talk about going home as soon as you can keep what's on your plate from coming back up, okay?"

"No, but do I have a choice?"

Frank laughed. "Nope. Oh, another thing. I don't want you living alone for several days yet. Do you want me to call your mom or one of your sisters?

"I, uh, that is, no, the dogs and I—"

He smiled. "Well, I could stop on the way to and from the office each day to check on you and the dogs. That is, I wouldn't mind if you needed me to call—"

I heard a commotion at the door, but I couldn't see around Frank, but he squeezed my hand hard. I winced. "Ouch, Frank. What on earth?"

A voice boomed from behind him. "No need to call anyone, she's coming home with me."

Enter, one angry-looking James Green.

Now, my wince was two-fold. First, J.J. embarrassed and intimidated Frank, and he only tried to help. Frank dropped my hand like a hot potato, and stood so fast he bumped the table and sent my new cup of water sliding off the end. He caught it on the way down and slapped it back on the table.

Second, J.J.'s voice reverberated through my brain like a herd of stampeding buffalo, the chair screamed in protest when it went flying across the floor and away from the bed. I didn't know whether to throw up or pass out.

J.J. stepped up to my bed and boomed, "Buzz, why are you crying? Do you hurt?"

Not giving me a chance to reply, he whirled on Frank. "What's the matter with this place? Can't you see she's in pain? Or were you so busy playing patty-fingers with my girl, trying to con her into going home with you that you didn't even notice?"

I couldn't believe J.J. misunderstood Frank. I tried to intervene. "Uh, J.J."

"That's okay, Buzz, I got this handled."

I peeked out from under the covers. "Uh, J.J., stop before you embarrass you and m–"

J.J. scowled at Frank. "Well, Beth?"

Frank was clearly baffled by J.J.'s verbal attack. "What are you talking abo–"

J.J. had a full head of steam going. "You know what I'm talking about. Just in case you didn't know, keep your damn hands off–"

"Uh, point of order." I raised tentative finger.

"Stay out of this, Buzz. Don't try to deny it, *Doc*-tor Beth. I know what I saw, and–what the–Buzz!"

J.J. jumped back as my ice water splashed on the floor and up his pant leg. I waited for the explosion from beneath my covers. The room was silent when I peeked out, and both men faced me-staring wide-eyed and open mouthed.

"Close your mouths, boys. You look like a couple of freshly caught Coho staring at me from Captain Bob's live well." My head began to pound. I felt nauseous. I looked around for a bucket or a pan. Frank grabbed the little tray from my hospital stash, and I promptly made us of it.

After heaving half of Lake Michigan into the pan, Frank took it away, and J.J. sat on the bed, anxiously patting my hand.

Frank wiped me off, rang for the nurse, and rounded on J.J., who dropped my hand and stood.

I took a big breath while they both looked ready for round two.

"Stop!"

They snapped their jaws closed. I tried for a smile and didn't get past grimace. They both stood silently; waiting for me to...I don't really know why, but I was glad they had shut up. "Better. Now, James Joseph Green, you apologize to Frank. I wasn't in pain until you started yelling. I guess my concussed brain isn't taking to the screeching of raging banshees very well."

Frank scowled. Hands on his hips. "She's not only sensitive to noise, her headaches are gargantuan, she's more easily upset, and when the pain gets too bad, she throws up."

J.J. looked at me. "Sorry, I didn't know..."

"Beyond the usual, she also might have lapses in memory, her coordination might be off, and even those indicators don't include what other symptoms might still show up."

J.J. ran a hand through his hair. "Whoa, I really am sorry about that, Frank. So, that sweet scene I witnessed when I came through the door you were trying to break it to Buzz–"

Frank closed his eyes. "That she either has someone live

with her full time for a week or two, she go to a rehab center, or I would have to arrange for a nurse to go to her house. I offered to check on her if she wanted. What I wasn't doing, was making time with—how did you so delicately describe her? Your girl? Geez, Green, take a pill, everyone knows she's hands off and your property."

He spun around to me. "Sorry about the phraseology, Buzz."

I panicked. "No nurse, J.J., no rehab, please. No strangers."

J.J. chuckled. "No strangers, Buzz? You already know everyone in town; there *are* no strangers."

"I just meant I only want, uh, I mean, I don't want anyone but, uh, oh damn," I whispered.

Rather embarrassed, I pulled up my blanket. My IV buzzed as the next dose of pain killer slid into my arm. I peeked out like Kilroy and shut up, my mind growing even more fuzzy than normal.

Frank sighed. "I knew she'd balk, so I just tried to lay it on her gently."

J.J. folded his arms. "Sorry, Frank, but it looked to me like you were 'laying it on her,' alright."

I could hear Frank becoming exasperated. My eyelids grew heavy, but I strained to hear what Frank had to say.

"For God's sake, J.J., don't be an ass. We've all known each other since we were all kids—what did you think I was doing? She asked if she could go home and I tried to explain it all. It's a little tough trying to be the physician and the friend, but I assure you, I wasn't playing 'doctor' with your girl, here. Get a grip, man!"

I couldn't help but smile. My brain might have been a little sluggish, but my comprehension skills were right on. The pain med must have kicked in, because as the two men continued to talk, I drifted into la-la-land.

When I woke again, Rosanna Delgado, Nazi Nurse from Hell stared at me from about three inches away from my nose. "Good, you up. I shake you lots. Woke you up. Doc says, gotta you eat. Chow time now."

I grabbed my head to keep it from falling off. "Yes Ma'am, could you whisper, please?" No one argued with an ex-army nurse. Just then, Fred tripped through the door–or rather, she walked through the door, and promptly tripped over the I.V. stand. Luckily, my body broke her fall. Unluckily for me, my head was jarred and pain exploded behind my eyes.

"Buzz! Oh my gosh, I'm sorry! Are you okay? I know, dumb question."

She reached in back of her and dragged some poor guy through the door. "You remember Mark Malone, don't you?"

I eyed him warily and shook my head "No."

Fred sighed. "You met him last Christmas in the pet store, remember? He and his brother Matt own *Cool Bean* coffee shop in town?"

Mark held out a cup of coffee. "Hi, Buzz, they told me your memory might be a little tricky for a while. Don't worry about it. I brought you a cup of the breakfast blend you like so well."

I sat up a little straighter. "I remember I love coffee, so I guess all is not lost. Sorry Matt, no offense."

Mark smiled. "None taken, and I'm Mark."

"That's what I said. Matt."

"But I'm Mark."

"Mark who?"

"Mark Malone. Coffee shop. The cute Malone brother?"

"Who? Have you been sampling my drugs? Don't you know who you are?"

"Mark."

176

Fred jumped in. "Never mind, he brought you coffee, and he is the cute Malone brother, so shut up and drink." She shoved the coffee into my hand. I pulled her close. "Hey Fred, is this guy on drugs?"

She tapped the coffee lid to make sure it was tight. "No, dear sister, you are. Drink your coffee, you'll remember him in a minute, and you're going to love him as much as I do. He's a great guy."

I pulled out the tab and sipped. Between the rich aroma and the warm slide of the black coffee down my throat, the experience was pure bliss. "Ahhh, I remember you. I looove you."

Mark's eyes lit up. "Who, me?"

"No, the coffee, silly. But you'll come in a close second, I'm sure." I sipped again. "Or maybe third, how cute did you say your brother was?"

Fred's eyes grew large. "Buzz, knock it off."

"Ahem, I think perhaps this is not an opportune time for visits, people. The patient is supposed to eat."

We looked up and saw Nurse Delgado standing by the door with her arms folded and her foot tapping.

Fred's lip curled as she looked at the milk, juice, Jell-O, and pasty soup.

"What's with the Elvis lip, Fred?"

"The Supper Nazi is booting us out so you can slurp slop."

"Aw, don't mind Rosanna Danna, she schleps the slop to several sick supper-suckers. She's pretty surly, too."

The nurse stomped her foot. "Delgado."

Fred looked up. "Huh?"

"Delgado. Nurse Rosanna Delgado-not Danna."

Fred smiled. "Guess you never saw much Saturday Night Live, eh? Rosanna Danna meets Dr. Joyce Brothers in the bathroom?"

Mark, Fred, and I laughed. I had to hold my aching head. Rosanna, however, did not look amused. She made shooing gestures at Mark and Fred. "You go now. The patient needs to eat and rest. Come back tomorrow."

I eyeballed the soup. Yuck. I could feel my lip doing the Elvis curl—hmmm, must be hereditary.

I heard Fred yell bye, and heard the door whoosh shut. Rosanna Danna's voice boomed across the room and she pointed her sausage-like finger at me. "You Miller girls. Always laughing. This ain't so funny, 'cuz you gonna eat, or you don-a go home no way." She shook her knackwurst-sized finger at me again. "I'm-a keepin' close watch on you, girly so no funny business." She nodded like a true Supper-Nazi, turned, and disappeared out the door.

The door whooshed closed. I carefully lifted the plastic lid off the soup bowl. It looked as if it already had been regurgitated from the guy across the hall. "I can't eat this sickly, sloppy, stuff, how am I going to ditch this without getting caught?"

An idea hit me. I sat up and waited for the room to stop spinning. *Whoa, Trigger.* I made sure Rosanna Danna, R.S.N. (Registered Supper Nazi) had closed the door tight. I panned in on the bathroom door. It looked like a football field away, but had to be no further than four feet. I saw a sign which said "Patient Is Not To Use This Bathroom Without Assistance."

"Huh. My butt. I can do this blindfolded, Roseanna Danna."

I took a deep breath and scooted to the edge of my bed. Getting ready for takeoff, I had second thoughts. "Whew, this might be a little tougher than it looks." I looked at the floor and it moved on its own. "Uh, I got a bad feeling about this."

I considered terminating the mission, but the thought of going to a nursing home gave me new strength. I grabbed the milk and stuffed it into my pocket. I snapped the lid on the soup container, and held on tight. I slid off the bed before I could talk sense into me, and steadied myself with the table. The Jell-O at the edge of the tray jiggled ominously, but held fast. I inched my way toward the bathroom, leaning my elbows on the table and using it like a rolling crutch. I had a death grip on the I.V. pole in one hand and held the soup in my teeth.

Sweat broke out on my forehead, and my knees wobbled. *Six more steps, Buzz.* Five, four, three...*smack*! The table hit the bathroom door jamb and I caught myself and the Jell-O before we both hit the floor. I wormed my way past the table and grabbed the rail on the wall by the toilet. I carefully peeled the lid off the soup. I looked behind me one more time, and dumped the soup in the toilet. I opened the milk and did the same with it.

Stuffing the milk container in my pocket, I grabbed the I.V. once more. I turned toward the table and leaned heavily on it. There I stood, in the doorway to the bathroom, hunched over the table. Heavy weariness pressed down on my shoulders, and dizziness washed over me. My head was about to come off, and I grabbed for my table. It wobbled, tilted, and I felt myself teetering. I let go of the table and stumbled backward. I felt dizzy and lost any balance. *Here I go, bye, bye Buzz!*

I stumbled, fell to the side, and sat hard on the toilet. I grabbed the rail with one hand and my head with the other. I let out a shuddering breath. "Hoo-wee Buzz Miller, you are not ready for prime time. This was not one of your better ideas."

I heaved myself up, and looked back at the toilet. "Oops, forgot to flush." I reached back and flushed the glop down the toilet. It took a couple tries, but the water in the bowl finally cleared. With renewed determination, I wheeled me, the I.V., and "Exhibit A" (the soup bowl and milk carton) back to the bed.

I slapped the empty bowl and milk carton on the tray, and eased myself into bed. I re-positioned the I.V. stand, and plugged it back in. Breathing hard and sweating like a rode hard horse, I used my sheet to wipe the sweat from my face, and slowly scooted myself back up the bed.

I had just straightened the covers and pulled the table up to my chest when the door slowly creaked open. An ominous figure stood backlit in the door. Rosanna stepped into the room. Scowl on her face and hands on her hips, she gave me the stink eye. "You okay? Your I.V. went off."

I grabbed the Jell-O and stuffed a spoonful into my mouth. "*Mmmph*, peachy. Okay for now."

I gave her a thumbs up, though I had an overwhelming desire to flip her off.

"Good. You eat, you go home."

The door closed again and I exhaled. Totally exhausted, I could barely pick up my spoon. I sighed a huge sigh of relief as I looked into the open bathroom. *Ha! A job well done. No one will suspect a thing, and I get to go home.* I smiled to myself and glanced back toward the bathroom. I blanched. I tried to blink away the picture before me. I couldn't be! "Hey, what is that sitting on the sink–"

My smile turned into a look of horror when I realized I left the lid off the soup bowl in the bathroom! I struggled into a sitting and my head swam. I squinted at the lid, hoping I had conjured tragedy out of thin air

"Oh, crap. I'll never make it back there. What am I going to do?"

I looked at the closed door to my room. *Please Fred, come back now. If I ever had psychic powers, please make one of my sisters hear my message. I'll even take Mom, Mary or one of the dogs. Please, anyone but Rosanna the Supper Nazi come back.*

Nothing.

I snorted. "Well, that went well, Buzz. What are you going to do for your next act?"

Frustrated, and near blind with a pounding head, tears stung my eyes. I grabbed the napkin and swiped them away. "Dang, Frank was right. I've turned into a wienie."

I flopped back on the pillows. Immediately sorry, I closed my eyes and breathed deeply. I tried one more time to conjure a family member through the door. *Maybe I can text Fred...* I looked around frantically for my cell phone.

Nothing. The Supper Nazi probably stole it.

I lay staring blankly at the stupid soup bowl lid. Since I couldn't scare up a family member, I tried my luck with the plastic lid, willing it to jump off the sink and into the garbage. No such luck.

What is the sense of having a psychic gift if I can't even move one little plastic lid from a sink to the waste basket?

I rolled my head toward the wall, gauging how many miles I had to walk back to get to it when a staccato clicking in the hallway had the hair rising on the back of my neck. *I know those stilettos.* The clicking grew louder and I felt the first tickle of panic. I desperately looked around for a place to hide. I realized then when I begged for any of my sisters to show up, I forgot to stipulate "with the exception of Al."

Murphy's Law! Salt in the wounds! Insult to injury! Mom always says be careful what you wish for-you said 'anyone'. Hide me quick! Woe is me, here comes Big Al!

Near panic, I grabbed the handrail on the bed. With bucket loads of adrenalin coursing through my veins, I gained super human strength and hoisted myself up into a sitting position.

I swung one leg off the bed, bile crept up my throat, the room spun wildly, and as I swung my other leg around, I knew I would be crawling to a unique destination when the rhythmic clicking stopped.

I froze in mid swing. I looked up to see my baby sister coming backward through the door and realized that yes, there *were* worse things in this world than being in the hospital with a gi-*normous* headache and "Felony Soup Dumping" hanging over my head. Being trapped in an enclosed room with Al with no chance of escape came to mind as a good example. *She'll tell on me, she's always been a squealer. I just know it! No amount of begging will work. She never forgave me for hanging Barbie in the crawl space...*

I deflated so fast I swore I could hear the fizzle. I gave it up and flopped back onto the bed. Breathing deeply to quell the panic bubbling to the surface, I turned my head toward Al and smiled.

"Alexandra, how nice of you to stop by."

Al spun around. She looked scared. "I must have the wrong room. What have you done with my sister?"

I flopped back. I had no reserves left. Knowing I was doomed, I had to choose between Al and Rosanna Danna. Al won hands down. "Al, come here, quick, I need you."

She hesitated, and then clicked over to the bed. "What's up?"

I squirmed up onto my pillows. "I need your help."

She raised an eyebrow. "And?"

I looked beyond her to the bathroom sink. The soup lid laughed at me. "I need a favor, and quickly."

She crossed her arms, leaned on one hip, and both perfect eyebrows rose. "And?"

I heard the food cart rattling its way down the hall and started to sweat. I took a breath. "Al, please. Go to the bathroom and grab the lid off the sink for me. Please."

She calmly looked over her shoulder. "Don't tell me. You don't want the Soup Police to know you flushed your supper, right?"

I blew out the breath I held. "H-How did you know? It doesn't matter, but you got it right. They won't let me go home unless I eat, and Lord knows I tried, but I just can't."

Al brightened and dusted her hands. "All-righty then! I always love a good cause."

She took two long steps into the bathroom just as the door whooshed open. All two-hundred-fifty-odd pounds of Rosanna, R.S.N. from Hell loomed like the Reaper-backlit from the hall. In my delirium and terror, I have to admit, she scared the crap out of me. *I think she does the nurse of death thing on purpose. She's more intimidating that way.*

The bathroom door popped open. Al popped out and bumped into Rosanna. "Oops! Oh, sorry." She pretended to crank down her skirt and clicked over to the bed.

"Visitors do not use the patient bathrooms." Rosanna looked around Al into the bathroom. I held my breath.

Al stepped toward the bed and pursed her lips. "Oh, I didn't use the bathroom. I'm just checking my lip gloss. It's a new shade, and I just had to hurry over and show my sister. What do you think, Buzz?" Al clicked over to my bed and we examined her lips in her compact.

"Lovely. A little on the neutral side for you, but I like it."

Al popped the compact closed and smiled a giant "May I take your order please" smile at Rosanna.

Rosanna gave Al a dirty look. "Lip color must be big deal while your sister lies near death in her bed."

I made to give Rosanna a piece of my fuzzy mind, but Al squeezed my hand and slipped the soup lid into it.

Rosanna sneered at the two of us. "She really your sister? She ain't nothin' like you. You pretty. She's, uh–"

"Beautiful, yeah Rosanna Danna, I know." Al gave the nurse the lethal-toothy smile. You know the one. So evil, just when you realize you are in really, really in deep trouble, Mom smiles her toothy smile, and you just know she came up

183

with an unspeakable torture to teach you a lesson, and very proud of it?

"Listen Nurse, what's your name again? I want to write it down so I can mention to the administrator at lunch tomorrow how you treat patients and visitors."

Ha! Even Rosanna was smart enough to back down.

"Uh, just picking up the tray. Be gone in a flash."

I needed a diversion, and fast! I licked the lid to the soup bowl. "*Mmmm-mmmm*. Rabbit stew. All done, Rosanna, you can take it away, please."

Rosanna looked stunned. "How, what–you ate it all?"

I examined the tray. "All but the juice. May I keep it for later?"

Rosanna nodded her head and nervously marked the clipboard hanging on the end of my bed, keeping one eye on Al. "Yeah, you keep. You know Dr. Beth, he will be very happy to hear this. He say, make sure dat girl eat or she not go home no how."

I blanched. "Uh, much as I'd like to, I think I'd rather be home with my dogs."

"No, no, you did good. Dr. Beth, he gonna like dat you eat good. Uh, I'm outta here." Rosanna grabbed the tray and disappeared out the door. I sank into my pillows and sighed. Al chuckled and I opened one eye.

"What's so funny?"

"You are, dumping your soup in the toilet. I'll bet you're not even supposed to be out of bed yet."

I sighed and eased back. "You'd be right, little sister."

"Boy, Nurse Kevorkian is sure a piece of work, isn't she?"

I closed my eyes. "Yup. I just want to go home. She and Frank are conspiring to keep me here against my will."

"Just like a Robin Cook novel. If they move you to an empty ward, be very afraid."

"Hey, I'm creeped out enough without adding Dr. Cook into the mix."

She held up her hands. "Okay, okay. Don't shoot. Here, I brought you some flowers. They're from my garden. I hope you don't think I tried to be cheap, but I thought they were pretty."

I looked longingly at the beautiful flowers on the table and melted. "Al, these are great-so much better than store bought. I sure wish–"

"You wish you could grow anything but weeds. I know, I saw your 'garden'. Uh, I don't want to be mean, Buzz, but it sucks."

I tried to work up some indignant anger, but couldn't. I deflated like yesterday's birthday balloon. "I know, I suck. I have a black thumb."

"Your flower garden sucks. There is a difference. I saw your fair tomato. You did real well on it, I was surprised-no offense."

I looked at the flowers and felt like a criminal. "No offense taken. Al, about the tomato–"

She patted my arm. "Hey, no worries, we put off the contest until next week. We didn't want you to miss it."

I don't know what came over me. It must have been the drugs making me confess. The more Al chatted, the worse I felt. Finally I couldn't stand it. I blurted it out like the sucker I am. "I might have cheated a little, Al. J.J. knew I'd croak my tomato so J.J. grew one as a spare."

Al sat up straight. "You what?"

"I cheated. Come on, Al, don't tell on me. I've been made fun of forever because I am a terrible gardener! Just this once, don't squeal, please!"

Al stared at me. She tapped a two-inch nail against her teeth. "That will be two giant favors you owe me. Are you sure you want to go through life with a debt like that hanging over your head?"

I thought about it for all of two seconds. "Yes, I am willing to take on the task. Just don't tell Mom, okay?"

Al suddenly leaned forward. "Deal. Now, I won't tell if you won't."

"Huh?"

She looked both ways. "I cheated too."

"What?"

She giggled. "Yup. I watered my seedling, and probably got it too wet, the soil wasn't sterile, and my tomato damped off. I even grew a spare, and drown the little sucker."

"Damped off?"

"Yeah, damping off is caused by fungus in the soil. The plant rots at the soil line and the plant falls over. There's no saving it. She bit her lip. "Normally I sterilize the soil when I plant seedlings, but I just threw it in a container and let it go. So one croaked by drought, one by flood."

"Oh." *Lesson One–Damped off. Remember to sterilize the soil, Buzz.*

"Yeah, dumb, I know, but by the time I realized what had happened, Freddie bragged all over the place about how well her tomatoes grew. Even you grew them successfully; I mean I thought you did, at the time."

Thinking back, I knew I had already replaced the first tomato by then, but kept quiet about it.

She leaned forward. "I even went over to Racine to buy a new one, because I didn't want to be recognized at the local garden center."

"No!"

"Yes, I did! I got an older plant and made sure I got rid of the container when I got home. Now I'm fertilizing the crap out of it...I sure hope it catches up."

I sighed. "I guess it's up to Mom and Fred to win the contest, now. We can tell them tomorrow."

She stood. "Oh no you don't. I cheated fair and square, and I deserve to win this thing. They won't know the difference!"

"But, Al, we'll know the difference."

"So?"

"So what?"

"So what if we don't tell them? Who's it going to hurt? Are we going to win a million dollars? Is it not only family? Don't be such a goody-two-shoes. Is our tomato contest going to change history?"

"Well, no, but–"

She stood. "But nothing. There is no prize. It's just for the bragging rights anyway. Come on, it's kind-of funny if you think about it."

For some reason she started to make sense... must have been the drugs. "Okay, I'm in. When is the judging? Sunday of the fair?"

Al hitched her purse. "You have been way out of it. The fair ended two days ago. We cancelled the judging until you got out of the hospital, remember? I just told you that about ten minutes ago."

I thought hard. Nothing. "Sure Al, must have been the drugs. Where are we going to uh, do this?"

"We'll do it at Mom's house when you've recovered. The Geriatric SWAT girls are planning the food as we speak."

She walked around the bed. "Who knows? Maybe I'll have ripe tomatoes by the judging."

I grumbled. "Who knows? Maybe I can kill mine by the judging."

Al laughed. "J.J. is taking care of it for you, so it will survive at least until you get home."

I stared, big-eyed, while she bent to kiss my cheek. "Hope you break out of here real soon, Buzz, I'll stop at the nurse's station on my way out. Let me know if I can sneak you in anything, I'll give you a call later."

"I uh, what? Hey lady, where is my little sister?"

"Don't worry, Buzz, I won't let it get around. I'll just say you hallucinated while on drugs." She stopped at the door. "But seriously, sis, don't overdo. I'll try to get back to dump your next meal. Call me if you need me." She twiddled her fingers. "Love you, Buzz," and was gone.

I sat, stunned into silence as she tapped out the door and down the hall. I waited until the sound faded into the sunset before I breathed again. I slowly shook my head. "What the heck? Yippee ki-yay, I *must* be hallucinating."

I thought some more and my head began to hurt. "Was Al just sweet to me? No way–that was not Alexandra." My eyes blinked slowly as I tried to comprehend what just happened. Another second passed. "Couldn't have been. Must have been an alien. Or the drugs." I closed my eyes and slept.

20

I felt a little better the next morning, until the breakfast tray arrived. Thank heaven Fred decided to stumble in bright and early. "Hi," she said as she bounced through the door.

I smiled. "Hey."

She looked over my breakfast tray, consisting of wallpaper paste oatmeal (Which looked suspiciously like last night's soup), a scrambled egg-like substance, more Jell-O, juice, and coffee. She snatched up the oatmeal and slipped into the bathroom. I heard the toilet flush and smiled. You gotta love Freddie.

She plopped the bowl on the tray. "Need to ditch any other evidence while I'm here?"

I handed her the Jell-O and half the scrambled egg. She sniffed them both and disposed of them as well.

"Don't take this wrong, dear Freddie, because I'm extremely glad to see you, but did you show up at this ungodly hour of the morning just to dump my breakfast?"

She smiled and patted my knee. "Of course I did. Al called me last night and gave me the scoop." She hopped up on my bed and patted my cheek. "She had an early meeting and called me in as the backup unit. Hey, I have to fly. Got to get to the store, but I'll be back. My poopy puppy papers await me."

"Yum. How do you do it, Fred?"

She laughed. "It's a labor of love. Hope they let you go today, Buzz. You need to be home. We'll work up a schedule so we can take turns taking care of you, but this place is doing you no favors."

About to agree with her, I struggled to find the right

words sans the sappy stuff, when suddenly she kissed the top of my head and bounced out the door. "*Ciao*, Buzzette!"

I sighed happily. "Gee, I am overwhelmed again. Thanks a lot, Fred. See ya later."

A little later I smiled benignly as the hospital staff praised my progress, removed my morning tray, and marked my clipboard. The SWAT ladies showed up for lunch, and Mary kept a sharp eye out for Rosanna Danna while Mom flushed the evidence. Al stopped by at suppertime and took care of the meatloaf surprise.

Some of the nausea abated by the next morning, and I choked down some eggs myself. I drank most of the nasty coffee, but by the time Fred showed up, I was sweating, hurting all over, and ready to give up. She took care of the rest of the tray, and received high marks because she brought me some real coffee from *Cool Bean,* and a bear claw from Jane's. Leave it to Fred to know the healing powers of excellently packaged caffeine, pastry, and raspberry–cream cheese filling... a little later the sugar made me a little queasy, but by 8:00 a.m., I felt much better.

Around mid-morning Frank Beth strolled in. "How are we doing this morning, Buzz?" He looked at the clipboard and looked at me. His brows crunched together and he eyed me over the tops of his glasses. He looked at the clipboard and looked at me again. I felt my ears grow warm under his scrutiny and made a show of straightening my blanket. *He knows!*

Frank smiled. "Your color is better."

Discretion being the better part of valor, I shut up.

Frank marked a couple of things on my chart. "By the looks of things, you're doing pretty good, Buzz. You're eating and you didn't ask for pain meds last night."

I began to squirm. "Yeah, well, I'm doing much better now. Any chance I'll be able to go home today?"

He pulled out his stethoscope and listened to my heart. "Heart rate is a little up." He stared into my eyes. "But I'm not worried about it much, it's pretty normal under the circumstances."

"Circumstances?"

He smiled. "Yeah. When someone is lying, their heart rate usually increases." He put his hands on his hips. "How did you do it, Buzz?"

"Do what?" I tried for an innocent look, but when I caught a glimpse of my face in the mirror on the wall, I looked guilty as sin.

Frank cleared his throat. "Forget it. Looks like you'll be good to go home today."

I brightened. "Great. If you could grab my cell, I'll call–"

Frank held up a hand. "I already made some calls this morning. J.J. said he'd pick you up and get you settled in at home. Since Rosanna Delgado has been your primary nurse, I can assign her to a home nurse schedule with you."

"No!"

He looked confused. "Excuse me?"

I crossed my fingers under the blanket. "I, uh... well, my family is taking turns round the clock. Someone should be with me at all times. I won't need a Nazi-I, I mean nurse."

I held my breath and prayed.

"But, according to Alexandra, the family is making up a schedule to cover round-the-clock Buzz-sitting for only a couple days."

I slowly let out the breath I held and smiled. "So they tell me. But really Frank, I should be okay in a day or so. If I'm not, Al is going to extend the "Buzz Watch" for as long as I need it. The girls will take care of the days, and J.J. will have the night shift."

Frank hesitated, and I went in for the kill. "Come on Frank, you know what a bee-ay-zich Al is when something

191

screws up her schedule. She alone will force me to comply with all in-house rules."

He beetled his brow and pointed a finger at my nose. "So she has assured me. But you *will* follow the program. You will eat healthy food, you will not engage in any sports, driving, or investigating until after your follow-up next week." He took a breath. Is that clear?"

I stared at my blanket. "If you say so, Frank, I promise."

He tipped my chin up. "Look at me, Buzz. This is very important. We're not dumping rotten soup down the toilet here. If you screw this up and re-injure your head, it could very well mean death. Is that clear enough for you?"

I blinked. "Uh, crystal, Frank. Crystal clear. I promise not to do anything stupid."

He smiled. "Don't make promises you can't keep."

I sputtered, but spared from comment by the whoosh of the door. Frank looked up, turned pink, and dropped my chin like a hot potato.

"Ahem, there he goes again, making time with my girl while I'm out fighting crime, eh, Beth?"

His eyes twinkled as he leaned against the jamb, arms folded over his chest.

Frank rolled his eyes and winked at me. "You cruise, you lose, law man. I'm the man of the hour. What are you going to do, shoot me?"

J.J. smiled. "I might." He looked at me. "Ready to go home, kid?"

I nodded. I must have looked really needy, because his eyes softened, and he came over to hug me. My breath hitched, and I said into his shoulder, "Take me home, Green."

He looked at me and his dimples deepened. "It will be my pleasure, my dear." He turned to Frank. "What do you think, Doc? Can I spring her from the joint sometime today?"

Frank smiled. "Sure Jim, as soon as I can get the

paperwork done."

"And don't worry about her, Doc, her family has the day hours worked out, but I'll be the night nurse, so we've got her covered."

He snapped his fingers. "Oh, one more thing, if you decide to make a house–call, you'd better knock first, if you know what I mean."

I could feel my eyes pop out of my head. "James Joseph Green! You know the dogs will bark and let us know someone's at the door."

Frank laughed and headed for the door. "I guess I'm safe then." Green, you are lame in the extreme. Seriously though, remember what we talked about earlier, and try to keep her and those rag-a-muffin dogs quiet for a few days, okay? See y'all later."

"Thanks, Frank, but seriously, I took a couple days off and will only go out in case of an emergency. I left the three stooges in charge."

"Nyuk, Nyuk, Sab-a-too-gie!" Frank waved and left. The door whooshed closed and I raised a weak hand and slapped at J.J. "James Joseph, you are so bad. Stop teasing Frank. And what kind of smack were you giving him earlier?"

He winked at me. "I didn't want to give him any ideas. You know, he's a big shot doctor and I'm just a rural sheriff. If I were you I'd probably be thinking, wow, here's this rich handsome guy who saved my life and, well, maybe you'd start thinking he was the better deal."

I tried not to grin. "Better deal? You mean the rich and very handsome doctor?"

He walked away from my bed and ran a hand through his hair.

"Yeah. No. Heck, I don't know. Maybe handsome isn't quite the word I'm looking for. How about...not exactly disgusting?"

He began to pace again. I said nothing, but really enjoyed watching him mumble to himself. "No, that's not quite right either. He's not so bad he'd make an onion cry, but definitely not the cream of the crop... and he does have that great place with the horses..."

"Please. Stop, James, stop now. If I start laughing, my head can't take the jarring. Leave poor Frank alone, and get me out of here. You should be ashamed, teasing me about Frank when you know darn well no one can hold a candle to your sorry butt."

He stopped and sat on the edge of the bed. He smiled. "I know that, Buzz, and I love your sorry butt too."

His fingers slid around the back of my neck, and he gently tipped my chin up with his thumbs. I felt the now familiar shiver of anticipation as his lips closed over mine. I never wanted to come up for air. Blood roared through my head. We were so involved, we didn't know the door opened until I heard Nurse Kevorkian yelling in my ear.

"Hah! I tell Dr. Beth, I tell him you can't be trusted. I tell him there's some funny business going on in 217, but does he listen? No way Jose. He say, don't worry 'bout that one, Rosanne. She go home today. I say, what? Her head's cracked open like a chicken egg dat fell outta the fridge!"

J.J. drew back and rested his forehead against mine. "That's Rosanna Danna, I take it?"

"Yup."

"Let's get you home. We'll continue this discussion later."

"Lead on, Macduff."

He kissed my nose. "My favorite Shakespearean misquote...makes me feel so manly."

I tapped his chest. "Then get me out of here in your oh-so-manly way."

"Done."

194

The release went off like gas through a funnel. Surprisingly, J.J. drove me home in Al's car. Good thing they didn't have to hoist me into his truck. I was really glad the hospital demanded I be wheeled out in a wheelchair. I'd have been dead meat if they expected me to walk out of there. The only hitch came when it was time to get in the car. It got a little hairy when I got up to walk from the door to the car. I blamed my wobbly knees on the fact I left one of the brakes off on the wheelchair. J.J. grabbed me and half carried me the rest of the way. He poured me into Al's car, and got behind the wheel. We took off and I let go of the breath I'd been holding.

My head, however, did not cooperate. The bright sun made my head hurt in a big way. Even with my eyes closed, the pounding grew worse. My head felt ready to explode, and a little whimper escaped my lips. It must have been louder than I thought, because I heard J.J.'s voice. "Hold on toots, I got this covered."

He plopped a wide-brimmed straw hat on my head, and slid Al's Jackie Kennedy sunglasses onto my nose. He pushed a bottle of water in my hand and said, "Here, take these."

I swallowed my pain meds, and sat back. "You are an angel, aren't you?"

He grinned. "Yup. You just remember that next time you're mad at me, okay?"

I touched his cheek. "Uh huh." I sighed and drifted off.

I woke to sloppy doggie kisses and lots of tail wagging. I was so glad to be home, I almost cried again. I was turning into a regular wienie. *Just call me Oscar Meyer.* I hugged first Wes and then Hill, then Wes again.

I looked up to see J.J. standing in the doorway. He smiled. "Gee, you're never that happy to see me. What's Wes got that I don't have?"

I rubbed Wes's ears. "A big hairy face, and no matter

how angry, or neglectful, or stupid I get, he never loses his temper."

"Ah, you got me there. I have this terrible habit of getting angry when you risk your life."

"See? Wes loves me unconditionally."

"He's just a sucker for treats."

Somehow, J.J. got me out of the car and into the house. As exhausted as I felt, I forced myself to stay awake as J.J. made us all toast. We sat at the kitchen table. Hillary leaned against one leg, and Wes laid his head on the other knee. I rubbed them both. "I missed you guys."

I didn't realize I drifted off until J.J. touched my arm. "Buzz?"

"What? Oh, sorry, did you say something?"

"No, but you're fading out. Are you ready to take a nap?"

I blinked. My eyelids felt as heavy as man hole covers. "Yeah, I think I'd feel better if went prone for a minute or two."

"Good idea. Come on, guys, let's put her to bed."

It could not have been easy for J.J. to half carry me down the hall while the dogs danced around his feet, but after minimal fuss, I found myself still in one piece and in bed. Wes and Hill inspected the area and decided I was safe for the moment. I rubbed their ears.

"I love you guys."

J.J. handed me a bottle of water and two more pain killers. "We love you back, Buzz Miller."

I might have been a little fuzzy, but the message was loud and clear.

J.J. sat on the bed next to me. I could only stare when he bent to kiss me. I gulped. "I guess all you need now is a hairy face, and penchant for snacks."

"Don't look now, Baby Cakes, but I haven't shaved in three days, and much as I would like to snack on you, you need your rest more, so I'll scrounge in the fridge for snacks."

I blinked. "Well, I guess I'm the lucky winner."

"Now that's a matter of opinion, isn't it guys?" he smiled down at the dogs. "I'm thinking we're the lucky winners. Now take your nap, and I'll make supper."

I settled back against the pillows. My eyes stung. The pain meds were kicking in and I faded fast. It seemed imperative I make him understand. "Hey you."

He turned. "Yeah, what?"

"I love you too, you know."

"Yeah, I know. Tell me again when you're not on drugs, okay?"

I winked and gave him the wobbly trigger finger like some drunken used car salesman. "You got yourself a deal, baby cakes." I closed my eyes and slid into oblivion.

21

Though I am the first to admit I am not the world's perfect patient, my family turned out to be worse at nursing than I am at gardening.

First, for breakfast, Al showed up with a large sippy cup filled to the rim with a green slimy-like substance, scaring the poop out of me. I promised myself I'd be nice.

"Al, what the heck?"

So much for nice.

She looked at the cup. Then she looked at me. "Alice Christine, get that Pop Tart out of your mouth this instant. You promised to follow doctor's orders."

I had the decency to blush and turn over the Tart. "Sorry Al, but J.J. got a call and had to respond to a PI accident by the interstate around five this morning. Wes here retrieved me some breakfast. He uh, would have made a decent one, but he had no thumbs to crack the eggs."

AL looked at Wes. "Traitor. You're supposed to be helping, not sneaking in junk food."

She patted his head absently, and held out the large glass with the green crap in it. "About breakfast, Buzz..."

I gulped and looked longingly toward the window. Nope. No escape route there. Maybe the closet..."

"Buzz, are you there? Earth to Buzz, I'm not going anywhere, so don't think for one minute you're going to dump it. Drink up, it'll do you good."

I eyeballed her from beneath my covers. "What the heck is it? Ectoplasmic residue?"

Al laughed. "No, Buzz, it's banana, mango, raspberries, and lettuce. It's so healthy your body will probably spaz. Are you going to drink it, or do I have to call Dr. Beth?"

I rolled my eyes and held out my hand. "Okay, okay. Hand it over." I sat on the edge of my bed, waiting for Al to leave. She stood in the doorway with her hands on her hips. I looked at the green stuff in the glass and looked at her. "Thanks Al, I uh, guess I can take it from here. Don't you have somewhere you have to be this fine morning?"

She smiled and a shiver went up my spine. She walked to the end of my bed and folded her arms. "Nope. I have all morning to take care of my big sister, so no mad dashes to the toilet... remember, I'm on to you. Chug it down, bunky. It will help you heal."

I took a whiff. "Hmm, doesn't smell like swamp water."

I dunked my finger in the glass and tasted it. "Hmm, doesn't taste too bad either."

I sipped from the straw, and found the swamp water absolutely delicious. When I came up for air, I looked at Al. "Alexandra Miller, you are a wonder. Would you write down the recipe for this stuff before you leave?"

She grinned. "You betcha I will. I even put the ingredients for it and others in your fridge. Gotta run now. I just wanted to make sure it went down your gullet and not the toilet."

"Aw come on, Al. Give me a little credit here."

She turned back at the door. "I do. That's why I stayed. Behave yourself now, Mom will be here in about fifteen minutes. The SWAT ladies decided to have their meeting here instead of Joy's this morning. Did you know Sylvia Green is joining them on a permanent basis?"

Some green stuff shot between my lips as I sputtered. It landed right on Wesley's head. Hillary calmly leaned over and cleaned it up.

"Wait, Al, don't leave me alone with the SWAT ladies!"

She smiled and yanked open the door. "By the way, if

you feel up to it, I left you a little something on the tray."

"What? Al what are you–"

I realized I sat yelling at a closed door, and slumped back on the bed.

I put the almost-empty glass on the tray and saw an unopened envelope sticking out from under the plate. In my haste, I upended the muffin on the plate and sent it sailing over the side. Good old Wesley caught it in midair and it disappeared in a couple bites-paper and all. I guess he didn't like floor muffins like he liked dirt toast. I could have used Wesley's talents in the hospital...

I tore open the envelope. A note from Al drifted onto the tray.

Buzz,

I looked up those names you gave me of the deceased seniors. Because they were all born around the same time, I cross-referenced the information to find out if they all lived in or around White Bass Lake at the same time. Turns out all but one lived in Lake Ivanhoe, and I can't make a connection with the guy found at the fairground until he is identified.

I found Ole's family lived in Lake Como, right outside Lake Geneva. All his family members had jobs on an estate but him.

Turns out, He worked at what we now call the French Country Inn as a bus boy. I found him when I checked with old records I have for the time period around Prohibition.

I also found The French Country Inn was originally called the Lake Como Hotel. The employee records must have passed down through the family until I ended up with them when they were donated to the library, along with boxes of other historical documents.

Now, according to the records of employees kept by one of the managers, most of the help in those days was day-help, and very few were live-ins. Some hired out for private parties, and so on.

I recognized the name "Walker" as one of the dead men, and surprise, surprise, Cab Walker and his brother Joey both worked at the Inn at the same time. So did Oly Norris-the man found in Baraboo. The only thing they all had in common was they, or their family members worked at the Como Hotel back in the fall of 1929.

Two women were also employed there at the same time. Cora and Fanny Jones. Fanny had two daughters, Sarah Jean and Iva Mae, who were not listed as employees.

It just so happens both Sarah and Iva disappeared from the records around October of 1929. Coincidence? Probably not. I could find no death notice for either girl, but that alone does not always mean foul play in the African-American communities back then. Record keeping tended to be entries in the family Bibles rather than notices in the papers.

I tried to track down any relatives of Fanny and Cora, but haven't turned anything up yet. Am following those leads now. I'll check in later-call me on the cell if you think of anything else I can check.

Hope this helps,

Al

I sat there in silence. Fanny and Cora Jones. The names sounded familiar but I couldn't place them. Fanny and Cora Jones. I grabbed the phone and dialed Mom. The phone rang and rang, but no one picked up. I about hung up when the answering machine kicked in.

"You have reached the Bill and Gerry show. If you are a telemarketer, I do not need gutters, shutters, windows, or doors. I don't need credit card insurance, my carpets cleaned, or new floors. Don't pitch me your rails, snails, nails, or pails. And you can keep your time shares, your home care, and your fancy-schmancy cook ware. So get lost, pal, and don't call me again.

Or if by chance you're friend or family, leave a message.

I stared at the receiver. I heard the beep and forgot why I called. The silence stretched as the phone and I had a standoff. The end beep sounded and the phone disconnected. The second beep startled me out of my stupor, and I realized the phone won the standoff. Shaking my head in amazement, I replaced the receiver.

"Well yippee-ki-yay, Mom."

She must have heard because my phone immediately rang and I jumped out of my skin. I grabbed it. "Hello?"

"Buzz? Mom here. I was just thinking about you and had a feeling you'd be calling me. What's up?"

Mom's ability to do her woo-woo thing still gives me goose bumps to this day. I looked at Al's note and remembered. "Yeah, well, I'm doing some research and thought you might be able to help. Did you or Grandma know a Fanny or Cora—"

"Jones?"

I jumped. "Yes. They lived—"

"In Lake Ivanhoe, Yes, dear, I know."

I began to hyperventilate when I heard in the background, "Third green house on the left!"

Confused, I stared at the phone again "What?"

Mom said, "That's Mary, dear. "She said the Jones family lived over by Lake Ivanhoe—"

"I know as much already Mom. I wondered if you knew anything about two girls."

I heard the speaker phone click on and chatter bombarded me from the other end. Seemed the SWAT Ladies were over at Mom's house. When they were all together, it usually scared the crap out of me, but for once I happily listened to the mad chatter; glad they were all together in one room—at Mom's and not here.

"Mom? Mom, can you still hear me?"

"What? Oh, yes dear. I was just telling–"

The phone clunked like someone dropped it. I heard a lot of scraping noises, heavy breathing, and muffled cusswords.

"Halloooo, Buzz! Joy here! My mother, rest her soul, knew Miz Fanny. Now she was Miss Cora's mother-in-law, and Miss Cora, bless her heart, was a widow-woman and had two daughters. They all lived together during The Great Depression, and all worked hard to make ends meet. Now Miss Cora–"

I heard more scuffling and cussing. Mom must have grabbed the phone. "Let me tell it, Joy. You'll just repeat all the old gossip. Buzz honey, the real truth is–ahhh!"

The phone clunked. I heard more name calling and Mary's voice blasted in my ear.

"Me, me! I know the real truth! I can tell it just fine. Hi, Buzz, Mary here. And if you want to know the dirty details about those Joneses, well, let me tell ya, and this'll knock your socks off–"

I blinked when I heard more clatter and a thunk. Then little bitty Jane yell in the background. *"Shuuut* your pie-holes, you old biddies! You don't know diddley about squat. Let Gerry talk to her daughter for a minute. When she's done, we'll have plenty of time to add the gossip and conspiracy theories."

Silence met with her statement. Conspiracy theories? I heard the speaker phone click off.

"Buzz? It's Mom again. Sorry about the confusion here. Do you want to do this now, or wait until we get to your house?"

"Now would be good, Mom."

I grabbed a pen off the tray and flipped Al's note over.

Mom cleared her throat. "Well, Cora and Fanny Jones lived over in Ivanhoe all right. They rented one of those shacks from old Anthony A. Parks The First. Nasty little

203

houses, really. Nasty little man, come to think of it. Well, he never did upkeep those slum digs worth squat, and when Fanny and Cora had a pipe leak or a gutter fall down, why, they were more likely to hire someone and pay them out of their own pocket than wait for that cranky old fart to fix anything. He had a kid, lazy as a hound dog snoozin' in the sun. Mean, too. Picked on kids too, a real bully. Anyway, the Jones women most of the time bartered with preserves, baked goods, and handmade lace. They took in sewing, and did laundry too. Lots of families did what they could just to survive."

"Yeah, Mom, great grandma did the same thing with eggs, milk, canned vegetables, and meat on the hoof. I sometimes wonder how folks made it at all."

"Things were different then, Buzz. People helped each other. Money didn't mean what it does today. Somewhere along the line the American Dream got screwed up."

"That's a good way to put it. Sorry to interrupt, Mom. Go ahead."

"Well, my grandmother met the daughters–Sarah and Iva were their names–one day down at Jane's grandpa's five-and dime. Grandpa Knight also ran a hardware store in the next room, rather like two stores in one. Cora and the girls had hiked to town to see if they could hire someone to fix the outside stairs and tack up a hanging gutter.

"Well, my Grandma Riley hung out there, eating penny candy with her friend Doreen, when the two Jones girls came bouncing in. Grandma said they took one look at the jars full of candy and she and Doreen could see from their faces they had no money for it. Well, Doreen had three pennies, and Grandma had two, so they pooled their money and bought candy for Sarah and Iva.

You remember Jane's great uncle, Chuck? Well, he was just a youngster then and Grandpa Knight let him run the candy counter while he waited on customers. Grandma always said Chuck was such a nice lad, he gave the Jones girls an extra peppermint stick so they both had three. They all became fast friends that day. After that, the girls always came to town with the elder Jones ladies, and Grandma Riley made sure she and Doreen were available to play.

"On one particular day, the girls chatted while Cora talked to Jane's Grandpa, and turns out, Grandpa Knight ended up doing the work himself. He borrowed Old Henry the mule and a wagon from my great grandpa, and let Grandma and Doreen ride out to the Jones house with him. They played with the girls while Grandpa Knight fixed the stairs and the gutter. That's when Grandma learned Cora and Fanny worked out at the Lake Como Hotel as day help."

The light bulb went on, sirens screamed, and Mom had my undivided attention. "Lake Como Hotel?"

"Yes, dear. The girls were excited because their momma had a special party coming up. They said some friend of one of the Seipp children planned on having a get together at the Seipp Summer House on Black Pointe, over on Geneva Lake, and their momma and grandma were hired to help over the weekend. Iva was especially thrilled because her momma and grandma said the girls could come along and help with the party. They had never seen the likes of a real mansion, and they could not wait to go. They'd also make some badly needed money. They said some real important people like movie stars and rich folks from Chicago might be there.

"On the way home Grandma asked Grandpa Knight if they could go and see the movie stars, and she said Grandpa Knight almost had a fit. She said he turned so fast, Old Henry almost fell over, and said, 'them kind of people is nothin' but trouble' and we were never to get near any place when 'Them People' were around."

Mom took a breath. I held my tongue and gave her time.

205

"Well, Grandma didn't even know who 'Them People' were, but she knew enough to stay away from Lake Geneva mansions.

"The next time Grandma attended a family get-together, someone brought up 'the tragedy' at Black Pointe on Lake Geneva. My grandma said when she heard Black Pointe; she was all ears, trying to hear the adults talk about it. That's when Jane's grandpa told the story of mobsters, a party on a yacht, and the accidental drowning-death of an up-and-coming starlet. He said rumor had it Al Capone was in cahoots with one of the Seipp brothers, seeing the Seipps owned a big brewery on the South Side of Chicago and Capone ran illegal liquor during Prohibition, but I think old women gossip was never reliable, so who knows if it's true."

I heard yelling in the background of "It's true! It's true!"

Mom sighed and covered the phone. "Stop it you two!"

Silence fell, and Mom took a breath. "Here's the kicker to the story; somewhere around a million dollars in diamonds allegedly went missing from Al Capone's summer house in Lake Geneva around the same time. Police tried for years to connect the two crimes, but they never found the body of the starlet, nor did the diamonds ever showed up on the Black Market, or anywhere else, for that matter. Today it's still an unsolved mystery."

I jumped in before she went on. "So why did Great Grandma eavesdrop?"

"Because dear, Black Pointe was the same party the Jones girls worked with their mother and grandmother."

"Mom, I'm not getting the connection. What does some mobster party have to do with Sarah and Iva Jones? Were they questioned by police or something?"

"No, Buzz, the Jones girls disappeared the night of the Seipp party and never were seen or heard from again."

22

Speechless and gasping, I sounded like Sniffy the Goldfish when I took him to Show and Tell without his fishbowl in second grade.

"Buzz? Are you still there?"

I pulled myself together like the trooper I am...Not.

"What? Disappeared? Just like...*poof,* you're gone?" *Think, Buzz, you have to think.*

"Buzz, dear? Are you still there?"

"Yeah I'm here. Listen, Mom, does anyone else with you know what happened to the girls, Sarah and Iva? Didn't anyone investigate? Were they killed, lost...what? Why do the other SWAT girls have gossip and theories to tell me? Do they want to tell me where they think the two girls went?"

"Yup. They are chomping at the bit to get this phone out of my hand. You'd better let them talk before they become and ugly mob."

I heard Mary say, "Hey, we're not a mob!"

Then someone else yelled, "But you sure are ugly!"

The speaker kicked on again and I heard, "Joy Broussard, you must be looking in the mirror!"

I cleared my throat. "Uh, ladies?"

"Oh yeah? Well at least my daddy didn't have tie a pork chop around my neck so the dog would play with me."

I cleared my throat louder. "Ahem, stop it, ladies. I'm trying to–"

"Well, you're so ugly, when you sit in the sandbox, the kitties try to cover you up."

That one got me and I snorted, but by this time, I had lost track of who was who. *How old were these women?*

"Mom, uh, Joy–"

"You're so ugly, you give Freddy Krueger nightmares!"

"Freddie Krueger? Who the heck is Freddie Krueger?"

"You know, *Nightmare on Elm Street* the movie?"

"They made a movie called *Nightmare on Elm Street*?"

"Oh never mind, Mary, I forgot how much *older* you are than me so I–"

"Older? I'll give you older, missy! I'll have you know I–"

"Did someone say old? I'll say! I swear, Mary, I heard you were a waitress at the Last Supper."

I gasped.

"Oh yeah, well, I heard you left your purse on the Ark."

"The Ark? Isn't that the new tavern in Lake Geneva?"

"No, you sillie old biddie. *The* Ark, you know, two-by-two? Noah, your next door neighbor?"

"Oh, *that* Ark. And here I thought I left it at Wal-Mart."

They all broke up and I sat there dazed.

"Buzz? Are you still there?"

I sighed. "Uh, yes, Mom, I'm here, but I'm very confused. Are you all finished beating each other up?"

"I'm sorry, Buzz, we're a little wound up. It's coffee day for the SWAT girls, but Mary found a new micro-brewery, and I guess while making merry, *some* of us got a little merrier than we had planned."

"Uh, Mom? Does anyone need a ride home? I'll come right over and–"

"Oh no, you don't, we're fine, thanks. Besides, you're not supposed to be driving. You're probably more dangerous on the road than Mary when she's toasted. But don't worry; since I'm today's host, I stayed sober so I could make sure everyone got home safe and sound, besides, I have to be at your house in...oh no, ten minutes ago."

"That's okay, Mom–"

"On no it's not. Give me twenty minutes to get rid of these soused mouses, and I'll hop on over."

I was hard pressed to believe she could break up the party that quickly, but with Mom, all things are possible. "Okay, Mom, if you're sure. Call me if you need me. Promise?"

I could hear the smile in her voice. "Promise. I'm as sober as a judge, Buzz."

"Not Judge Henford, I hope!"

She huffed. "Certainly not Henford. He hasn't been sober since 1953. More like, uh, Judge Judy."

"Hah. Whatever you say, Mom. Just be careful, okay?"

"Ahem, Don't look now, but I'm not the one sitting at home because I cracked my gourd open, Alice Christine."

I winced. "Uh, yeah, I forgot. Got your point, Mom. Say, when the other ladies sober up, ask them again about the Jones girls, would you? I think it might be a vital connection."

Sure thing, dear, now take care of your noggin, and I'll see you around ten. Love you, Buzz."

"Yeah, love you too, Mom. See you later."

"Toodles!"

I hung up and stared at the phone. "Toodles? And she claims she's not drinking?" I dialed the sheriff's office and asked Edie to have Moe drive by and make sure the Miller farm was still in one piece. I knew he'd make sure the ladies made it safely home, as long as they gave him cookies, and they always had cookies.

I sighed and turned toward the white board. Armed with this new information, I promptly forgot my aching head. I gathered my notes and picked up the phone.

I got Al's voice mail. I outlined my conversation with Mom, and remembering Fred signed up for the early evening shift, and I told Al I'd ask Fred to stop by the library and pick up copies of any old newspaper articles regarding the incident on Geneva Lake.

Al called back about ten minutes later and said she'd do the research and pull what she had. I smiled as I hung up and wondered briefly why Al remained such a thorn in my side for so long. Then I thought about growing up, and I came to my senses. *But people can change, Buzz Miller. Add a few years, college and a career, a lot of maturity...yours too, Buzz.*

I blinked a couple times to clear my head, and called Fred. The cacophony of sound which greeted me when she answered almost knocked me over. The squawking, barking, meows and other jungle sounds made my eyes water and my headache rage forth.

"Miller's Menagerie! The one stop shop for all your pet needs!"

I squinted as the noise sent ice picks stabbing through my temples. "Damn, Fred. How can you stand the noise? And what are you so chipper about?"

"Buzz? I can't hear over the kids here. It's feeding time, you know, and it always gets a little loud. Did you say you want some slippers? I can stop at Wal-Mart on my way to your place if you want."

I must have rolled my eyes, because the movement had me grabbing my aching head. I took a big breath and tried again.

"Not slippers, chipper! I said you sounded cheerful, you dope!"

"Hope? Yeah, I hope they have slippers too. I'll try to find green ones, but you may end up with fish heads or Packer helmets for all I know. Anything else you need before I feed the masses here?"

I gave up. "No, no, That's all. I'll talk to you when you get here. See you in the funny papers."

"Poopy papers? No, I already cleaned the puppy cages, so I'll be at your place in about an hour-and-a-half. Bye, Buzz!" *Click*.

I hung up the phone and stared at it. I marveled at the fact Fred was becoming more like Mom every day. My watch said Fred would arrive approximately seven hours early. I sighed and looked at Wes. "Am I the only sane person in my family, Wesley?"

Wes grinned and shook his head A thin stream of doggie slime wrapped itself around his snout. His tail thumped happily. I laughed and looked at Hillary. "Hill? What do you think?"

Hillary wiggled and passed gas.

I covered my nose and threw the sheet over my head. "Uh-huh, just as I thought; a unanimous vote."

As it turned out, I forgot to ask Fred to stop at the library, so Al faxed the news article copies to the Sheriff's office and J.J. brought them over to the house. It seemed as though Al made some sort of connection in the mystery surrounding the disappearance of the Jones girls and wanted to strike while the fire was still hot.

J.J. walked through the door just as I tried to haul an ecstatic Wes the off Fred. Freddie had an almost eerie way with animals. They loved her and she adored them. Wes had no idea he outweighed Fred by a hundred pounds.

I remember once, Mag and I found baby skunks under the machine shed, and Momma Skunk sprayed the crap out of us. Fred went back later and gently moved the family to a more remote location and came back smelling like a rose. That she brought back a sickly skunk runt and nursed it back to health was typical. A de-scented Rosie the skunk followed her around for years, and became the charter member and mascot of Miller's Menagerie–Fred's pet store.

Wesley, however, remains president of Fred Miller Fan-

211

imal Club. Fred's relationship with my dogs is more of a mutual admiration society, but my dog far outweighed my sister, and sometimes I feared she'd disappear under all the doggie lovin' and not be able to breathe.

J.J. grabbed a fistful of hair and Fred popped up under Wesley's elbow, bangs in her face and dog hair all over. "Whew! Oh, hi, J.J. didn't see you come in. I thought I had the noon 'Buzz Watch'. I brought over Chinese for Buzz and me, but there's plenty to go around. What's in your hand? Notes on the case? Let me see 'em; maybe I can help. You know I did a great job on the South American caper I helped Buzz with. Maybe I can put some facts together you guys might have overlooked."

J.J. smiled and held Fred off. "Thanks, Fred, but, this is just boring stuff. Nothing here would be of interest at this stage. But if something comes up when we get rolling, I will give you a shout."

"Well, all right...maybe later."

She blinked at him with her big blue eyes and I could see J.J. begin to cave. I thought it would be a good time for back-up. "Hey, Fred, what about some Chinese? I am kind-of hungry, and you are a credit to our species for bringing it over."

"Oh, poor Buzz, I'm sorry, where is my brain?"

"Oh, I don't know, maybe it's at Wal-Mart with Mary's purse."

She stopped and stared at me. "What?"

I sat on my bed. "Nothing. I heard Mary left her purse somewhere, that's all."

She gave me a dubious look. "Um, All righty then. Say, J.J., would you help me in the kitchen for a minute?"

He looked at the papers in his hand and at Fred. She had her teeth clenched and signaled with her head toward the door. I almost laughed out loud at the look on her face.

J.J. dropped the articles on my lap and followed her out the door. I supposed I should have explained to her about the conversation I had earlier with Mom and the SWAT ladies, but decided to let it be for now. Mom would tell her later, along with half the town.

I read through the articles about the missing diamonds, the missing starlet, Al Capone's fateful party, and the missing yacht, yet I found no mention of the Jones women or the disappearance of the little girls. The police tried to connect the Seipp family with Capone, but the trail left too many loose ends. It ended up being a game of connecting circumstantial evidence with a lot of conjecture, trying and failing to force a mob connection.

Thumbing through the rest of the paperwork Al faxed over, I found little I could use until I ran across a small article on an opposite column about a pro football player named Sweetwater. I froze and my breathing became shallow. Why did the Sweetwater name sound familiar?

I shuffled through the articles again, and searched my desk, skimming my notes on the last body we recovered. "Sweetwater. It's somewhere here, I know it is. Sweetwater..."

I turned to the cork board and the name jumped out at me. Written on the piece of paper recovered from the body at the county fair I found the word Sweetwater. Grandpa Iggy. Sweetwater. "What the heck?"

I absently rubbed Wesley's ears and concentrated on the board. The body from the fair. The missing girls. Sweetwater. I grabbed the phone and dialed my illustrious little sister. Sure enough, Al still slaved away at her desk.

"Buzz, what's up?"

"Al, I need you to do a name search. You can do cross reference stuff, right?"

"Well, yes, but–"

"I think I might have a link. Look in sports figures of the thirties. Green Bay, I think the article said. Looking for anything on a local guy named Sweetwater. It may be connected."

"I am confused, but I'll get back to you as soon as I find something."

"Thanks-you might just find a missing link."

"Or better, some answers. I'll get on it now, see ya, Buzz."

"Yup." I hung up the phone and called for J.J.

He and Fred came back in the room. Smiling, J.J. came to stand next to me. He gently rubbed the back of my neck. "What's the good news? Are you feeling better?"

"Yes, but it might just be adrenalin. Look at this, I might have a connection. Al is checking it out right now. I ran over the facts as I knew them, updating the board as I went. I got to the piece of paper I called Al about, and J.J.'s hand stopped massaging my neck. I stopped yacking and he pointed to the copy of the paper from Iggy's pocket.

I picked up a piece of yarn and tacked one end to the Jones girl's names and the other to the name "Sweetwater."

"Buzz, what is this?"

I looked up. "Sweetwater. This is the paper I babbled about when you took me to the hospital. Malcolm found it in the change pocket of Iggy, the dumpster guy at the fair. You had gone back to check on Edie, I guess, and I forgot about it until a little while ago when I read the old newspaper Al faxed over. I'm having Al cross reference the name with local families and–"

He held up his hand and I stopped. He slowly stepped forward and pulled the tack out of the cork. He stared at the paper for so long I began to feel a little unsteady on my feet. I hobbled over to the chair at my desk and sat. J.J. didn't even notice I left. He looked up from the paper.

"Joe."

I blinked. "Joe?"

Eyes never leaving the paper, J.J. nodded. "Yeah, Joe Sweetwater. He and his wife moved out here when he started playing ball for Green Bay. When I was little, they lived in our neighborhood." He pinched his nose and walked across the room. Alva came back after Joe died in the early nineties."

"How come I never met them?"

"They only lived up here part time after Joe got sick, and you guys live out of town. I was still pretty young when they moved south. Alva came back after Joe passed, and now lives in the assisted living facility at the edge of town. I get over there to visit when I can."

He suddenly looked up and snapped his fingers. "Holy cow, Buzz. I swear she's in the same facility Cab Walker lived in. She's a wonderful woman, and come to think about it, she knows a lot about local people and places. She might be able to shed some light on our problem."

"J.J.? Do you think this Sweetwater woman might be connected to the Sweetwater in the newspaper?"

J.J. stared into my eyes. "I'm sure of it. Hey, I gotta go." He dug for his keys.

I grabbed his arm. "Not without me, buster."

Fred stood holding a bowl of soup. "Ahem, what about me?"

We both stopped and stared. J.J. recovered first. "She's staying. With you."

He turned to go. I had a hold of his arm. J.J. tried to shake me off, but as he walked to the door, I skid across the floor in my stocking feet. When he stopped, I still had a hold of his arm. "I'm going."

"Buzz. I can't drag you all the way across town. How about if I finish up at the office and pick you up on my way

215

over to the nursing home? We don't want to barge in on a ninety-some year old woman out of the blue, so let me make arrangements and give them warning we're coming."

I dropped his arm, knowing he had the right of it. "All right, I'll call the assisted living place. You have enough on your plate without worrying about a phone call. I'll put on real clothes, and be ready by the time you get back."

"Deal." He kissed my nose and turned to go.

He spun me around and wrapped me up in a bear hug. I felt him nuzzle my neck and felt dizzy all over again. His voice was muffled. "You know what, Miller?"

"What?"

"I think I'm really diggin' this relationship thing."

I looked up into those green, green eyes. I smiled. "It's about time you caught up, James. I've been diggin' you for a long, long time."

Those long dimples creased his face as he turned to go.

23

I felt all warm and fuzzy, but then the phone jangled and almost sent me through the ceiling. I screeched, Wes woofed and Hillary opened one eye. I grabbed the phone and flopped in a chair–not a good thing to do when my head felt like it did. I had one hand on my head and one on the phone. "Oh, man, hello?"

"Catch you at a bad time, big sis?"

"Uh, no Al, I just moved too fast and my head barked back. Did you find, anything?"

Fred shoved the chicken soup under my nose. I smiled gratefully and told Al I had a soup emergency.

"Fine, fine, slurp away. As a matter of fact, I did find something. Without going into long ugly details, here's what I pieced together so far..."

The longer Al talked, the more I knew we were on the right track. My mind raced. I suddenly couldn't wait to get to the nursing home. *I promised J.J. I would wait for him, but maybe I could tell him I forgot because of the head injury. Oh crap, the head injury. I'm not supposed to drive, but how else am I going to get across town to the nursing home?* I suddenly realized Al had stopped speaking. "Al?"

"Yes, Buzz?"

"Are you going to offer me a ride downtown to the nursing home?"

"Why do you want to go to the nursing home, and you're right. You shouldn't be driving. I'd come get you, but I have an appointment in fifteen minutes. Bucket the Clown wants to come over and book next year's fair."

"Already? Isn't the timing a little weird? After all, this

year's fair just ended."

"It's not so weird when you think of it. He might be nailing down next year's bookings early. I personally think it's because of the fiasco with Snoodle the Poodle. He might think we won't want him back after he punted a poodle, and wants a contract in-hand before we can change our minds or find a more animal-friendly clown."

Something sparked in the back of my mind. "Maybe finding a new clown's not such a bad idea, Al. Why don't we look around? You know, not decide right away. Besides, Mom and Mary Cromwell think he looks like John Wayne Gacy. Can you call and cancel your meeting? Come on over here and we can all go over to the nursing home."

"I would if I could, Buzz, but it's really too late, and I'm sure Bucket has other rodeos he has to get to."

I thought a bit. "Al? What rodeo company did Bucket say he clowned for?"

"I'm not sure. I thought Rudy Meyer said Circle K or Logan's, why?"

My mind tried to collate and disseminate, but I found it difficult to slog through the injured grey matter and make sense of it all. "I don't know, but I have a bad feeling about this.

"Hah! I thought I smelled rubber burning. Don't hurt your brain, there's not much left to produce cohesive thought when you're healthy."

"Ha, ha. Why don't you call and cancel old Bucket, and come meet a nice old lady with me?"

She hesitated. "Like I said, I wish I could, but this was the only day he could make it. Hmm, that's funny I thought everyone left for the day."

The hair on the back of my neck stirred. "What's funny, Al?"

"Hold on." I heard her in the background talking to

someone.

"Al? Do you need to go?"

"Uh, yeah, Buzz, sorry. Tony just walked in, and I'm not ready. I have papers all over and the contract is in a pile somewhere."

"Tony? I thought you were meeting with–"

Al almost whispered. "Parks. Tony Parks is Bucket the Clown. He stepped out to go to the bathroom so I just have a sec. He hates to be called Bucket when he's not in make-up. He went off on Ted when he hailed him from across the street the other day. I really thought he was going to hit Ted. He got all up in his face and screamed at him like a lunatic. I'm surprised Ted didn't wet his knickers. At the time I discreetly locked my doors Bucket went so whacko."

The hairs on my neck stood on end now. "Al? Are you sure it's okay to meet with him alone? How about you put him off until he gets back from his vacation?"

"Come on, Buzz, you know how anal I am. I have to finish this or I won't sleep for weeks. Oh, hi Tony, come on in, I'll just be a minute. I'm finishing up with my sister."

In the background I heard, "The spaz or the one who can't mind her own damn business?"

"Hey Al, ask him what he means by that crack? I don't even know the dude."

I heard Al smooth over his ruffled feathers as she gently replaced the receiver. I stared at the phone and thought a moment. I hung up and started for the bedroom to change. I hesitated and grabbed the phone. Edie picked up on the first ring. "Sheriff's Office."

"Edie? Buzz."

"Hi, Buzz, Sheriff Green told me to tell you if you called to tell you he had to run over to the Greeley's and feed the llamas. Bud Greely slipped and hurt his ankle. Shirley has him over to the ER right now, and their son Sean can't cover because Sue is having her baby and Sean's at the hospital himself."

Curiously deflated, I tried to think. "Oh, uh, well, llamas? Tell him I talked to the nursing home, and uh, I'll meet him there."

"But, Buzz, J.J. told me–"

"Hey, Edie, can you do me a favor? Al's at the library at a late meeting, and I have a feeling it might not go well. Can you have one of the squads drive by and check on her without her letting her know she's being checked up on?"

"Sure. Phil's meeting a Rock County squad at the county line to turn over a prisoner right now, but he should be clear in a bit. You know how sweet he is on Alexandra. He'll break land speed records to check up on her for you. If twenty minutes isn't quick enough, I can run over–"

"No Edie, don't do that. It's not a big deal. I just had a funny feeling about the client she's with, and it will make me feel better."

"Funny feeling? You? Holy crap, Buzz, maybe I should call in Daryl at home. I know he'd–"

"Good Lord no. Let the poor man rest. Al told me it's not a big deal, and just because I don't care for the guy doesn't mean he's a masher or anything, but–"

"Who is it?"

"That Bucket the Clown guy. He's signing his next year's fair contract. He claimed now is the only time he could do it. He's there now, as a matter of fact."

Silence.

"Edie?"

"You do know he looks like John Wayne G–"

"Gacy, yeah, I know. That alone doesn't make him a criminal, just creepy."

"I'm calling Daryl."

"No, Edie. Say, why don't we just forget it? It's not–"

The radio crackled behind her. "221-Dispatch?"

Edie whispered, "Hold on, Buzz. Dispatch-221, go ahead."

"Yeah, Dispatch. I just T.O.d the male subject to Rock, and I am heading back in."

"10-4. Are you going straight home Phil, or are you stopping back in town tonight?"

"Either way. Why? Got anything else for me before I call it a day?"

"Maybe. Would you 21 me here before you go off duty please?"

"10-4, will do, 221 out."

"10-4."

Edie sighed. "Buzz? You still there?"

"Yeah, Edie. Listen, I really appreciate this. I know it's nothing but please tell Phil I–"

"I know, Buzz. It's my pleasure, and Phil's too, I'm sure. Hey the main line is ringing, so I'll let you go. You be careful now."

"Thanks, Edie, take care."

"Will do, bye, Buzz."

"Bye, now."

I hung up the phone and grabbed the phone book. I found the number I needed and dialed.

"Home Sweet Home, Lynn speaking. How may I assist you?"

"Hi, this is Alice Miller, Is Patti Miller in, please?"

"Sure, Buzz. I'll put you through."

It took about three seconds before Patti picked up. "Hey cuz, what's the Buzz?"

"You weirdo, does razzing me never get old?"

I heard her giggle, "Nope, never. What's up? You never call me at work. Is everything okay? Aunt Gerry and Uncle Bill all right?"

"Yeah, they're good. I need to speak to a client of yours, if she's okay with it. Alva Sweetwater. Is she—"

"Alva? She's great. She'll outlive you and me. Sure, come on over. I'll let Alva know you're coming. I know she'd love the company."

"Thanks, Patti."

"Any time, cousin. See you in a short."

"You betcha, and thanks, Pat."

"Pat is my mother. Call me—"

"Yeah, yeah. Bye-bye, Pat-tay."

I hung up and slurped the last of Fred's wonderful soup. She popped her head around the kitchen door. "Anything else I can do for you before I take off?"

I eyed her and smiled. "As a matter of fact if it's not too much trouble, I could use a lift..."

* * *

The room was spare. A double bed shoved against the far wall and a three-drawer dresser sat across from the foot of the bed. Lacy curtains hung over the one small window and cast muted patterns over the tiny body in the wheelchair. Her eyes were closed and her silver head bent forward, her hands folded in her lap. I touched her shoulder.

"Mrs. Sweetwater?" No response. I walked around so I faced her. I gently rubbed her spotted hand and I felt a light breeze wash over me. She opened her eyes, and a feeling of calm and of acceptance stirred the hairs on the back of my neck and tingled in my fingers.

"If you will pardon me ma'am, you have a beautiful soul, Mrs. Sweetwater, and I am very happy to meet you. I can feel the goodness in you. But I feel something else as well. Are you...waiting for something or someone?"

Alva Sweetwater's mouth twitched. A half-smile lifted her lips and she turned her hand over to grasp mine. Her tired face crinkled into a lovely smile. She opened her eyes and looked into mine. "Yes, Alice Miller, I am waiting. The Lord is going to call me home soon, and I'll be with my Joe."

I smiled, "Joe, your husband, right?"

She patted my hand. "Yes, dear. But I still have unfinished business, and you are connected with it. Am I correct?"

I returned her smile. "Yes Ma'am, I believe I am. Thank you for allowing me this interview. Do you feel like speaking with me at this time?"

"I'm thinkin' God won't call me home until I come clean, so to speak. I also fear I may be the next to be murdered, and if that happens before I spill the beans, no one will know the truth of this whole awful mess. Yes Alice, I will tell you what I know—and call me Alva, please."

I smiled and nodded. "And I'm Buzz to my friends, if you would do me the honor."

"Of course, Buzz."

With her hand still in mine, I slowly sank into the chair across from her. I pulled my digital recorder out of my pocket. "Do you mind? I had a recent head injury, and wouldn't trust my memory as far as I could throw it."

She chuckled. "I heard. I can't trust mine anymore either. Go ahead and record, it's quite a long story."

"You've held your story a secret for many years, Alva."

She chuckled. "That is a fact my dear, I have, indeed. I promised my mother when I was a little girl. Neither my husband nor my children ever knew what I am about to tell you. I feared for their safety should the story become known."

"I understand. Start whenever you feel comfortable."

She touched her bottom lip with a forefinger. "Let me see, where to begin?"

She thought a little more and sighed. "All right. Did you know during prohibition many members of the Italian Mafia from Chicago had summer homes or retreats right down the

223

road in the Lake Geneva area?" She tapped my knee. "Well, of course you do, my apologies."

I nodded. "Yes ma'am. I also know The French Country Inn on Lake Como hosted many a mobster get-together."

Sarah snapped her fingers. "That is correct; which brings us to where I come in."

"Off the subject, Alva, do you remember a man named Olin Norris?"

She hesitated. "Of course. I remember Oly and his family very well. Didn't they move up north?"

I nodded. "Baraboo."

She looked thoughtful, as if waiting for me to go on, but not wanting to know what I had to say.

I patted her hand. "Okay, back on task, Please take your time Mrs. Swee–"

At her stern look I correct myself. "Alva."

She smiled and continued. "Now back in those days if you were black you were a servant, and day help did not live in town. Our community was a few miles east of Lake Geneva.

"My momma and my grandma walked to town every morning in the rain, snow, sleet, or hail to work at what is now called The French Country Inn in Lake Como. They worked in the laundry, they worked as servers, and if a special party requested a certain servant for the duration of their stay, they might get assigned to the party. Momma would sometimes have to stay over at the Inn. It meant more money for us, and we stayed with Grandma Cora while Momma was away."

All my senses hummed on high alert. Sirens screamed, whistles blew, and red lights flashed. I touched her hand. "Your mother was Fanny."

She nodded slowly.

"Then you are Iva or Sarah Jones."

She smiled gently. "Sarah, dear, but we are getting ahead of ourselves."

A shaky hand reached over and plucked a tissue out of the box on the table. "One day Momma told us she had a private party at a summer home in Lake Geneva for a big meeting and party. Grandma went too, so she told Iva and me to come along and help."

Her eyes twinkled "My, my. We were so excited, you see, because a lot of fancy people were to be in attendance. The party took place at the Seipp summer home on Black Pointe, on Geneva Lake but by golly it turned out to be a huge mansion. I hear they give tours there now."

I nodded but didn't want Alva to get distracted. She sighed.

"I was twelve and my sister Iva was ten at the time, and Momma brought us along to help behind the scenes folding napkins, doing laundry, fetching specialty items from the local stores, as well as a host of other menial tasks, so she and Grandma could attend the guests. I tell you; even with us there those guests ran those women ragged with their special orders and lah-dee-dah requests. As long as Iva and I stayed invisible and silent, we were allowed to help. We didn't get paid but if the guests liked the service, they tipped Momma and Grandma generously–which amounted to more than they'd have paid two little black girls.

"On this particular day, most of the guests were goin' down to Geneva Lake, sailing. I knew this because me and Iva delivered huge picnic baskets full fried chicken, potato salad, crackers, spreads–you name it–to the boat."

She raised her hands over her head. "Boxes piled on boxes, I tell you, and they all sat on the pier. One box held nothing but drinks and glasses. They also brought along fancy little tables and umbrellas, suitcases full of what-nots and extra chairs–you know, the loungin' kind.

"Well, Joey and Cab Walker worked at loadin' up the boat so Iva and me stayed to help 'em get everything on board. They had to hurry because Joey Walker was goin' along on the boat as a house boy, and needed to be changed into his white uniform in time to greet the guests."

Alva leaned forward; her face took on new animation. "Then, along comes the most beautiful white woman I ever saw; skin like cream and eyes like sparkling blue sapphires. Tall, blonde, and stunning, she hardly wore a thing! She wore these white shorty-shorts and a matching halter-top. She had a sheer white robe over the top with white feathers around the collar and down the front, and trimming the hemline all the way around."

Alva gestured with her hands, her fingers fluttering in the air, and I could tell she still saw the beautiful woman in her mind's eye.

Alva continued. "She seemed to float down the hill to the dock like a fairy princess on a cloud. I had never before seen such flawless perfection—or so much white skin. Iva and I had never seen a picture show, but we figured she must be one of those movie stars we always heard about.

"The lady smiled at us when she approached the dock and Iva ducked behind some boxes. The woman asked if I could help her get settled in her cabin. I said okay and she gave me a nickel. I gave it to Iva and told her to tell Momma where I was. She ran off, and I picked up a basket, while Joey Walker grabbed her cases.

"I followed the lady onto the boat to a big room just like in the hotel. Joey dropped the cases and left. I remember the large bed was cotton candy pink. The pillows were fluffy and plentiful. She looked like a princess in a fairy tale room. She had me empty her make-up box and line up all her little bottles, pots, and tubes on the vanity. I remember she had a beautiful silver brush set, and I pulled one long blonde hair

226

out and gazed at it in awe. She laughed at me and patted me on the head. She asked if I liked the brush set."

"I nodded, because I couldn't speak if my life depended on it. She smiled at me and patted my head. "You may have it for being such a good girl. You are a beautiful girl, and beautiful girls should have beautiful things. What is your name, child?"

"I whispered my name was Sarah. She insisted I take the brush set though I tried to tell her Momma wouldn't let me take things from strangers. I kept staring at the silver brush set and I couldn't make the words of refusal come out. She held out the brush and my little fingers closed around the handle.

"She told me her name. It was Alexa, and I could call her Miss Wentworth in the event other people came in. Alexa was lively, vibrant, and giggly and she called for champagne to be brought to her cabin.

"I carefully hung clothes of the likes I'd never seen before, when Joey Walker brought in a bottle and un-corked it for Miss Wentworth. I remembered thinking the silver bubbles floating to the top of the glass reminded me of the color of her hair. She drank and danced around her bed while I arranged her shoes in the small closet. I felt light and happy, and floated along on her buoyant mood."

Alva stopped talking and stared at the floor. She had a death grip on the tissue in her hands, and small tremors shook her frail body. She closed her eyes and took a couple of slow, deep breaths. I reached out and patted her hands, and curled my fingers around them. The vertigo hit me like a sledge hammer and before I could catch my breath I hurtled through time and my the picture opened in my mind, in a tiny closet on a boat in a twelve-year-old body.

In my hands I hold a silver mirror and brush. A complex design of flowers are engraved in the back with a scrolled

227

"AW" in the middle. I lay the brush carefully aside and pick up a pair of white open-toed shoes with spiked heels and feathers across the toes. A silver clip is nestled in the center of the feathers, and sparkly stones gleam from its center. I could feel the soft feathers in my small, fine-boned hands. The contrast between the white feathers and the my caramel-latte colored skin reminds me I am only a visitor in this woman's life. I shrug my shoulders in my too-small dress. My pinafore pinches me in the armpits. Momma promised me a new dress this fall and–

I hear a footfall and a bang, and cringed into a corner of the closet. I heard muffled noises coming from the bed room I want to look but am terrified of what I might see...

Alva broke her connection to me with a flick of her wrist and I found myself in a moment of panic, trying to calm the hysteria which threatened to bubble over. Alva took a couple of calming breaths, clutching the arm rests of her wheelchair. I turned from her to give her a moment to collect herself, and glanced around the room. I felt drawn to the dresser, and didn't realize I drifted across the room until I stood staring at the silver brush and mirror sitting atop a hand–tatted doily. The engraved pattern on the back was a chrysanthemum flower design, and in the center in looping scroll I saw the "A. W." I already knew I'd find. Alva stared at me and at the silver brush in my hand. Lifting her chin, she continued her story aloud, and I stood trapped in her nightmare.

"The door suddenly slammed open and a huge man entered. He kicked the closet door closed and I sat huddled in the corner, trapped inside. I stared through the hole in the lock, and saw Alexa backing toward the bed, a frightened look on her face. She opened her mouth to scream and I saw an arm flash across my field of vision as the big man backhanded her across the mouth. The blow snapped her head back and sent her flying backward toward the bed. A line of red appeared where his ring caught her on the chin. Alexa screamed and grabbed her chin, tumbling to the floor. The big man grabbed her hair and lifted her off the floor, tossing her onto the pink bedspread."

Alva stopped and looked up at me with frightened eyes. "It's too horrible. Even after all this time I can't tell the story. Help me, please."

She grabbed my hand with both of hers. I barely had time to breathe before I tumbled with her back into the closet on the sailboat.

24

From the closet, I saw the woman on the bed, her hair spread around her head like a halo, and blood dripping from her chin. She is missing one shoe. I want to cry out but instinctively I know to stay invisible and keep silent.

The man fisted her robe in one hand and dragged Alexa toward him. "Where is it?" He yelled.

"Where is what?" She cried.

"You know damn well what! The bag! I want the bag now!"

"But Johnny, I don't have a bag, honest! What do you think I did, steal something from you?"

The big man named Johnny slapped her face and grabbed her by the throat. Alexa clawed at his hand, fighting for breath. He got real close to her and spoke real quiet-like.

"You know you did, you lying bitch! You and those South Side scumbags you brought with you! Mr. Capone offers his hospitality to you and this is how you repay him? You steal from him? The stones are gone, and your friends skipped. You are one stupid, dead, wannabe actress, baby."

"Wait, no, Johnny! I don't know–ack! Let me go!"

I hear choking noises and bumping sounds, but I'm too terrified to look. I push behind the shoe rack and under a low shelf. Hoarse screams erupt from the bedroom and are abruptly cut off. Clutching the silver brush and the feather shoes in my hand, I crunch my eyes shut–willing the big man to go away and stop hurting Alexa.

From far away, and I try to claw my way back to the reality of Alva's room. I can hear Alva's voice, but the pull of the darkness drags me down, the smells of perfume, talcum powder, and feet engulf my soul and swallow me whole. The scratch on my knee from the shoe rack stings like the dickens. The darkness is my only reality now. I strain for a deep breath and fight the panic threatening to overpower me. I took a large breath. I'm again in the closet, a little girl, alone in a waking nightmare.

I hear a grunt and a bang, and can almost feel a large object (Alexa?) slam into the closet door. I hear the door handle jiggle and the hinges squeak. From under my shelf I can see a wedge of light. Johnny opened the closet! I can see the shoes disappearing off the rack and thudding on the carpet behind him. He's getting closer. Any second he will see my feet and I will be dead. I know this as sure as I know my mamma loves me. I hold my breath and press my face into the carpet. I pray to the Lord above, I can hear my heart pound against my chest–can't the bad man hear it too?

Suddenly, the clothes above me move. I hear ripping of fabric and the squeak of the hangers as they drag across the bar. I realize Johnny is looking for his missing bag and not me. I feel something slither across my ankle and I almost screech. Clothes. He dropped some clothes. I sure hope whatever fell on me covers up my scuffed Mary Janes.

A soft clunk and a puff of air right next to my ear startles me and makes me flinch. I crack and eye open and see an object tip and fall right at the end of my nose. I press my face harder into the carpet and I see a large hand with sausage like fingers grope blindly behind the shoe rack for whatever fell. I suck back against the wall one more millimeter.

A large square ring appears in front of my face. It is silver and has a snake on the top. The snake has a large ruby red eye and a white fang. The ring has a smear of red across it, and I can see a piece of skin on one corner. I need to throw up. I have to go potty. I dare not breathe. Tears leak out of my eyes and my nose is running. I am dead. I'm sorry

231

Momma, I'm sorry Grandma, I love you Iva...how does he not hear me?

I can smell his B.O. His fingernails are dirty. He ate garlic for lunch–yuck. The white shoes are clasped tightly against my body. The spike heels are punching holes into my flat chest, but I barely feel the pain I am so very frightened. Where is Alexa? I hear a kitty mewing somewhere, but I can't think about that now.

The snake ring stops moving and draws away, bringing with it a shiny flat box like the ones fancy ladies keep their cigarettes in. He is still standing at the door to the closet, the man she called Johnny, because I can see the shadow of his shoes move as he prepares to leave. I dare not move a muscle, but my breath hitches.

Mr. Johnny the Snake Ring man stops. I know I am about to die. The shadows shift, the hangars squeak, he kicks the shoe rack which slams into my knees, and–?

The shadows shift again and the door closes with a soft click. My mouth hangs open, tears pour down my nose and soak into the carpet just like the blood poured off Alexa's chin and soaked into the cotton candy bed spread.

More shuffling, a door slams and there is no more sound. He must have left. Out of the silence I hear the kitty again, and I wonder if Mr. Johnny the Snake Ring man hurt the kitty like he hurt Alexa. I dare not move even though I am in the dark.

Time passes and still I lay huddled in the closet. The adrenalin stopped pumping and my heart stopped pounding. I felt really tired. A floaty feeling is with me and my tummy feels a little funny. The gentle rocking soothes me and my eyelids are getting heavy. I clutch the brush and the pretty shoes to my chest like my favorite Teddy bear and drift off.

I dream my Momma is calling me. I can hear her voice calling, "Sarah Jean, where are you?" Something grabs my

232

wrist. I heard, "There you are!" And stared into the big man's face. "I've been looking for you, Sarah Jean!"

My eyes flew open to find Alva Sweetwater gripping my wrist as I held on to hers. Her faded chocolate eyes bore into mine as I fought to surface from the vision. Her labored breathing was fast and erratic. Her voice shook with emotion. "You were there. You were just with me in the closet."

I nodded, weary beyond belief. "Yes. You are Sarah? Your real name is Sarah Jean Jones."

Tears welled in her eyes and she nodded slowly.

I gripped her hand. "You must have been terrified."

"I'm terrified now, but I have to keep going. Someone has to know before the truth dies with me."

"I understand Mrs. Sweet–Sarah, Alva, what do I call you?"

"I have been Alva for over eighty years. Sarah ceased to exist a long time ago on a sailboat in Lake Geneva. I am comfortable with Alva. I *am* Alva." She sighed and I watched her crooked fingers fidget in her lap.

"Alva, if you'd like to continue this tomorrow–"

"No, no! It has to be today. Now, don't you understand? Please help me do this. It has to be now, before he comes. We cannot afford to wait any longer. Can't you see? I have to tell because of Cab, Iggy, Ole, Joey, and the rest!"

The names fell into place. I screamed inside, but I stroked her trembling hand. "Okay, okay, take it easy Alva. We can do this now if you're up to it. Please let me make a call to Sheriff Green first."

She agreed and I called J.J. I told him the situation and predictably, he cussed a blue streak, asked if I felt okay, and told me he'd be there in ten minutes. He made it in six, and proceeded to badger me like my mother did when I was seventeen and late for curfew. Alva stared, one eyebrow raised, her head bobbing back and forth as if she watched a particularly hot Ping-Pong match.

J.J. finally ran out of steam; a fact of which I will be eternally grateful. He needed no introduction to Alva, as he grew up across the street from her and her husband. He touched his ball cap. "Afternoon, Miz Sweetwater. Are you keeping all these men in line around here?"

J.J. bent and kissed her cheek. Sarah smiled and smacked him on the shoulder. Her entire face crinkled when she smiled. "You're full of sass today, young James."

At his startled expression, I gave Alva the thumbs up. "I tell him he's sassy at least once a day."

Her eyes twinkled and her gaze darted from J.J. to me. "Oh, I think you give as good as you get, Alice Miller."

J.J. hooted. "You call her Alice and she doesn't shoot you? I only call her Alice when there are no sharp objects in the near vicinity."

Alva smiled. "You, James Green could try the patience of a saint, but it's a lucky woman who ends up with you." She looked at me. "I hear you are the lucky woman who is applying for the job."

I laughed. "I'm no saint, Alva. There isn't a woman alive who could keep this rascal in line."

Alva smiled her Mona Lisa smile. "But what an adventure it will be! Don't wait too long, you two. Life picks up speed the older we get."

J.J. laughed and threw an arm around my shoulders. He winked at Alva. "I'm working on her, Miss Alva. I think she's beginning to cave in and accept the idea. She'll be taking me home in shackles before you know it."

I elbowed him in the ribs. "He wishes. Ignore him, Alva. He's a big talker."

Alva smiled. "Better make it soon, James Green. Time is the only thing I don't have. I want to dance at your wedding, you know."

J.J. sobered. "I will reserve the second dance just for you, Alva."

Alva's eyes teared up and J.J. reached for her. She swatted at his hands and I pressed a tissue into her palm.

She smiled. "Thank you, dear. Now, let's get back to business, shall we?" She thought a moment. "Ah yes, Sarah Jones."

J.J. looked at me and mouthed "Sarah Jones?"

I nodded and patted his leg. "*Shh*, just listen."

25

Alva began slowly. "Yes, I was born Sarah Jean Jones. I was Sarah for twelve years. After that horrific day on the sailboat, Iva and I were packed up and sent to Charlotte to live with my mamma's cousin Calvert Jefferson and his wife Mimi. Calvert and Mimi had a good life, but no children. They were thrilled to have Iva and me come live with them.

Calvert owned a shoe repair–rare as it was back in those days for a Negro to own a business, but Uncle Calvert was an artist. Mimi tatted lace for fancy hats and dresses." She nodded toward the intricately tatted doily on her dresser. "That's where I learned to make lace. Mimi was also an artist, and had all the patience in the world for two lost little girls. We struggled at first, but eventually Iva and I came around. I grew up Alva Jean Jefferson, but Iva never did change her first name. She could never remember who to call what."

Alva stopped for a moment and drew in a deep breath before continuing. "So we settled in. Mimi had orders all the time, so it followed Iva and I learn her craft to help out. We grew to love them as our parents. They were good people and I miss them every day of my life."

Alva dabbed her eyes and began again. "My Momma stayed on in Lake Geneva for a while. She didn't want anyone thinking she knew anything about what went on that day on the boat. If two little colored girls disappeared from the area, well, no one cared enough to question it. No one knew I worked at the hotel that day, let alone I boarded the boat, but Momma always thought someone might let it slip."

"Momma didn't even write for the first year, but afterward she and Grandma moved to Kansas City and again, to Atlanta. Grandma went on to Mobile for about three years, but moved back up with Momma in Atlanta. Grandma Cora passed a short time later, and left Momma all alone. Momma felt safe enough to keep track of us through Mimi. Finally when I turned seventeen and Iva fifteen, Momma surprised us and moved to Charlotte. Cal and Mimi insisted she live with us, and we were one big happy family again.

"It didn't matter to Momma we called Mimi and Cal Momma and Daddy. Momma said it was important to keep up appearances.

"I met Big Joe Sweetwater in high school. Big, tall, and brawny, my Joe played left tackle on the varsity squad. One night while we worked on the Homecoming float at Steffie Sparks' house, a bunch of rowdy football players showed up and began to mess up the works. Joe was in the process of shredding tissue paper so I march up to him, snatched the tissue paper away, and slapped his hand. Everyone stopped talking and stared at us. I told him he should be acting with the good manners his momma taught him. He bent down to look me in the eye and smiled a big old sloppy smile.

"He said, 'Who are you, girl?' I slapped him on his big old barrel chest of his and told him it was none of his business."

I covered my mouth to keep from laughing. "Alva, what did he do?"

Her face creased and she shook with mirth. "He grabbed me by the front of my sweatshirt and lifted me all the way up so my feet dangled off the ground. Everyone around us yelled at him to put me down. More mad than scared, I just looked him in the eye, crossed my arms over my chest, and dared him to do his worst in front of witnesses."

"Oh my gosh, Alva, what did he do?"

"He planted a big old kiss right on my lips and told me he hoped our kids had half my sass."

I gasped and flopped back against my chair. "You're kidding, right?"

Alva chuckled and slapped her knee. "After that, I couldn't get rid of the man if I called out the National Guard. After graduation he finally wore me down and married me. He went to Notre Dame on scholarship and got him himself drafted by the Green Bay Packers, of all teams! He missed World War II by a hair, so he played football, and I tatted lace. We had a good life together."

I stopped her. "You mean to tell me you married Hall of Famer Big Joe Sweetwater? He was ground breaking. He was one of the first African Americans on the Packer defense, and still holds a couple team records."

I turned on J.J. "Why didn't I know this?"

J.J. put an arm across my shoulders and patted my arm. "Calm down, Buzz. I thought you knew. You being the sports guru, and all. Everyone else in town knows."

I sat fuming while J.J. and Alva spoke a few minutes about Joe. Alva reached over and patted my knee. "My Joe passed when you were still a little girl, Buzz. He's the only reason I came back here at all. I met up with J.J. here when I came to a Packer reunion where they honored Joe and retired his jersey. I stayed on here because nearly all my family had passed by then, and no one here made the connection to me and Sarah Jones."

She looked away and dabbed her eyes with a tissue.

I sucked in a breath. "Until now."

She nodded. "Until now."

"I'd like to get the rest of your story on tape if you're up to it, Alva."

She smiled. "I think the question is are you up to it, Buzz?"

"I'm okay, thanks. Now where were we?"

J.J. removed his arm from around my shoulders only to

rub my back. It felt so good I wanted to curl up around him and purr, I instead gave him the fish eye and asked, "Don't you have crime and staff to tend, Green?"

He patted my butt. "I'm tending, I'm tending. I'm participating in an interview which is vital to our most important investigation at the moment."

I poked him in the ribs. "It's the only investigation we have going at the moment." I turned to Alva. "Now where were we?"

Alva smiled sweetly and continued. "Still in the closet, Buzz. I stayed hidden, and the only thing I could still hear the sounds of the kitten. The floaty feeling in my belly came back, and I guess it struck me for the first time we had sailed out on the lake. I panicked and began to cry. I knew if they threw me overboard I'd drown because I never learned to swim. I thought maybe Alexa would come back and save me, and peeked out of the closet to see if she had stayed behind."

She stopped. I tensed. "What did you see when you looked out the closet door, Alva?"

Her eyes filled with tears and she squeezed them shut. Her grip on my hand was fierce. "I–I saw her. She was there, on the floor. Her, her h-hair, her beautiful blonde hair spread out like before, only this time red covered the blonde. Her face horribly battered and her lips split and bleeding, she could barely speak. I looked down and saw teeth scattered on the floor. Her teeth.

"I realized then there was no kitten. The mewling sounds came from her. She couldn't talk. She barely breathed. Her jaw sat at a funny angle. I didn't know what to do, so I sat next to her clutching the shoes and hair brush with one arm and rubbed her chest like Momma did when we felt sick or scared.

"I heard noises in the hall and Alexa tried to talk to me. I rubbed her and cried–telling her help might be coming.

239

"She touched the pretty white shoes. I couldn't make out any words, so I moved real close. I barely heard, 'Shoes. Take them. Hide.' I dove into the closet and squeezed under the shelf, making sure I tucked my feet in this time.

The door banged open and someone said, "There she is. Bitch wouldn't talk."

Another voice. "Well brainless, you fixed it so she'd never talk again, right? Now we might never know where Capone's diamonds are."

"Someone else must know, and we'll get 'em, Sonny."

"Not if we have to keep cleaning up after your messes, we won't. Come on, Johnny, let's take care of her. Jake told me the water's about seventy feet deep around here. They won't find her for a while."

Laughter. "Hah! If ever. I'll pack everything up. You and Tony take care of her. I'll meet you on deck, and for Christ's sake, don't forget anything!"

"I heard you the first time."

Alva opened her eyes and forced herself to continue. "I heard the outer door slam and the closet door flew open. I saw the snake ring reach in and take Alexa's suitcase out. I don't think I breathed the whole time. The other case disappeared as well, and the clothes in the closet were ripped off their hangars and thrown in the case. The door to the cabin opened again and there I heard a lot of feet clomping and bumping noises. Alexa squeaked and moaned. Just then I put two-and-two together and it hit me they planned on throwing Alexa overboard in seventy feet of water. Alive."

Alva stopped, closed her eyes, and drew in a long, shuddering breath. She laid a hand over her heart. Very softly I asked, "And then?"

"Then I crawled out of the closet and looked around the room. Everything vanished. It looked like she never existed, except for the splotch of blood on the bed, and the large puddle on the floor where her head bled.

"I wandered over to the little window in time to see a flash of white streak by. I will live with the vision forever of her hitting the water, her hair floating around the face of an angel as she sunk out of sight. The suitcases were tied to a chain, dragging Alexa to her death. The water closed over her and all what was left was the dark rippling surface of the lake, bathed in moonlight and hiding its secrets."

I shudder. "I should say so. How did you escape?"

"I crawled back into the closet under the shelf, and waited. A motor I had not heard before started up and they drove the boat to the dock at the Seipp pier. Everyone got off the boat, and unloaded whatever they brought on board, but still I waited. It could have been minutes, it could have been hours. I don't know how long I sat there before I worked up courage enough to make my way up the stairs and off the boat.

"I ran all those miles home as fast as I could and collapsed on the doorstep of my house. It was well past daybreak by then, and Momma came out and carried me inside. She took one look at my blood- stained pinafore and had me stripped and in the tub in no time. They had to pry my fingers from around the shoes, brush, and mirror I didn't even remember holding.

"The hot water and the warm presence of Momma and Grandma eventually loosened my tongue and I told them everything. Frightened out of their minds, Momma said we had to pack me up. Somewhere they decided Iva had go to as well, and Grandma and Momma tried to make it seem like a great adventure. Grandma, always the voice of reason, decided Uncle Calvert and Aunt Mimi had to be contacted, and Iva and I were to be shipped off to them. Momma and Grandma would continue to work until they felt safe enough to leave.

"As it was, Joey Walker disappeared after that night, and his body never found. Cab stayed ashore. I don't know what they told Cab's family. But I know they killed Joey because he saw what they did, and I lived in fear they would somehow find out I was there." Alva sighed. "Poor Cab and his momma. My momma couldn't even tell her what happened to her baby boy."

She sat quietly as she thought about the past. With an odd look in her eye, she glanced up first at me, and at J.J. She sighed and lifted her chin. "That is what I know. Now what can you tell me I don't already know?"

I looked at J.J., and he nodded. I took her hands in mine and for a second marveled at the calm acceptance of what she would face. I knew telling her anything but the truth would be a stupid waste of time, and time was something we did not have on our side.

"Alva, I believe someone who believes the tale of the lost Capone diamonds is looking for the loot, and is systematically killing off anyone who he thinks knows anything."

She bent her head for a moment. "Cab and Joey, such nice boys."

She took a breath and with new resolve, rolled up to J.J. and me. "The murderer can't be one of the people who were present on the yacht that day, so we have to be dealing with a descendant of someone who was there. Do we all agree?"

J.J. and I nodded.

"Then whoever it is must believe they have the whole story by now, and quite possibly they do, except for one thing." Alva wheeled herself over to the closet. She pulled out a battered metal box. I held my breath. I gripped J.J.'s hand. It couldn't be. Alva lifted the lid and removed a package wrapped in tissue. J.J. and I didn't move a muscle as we watched Alva slowly unwrap the tissue. I wanted to grab the box out of her hand and rip it open, because I knew what we'd find inside. I hyperventilated and broke out in a sweat by the time Alva spread the tissue wide and reached inside.

She gently withdrew a lovely pair of white heels with feathers across the toe, and a delicate silver clip on top. My heart stopped. "Oh my Lord, Alva. Don't tell me–"

"I never told Iva, Momma, or even Auntie Mimi. You are the very first people I've ever shown."

I still reeled from the shock of finding the story of Alexa, the mirror, and shoes remained a secret all these years. I stared at the white feathers on the toe of one of the shoes.

Alva cleared her throat. She picked up a shoe, while a secret smile played about her lips. "Hold out your hand. I found this in the toe years later when Iva and I lived with Aunt Mimi. She reached into the toe of the left shoe and pulled out a small velvet bag. I squeezed J.J.'s arm. Hard. With the other I reached toward Alva. A whisper of a smile crinkled her face as she pulled apart the strings. She gently shook the bag over my trembling hand. Three sparkling pink stones rolled across my palm and stopped short of tumbling to the floor.

The three of us gazed at the sparkling gems.

J.J. made a gurgling sound. I could barely breathe. "Oh my God Alva, the missing diamonds."

"You see why I have kept this to myself?"

"You've had these all these years and never told a soul?"

"Never a soul. These stones hurt so many lives; I could not risk my loved ones. I couldn't turn them in without big media attention, and jeopardize the safety of my Joe or my children, and their children–do you see where I'm going?"

I nodded. "And now you have no choice, because whoever is killing people has figured out the what, just not the who, am I correct?"

Alva sighed. "These stones are still responsible for the

243

deaths of, what–two people?"

I held up three fingers. Alva made the sign of the cross and bowed her head.

I dropped the diamonds into the velvet bag. "I looked at J.J. and Alva "What now?"

Alva cleared her throat. "I decided all those decades ago not to do anything with them until such a time arose when someone found out about the stones, or I could find someone who could be trusted to do the right thing with them."

"But, but–"

"I figure whoever lost the stones collected the insurance money decades ago, and whoever stole the diamonds should never have profited off the backs of dead innocents."

She looked at me. "But the time has come where the truth must be told, and I know I have met the person who will make sure the right thing is done. She reached out and curled my fingers around the diamonds. "So now is the time, and you are the right person, Alice Miller."

Stunned, I pulled my hand away and dropped the diamonds in J.J.'s hand. "I'm honored, Alva, but why me? Why now, almost eighty years later?"

"Because this mystery needs to be solved, and the murderer needs to be exposed and stopped."

She grasped my hand and folded my fingers over the hairbrush. "Without you and J.J., the truth dies with me. You alone cared enough about two little nobody black girls to want to know the truth."

Alva sat back. "Someone obviously knows, or thinks he knows, and poor Cab Walker has died because I was too late in coming forward, and too scared to go after the person myself. I thought it was all laid to rest a half century ago."

J.J. stuffed the pink diamonds back into their bag and dropped it in Alva's lap. I didn't see her nod and his wink, because I was too busy pacing up and down the room, talking out loud to myself.

"The killer does not know the entire story, or our murder victims might not have been tortured and killed after the killer drained them of information regarding the incident off Black Pointe."

I sucked in a horrified breath. "Oh my God, J.J., I'll bet Mary Cromwell *was* being stalked, because she looks about a-hundred-and-ten years old. Maybe the murderer didn't believe her. Good thing she had her ten-pound purse with her." I thought a second. "We also know now our murderer is definitely a man. Mary identified her stalker as a man she thought did Cab want to play patty-fingers out behind the beauty shop. Wow, she could have been a victim."

An idea hit me like Mary's pink purse upside my head. I turned to J.J. "Help me out here. Just listen."

I saw J.J. wink at Alva and I shot him an evil grin.
"What if the killer targeted people who could have witnessed what happened that night? Anyone on the yacht or working at the party could have heard Big Johnny with the snake ring yelling at Alexa about the missing diamonds. Someone either figured it all out or thinks he knows of the existence of the diamonds. But no–if they figured it out; they wouldn't have to kill anyone. It's got to be a relative of someone who was there–someone has heard the stories, who thinks they know, and put two-and-two together and got three."

Alva gasped. "You're saying someone is just killing old people on a whim, just in case the legend of the missing diamonds is true?"

J.J. looked baffled. "How would they know the diamonds even exist? They could be in 150 feet of water with Alexa for all anyone knows, or just a myth. No one knew they were real."

I grew frustrated. "J.J., *someone* had to know they were real, and they were truly stolen by Alexa or her friends. When

245

you think about it, the diamonds have to be the connection here, don't you see? The first person murdered in Baraboo, Oly Norris? A baggage boy for the French Country Inn, and probably took the baggage from the hotel to the Seipp residence. He'd have been there at the docks loading luggage and supplies on the boat. I thought his death a coincidence until I heard about the torture and murder of Cab Walker. Remember his brother Joey was the cabin boy on the yacht."

J.J. ran a hand through his hair and pinched the bridge of his nose. "I agree we can connect the dots there, but what about the man in the dumpster at the fair? What the heck was his name?' he thumbed through his notebook, "It was Iggy something."

I spun at the sound of an indrawn breath. Alva stared at us in abject terror. Her hand covered her heart, and she was shaking and pale. I dropped to my knees, taking both of her trembling hands in mine. "What is it, Alva?"

J.J. held onto her shoulder and we both leaned close. Alva closed her eyes and a tear ran down her cheek.

No one said a thing. Alva squeezed my hands. "Iggy Adams," she whispered.

I waited until she looked at me. "Alva, you knew Iggy."

She nodded. "I saw him just for a little while about three weeks ago. His momma named him Ignatius Delford Edward Adams. She smiled and sniffed. "He always called himself the 'IDEA' man because of his initials. He was a neighbor boy who played with Iva and me a lot when we were kids. He was full of life and could charm the socks off just about anyone."

She wiped her eyes and chuckled. "We used to get into the darndest scrapes, 'cause the 'Idea Man's' ideas usually proved to be pretty bad. He was a very nice boy, though. Some of the other kids would pick on him because his family had even less than we did-especially that nasty Anthony Parks."

"The one who owned your house?"

"That was Anthony Senior. I'm talking about his son. Anthony Senior would bring his son along to collect the rents, and Junior–we called him Number Two– would come with him, probably so he could learn how to bully poor folks so he could carry on the Parks cruel legacy. He was much older than we were, lazy and mean. He would tease Iggy something terrible, he'd beat him, up or throw stones at him.

"Momma told me Junior Parks grew up and had a boy just as mean as his daddy. Anthony the Third, they called him. Heard tell he bullied children and tortured animals. They say he ran off to Chicago to make it big, but Lord-a mercy, I'm just glad I never ran into him

Alva thought for a moment. "You know, Iggy had a hard life. He didn't do anything the easy way. He always had an angle. I heard he got drafted in World War II, came back with alcohol problems, left his wife and little girl to fend for themselves, and just drifted away. He told me he came here to meet his granddaughter."

"Deserae," I whispered.

Alva nodded. "But after talking with him, I thought Iggy came to see me because he wanted to know what I knew about what happened way back then. I figured old Iggy had a new angle to play, and thought maybe I could help him help himself to the diamonds.

"You see, he knew my Aunt Mimi, and he would have pestered my momma fierce when Iva and I disappeared if he thought we were there. When I asked him how he found me, sure enough, he tracked me through Aunt Mimi, and then Joe. "Poor Iggy. I wonder if he ever found Deserae."

I placed my hand on her knee. "Poor Iggy probably pointed the murderer in your direction, Alva."

She shrugged. "If Iggy found me, someone else can. The proof is in the box. For years I tried to find out bits and pieces about what happened and where all the players ended up. Thank goodness for my Joe. When he bought me a computer with Internet, I never looked back. I could read papers from all over the country, and no one could track my subscriptions."

My head spun with the information we learned thus far.

Alva cleared her throat. "You will find one more connection of the dots you don't even know about. Bobby Morelli, alias Roberto 'Boom-boom' Baffone, was a mob-employed patch man in Chicago, and a grandson of one of the men who murdered Alexa. He was found last month, dead in an alley off 22nd Street in Chicago near Chinatown."

She waited a beat. "Boom-Boom had a partner, Victor Parco, a very bad man. My research man turned up some fascinating information on Slick Vic–"

I interrupted. "Alva, we're talking about Iggy. Now if he knew–"

Alva slapped the arm of her wheel chair. "Wait, don't you see? It's the only thing that makes sense. The connection. This Victor Parco has got to be connected to whoever is after the diamonds. He's getting closer, and I think through Iggy he must now know I'm alive.

"That's why I needed to tell you the story because I am going to will the diamonds, or rather the metal box and complete contents; the silver set, the shoes and the velvet bag with contents to someone who will do the right thing with them."

I started to get a sick feeling in my stomach, but Alva barely took a breath. "Someone who will not live like a coward and in fear of discovery for eighty years. Someone who might find Alexa and put her to rest."

She took my hand. "I've watched you grow up through pictures, news stories, and talking to people, Alice Miller." She squeezed J.J.'s hand, "People I have known who know

248

you. You are that person. You are strong, you are honest. You always do the right thing, and I know through this, you will do the right thing for Alexa and the diamonds."

I had no words. I stuttered and stared. J.J. squeezed my shoulder and spoke for me. "I think what she is trying to say is thank you for the gift, she will do her best to find closure for Alexa, and she will treasure the shoes and mirror set forever."

I wiped the tears from my face and said, "I will tell your story someday, Alva. I will tell the story of a brave little girl who survived against all odds, and kept a secret for almost eighty years."

Alva smiled and put the diamonds back into the box. She finally relaxed, and sat back in her chair. "Just one more thing. I now believe I know who might be behind these murders, and so do you."

J.J. leaned forward. "What? You have my attention. Who?"

I stared at her. I swallowed a smile. "Wait a minute. You're not telling us this Victor Parco is our murderer, are you? Every bad guy in every 'B' movie was named Victor something-or-another. What a hokey name for a bad guy. Are you really saying this is the person who has been murdering our senior citizens?"

Alva placed the shoes in the box and tucked the velvet bag inside the toe of the left shoe. "What would you say if I told you I believe I saw the snake ring or an exact replica of the ring the killer they called Johnny wore the night Alexa died?"

I waited. Alva shuddered and pulled a shawl over her shoulders, and grabbed a tissue. "I saw the ring. This morning, I sat in the park across the street from here, watching my great grandson play. A hand slammed onto the backrest of my bench, next to my left shoulder. It startled me

249

so much I jumped out of my skin. I looked at the hand and saw the ring. I couldn't breathe. I slowly looked up, and into the dead eyes of a huge man. He didn't say a word, he just smiled."

Alva tore at the tissue in her lap. "I didn't even know if he knew who I was, but he probably guessed by my reaction to the ring. Well, I grabbed up my great grandson and dragged him back here. Later I told myself it was my imagination playing tricks on an old woman, but I realized my time in anonymity had come to an end."

She sighed. "I am a tired old woman. I'm not afraid of death, and I am not going to run again."

She locked the box and handed it to me. "Take it and put it somewhere safe until the time comes, would you?"

I nodded automatically and wondered briefly what time she meant. I hated to ask the question for which I wasn't ready to hear the answer. I looked at the still silent J.J. He nodded encouragement. I drew a breath. "Alva, who was the person wearing the ring? Was it this Victor Parco?"

"You didn't guess yet? His rap sheet would list him as Victor Antonio Parco, grandson to the late Antonio Giovani Parco, known as Big Johnny. He was one of Capone's body guards, and the man who murdered Alexa Wentworth."

Totally confused, I looked at J.J. He looked as lost as I was and asked, "Alva, why do you think we know this Victor Parco?"

"You must know Victor Antonio Parco is from Chicago. The Italian translation for 'parco' is park. You know him by the name Tony Parks, a.k.a. Anthony Parks The Fourth."

"Holy cow."

J.J. nodded. "It makes sense. The Anthony Parks, your momma's slum lord was actually an enforcer for Al Capone. That he, who allowed his son to beat small children and burn the neighbor's cat brought up his son to be a murderer as well."

I butted in. "And a greedy one too. He who killed the actress while you were in the closet, and what's more, I suspect you really did see the ring that has haunted you all these years, and it is right now sitting on the finger of our murderer."

She hesitated and I didn't move a muscle. My mind raced. Al. Oh my God, I wondered if Parks knew we were investigating the murders.

Alva smiled a sad little smile and patted my hand. "Tony Parks is now back in town but in disguise. Most of us know him by the sight of his big red nose, and size twenty cowboy boots, but by yet another name, don't we?"

My stomach jumped. My heart stopped. It took a second to digest her words. The three of us whispered together, "Bucket the Clown."

"Ohmygod, Alexandra!"

I grabbed my cell. I felt J.J.'s hand on my shoulder. "Take it easy. See if he's still in her office first."

I listened to Al's phone ring. J.J. flipped open his cell and called Edie.

Al picked up. "White Bass Lake Library."

My sweaty hands clutched the phone. I took a deep breath. "Hi Al, this is Buzz. Is your meeting over with yet?"

"Hi, Buzz, No, I'm still here. Pizza? Your house? Tonight? Why sure, I should finish up here in the next ten minutes or so and I can be at your place in about a half hour. Sound okay to you?"

I had a death grip on the phone now. "Al, is Bucket still there?"

"That's right, a half hour. You know how anal I am. Got to leave the office neat as a pin."

"Al, listen to me. Is this Parks guy wearing a ring with a snake on it?"

251

"Why yes, and it looks like he's going to book our fair for 2013. Good thing we got him before Jefferson County grabbed him."

"Al, I need you to get out of the building right now. Can you do that?"

"No way, Buzz. I have to go home and change clothes first, you know me. Just start without me, okay?"

I shook with rage and dread. "Al, don't panic. I swear to God I will get you back. Do you know where he is taking you?

"Yep, I know you will. Tell Dad I hope his ankle is better soon. Mom can feed the llamas for a couple days, it won't kill her. Well, got to go sis, See-ya-bye."

"Al!"

The phone went dead. J.J. pried my fingers off my cell, and held my hands in his. "Look at me. Buzz, Look at me damn it!"

I looked up and whispered, "He's got Al. He's got my baby sister."

26

The room closed in and I started to shake. J.J. squeezed my fingers. I felt fractured, like glass shattered into a thousand pieces. I barely heard J.J. He shook me a little and I blinked. J.J. came into focus in front of me.

"Buzz, stop. I need you now, babe. We'll get Al, and we'll get him, but I need you focused here."

I took a shuddering breath, and blew it out slowly. I did this twice more and felt the pieces come together. I looked at J.J. and a calm settled over me. J.J. must have felt it too.

"That's my girl. Now tell me what went on. What did Al say?"

I thought. Snake... llamas... pizza... the thoughts swirled in my head, and aligned themselves on my subconscious. As I cut and pasted them into some semblance of order, J.J. stood in front of me and didn't say a word.

I reiterated almost verbatim, my conversation with Al. When I finished, J.J. put his arms around me and pulled me close.

"Now let's make sense of it all."

I thought another second. "Okay. We know Parks is still in her office, and he is wearing a snake ring. We also know he is probably taking her over to Greeley's farm."

J.J. picked up his cell. "Luke's still at the morgue. I'll have him tail Bucket."

While J.J. spoke with Luke, I patted Alva's hand. "You doing okay, Alva?"

Alva leaned forward. "Yes, I'm fine, but Greeleys? How do you know he's taking her to Greeley's farm?"

"My folks don't have llamas, and Greeley's do. Al also

hates pizza, so I knew she wasn't really talking about coming over, and the Greeley's own a pizza franchise across the street from their petting zoo."

J.J. smiled. "Bud Greeley sprained his ankle at the fair last week, so Dorothy packed them up, hired Chris Pyle to take care of the animals, and she dragged Bud to her sister's house in Highland Park for a couple weeks."

"So she really wanted you to know where she was going. Well, now what do we do?"

J.J. stood. "You, Alva? You do nothing. I'll call in one of my deputies to stay with you until this is over. We'll move you to–"

I jumped in. "My house. We'll move you to my house. It's small, so it's more easily guarded. It's a ranch, so you can maneuver your wheelchair around easily, and it comes complete with two of the best bodyguards around."

Alva's eyes widened. "Bodyguards?"

"No one gets past Wes and Hillary."

Alva eyed J.J. "Why are you laughing, young man?"

"Uh, Wes is about 180 pounds of Newfoundland dog, and Hillary is a retired cop, who also happens to be a sweet but somewhat flatulent Bulldog."

Alva clasped her hands in front of her. The anxiety seemed to melt away from her body. "Joe bought me a bulldog for company when he went on the road. He called him Curly, after Earl Louis Lambeau."

She sighed. "We had Curly for twelve years." She looked at me with shining eyes. "But I'll never in my life forget the smell, and at the most inopportune times! Curly was especially fond of hot dogs, popcorn, and liverwurst on crackers." She leaned toward me. "I always told him how indelicate it was to poot in polite company, but Curly and Joe loved to watch football and eat liverwurst and crackers."

J.J. had a duffel bag in one hand, and a cell phone in the

other. Since I knew I would be absolutely no use to him, I helped Alva pack the duffel, and went to notify the staff she would be going with us.

I walked back to Alva's room by way of the ladies room, and as I turned the corner by her room, I saw an orderly turn at the opposite end of the hall, pushing a wheelchair. The figure in the chair slumped forward as if she were sleeping, and I entered Alva's room as J.J. put his cell phone in his pocket.

He grabbed the duffel. "Boy, they sure were fast. The orderly just picked up Alva. I told him to meet us at the front so we could sign her out."

I grabbed Alva's robe and toiletry bag and headed for the door. "I told them not to send an orderly. We would take her out ourselves."

J.J. whipped his head around to look out the window. "Alva—"

I turned and was out the door and running before J.J. had time to finish. We hit the side door of the facility as one, only to find an empty wheelchair on its side, one wheel turning slowly in the breeze, and not a vehicle in sight.

"Alva."

"Now, Buzz, don't jump to conclu—"

My cell phone rang. I almost didn't answer it, but glanced down and saw the caller I.D. "J.J., it's Al's phone."

I punched speaker. "Al, thank God you're okay. Listen, I think—"

A gravelly whisper sent chills up my spine.

"I have your sister."

27

My throat wouldn't work. Terror struck my soul and I couldn't even think. The voice spoke again, and I almost missed the first words. "Not so smart now, are you, voodoo lady? I got the old lady too, but it's you I really want."

J.J. stayed silent, but poked me on the shoulder and startled me into answering. "You want me? What for? Let me talk to my sister, Bucket. Now. Put her on the phone."

"Bucket my ass. Now you listen to me and listen good, or your sister and the old lady are toast." At my silence he chuckled. "I see we understand each other."

Rage hit me instantaneously. "You hurt either one of those women and I'll hunt your rotten carcass down and—"

I heard a loud metal-on-metal clang and a high-pitched scream. The hair on the back of my neck stood on end, and I held my breath.

Bucket chuckled. "That was just a broken finger, smart ass, next time you spout off it'll be a busted kneecap, so shut your yap and listen up."

I swallowed hard and exhaled. "I'm listening."

"You got somethin' I want, lady, and if I don't get that box, you can say bye-bye to Granny first, then listen while I carve up your sister. I promise she won't be so beautiful when I get through with her."

J.J. squeezed my arm, and I pulled it together. "I won't insult your intelligence and ask what box, so just tell me when and where, and you can have the damn box. I never wanted it anyway."

I heard laughter. "That makes you a liar, or stupid, or both, lady. You just make sure you're around to answer your phone at five. Get the box and be ready."

"Okay, I'll be ready. Let me talk to my sister–"

The line went dead.

* * *

I stood looking at my cell phone. J.J. pressed the emergency signal on his police radio before I could stop him. "Attention all units, attention all units, report to the station A-sap. Repeat, report to the station, we have a situation."

J.J. picked up the duffel bag and ran to his squad. I piled in the other side and we rode lights and siren back to town.

I fastened my seatbelt on the fly. "You realize what you just did, right?

Gravel flew as we took a corner a little too sharp. The squad fishtailed and righted itself, sliding to a halt. The tires chirped and we took off again. "Yeah, yeah, I cut the corner a little too close. Leave off me, Buzz, and let me drive."

"You know, Green, you could slow it down to ninety and we could arrive alive."

"What a novel idea." The wheels screeched as he whipped left at Main. "Now what did I do that was so awful?"

I crossed my arms. "You'll see in about thirty seconds."

J.J. tore around the corner and came to a sliding halt at the driveway to the Sheriff's Department parking lot. There were so many cars and people jammed in the lot, he couldn't have pulled in even if he wanted. "What the–"

I barked out a laugh, despite the terror I felt. "Rule Number One: Always remember the little old ladies in this town all have police scanners and cell phones."

The crowd parted like the Red Sea as we hurried to the building. J.J. bypassed his office and opened the doors to the auditorium.

I yelled above the din. "SWAT ladies, front and center!"

J.J. grabbed my arm. "What are you trying to do, cause a riot?"

I patted his hand. "Wait and see, my love. I have an idea. Why don't you brief your guys, I'll break the news to the SWAT team and we'll put it together in let's say," I looked at my watch, "fifteen minutes?"

He raised his eyebrows and went to the front of the room. The crowd parted again, and Mom, Mary, Jane, Joy, and Silvia tottered forward. I pointed to my left. "Ladies? Conference room." I turned, knowing they were on my heels.

I went to the head of the table and saw Mom bumping the door on someone's foot. "No, Edie, you can't come in. You are not an official member of SWAT." I heard murmuring and more bumping. "I know you're a senior, and you have a scanner, but you never come to meetings and—"

I'd had enough. "Mom, stop messing around and let Edie in. We need her for communications liaison, if nothing else."

"Oh, well okay, get in here, Edie, but make it fast, I'm slamming the door on the next wannabe who tries to muscle in."

Edie slid through the door and I heard a slam, a thunk, and "Ouch, that hurt!"

Joy piped up. "Who'd you nail, Gerry?"

Mom rubbed her hands together and hooted. "Hah! Rosie." She held up a high heel. "Broke her stiletto off when she stuck her foot in the door and landed on her butt."

They all laughed and I banged on the table. "Knock it off, right now." They were immediately silent.

I drew a breath. The picture of the crunch of Al's finger, and her scream of agony rolled over and over in my mind.

"Listen up ladies, and do not interrupt. Some events have happened I think you should know about, and J.J. and I will need your full cooperation."

"But why—"

"Not now, Mom."

"But, Buzz!"

"Mom. Stop. Listen, just this once, please. You'll understand in a minute."

I turned to Joy. "Joy, can call your niece Jody and order a pizza? Then ask her if Chris Pyle's pickup is at the Greeley's place. If she asks why, tell her J.J.'s going to stop by and help him if he still needed help."

"Done."

"Mary?"

"Sir, yes, sir!"

"Do you still have the surveillance equipment J.J. told you to get rid of last winter?"

"Well, yes, but what do we need it for, any-who?"

"Mary, I'm serious. We'll need it, and J.J. won't care."

Five sets of wide eyes stared at me, and I knew I had to break the news. "Here's how it goes, and Mom, don't freak."

They all leaned forward. Mom sucked in a breath. "It's Alexandra, isn't it?"

I nodded slowly.

Joy stood up. "Gerry, sometimes you are way too creepy."

Mom, Mary, and Silvia stood. "Shut up. Joy!"

I waited until they settled in their chairs.

"The good news is we've solved the dumpster murders. We know who the killer is." I took a breath. "He's kidnapped and is holding a woman named Alva Sweetwater."

Silvia drew in a horrified breath. "I know Alva. She's a wonderful woman. Why would someone want to–"

I interrupted. "That's not all, ladies."

All action stopped. Their eyes stayed glued to mine. I took my mother's hand.

Mom gasped "Oh no, he's–"

I put a hand on Mom's shoulder and looked at the others. "He's got Al too."

Pandemonium is the only way to describe the conference

room. I tried to calm them, but they were inconsolable. I had to regain control somehow, so I resorted to shock treatment. I picked up Mary's purse and emptied it on the table. The cacophony of sounds drew a hush inside the conference room, and mass confusion outside the door. I ran to unlock it, even as J.J. barged his way in; followed by half the town. Rosie brought up the rear.

J.J. and his deputies ushered the crowd out the door. I pulled Mom aside. Jane, Joy, Mary, and Sylvia followed. I held Mom's hand. "If you can't handle this, go home, we'll understand. I'm counting on all of you to hold it together so we can help get Alexandra and Alva out alive. Now Mary..."

"Got it all, Buzz. Bugs, scopes, satellite, wires, sound equipment, cameras, GPS, lock picks, got me a TASER, night goggles-it's all in the Vic."

Good. Let me fill you in on what is happening..."

* * *

As we entered the auditorium, J.J. almost had the crowd under control. "Folks, if you'll take a seat...Ladies and Gentlemen, if I could have your attention, please? Look guys, we need to–"

Jane's cane whizzed past my ear and banged on a table. The noise silenced the room in seconds. "Y'all just shut your pie holes a minute and listen up. We need to act, and act fast. Lives are at stake here, so shut up long enough to let Sheriff Green do his job."

She cleared her throat and looked at J.J. "Carry on, young man."

J.J. glanced our way and nodded. "I just heard from Luke Hall. We have a situation over at Greeley's farm, people. Two women are being held hostage there. What we don't want, is this to turn into a deadly situation, ending in a bloody shoot-out."

Mom whimpered and Mary clutched her hand.

260

J.J. held up a hand. "We need organization and we need cooperation. I already have a plan–"

The sudden burst of the *1812 Overture* startled the crowd. J.J. turned beet red. "Who the hell has a cell phone on?"

Joy stuck a finger in the air. J.J. geared up to yell and I stopped him. "Wait".

Joy covered the phone. "My niece Jody said Chris Pyle's truck is in the driveway, but she doesn't see him, and the llamas are waiting at their gate like they haven't been fed yet. She wants to go help him out. What do I tell her?"

I spoke. "Tell her J.J. will come over, and do not leave her job. Tell her you and the SWATS are coming over to the pizzeria for a party instead. Tell her to hang streamers or blow up balloons. Play the mean Auntie if you have to, but keep her off that farm and in the pizzeria. Can you do it?"

Joy stuck a thumb up. "You betcha I can!" She walked toward the back of the room, speaking tersely into her phone. The auditorium looked like an old E.F. Hutton commercial, everyone sat still; no one moved, no one spoke, but every last person stared at Joy Broussard.

Joy ended with an, "And I mean it, young lady," and calmly closed her phone. She smiled at J.J. "Done."

J.J. spread papers across the large table. "All righty then, here's how it's going to go down..."

28

After many arguments and adjustments later, J.J. ran a hand through his hair. Fatigue etched new creases on his face as he scowled at the audience. "Now I didn't want to involve civilians in this, so if even one of you gets out of line or decides to play cowboy, Alva Sweetwater and Alexandra Miller are dead. We are dealing with a psychopath, and nothing," he glared at the SWAT ladies, "I mean *nothing* can be out of sync on this. Are we clear?"

Heads nodded all around.

Silvia cleared her throat. "What do you want us to do, Jim?"

J.J. gestured to the paper. "Here's what's going to happen. SWAT ladies, you're going to have a rousing pizza party. Pick out someone to have a birthday bash at Greeley Good Pizza, and stay there. Got it? You will stay in the building, and will not come out until I come for you. Are we clear?"

Five grey heads bobbed and huddled at the far end of the room.

He looked at the rest of the crowd. "Little by little the rest of you will trickle in and the party will become louder and more boisterous. I will need this distraction so my deputies and I can find out the wheres, whats, and hows as to getting in and getting the women out safely. Backup is going to be slow in coming, and the bad guy is a ticking time bomb, so we all have to stick to Plan A. Clear?"

A voice from the back yelled. "Crystal!"

I heard Mom mumble, "Crystal who?"

J.J. turned to look out the window. "Where the heck is

Moe?"

Just then, spinning tires and spraying gravel had the entire crowd at the window. We saw Moe jump out of the car with a metal box. Whatever was inside rattled and clunked against the side. "Got it, J.J., just like you said. I found it in your dad's old stuff in the back of the garage."

Moe held up an old ammo box which was battered enough to look like it came from the Revolutionary War. "I threw a couple Muskie lures inside so it sounds like something good is in there."

"Good Job, Phil. Now before we—"

A cell phone ringing broke the silence, and it was a second before I realized it was mine. I didn't recognize the number, and almost ignored it. Something told me to take it and I punched the answer button. "Buzz Mil—"

An urgent whispering voice called, "Don't hang up, it's me, Chris Pyle."

"Chris, are you at the Greeley farm? Don't feed the llamas, and do not go near the barn!"

"Will you give me a minute without talking?"

"S-sure. I'm putting you on speaker phone."

"No, wait! I don't wanna talk to the whole damn town! Just you and the cop. C'mon, this is important, and I only have one bar left on my phone."

J.J. came over by the window. "Okay, Chris. We know you're at Greeley's farm, and we know Bucket the Clown is holding Mrs. Sweetwater and Alexandra Miller, but I'm not sure where."

"I do, man. He's got them in the dairy barn. Al, I mean Miz Miller is tied to a milking stanchion and Miz Sweetwater is layin' on the floor. She don't look so good, but I don't think she's dead or nothin' yet. I'm afraid to do anything in case the whacko goes postal. I thought maybe I could—"

"Don't do anything, Chris. Do you hear me? Don't do

263

anything. We'll be there later, after the clown calls me back. Put your phone on vibrate so you don't give yourself away. I'll meet you behind the old silo near the haylage wrap. Don't move from there, okay?"

"Okay." Click.

I turned back to the crowd. "Okay, town folk. Are we all on the same page?"

Much head bobbing and murmuring ensued. A hand went up in the back. Brett Hinkston said he and a group of businessman downtown decided to bring a couple picnic tables to Greeley's to accommodate the crowd, and Cam McKenzie and the boys are supplying the music for cover noise.

It all seemed to be coming together; all we needed was the bad guy to call.

29

With the box clutched closely to my chest, I waited with the others for my cell phone to ring. The SWAT team already left for Greeley Good Pizza, hooting like they already had a snoot full, and bent on a party.

With the exodus of the second wave of partygoers, I hopped inside my cousin Dan's truck; squished between two other linebacker-sized, career cop Miller cousins, Paul and Chuck, who were sweating like it was the fourth quarter during a September football game.

We rolled past the pizza parlor, straining to see anything out of place across the street at the Greeley farm. A light shined through a window in the barn, but nothing moved.

Dan pulled onto an access road about a hundred yards down from where the barn sat, and we piled out and pow-wowed over the air with Mary's Super Spy Walkie-Talkies.

I picked up my back pack and almost jumped out of my skin when a body jumped out from the corn field behind me. "Miz Miller, glad you're here. You won't believe what's goin' on over at Greeley's! I–"

I grabbed his shoulders and he stopped talking. "Christopher Pyle, you scared the bejeezes out of me. You're supposed to meet me over behind the silo. Did he see you or something, or do you know anything else, like where he is and what he's doing?"

Chris smiled the very first smile I ever saw out of him, and held up a small rectangle. "I got me a digital recorder. You gotta hear this."

We all gathered around while Chris readied the recorder.

I heard Al's voice loud and clear. "Come on, please don't

touch her again. She's about a hundred years old, Bucket. You kill her and you'll never get whatever you're looking for. You already know my sister has the box, and she's bringing it."

"As long as I have you, I don't need this dried up old broad anymore."

"Yes you do, because I don't know what the heck you're talking about, and if my sister doesn't have all those alleged diamonds you're looking for, and the old lady is dead, you're screwed, pal, because like I said, I don't have a clue."

My throat tightened and my stomach clenched. Al. Baby-sister-pain-in-the-ass-Alexandra. I gasped for air and realized I had been holding my breath. I looked up and every face around me had the same horrified look I felt I wore.

I cleared my throat and fought back the tears. *Focus Buzz, or get out. Come on, deep breath. Breathe out slowly. Yeah, that's good, one more.* I looked up. "Okay, at least we know they're alive. Are we ready?"

"Uh, Buzz, uh, Miz Miller?"

I whipped my head around and Chris Pyle's face was about two inches away. "What?"

He bit his lip and looked at where I grasped his hand and the recorder. The tips of his fingers were dark red and where I had a death grip, and his hand was white-turning-blue. I let him go. "Oh my Lord, Chris I'm sorry."

His pained expression eased as he shook out his hand. "No prob-if it was my baby sister, I'd be freakin' too." He held up his discolored hand. "See? It's better already."

I rubbed his fingers and hugged his thin shoulders. For the first time since I'd ever known him, he didn't jerk away at human contact. "Thanks, Chris, I guess I am a little tense. Can you tell us anything else about the barn, or where exactly the two women are, or did you hear the clown say anything, or are the women hurt, or are there any animals in the barn–"

J.J. put a hand on my shoulder. "Buzz, stop. Can I take

over here?"

I shrugged his hand off. "I got it. It's my sister."

He gently took my shoulders in his hands and ran his hands down my arm. He leaned close and spoke in my ear.

"Listen, Honey, she's like my sister too, and she's my future sister-in-law, so I have a stake in this as well. You are way too close to the situation. I think you're scaring Chris, because I know you're scaring me. Let me talk to him, okay?"

I didn't make it past the "my future sister-in-law" line. I caught the intense gazes of several people around me. I shook my head to clear it; I'd deal with the sister-in-law later. I'd bet he didn't even realize he said it. I also realized in a flash I *was* too close to this situation, which would definitely impair my judgment, not counting the concussions I still dealt with. I knew from this point, I could only hurt the entire operation by insisting on leading and not following. I flushed in embarrassment and stepped back. "I'm sorry, J.J. I'm not even a cop anymore. It was an automatic reaction. Al's my...my..."

I sniffed back the tears and he kissed my forehead. He put an arm around my shoulders and turned to Chris. "Chris, you seem to be the only one of us who knows what's really going on. Why don't you step over here with me and the boys, and we'll figure out how we're going to save the world."

I watched the transformation in Chris as his shoulders straightened and he stood a little taller. The beaten expression vanished from his face, and was replaced by a resolve I had never before seen in him. He let go of my hand and walked with J.J. to the back of the truck, where they huddled with the other deputies and talked.

Moe broke away from the group to fetch me. He didn't look happy, but at least there were no snide comments; a fact I greatly appreciated. "He wants you."

I knew Moe meant J.J. and vowed to myself to reassure Moe I was not now, nor would I ever be after his job. I followed Moe back to the truck and J.J. drew me into the circle. He looked at me hard, and raised a thumb. "Okay?" I nodded and he turned back to the rest.

"So I'll have Buzz and Chris with me. I'll drop them at the milk house and S.W.A.T. will follow."

He gave us both a stern look. "Observation only. We'll go in through the milk house, and you two," pointing at Chris and me, "Will do nothing more than hold the doors open for the S.W.A.T. team to enter. Chris, you keep recording, Buzz, do nothing. I repeat *nothing*. According to Chris, Bucket is holding the women on the other side of the barn, and I want you to stay in the milk house."

I stared at him.

He glared back.

I opened my mouth.

He slapped a hand over it. "Promise, or you don't go."

I narrowed my eyes and nodded.

"That was a promise?"

I blinked, and he turned me loose.

* * *

The plan was for me to call from the milk house that I had the box Bucket wanted, while J.J. and the fourteen other cops from three counties who showed up slipped into the barn behind where Al was tied. Bucket thought he had a straight shot toward the door, but hopefully, I could draw him toward me and away from the two women. While Bucket followed the lure I laid, S.W.A.T. would blow through the door and nail his sorry ass, and J.J. and the boys would create a wall of cops between him and the hostages. They would close in on him and bring him down if necessary, while my cousins got my sister and Alva out of the barn and out to the Randall Township ambulance. I was just sorry I wouldn't be able to get off an accidental shot to his head in the process.

With the multi-county S.W.A.T. in place outside the

milk house, the surrounding jurisdictions on the opposite end of the main barn led by J.J, and Chris and me at the milk house door, all seemed to be in order. One of the S.W.A.T. guys flipped up his face shield, held up a cell phone, and took my picture. "Hey pal," I whispered, what's with the camera?"

He grinned and pointed to my arm, where Mary's giant pink purse hung. I rolled my eyes, "It's not mine, but our equipment is in there."

He winked. "It goes with your sneakers, Buzz."

I hitched it further up my arm. "Shut up, Polansky. You're just jealous because you don't have one."

One look from his commander had Jim Polansky in line, shield down, and cell phone gone. I felt the weight of Mary's purse, and for the first time in my life, thanked my lucky stars Mary was a pack rat and Mrs. Murphy stayed home. Nothing was going to go wrong.

On a nod from Commander Mike Jeters, I slipped inside the small milk house, Chris silent on my heels. I had Mary's bird watching binoculars in my left hand, her purse on the same arm, and my HKP9S in my right hand (I still had hopes of the head shot).

The door to the main barn cracked open and I could see everything clear as a bell. I turned on the camera–we had one monitor set up back at the pizza parlor, and one at the truck. We were on silence status, but I heard J.J.'s whisper, "Good picture." I licked my finger and stuck the camera's suction cup to the milk house door. Chris went left, and I stayed right next to him. We settled in to watch on my tiny monitor, and wait for the nod from Commander Jeters.

Now I swear I had every intention of sitting quietly in the milk house and letting the boys do their magic, but I guess something somewhere must have gone awry, or the long arm of Murphy's Law grabbed a hold of the game plan and twisted it with a vengeance.

30

I watched Al as she tried desperately to attract the attention of the monster hovering over Alva Sweetwater. Bucked stood over Alva and held a knife close to her cheek. Alva was so weak he didn't even have her tied, and it looked like Alva was almost at the end of her endurance.

Tied to a milking stanchion about ten feet away, Al did her best to play the whiny diva.

"Ouch, these ropes are really cutting into me! Am I bleeding? Hey, I broke two nails and my shoe fell off. Is my ankle bleeding? Oh, would you look at this? I have a run in my stocking. Hey mister, get me my purse, would you? I have to fix a couple things here."

Bucket's makeup smeared across his face, and two claw marks marred his cheek. *At least Al's broken fingernails went to a good cause.* The oozing trail cut through the leftover grease paint, giving him a hideous appearance, and his nose shone big and red, but he wasn't wearing the rubber one.

His head spun toward Al and spittle flew from his lips. "You better shut up now, bitch, you already did enough damage with those shoes of yours. I oughta break your toes like you broke my nose. An eye for an eye. You wouldn't walk far in those four inch heels, then, would ya?" A high pitch giggle raised goose bumps on my arms. *Careful Al, this guy is totally bonkers.*

"Oh pooh. I didn't mean to kick your nose in, but when you broke my finger, my leg had a spasm."

Oh pooh? You never said oh pooh in your life, Alexandra Miller.

Bucket's grotesque face turned toward Al. "You'll have

your last spasm if that uppity sister of yours doesn't show up soon. She's got about four minutes before I start carving on the old lady."

Bucket took two steps toward her and at Alva began a slow slide toward the ground. Al struggled against the ropes holding her and Bucket grabbed Alva by the front of her dress. He shoved her in a rickety chair. "Old woman, you'd better stay there or I'll tie you there."

I saw Alva's head barely move, but the clown's attention shifted to the racket coming from Al and the cow stanchion.

Every move Al made had the metal pipes clanging like country church bells. The good news? The more she moved, the less attention the whack-job with the red nose paid Alva. Alexandra's broken pinky must have throbbed like a mother, but she kept clanging around, probably thinking we'd would find it easier to locate Alva and her, plus, she'd have the advantage of cover noise when we finally came to the rescue, if the whacko didn't kill them first.

Chris had his recorder on, and the "Super Ear" I dug out of Mary's purse picked up Al's whisper. *Thank heaven for these days of wireless.*

"What the heck is keeping Buzz? It's funny, really. You'd think I'd be hoping J.J. or Superman or anyone but Buzz rescued me. She's always hated me, so it's too weird to think Buzz as the only one I thought of...but I know she'll come... I'm sure she'll come...Geez, Buzz, if that stupid Irish woo-woo thing you have ever worked at a crucial time, let it work now."

I came up out of my crouch and felt Chris holding on to my shirt. I made to move, and he snatched me back. I realized Chris had kept me from blowing through the door and mucking up the whole ball of wax.

I stuffed the HK in the back of my pants, dug the box with the muskie lure out of the purse, and looked across at

271

Commander Jeters. He held his fist in the air. We all held our collective breaths. I heard a soft. "ready," from the guys on the other side of the barn. Commander Jeters silently pulled his face shield down and I watched as he held up three fingers. Two...one...and he pointed at me. I stepped forward; Chris flinched, and fell over an old milk can. The can made enough noise to wake the dead. One of the S.W.A.T. guys grabbed Chris and held him down, while another up-righted the milk can. The silence was so thick you could cut it with a knife.

"Millerrrrrr?" Bucket's startled me. I turned for a quick look at Jeters and I clunked my head against the door jamb. I saw stars and stumbled forward which put me half-way through the door. I was about to push the door all the open when Jeters grabbed my shirt. "Delay going in as long as you can. I'll call Green."

He let go of my shirt and I stumbled the rest of the way into the barn. I stayed as far behind the open door as I could, I hitched Mary's purse up my arm and stepped to the left of the door.

"Bucket? It's me, Miller. I have the box. Please put down the knife it's all but over."

"Are you alone? I told you to come alone."

"I am alone, I just fell over a can."

His voice climbed higher and I could hear him breathing like Darth Vader after a 6K run. "What was that noise? Is somebody with you? I swear I'll–"

"I fell. That's all, Bucket. Tripped over an old milk can and fell against the damn door. Chill out and give me back my sister."

"You came in the wrong door. I ought to kill your sister and the old lady right now. You were supposed to come through the right door. Why did you come through the wrong door? Come out where I can see you."

272

Oh-oh. He's losing it fast. Go girl, go!

"I didn't know this was the wrong door, Do you want the diamonds or not?"

Bucket grabbed Alva's hair and put the knife to her throat. Alva whimpered but didn't struggle. I stayed put.

"My hand's a little shaky, Miller. Move along the wall there and hold up the box or I'll cut her."

I held up a finger. "Hold on Bucket. I'm here but I'm hurt. Let me pick up the box, we'll make the exchange and you can leave."

The knife pricked Alva's neck and blood seeped out of the shallow gash. "I don't think so, lady. You think you're so smart, but you ain't got nothin' on me. Get in here where I can see you."

"Okay, okay. Here I come." I opened the door a little and led with the box. I shook it so thee Muskie lures rattled inside. "See? I have the diamonds. Put the knife down, Bucket, or John, or Tony, or Victor, or whoever the heck you are. A deal is a deal. Alva has delivered what you want."

He licked his lips. The knife hand moved slowly away from Alva's throat. He didn't even notice when she slid to the floor. I could hear him breathing. I could smell him clear across the barn. Knife in hand, he walked toward me like he was in a trance.

"Come on, Bucket, I have what you need."

I stepped one step out of the milk house and someone behind me grabbed my shirt. I stopped and held up the box. "See? No tricks. You can have the box. I—"

A muffled roar came from my left. A crowd at the party cheered and Bucket froze. He dropped the knife and I breathed a sigh of relief. He looked at me and looked off toward the west end of the barn. "What's that?"

I never took my eyes off him. "Don't worry about it now. Come get the diamonds. Come on."

He took a step toward me, but the noise of the crowd pulled him toward the window.

"What the–"

He looked at me and looked at the window. He stepped closer to me and I slid to the side of the door. Bucket looked at the window again and I moved in the same direction he did, clearing the way for Jeters and the boys. Al clanged across the barn and the crowd at the pizza joint cheered again.

Bucket's confusion grew, and he was beginning to lose focus. He whipped his head back and forth; first toward the window, then toward Al, and then me.

His breathing became erratic, he began to panic. Sweat poured down his face, and he looked around frantically before zeroing in on me. Our gazes locked and we slowly moved parallel to each other. I led him away from the door and closer to the window. He suddenly lunged. I ducked and sucked back. His big clown boot caught on a loose floorboard and he stumbled and launched himself forward. I jumped backward but his right shoulder hit my left, knocking me against the outside wall. The back of my head and his face plastered into the barn wall, and he screamed as his already crunched nose took another hit. I fell to the side, but Bucket came with me, shoulder on my collar bone, screaming and bleeding all over my shirt. We hit the floor hard and I heard Mary's bag clank against the cement. I rolled to the side and he caught me by the hair. A snub-nosed pistol was shoved under my chin. I froze as I felt the cold steel touch my skin.

Another high pitched giggle escaped him and he shoved his face up to mine. "Who's smarter now, Miss I'm- Smarter-Than-The-Whole-World Miller? I'll show your uppity ass just how smart I can be."

He twisted so he had his arm under my armpit, my elbow bent backward and my fingers in his. The gun pressed hard against the back of my ear.

"Good move, Bucket. What do you do for your next act?"

Another roar went up across the street and shoved me forward toward the window. I groped behind my back with my free hand, trying to reach my gun. Mary's purse still hung from my arm, and there was no way I could reach my HK. *Crap. It always worked in the movies...but Bruce Willis never carried around a ten pound pink purse.*

Bucket shoved me up against the wall next to the window. He moved his head so one eye looked out across the street. I chanced a look and saw a rousing game of horse shoes and a "Happy Birthday Gerry" banner strung across the front of Greeley's pizza parlor. Food and drink flowed freely and Bucket looked for any sign of foul play. Seeing none, he drew back from the window and looked at me. "The box. Where is it?"

I held up my empty left hand. "You knocked it out of my hand when you tackled me, you wimp assed moron. Give me my sister and take the stupid box."

He backed up a step and brought up his weapon. The gun came level with my eyes and I looked down a .44 bore. My body went liquid. I could see my head exploding like a soft tomato, and I became a little light headed. Bucket was screaming in my face, and I saw movement near where Al was tied.

"Where are my diamonds, you useless bitch? Where'd you drop them?"

"Oh my, the box...where's the–" I pretended to swoon, my back to the window.

I leaned on him hard on him and he stumbled. "What the heck?"

While Bucket teetered off balance, I hauled back in one fluid motion and slammed my forehead into his flat, broken, blob of a nose. Screaming like a girl, he wobbled but held his ground.

My head spun and my stomach lurched, but the head butt did the trick, and he finally let me go. With super human strength that comes with panic and adrenalin, I grabbed Mary's purse in both hands and swung it as hard as I could.

Bucket struggled to stand a split second before all ten pounds of pink slammed into his right right jaw, sweeping him about two feet backward, and laying him out flat.

I spun in another circle and Mary's purse fell to the floor. The loud report of gun fire deafened my ears. I staggered to my feet, my head spinning and blood–I didn't know whose blood at the time–stinging my eyes.

I drew my HK from the back of my jeans and yanked the slide backward. It slipped through my bloody hand, slammed forward, and I heard the first round chuck into the barrel.

Bucket struggled to his elbows, the box with the Muskie lure in his hand. I jumped over his big feet and landed on his ribcage. Bucket expelled air like a fizzling balloon, and my knees slammed into his biceps, pinning him to the ground.

I grabbed for the front of his shirt, and shoved my HK onto what was left of his blobby nose. He looked at me with wild eyes, tears streaming down his face, his clown makeup almost gone, whimpering like the sad sack of crap he was.

My ears buzzed. My head swam. I could barely see, I couldn't hear a thing, but I had my finger on the trigger, and I knew with deadly finality this son of a bitch was about to die. The world closed in and it was only me, and the clown.

My gun dug into his face and my hand trembled. My chest heaved as I dragged air into my lungs. My finger twitched and the trigger moved. I gritted my teeth and the faces of those he murdered flashed through my mind. Tears gathered in my eyes and mixed with the blood, and my trigger finger itched to move one more time.

Sounds penetrated the deep fog of my mind. "Buzz,

no…me. J.J."

Voices. I heard voices. No, a single voice. J.J. I heard J.J.

My world expanded. The clown slowly came back into focus, and sound began to return to my ears. J.J spoke softly to me.

"Easy, Buzz. Come on, back off, baby. You got him. Al is safe. Alva's alive.

Al. My sister was alive. I exhaled slowly, and my trigger finger eased back.

"Buzz, honey, listen to me. Come on now, you got him and everything's okay now. That's right, good girl. It's over, honey. We won."

I wondered for a brief second why he sounded weird, when the world came back with such a rush it was like being sucked through a tunnel. My hand steadied, and my finger lowered to the trigger guard. I felt a hand close over mine.

I stared at the clown and realized I sat on his chest. I noticed my knees on his arms and his pulverized face contorted into a sniveling mess. J.J. gently backed my hand away from Bucket's face, and removed my weapon from my frozen fingers.

Another hand pried the clown's collar out of mine. Chris. Steady as a rock, and working my fingers open. I finally let go of the shirt.

I laid my trembling hand on Chris's face, and he smiled. "Geez, Miz Miller, you are one kick-ass bitc–uh, chic, uh, lady."

I think I smiled as I wiped my sleeve across my face and took a deep breath. I looked up to see forty-some cops surrounding me, guns still at the ready, and their mouths hanging open.

I watched Polansky flip his face shield up, and hold up his cell phone. He clicked off a picture and showed it to the

277

guys around him. They nodded and he looked at me. Holding up a thumb, he grinned. "This is going on my Face Book page for sure."

That broke the ice and they laughed, pounding Polanksy on the back.

Jeters watched and just shook his head. "So why did you bother calling us in?"

J.J. hauled me off the clown and Moe and Jeters moved in to cuff him. J.J. caught me up in a bear hug and I hugged him back, feeling blessed and very glad to be alive.

I heard a squeak and a sob and turned from J.J. in time to be smothered by Al. We held on to each other like we never had before. My throat grew tight and I sniffed. "Don't think for a minute this means I'll stop making fun of your stilettos."

She backed off and pushed the hair out of my eyes. She rested her forehead against mine. "And don't think for a minute this absolves you from being guilty of murdering my Beach Party Barbie under Mom's house."

I kissed her cheek and hugged her again. "Just so we understand each other."

She smiled. "We do." She turned toward J.J. "We certainly do."

I took Chris's arm and Al took J.J.'s. J.J. grabbed my other arm and the four of us marched out of the barn. The ambulance finished packing up to take Alva to the hospital. I surged ahead and grabbed the door. I hopped up into the back and no one stopped me. I picked up Alva's hand and brought it to my cheek.

Her fragile fingers touched my chin, and she pulled me close and whispered, "I knew I was right about you. Thank you child, you truly are one of a kind. I know you will do the right thing with the pink diamonds."

"I'll try, Alva. But you worry about getting patched up. We'll talk more later."

I bent low to hear her words, and I felt tears gather in my eyes as her lovely face crinkled into a sweet smile. "No, it must be now. I know the diamonds will go to the authorities, but the shoes are for you. Promise me you'll keep them, sell them, but they go to you."

Confused, I promised. At that point, I'd have promised to kiss Ted Puetz on the lips in public if it would make her happy. "You get better now, Alva. I'll see you later at the hospital."

A single tear slipped out of her eye. "I don't know Buzz, I'm a tired old woman, and if the good Lord is ready, I am ready for him to take me home. I want to be with my Joe again, and I believe His Plan is now complete. You go to your man, Alice Miller, and thank you, for who and what you are."

I held her hand in both of mine. "Alva."

Tears ran down my face and I could feel her slipping away. I felt a warm wisp of air caress my face as Alva Sweetwater's eyes closed and a gentle smile crossed her lips.

She was still and silent, but I swore I heard, "I'm still going to dance at your wedding, child."

I kissed her hand and laid it on her chest. Paramedics jumped in front of me and pushed me backward toward the door. Orders flew as they worked to bring Alva back, but I knew she was gone. As I crawled out of the ambulance, J.J. caught and steadied me.

He looked into my eyes. "Is she?"

Tears filled my eyes again and I nodded. "But she said she's still going to dance at our wedding." He wrapped his arms around me and we stood amidst the chaos, holding each other as we watched the ambulance as it disappeared over the rise.

31

Several weeks later found us in Mom's back yard, gathered with half the town around a huge bon fire at twilight. I didn't quite get what the celebration was about, but apparently no one else did either, so I just kicked back and enjoyed watching the sun set.

The frosty bite to the air was a perfect complement to the raging heat thrown off by the fire. It gave me the perfect excuse to snuggle closer to J.J. Wesley sprawled behind the log we sat on, as he reveled in the frosty evening air, and Hillary snuggled up next to him, lolling in the overabundance of body heat and long hair.

I looked across the fire to see Al gobbling up S'mores, wearing the flannel shirt she got from our friend, Evo Castillo. Her wooly socks stuck out of her hiking boots, and if it weren't for the designer jeans, she'd have been an ad for outdoor life.

J.J. poked me. "What's the sigh for?"

I pointed. "Al. Look at her. I haven't seen her this loose in forever. I checked out the designer jeans, though. Definitely not Wranglers."

He laughed. "Cut her some slack, Buzz. She's come a long way."

I laid my head on his shoulder and snuggled closer. "That, she has. Would you ever, in your wildest dreams picture Al with marshmallow on her chin. . .in public?"

Al looked over at us and waved. She had marshmallow from her eyebrows to her chin, and I thought she had never looked more beautiful. But don't go by me, I have a skewed notion of what beautiful looks like.

Judging from the look of the guy sitting next to Fred, I wasn't the only one. I nudged J.J. "Who is the guy next to Fred? He looks like he's going to have Al for dessert."

J.J. slowly turned his head. "Oh, that's Matt Malone. He's Mark's brother. You know the Malones brothers, who own the *Cool Bean* Coffee Shop in town?"

I smiled and butted my head against his arm. "Of course I know *Cool Bean*, but I've never officially met Matt. He was only here for a short time last Christmas for the store set-up. Matt is the money-man. So why is the big-shot brother back in town?"

J.J. shrugged. "Maybe they're opening a new shop and Mark will be leaving soon. Matt might be covering *Cool Bean* while Mark is gone. That would be a shame, because Fred was really looking forward to some quality time with Mark."

A boney hand on my shoulder told me we were no longer alone on our log. "Sweet Schmeet! That girl is head over heels if I ever saw one. Too bad that Malone boy is always leavin' town. It's like bein' in love with a sailor. Here today, gone for six months. Goll dangit, the thing is, we ain't never gonna get you Miller girls married off if you can't nail down a groom!"

I turned and saw Mary with a beer in one hand, and her other arm locked around Mom's waist. I turned back to J.J. his arm tightened around me. "Do you think they're propping each other up?"

J.J. smiled. "With the death grip she's got on your Mom, I'm afraid if Mary teeters, they'll both go flying. Let's get them to a couple chairs."

"Right." We stood and each took an arm. J.J. tossed Mary's beer in the garbage can on the way to the camp chairs set up near the food tables.

I always thought the best thing about camp chairs was

when you have tipsy little old ladies and you plunk them in a deep pocketed, comfy camp chair, they get stuck and can't wade their way out. That way no one has to worry about them wandering off and stepping in a rut, breaking a hip. It's a well-known fact of small-town and country life.

With Mom and Mary settled in their chairs, J.J. ran to fetch sodas for both. They well knew what we had just perpetrated, but let us pretend we suckered them.

Mary's feet dangled off the ground, so I slid a milk crate under her feet. She winked at me when J.J. handed her the soda. "Speaking of sweethearts...."

I narrowed my eyes at her and popped the top on her can. "I wasn't talking about sweethearts, Mary."

"Well, yesh you were, Muzz Biller...." She looked confused for a second. "I mean Buzz Miller. I distinkitally...uh, I mean dishtinct-tal tally..." She looked at Mom for help.

Mom smiled. "I think she means distinctly."

Mary slapped a hand over Mom's mouth. "Yup, that's what I said. Extinct...in-sink" She scratched her head with her free hand. "D-dis-stink–hmmm, dangit, that ain't right either."

She pointed a thumb at Mom. "You know....what she said."

I looked at J.J. "They lost me after 'distinctly'."

He put a finger to his lips. "*Shh*. She's on a roll."

Mary finally remembered what she had previously tried to say, and I watched her gather steam. "All this talk about marrying off those Miller girls gave me an idea."

I became very afraid. "Now, Mary, we talked about this before. You can't be plotting and planning for people. If things are going to work out between Mark and Fred, they will happen in their own good time."

Mary became indignant. "I didn't say nothin' about Freddie." She slapped her orthopedic shoes on the milk crate, making a noise loud enough to attract the attention of a few more people. That would have been bad enough, but J.J. seemed to be blissfully ignorant to the fact that he was about to become the center of attention. Again. I backed up, looking for an escape route.

Mary took a slug of her soda and cleared her throat. "Well, I always said Mother Nature could use a helping hand once in a while, so why not now?" She struggled to escape her chair, but sure as if we had duct-taped her to it, she was definitely stuck. Her arms paddled in the air while her feet clunked against the milk crate.

I pulled on J.J.'s sleeve to get us away before Mom or Mary could use me as a tool to embarrass Fred and Mark, or even worse, J.J. and me.

We backed away a couple more steps from Mom and Mary and I nearly fell over Fred in the process. "Whoa, Buzz. Watch out. What's going on over here? Mark and I were talking to Mark's brother, and I saw the gathering crowd. What are you guys doing over here?"

I panicked. "Nothing. Mom and Mary have been tipping the sauce again, and now they're all about making announcements."

A commotion near the barn had us all looking to see what was up.

Luke and Ollie Boothe from The Olive Branch Garden Center, and a couple of her kids carried plants over to Dad's hay wagon. They lined them up next to each other and I must have let out a groan, because J.J. poked me in the ribs. "What's going on, Buzz?"

I leaned over and whispered, "I think our tomatoes are about to rear their ugly heads once more."

He stretched to see over the crowd. "You've got to be kidding me. I thought that all went away. What now?"

Ollie cleared her throat. "Uh, may I have your attention,

please?"

A voice behind Mary yelled, "Getting Married! They we're talking about Miller girls getting married."

Mom shushed her. "Mary, be quiet, it's tomato time. The tomato contest, remember?"

Mary tried to focus her bleary eyes on the hay wagon, but instead, ended up digging in her pink purse for her binoculars. "Oh, I got 'em now. Hoo-wee, Gerry, yours sure is purty! Which one did Buzz kill...I mean grow?"

The crowd laughed and I turned a lovely shade of pink, and you all know how I hate pink.

Ollie waved her hands in the air. "Attention people, we have unfinished business up here. As you all know, the first annual Miller sister's grow-off has come to an end."

Some smart ass in the back row yelled, "So which one did Buzz kill?"

I yelled back, "I bought the beer you're drinking, Tom Sanders!"

"Oops, sorry, Buzz, lovely tomato, just lovely."

Ollie sighed heavily. "Okay, all, I was tricked into judging this year's specimens, and before I announce the winner, I'd like each contestant to tell us a little about their tomato. Buzz, you start."

I took a long swig of my beer and stood. I opened my mouth and J.J. pinched my rear. I squeaked and jumped about a foot in the air. I backed away from his pinchy fingers and smiled at the crowd.

"Well, first I got a large container so the roots had a place to grow. I used well composted duck doo added to my secret recipe potting mix, a little bone meal and pulverized egg shells for added calcium, some pelleted fertilizer, and a little of that water-retentive crystal stuff in case I forgot to water them later. Then I took my tomato plant, and I plucked off the leaves until about four inches of tomato were left. I planted it real deep so it would grow a healthy root system, and put her in full sun."

One of Ollie's kids, I think they called him Shroom, held up J.J.'s lovely tomato. There were two bright red medium sized fruits, and several more ripening. The crowd cheered and I felt like Benedict Arnold.

Ollie held up her hand. "Alex Miller? You're next."

Al stood and crossed her arms over her chest. "Last year I dug garden dirt, added some horse manure, and stuck mine in a five gallon bucket. I used liquid fertilizer, but my tomato did not fare as well as Buzz's plant, because she amended her soil and mine was rock hard. When I watered it, most of the water just ran off, and I don't believe my tomato got enough water or fertilizer."

It was evident Al's tomato had problems last year, because some of the bottom leaves were yellowing, they shriveled, and the poor plant had a couple of marble-sized green tomatoes on it that rotted before they ripened.

Alexandra smiled. "But this year, I got smart. I stole some of Buzz's potting mix, and I used water from the fish tanks and some lawn fertilizer from Dad's barn. I needed a tomato plant fast, and figured the fertilizer would do the trick and grow one real quick."

I felt worse because Al worked so hard and I cheated. I brightened a second later, because I remembered Al cheated too, but I kept my mouth zipped.

The kid named Shroom picked up a five gallon bucket with a tomato plant that bushed out three feet high and at least that wide.

Al sighed. "But you can see, by using the nitrogen rich fish tank water and the nitrogen rich lawn fertilizer, I grew a beautiful jungle plant, but it has no tomatoes. Ollie says the imbalance of nutrients was my problem." She smiled and sat.

Fred popped up and stuck her thumbs in her pockets. "I

285

didn't do anything special, but I used liquid fertilizer and poof, my tomato is doing fine."

I looked at the thick stemmed, robust tomato Shroom put out on the wagon, and marveled at the four medium sized fruits which were almost ripe. I saw a black spot on the bottom of one of them, and was sure Ollie could see it as well. Ha, I thought. Blossom end rot. Mrs. Simmons told me about it last year. Not enough calcium in the soil prohibits the plant from taking up water evenly. The fruit was rotting from the blossom end, and would keep rotting. Fred would have no viable fruit.

Mag stood. "I was disqualified from this year's contest, because my plant boy has been working on several new strains of hybrid tomatoes, new organic fertilizers, and soil conditioners, and I kind-of took advantage of that."

From the back we heard. "Admit it, Maggot, you cheated!"

Mag scuffed her toe in the ground. "Yes, I might have taken a few liberties, but this year was a whole different story."

She smiled smugly, and the same smart ass in the back yelled, "Yo Mag, I heard you left yer 'mater outside and that cussin' cock-a-too of yours ate your whole plant to the ground."

Mag aimed her beer can for Tom Sander's head and was rewarded with a howl of pain, and then silence. She smiled at the crowd. "Rumors, folks, vicious rumors."

Just then, Shroom plopped a large container with a greenish-brown nub in the middle. Mag turned a bright shade of red, and Ian Connor grinned from ear-to-ear. He stood and hugged Mag. "What Maggie has grown, Kitty has put asunder."

Fred piped up, "That's why that silly bird is once again at my pet shop."

Mag grumbled. "It was either your store or Thanksgiving dinner for that mangy bird."

Ollie laughed. "And the winner is, Buzz Miller! Come on up, Buzz."

I felt terrible. My stomach churned. My old ulcer threatened to fire up, and I swear I felt residuals of my concussion thundering inside my skull.

I stood and felt the blood in my head dive for my feet. I looked behind me and J.J. winked and smiled. Even my dogs were wagging and smiling at me. I took a step forward and stopped, knowing I cheated and feeling tons of Catholic guilt pressing down on my Protestant soul.

Taking another step, I looked at my sisters' tomatoes. Dragging my feet, I made my way slowly to where Ollie held up a trophy with a cornucopia on top. I was close enough to see the name plate on the base. My eyes watered as I held out my hand, and the trophy burned as I took it from her. I slowly turned toward and forced a smile to my lips. *Just say thank you and bolt, Buzz. Say thank you and bolt. Easy. Two words. Say them. Now, Buzz. Everyone is staring, you idiot.*

I opened my mouth. "I cheated."

The silent crowd stared first at me, then at Ollie. I saw movement in the back and thought Tom Sanders had come to. No such luck. *Oh no, Rosie The News Whore. She's going to be rubbing her paws together over this one, Buzz. You should have just cried off. How are you going to stomach an interview with her? How does that saying go? Losers never cheat, and cheaters never lose? No, that's not right. Winners never lose and cheaters do...no, how the heck–*

Somewhere during my conversation with myself, I realized Ollie didn't take back the trophy. I looked at her and she just stood there, smiling serenely.

"Ollie, did you hear me? I said I cheated. J.J grew this tomato in case I croaked mine, and when I got hurt, I never thought of watering my own, it croaked and J.J. gave me this one. So it was a foster tomato. It was mine, but J.J. raised it."

Ollie nodded. "I know you cheated, Buzz, but I'm thinking you're not the only one."

Ollie turned to Al. She nodded. "Yup, I confess. The reason I needed to grow a plant fast was I forgot to punch holes in the bottom of my bucket and drowned the first one." She smiled and schmooshed a marshmallow between two graham crackers.

I looked at Fred. She smiled and sighed. "Count me in as a cheater too. I thought mine was too sickly, and by the time I realized it wasn't getting enough sun, it was almost August, so I ran over to Ollie's place and picked up a patio tomato. Ollie recognized it right off; I think Shroom over there squealed on me."

The kid smoothed back his jet black hair and slid a pair of shades on his nose. "I may be a punk, but I got my pride, yo. You cheated, man."

Fred smiled large. "Yes I did."

Mag jumped up. "Am I the only non-cheater here? What's up with you guys, we were raised better than this."

We all looked over at Mom; shame hanging over us like we were little kids caught flinging mud pies at cars.

Mom smiled. "Ollie, break out my tomato now, would you please?"

Ollie nodded at Shroom, and the kid pulled out a beautiful little plant, just the right size, and covered with perfect little tomatoes. The entire crowd *oo*'d and *ahhh*'d.

Fred stepped in front of me. "Oh wow, that is the most beautiful tomato I have ever seen."

Al smiled. "You go, Mom. Jerry Baker would be proud."

Mag just stared, open mouthed.

I let out a long sigh. "Oh, Mom, how did you do that?"

My sainted mother stood proudly, took a breath and with

the rest of the SWAT ladies surrounding her, they all yelled, "She cheated, how do you think she did it?"

The crowd went wild. Mary yelled, "She plied me with booze and made me promise I wouldn't tell!"

My sisters and I got up close to the hay wagon and stared. I started to laugh, Mag snorted and guffawed, Fred and Al held on to each other to keep from falling down, and Ollie just grinned and nodded. "Pretty ingenious, eh?"

There sat a perfect little tomato plant, with ping pong balls painted red and hung on the plant with fishing line. From a distance, it looked just like perfect little tomatoes.

The SWAT ladies finally made it to the hay wagon, and they all chatted at once.

Jane patted my mom on the back. "It was all Gerry's idea."

Joy chimed in. "I had the ping pong balls."

Mom cleared her throat "I um, bought the red paint."

Silvia whispered, "I stole the fishing line from my son's tackle box."

J.J. shouted, "I heard that, Mom."

Mary piped up. "And I brought the Hennessey's."

Ollie's blue eyes twinkled. "And I kept their secret!"

I watched Mary throw an arm around Rosie. "Let me tell ya all about it, Rose…"

I still held the trophy in my hand and turned to give it back to Ollie. She shook her head and pointed to the plate. "Read it."

I looked at the inscription and read it aloud. "Winner 2013, J.J. Green."

Ollie smiled. "He may not be a Miller sister, but he was the only one who ended up the year with the same tomato he started with."

I spun around. "Hey, J.J., did you know about this?"

He shook his head and held out his hand. He read the

plate, his dimples creasing his cheeks and he shook his head. "Nope, but at least I'm not associated with a bunch of cheaters like you girls."

I reached over and plucked a grey hair out of Fred's head. "Huh. Girls, eh?"

Fred reached over and grabbed a handful of my hair. "Oops, too many grey ones, you can't pull just one."

"Ha-ha. Very funny."

Al clumped over in her new hiking boots. She looked at both our heads. "Why are you talking about grey hair?"

Fred and I looked at each other. We looked back at Al. "Shut up, Al."

She ducked and laughed. "Can't help it I'm the young one of the group. Where's Maggie? Maybe we can make fun of her grey hair too."

I gave her the evil eye. "The Maggot just might kill you."

"Oops, you are so right."

We mingled with the crowd, and it wasn't long before talk returned to Bucket the Clown and the showdown at Greeley's.

Frank Beth chuckled and toasted us with his beer. "Gotta admit there, Buzz, it might not always be pretty, but the Miller sisters are most assuredly entertaining." He looked at J.J., still grinning and holding his trophy. "Yup, certainly entertaining."

Now that the excitement was winding down, I noticed my pain meds were wearing off. My face hurt, and I touched the fading colors of my black eye. "Thanks, Frank."

Frank smiled. "Hey, what are friends for?"

"To remind me three concussions, a broken bone in my left eye socket, two cracked ribs and a torn meniscus is a little extreme for a retired cop?"

J.J. poked me. "Would that be the same retired cop who

was supposed to be observing and ended up taking out Psychos-R-Us single handedly?"

Al shuddered. "At least he's someplace where he can't hurt anyone any more. All that death for a couple of stupid diamonds."

Mary murmured, "I still think he looked like John Wayne Gacy."

I looked at Mom and the SWAT girls and they all nodded. They all grabbed the camp chairs and plopped down, having a front row seat to everything.

I felt a wave of sadness wash over me thinking of Alva Sweetwater. Her family made her funeral a wonderful celebration of her life. I think every person came away smiling at the joy Alva brought to her life and to the people who knew her. I nudged J.J. "Yeah, remember Alva said she wanted to dance at your wedding? I'm sorry she'll miss it."

He nodded. "Yeah, which reminds me."

Puzzled, I asked, "Reminds you of what?"

J.J. opened his mouth to explain when Frank evidently passed too close to Mary, and she caught a hold of his sleeve. When he tried to walk away, Mary popped out of the camp chair and centered herself in the circle of people. "I got an announcement to make, so all of you just brace yourselves."

The crowd closed in. I laughed. "Boy, Mary sure loves the attention, doesn't she?"

J.J. had his arm around my shoulders and rubbed my arm. "She sure does, but listen, Buzz. I have something important—"

I patted his hand. "*Shh*. Mary's about to impart her special words of tipsy wisdom on us mere mortals."

Mary waved her arms to the SWAT ladies, and Joy, Jane, Silvia, and Mom tottered into the middle of the circle. A warning bell went off in my head. "Oh-oh."

J.J. grinned. "Yeah, I saw. Someone sprang your mom

291

from the chair."

"No, J.J., that's not what I mean. I got a bad feeling about this."

I started to pull away and J.J. pulled me back to him and put his mouth right next to my ear. "Well, I have something to discuss with you and you are not cooperating. As a matter of fact, this whole party is very distracting. How about if we pack up the dogs and go home?"

"Hmmm? Yeah, okay, but let's wait until Mary says what she's going to say. Aren't you interested, J.J.? I mean, it looks like both our mothers are going to be involved."

He sighed heavily and sat us both on our log, acting totally irritated and scratching Wesley's ears. "We could go home and find out tomorrow. Come on, Buzz, let's go."

I realized he wasn't kidding. "Sure, I'm more than ready, don't forget your trophy, I'll meet you at the–"

Fred and Mark came to sit next to us. Fred looked a little peeved. "What's up, Fred?"

Nothing much, except Mary's going to steal my thunder. Mark and I were going to–"

I held up a hand. "Hold that thought a second, Fred." I watched Mary. "Wait, there she goes. What the heck?"

Mary held a vest in her hands. She raised it high and turned it around. Across the top, the words "Mad Dog Mary" stood out against the black leather. The hair on the back of my neck stood on end. My fingers sunk into J.J.'s sleeve. "James, I *really* have a bad feeling about this."

He grumbled. "Told you we should have snuck out while we could."

Mark patted Fred's hand. She pouted on the log next to me. "Now I don't even want to do it. I'm with J.J. Let's just go, Mark."

Poor Mark opened his mouth to speak, and I butted in again. "Oh wait, just hush a minute. Look, Mom has one too, oh no."

There stood Mom, in the center of the circle, holding up a vest which read "Gerry The Grist-Miller."

It hit me upside the head. I jumped up. "Fred, those look like motor cycle vests. Mom, do *not* tell us you're thinking of–"

Mary jumped up and down. "Hey, Buzz, pretty good guess work! Next summer me and the SWAT girls are gonna rip up the big slab and hang out at next year's Harley Davidson 110th Anniversary at the Summerfest Grounds! Maybe we'll even go to Sturgis!"

I opened my mouth, but no sound came out. Fred opened hers too, and our mouths worked like two goldfish out of water.

Mary shouted above the racket of the crowd. "We figure we got all winter and spring to practice and get our licenses, and come next summer, we'll make the hopper on the chopper and hammer down to Milwaukee!"

The crowd went wild. I stood. J.J. stood. Wes and Hill stood. I took a step toward Mom, and J.J. grabbed my hand. "We're going. Now."

"But, but…"

Fred grabbed my arm. "Buzz, wait, I wanted to tell–"

I yelled above the din. "Tell me what?"

J.J. dragged me, I dragged Fred, everyone else yelled and cheered, and Mark had Fred's other arm. The crowd parted like the Red Sea, and our loud and clumsy conga line snaked a path toward the driveway. Neither of us realized a hush had fallen over the crowd.

I took a breath and yelled, "Tell me what, Fred?"

She pulled on my arm and yelled "Mark and I are getting married this Christmas!"

J.J. stopped and we all crashed into each other like a NASCAR pileup. I grabbed Fred with both hands. "What?"

Fred's big blue eyes looked misty, and she nodded. Mark looked embarrassed and looked around at the crowd of people—most of whom he met less than a year ago. He nodded as well.

I stood in the driveway, flabbergasted. "Wow, great." I thought a second. "But that's only a couple months away!"

Fred nodded, and the crowd began to move in on her and the noise level picked up again.

I tried to hear what she yelled back, but J.J. had a hold of me again. "We're going. Now." He looked over his shoulder at Mark and Fred. "Congratulations Fred and Mark. We'll call you tomorrow. We have to go now." J.J. hustled the dogs and me toward J.J.'s truck.

I felt kind-of lost. I wanted to stay, but I wanted to run as far and fast as I could. "But. . .but. . ."

J.J. turned to go. "But nothing. You heard them, we have all winter to yell at our moms and their hair-brained schemes. Your sister is not getting married until Christmas. And you me, and the dogs? We're outta here. We have important stuff to do too. Say goodbye, Buzz."

I raised a hand. "Goodbye, Buzz," and J.J. half dragged half stuffed me to his truck. The dogs piled in and he peeled out of the driveway.

I was still trying to compartmentalize the motor cycle announcement and the wedding announcement, and dig for my pain pills when J.J pulled into my driveway. I popped a couple ibuprofens, and swallowed them dry. Wes dug up a half empty bottle of water and dropped it over my shoulder. I eyeballed him. "Sometimes you're very scary, Wes."

Grin, wag.

The dogs hopped out to do their thing in their own yard, and J.J. took my hand, only to drag me to the door. The dogs squeezed through and settled in the living room.

"J.J., what on earth has gotten into you? Stop dragging

me all over the place. I can walk."

"I'm a man on a mission."

"Is it Mission Impossible? Can I call you Mr. Phelps?"

"No jokes, Buzz."

I admit, that stung a little. "Okay, no jokes, but why didn't you just tell me earlier?"

"I've been trying to tell you all evening. Me and Wes, we've been doing a lot of thinking.

Oh-oh. What the heck is going on now? Should I run away, or hang around for the bad news? Is he sick? Is his mom sick? Is he sick of me? Oh crap, my head hurts.

I led us to the kitchen table. I grabbed a couple mugs and nuked some coffee. My shaking hands almost dumped the mugs on the way to the table, but I sat and watched as J.J. struggled to tell me what bothered him.

He took a deep breath. "Buzz, we've known each other for a long time, right?"

Hmmm, what kind of question is that? "Yeah, so?"

"So now the whole town knows."

"It would be kind of hard not to notice, J.J."

"Uh, yeah, you're right. Well, I just wanted to clarify the point."

I just nodded. "Go on."

He looked at me and quickly looked at the table. "Uh, yeah, well, I love you, you know."

I smiled. "And I love you too, you know."

He scowled. "Don't make fun of me, I'm on a roll."

"Sorry, but I'm not sure where this is going. You're uh, not going anywhere, are you?"

"That is part of what I need to talk about. We hung out as kids, we grew up and life sort-of happened. We each went our own way, and some of those roads we travelled were pretty rocky. But it never mattered what path we took in life, all roads led back to right her and right now. You, me, and the dogs."

I gasped. "You *are* leaving." Tears stung my eyes, and I tried desperately to blink them back.

"No, why would you think–no, I'm staying, probably for good, but that depends too."

I leaned forward and sniffed. I was reduced to whispering. "Depends on what?"

He ran a hand through his hair. "Oh man, I am not doing this very well, am I? Don't cry, Buzz, it's not bad, well, I don't think it's bad, but that depends too."

I couldn't stand it anymore. "Depends on what, Green? Just spit it out, I can take it."

He sighed and just looked at me. He shook his head and went on. "You know, I meant to get around to this several weeks ago, but then you got hurt and it drove me crazy to watch you suffer, then the fair happened, you got hurt again, and I was crazy again, the murdering psycho clown happened, you got hurt yet again, and I almost lost it, and aw hell, I'm just not doing this very well."

"What?"

He looked confused. "What?"

I started to sweat, but needed him to go on. "Sooo?"

He looked at me with stricken eyes. "So I don't want to lose you, that's what."

The tension in me fizzled. *Whew!* "Lose me? I'm not going anywhere, James."

"Good, because I can't imagine not having you and the kids around, so–"

He reached across the table and took my hands in his. I stared into those green, green eyes. My mouth was dry and my tongue would barely move. "So what?"

He kissed the end of my nose. "So are you going to marry me or what?"

Gale Borger, author of the hilarious Miller Sisters Mystery series, brings to life the small town of White Bass Lake, Wisconsin and its wacky inhabitants in *Totally Buzzed* and *Totally Fishy*. 2013 sees the addition of book three in the Miller Sisters Mysteries, with *Totally Evil*.

Totally Decked, was out in time for Christmas, 2010. This bestselling short story has love brewing for Fred Miller and the owner of the coffee shop next door, Mark Malone. Christmas 2013 will be the year Mark and Fred plan to get hitched in *Totally Sleighed*-that is, *if* Fred makes it to her wedding alive.

The Olive Branch Mystery Series is a six-short story YA eSeries for teens. Now available in print as well, *Death of a Garden Hoe* follows five street kids as they try to find a murderer, but they find trust, friendship, and themselves along the way.

With over 20 years in law enforcement, Gale has extensive experiences from which to draw material for her books. Growing up in a hilarious household lends humor to her writing. Gale says, "I've always been told 'write what you know,' and I know bad guys and funny stuff, with a little gardening thrown in for good measure."

Gale has a Bachelor's degree in Criminal Justice and a Master's Degree in Education. She lives in southeastern Wisconsin with her husband Bob, their sometimes-seen college student (dragging behind her a trombone, and her dirty laundry bag), two cats, about 1,000 tropical fish, a turtle, a horned frog, and more flowers in her yard than grass. Visit Gale at *http://galeborgerbooks.com*